Special thanks to the following people for breathing life into the Godsverse when I thought its light had been blown out:

Katrina Roets, Pat Shand, Starr, Ernie Sawyer, I'm a Ninja, Logan Waterman, Matthew Johnson, Gary Phillips, Ramsey Church, Phil, Melissa Hooper, Jean Lau, Eric P. Kurniawan, Peter Anders, Collin David, Nikres. Joshua Bowers, Jeff Lewis, Emerson Kasak, Linda Robinson, Susan Faw, Talinda Willard, Courtney Cannon, Dave Baxter, old_fogey@yahoo com, Nick Smith, Charlotte Organ, Chad Bowden, Jason Crase, John L Vogt, Philip R. Burns. Bloodfists, Death's Head Studio, LLC, Daniel Groves, Rodney Bonner. JF weber, Walter Weiss, Mitch Fittler, Stacey Henline. Stephanie, Kathy Ash, Charlotte Ulla Pleym, Ray, Jason Schroeder, Chris Call, Maximilian Lippl, Andrew Rees, Tawnly Pranger, Minarkhaios, Vincent Fung, Dave Kochbeck, and Bob Jacobs.

GODSVERSE PLANETS

1000 BC – BETRAYED (HELL PT 1) /PIXIE DUST
500 BC – FALLEN (HELL PT 2)
200 BC – HELLFIRE (HELL PT 3)
1974 AD – MYSTERY SPOT (RUIN PT 1)
1976 AD – INTO HELL (RUIN PT 2)
1984 AD – LAST STAND (RUIN PT 3)
1985 AD – CHANGE
1985 AD – MAGIC/BLACK MARKET HEROINE
1985 AD – EVIL
1989 AD – DEATH'S KISS (DARKNESS PT 1)
2000 AD – TIME
2015 AD – HEAVEN
2018 AD – DEATH'S RETURN (DARKNESS PT 2)
2020 AD – KATRINA HATES THE DEAD (DEATH PT 1)
2176 AD – CONQUEST
2177 AD – DEATH'S KISS (DARKNESS PT 3)
12,018 AD – KATRINA HATES THE GODS (DEATH PT 2)
12,028 AD – KATRINA HATES THE UNIVERSE (DEATH PT 3)
12,046 AD – EVERY PLANET HAS A GODSCHURCH (DOOM PT 1)
12,047 AD – THERE'S EVERY REASON TO FEAR (DOOM PT. 2)
12,049 AD – THE END TASTES LIKE PANCAKES (DOOM PT 3)
12,176 AD – CHAOS

ALSO BY RUSSELL NOHELTY

NOVELS
My Father Didn't Kill Himself
Sorry for Existing
Gumshoes: The Case of Madison's Father
Invasion
The Vessel
The Void Calls Us Home
Worst Thing in the Universe
Anna and the Dark Place
The Marked Ones
The Dragon Scourge
The Dragon Champion
The Dragon Goddess
The Obsidian Spindle Saga

COMICS and OTHER ILLUSTRATED WORK
The Little Bird and the Little Worm
Ichabod Jones: Monster Hunter
Gherkin Boy
How NOT to Invade Earth

www.russellnohelty.com

RUIN

Book 8 of The Godsverse Chronicles

By:
Russell Nohelty

Edited by:
Leah Lederman

Proofread by:
Katrina Roets & Toni Cox

Cover by:
Psycat Covers

Planet chart and timeline design by:
Andrea Rosales

BOOK 1

"Mystery Spot"

CHAPTER 1

"I don't gotta do nothing no colored woman tells me to do," Duncan Lewis sneered at me. I planted my feet and gritted my teeth, trying desperately not to march over to his desk and scratch out his eyeballs.

The classroom "oohed" and "ahhed" as their eyes ping-ponged back and forth from the hulking brood at the other side of the room from me, the perturbed, black teacher standing at the front of it. Duncan was a behemoth of a man in a boy's body. He stood six foot three with buzzed, blond hair and bloodshot, brown eyes. His thick forearms folded across his chest, which swelled with pride at his racist statement.

"I'm not going to tell you again, Mr. Lewis," I said, trying my best to project authority when I had clearly lost any that I might have had. "Go to the principal."

"Make me, Ms. Freeman," he replied.

Any shred of respect the students held for me had dissolved five minutes ago when Duncan hurled a spitball into my long, straight, bleached white hair. It stuck in like glue, leading the whole room to burst into laughter. Still, I didn't back down. "I'm waiting," I said, glaring.

"I can see that, Julia," he replied, stoic. "You'll be waiting 'til the cows come home."

I fought the urge to leap across the desk and toss him through the window that backlit his broad shoulders. The way he sneered my first name like he knew me. I wanted desperately to fight, but that wasn't how I was taught. My mama taught me to capitulate to white folks because they will string up uppity negros as a lesson to others. I knew that truth all too well.

I combed my fingers through my hair one more time to pull out any spit left on it. My hair didn't use to be straight and bleached. I used to have a big, beautiful afro that would turn Pam Greer green with envy.

But that was back in Chicago. Back when I was in school before I moved home to take care of my mama in Chandler, Colorado. In this town, black folk lived on the other side of the tracks, where they wouldn't offend the sensibilities of good, Christian, white folk.

I dared to step across that track and apply for a job at the school all the white kids attended. Sure, segregation had been over for some years by 1974, but it's not like black folk could just move across town on a moment's notice, especially not to a house that cost double what they could afford, so they just stayed put and kept going to the same school just like they always had.

There wasn't really a black school and a white school anymore, not legally, but things hadn't changed so much since the 50s around here—no matter what the courts said.

The principal gave me a job teaching history, somehow, but nobody was happy about it. They called it affirmative action, and they called me a "token," but here at George Washington High, the pay was a lot better than across the tracks at William Howard Taft High, and I deserved that money. I worked hard for six years to get a Master's in history, but to get that money, I had to capitulate to make the white folks happy.

That meant I couldn't keep my afro. Now, my hair was "appropriate" for school and appropriate for Chandler; but that didn't matter. I still didn't get any respect.

"You are ruining your peers' education," I said.

"No more than you," Duncan replied to a room of chuckles. "I ain't the one tainting the classroom with my colored ideas."

I didn't know what to do. I couldn't back down, and I certainly couldn't take him on myself. I'd tried calling security into my classroom a dozen times before, and they were about as helpful as Duncan. Nobody wanted me here except for me.

It got deadly quiet in the classroom as we stared each other down. The air left the room, replaced with swirling eddies of tension.

Thankfully, the bell rang, breaking the spell. The students groaned under their breath as they collected their things. They wanted a fight. They might still get one, but not today. There would be plenty of time for fighting in the future, though. Tensions don't just fade away in Chandler; they built under the surface until something snapped.

"Alright, class," I said with a smile. "Since this distraction didn't give us any time to study, we'll have our quiz on chapters seven and eight next time without any preparation. Please study these chapters."

The class groaned again as they walked out of the classroom. They all wanted to be Duncan at that moment and stand up to me, but the truth is that Duncan was pathetic. He was the star football player, and he was dumb as a rock. Teachers passed him because he could hit people well and catch a ball. He would get to college on a scholarship if he managed not to blow out his knee, but eventually, he'd be back here working in a gas station, dreaming of his glory days for the rest of his life. Then again, I ended up back here too, so what does that say about me?

Duncan strolled up to the front of the room and cracked his knuckles on my desk. "I think I'm just gonna take the A and skip that test, Julia."

I laughed, looking him straight in the eye. "You don't have to come to class, but you will get an F."

"You don't know how this works, still, do you? You're the token hire, the joke. Nobody wants you here."

I leaned over the table. "Then we have something in common. Neither of us wants the other one here."

The loudspeaker creaked and crackled as it screeched through the room. "Ms. Freeman, please report to the principal's office."

Duncan pointed to the loudspeaker. "See?"

He strolled out as if he owned the place. He did, of course. In Chandler, he mattered more than me. That fact stung every day, but my mother beat it into my head enough. At least if you know the system, you can work around it.

***

"I don't know what to tell you, Julia," Principal Anderson said, shaking his shiny, bald head. His jowls slapped the sides of his face as he stammered. "The parents have complained, again."

It wasn't Principal Anderson's fault that the parents complained, but I couldn't help resenting him for it. "What is it this time? Way I chew my gum? Way I say hello? What could they possibly have to complain about now?"

Principal Anderson cleared his jowly throat. "Well, it's that hair, Miss Freeman. They…don't think it's appropriate."

I scoffed involuntarily. "I only have this hair because they told me they didn't like the cornrows, and I only had them because they didn't like the afro. I wake up at four am to straighten this goddamn hair."

I could tell my terse tone, and the fire in my eyes frightened him. That sort of thing, well…it scared white people, especially weak ones like Principal Anderson. They thought I was a wild animal, ready to strike at any time. Even the smallest hint of a temper sent them running for the door. Something about black people getting angry put white people on edge, even though they have all the power. Maybe it's because they have all the power, and they're worried we're gonna steal it back.

Principal Anderson scooted back in his chair, away from me. "I-I-I—"

"Speak up, Bob." I spat the words.

I had no patience for this back and forth. In the three months I'd been teaching, Principal Anderson and I had already held seven meetings about my appearance. Still, I wasn't supposed to be rude.

My mama taught me that—how to hold my tongue even when there was some nonsense taking place. She taught me to behave, to smile, to never raise my voice, and I didn't, for eighteen years. It's what got me out of this town alive when so many didn't, but after going to Chicago, and seeing a place where black people got along just fine, weren't looked at side-eyed when they walked into a restaurant and could puff out their chest with pride without fear of getting beaten, at least in the right neighborhoods, it was hard to act like a meek, obedient child again.

"I don't know what to tell you, Julia," Principal Anderson finally managed to say. "They don't like it. They think it should be shorter, more professional. They also have a problem with…"

His eyes tipped down to my clothes, a tasteful pantsuit that couldn't help but accentuate my curves. The parent-teacher association had a problem with me wearing slacks and a collared shirt now. Those bitties would say anything to get me fired.

"I am a curvy woman, Bob. I can't hide that."

Principal Anderson sighed. "The mothers would like it if you dressed more…matronly."

"I'm twenty-five years old. How matronly can you look at twenty-five? Do you want me to gain fifty pounds to keep this job? Cuz I'll do it, Bob. I'll do it."

He chuckled uncomfortably. "It wouldn't be the worst thing in the world."

I lowered my voice and dropped my eyes. "I need this job, Bob."

"I know, Julia. That's why I gave it to you. You're a damned good teacher, and your credentials are stellar. I want to keep you around, but it's only been three months, and you've gotten twenty complaints—"

"None of which are for my teaching."

Principal Anderson shook his head, disappointed. "And now I hear students are harassing you, too."

I took a deep breath and let it out slowly. "I'm losing their respect."

Principal Anderson placed his hand gently on the edge of the desk, expecting me to take it. "Don't take this the wrong way, Julia, but you never had it."

I was supposed to act like a meek teacher and tell him he was right, but I just couldn't. "It's always hard for all new teachers. I'm working on it, Bob. I'm getting through to some of them."

"Not enough, though, Julia. Not nearly enough."

I looked him in the eyes. "Are you firing me, Bob? Tell me straight."

He shook his head. "Of course not. Not yet, at least. I'm just saying you might be more comfortable at the…other school."

"You mean the black school across the tracks, right?" I said, pointing out the window behind him. "The one I came up through. The one no respectable white kid would attend even after everything that's happened in the last twenty years?"

Principal Anderson nodded, timidly. "There are a lot of good teachers over there."

"Then why ain't they over here, too?"

"Because they like it there," Principal Anderson said, smiling. "They're happy. They're respected. There is nothing wrong with that school, just because you say it's a black school."

"I didn't say there was anything wrong with it," I shouted. "That's not the point. Point is that I applied here, and I got hired here, not over there, and I should be able to work where I want as long as I'm doing my job right."

"I agree, but…that's just not how it is, and you know it. How are you going to feel when these kids get a lesser education, not because of anything you did, but because the other students don't respect you?"

I looked down at the ground. I couldn't deny that giving the children the best education was my top priority. "I would feel terrible."

"And how are you gonna feel when those really smart ones start to talk about you behind your back because you're a distraction to their education?"

"I'm gonna feel really bad about it," I replied. I could see him baiting me. Damn it, this wasn't on me. Not this time. "But how are you gonna feel, Bob, when I leave this school because those women wouldn't let me do my job? How will it feel when you let a bunch of old, white women convince you to fire a good teacher just because she's black? Are you gonna be able to look at yourself in the mirror and be okay with that?"

"I can look in the mirror fine, Julia. Just fine. My duty is to the students and make sure they get the best education possible. That is why I hired you because I thought you could provide that to them."

I stood up, seething. "I know why you hired me, Bob. We all know why you hired me. Thing is, I have more education than most of the teachers in this place. I got a Master's in history, Bob. How many of your teachers have Master's degrees?"

"Not many…"

"And how many have that Master's degree from Northwestern, huh? How many have them from one of the best schools in the country?"

"Not many."

"Not one of them do. Not one of them but me. I'll bet I'm the most qualified first-year teacher you've ever hired, and I'm gonna be the most qualified one that you've ever fired, too."

"I hope that's not true."

I headed toward the door. "You can tell those old bitties I'll start to wear my hair in a ponytail, and I'll wrap myself in a sweater whenever I'm in school. I promise you that, and if they ever want to talk to me—well, my door's open. Funny thing, though, Bob, I haven't ever heard from one of 'em."

"They won't talk to you except through me."

"I know they won't, Bob, and look. I know what you've done for me, giving me a chance to come back here and be with my mother. I know it's not easy for you."

Principal Anderson nodded. "Every day, it's something else. I'm trying, Julia. I'm really trying."

"And I appreciate that, Bob. I do, but I'm a human being with a goddamn Master's degree from Northwestern. I'm nobody's fool. I understand this game, and next year I might be right back over across the tracks where I came from, but until they kick me out of here, I am not going anywhere."

"I understand." He cleared his throat. "Uh, Julia, could you do me a favor?"

I stopped in the doorframe. "If I can, Bob."

"Don't tell anybody else you talked to me the way you did today, okay?"

"I was raised here, Bob. I know what's expected of me. Consider me the perfectly behaved teacher outside this office."

CHAPTER 2

They used to play this show, Leave It to Beaver, when I was growing up, and it reminded me of Chandler. From the outside, Chandler didn't seem so bad. Hell, from the outside, it looked downright cheery, just like every other sleepy, little hamlet across this country, complete with smiling, happy people, clean streets, and perfectly painted houses. They could have shot Leave it to Beaver right down the street from school, that's how wholesome it was here.

But that's just a veneer.

Funny thing was, you didn't see a lot of black folks in that show. I'd love to see how Wally and the Beave reacted to a black teacher. Something tells me Ward and June wouldn't like it much. They might even complain to the school about their precious child being taught by a colored woman. It was hard being black in Chandler now, but it was harder when I was growing up.

Hell, if you were a white kid in Chandler, Colorado, in the 1950s, things were hunky-dory for you. Things came up aces again and again. Your parents had work. They had a house. You had friends. You had some money. Your future looked bright as can be.

But that was just one side of the train tracks. There was another side to Chandler, a darker side, and I mean that quite literally. It was the side the good, old white people of Chandler didn't talk about or visit, and they didn't want us visiting them, either. It was the side where black folks like me lived.

***

By the time I stepped out of George Washington High School, it was dark out. The dead of winter's crisp wind nipped at my nose. The cold never bothered me, but I didn't like the night. The streetlights lit up the streets, but I didn't trust it. Bad things happened in Chandler at night.

I stood at the top of the steps looking out at the quaint square that made up downtown Chandler. Restaurants and shops lined the square, and at its center was the park that made us famous, Mystery Spot Park.

Mystery Spot Park wasn't like any other park I'd ever seen. It wasn't even like any other park in Chandler. This park, well, it had something special. Right there, in the middle of the park, was a giant hole that led to nowhere. You could throw a penny down into the hole, and it would never hit bottom.

Before I left Chandler, they fed a rope down into that hole ten miles and still never found where it ended. It was one of the great mysteries of eastern Colorado, and people came from miles around in the summer to play with it, to feel the weird electromagnetic energy that made your hair stand on end. On a hot summer day, there was a line twice around the block to get a peek. This was the dead of winter, though, and nobody came to Chandler in the winter. The spot was special, but not that special.

I walked down the steps of the school toward Mystery Spot Park, clacking my heels faster with every step. I loved it there. One of the only joys left in returning to Chandler was my nightly walk through the park when the cold air drove everybody away, and it was quiet and peaceful.

I couldn't explain it, but the mystery spot seemed to draw me toward it like it had a magnetic charge I couldn't control. Of course, most people thought that, which is why they came from far and wide to see it and waited all day to stare into the abyss. There was something magical about that hole. Of course, that was crazy because magic doesn't exist.

Electrical charges crackled sparks through my hair as I danced along the edge of the spot, just like I had done so often in my youth. I closed my eyes and spun as fast as I could until every hair on my head stood straight up into the air and twisted together in a ponytail.

"Hey!" A man's voice shouted at me. "Quit spinnin'. It's not safe to spin so close to the—"

I turned around to come face to face with a familiar face, Chuck Dixon, father of one of my most well-behaved students and nighttime security guard for the park. "I'm sorry, Mr. Dixon. I'm just strolling on the breeze and lost track of time."

"Oh. Sorry, Ms. Freeman. I didn't recognize you in the dark." He tipped his cap to me. "How is everything tonight?"

He was a handsome man, so I gave him my most flirtatious smile. I always knew how to smile right. "It's going just fine, and how is our lovely park tonight?"

He nodded. "Lovely as ever, my dear."

If I didn't know any better, I would think he was flirting back. The creases on the sides of his mouth turned up on the edges, and I was pretty sure he winked when he caught my eyes. Mr. Dixon's wife passed away some years ago, and, like my poor mother, he had to raise his child all on his own.

The neon sign above Charlotte's Diner crept into my periphery, and I remembered I was late to meet my mother for dinner. "I should be going, Mr. Dixon. Mama will be waiting for me."

"It's a pleasure, ma'am, and please, call me Chuck."

I strolled away from him, letting his eyes linger on me for a long moment as I walked. "I don't think I'll be doing that, Mr. Dixon, but thank you for the courtesy."

I always did know how to play the game.

CHAPTER 3

Mama never liked to eat at home. Home was a cold, dark place on the outskirts of town that she only visited when she needed to sleep. It used to be a warm, welcoming place with a down to Earth charm to it when I was growing up, even in the worst times. But since I'd left for school, it turned into a place I barely recognized. The furniture was the same, but the soul had gone from it.

Mama raised me by herself, which meant she hustled and bustled my whole life. When I was a kid, she ran a daycare out of our backyard. She kept her rates low since our neighbors couldn't afford much, which made her very popular. Our house was always full of kids, laughing and playing. Mama loved kids, but the daycare was about more than that. It was about survival, and in my neighborhood, you did what you had to do to get from the beginning of the month to the end of the month without going belly up.

It ran her ragged, though. To eke out a living, she had to take on a lot of kids, and the more kids she took on, the more help she needed, but that meant paying people, and she couldn't afford to do that without eating up every dollar she made. So, she ended up with too many kids and too little help, which made her entire life…challenging.

When I got up in age, I tried to help after school, but Mama wouldn't hear of it. She worked extra hard to make sure I could study and focus on school. She wanted to make sure I could leave if I wanted, even if she didn't think I'd ever want to go somewhere else.

She was wrong about that. I'd wanted to leave Chandler from the moment I exited the womb. What I never wanted to do was come back, but that's all that Mama wanted for me. Sometimes, I think she got old just to spite me.

When I got back to Chandler, things were different for Mama. She treated herself to the finer things since the house was paid off, and she got a social security check every month. It didn't hurt that I had a decent salary and could pay for a few of life's niceties which passed mama by in her younger days. I didn't mind spoiling her a bit, either. After all, she raised me. Back when I was a kid, we could never eat out. Money was always tight, like ketchup on bread tight—and stale bread at that, so we didn't leave the house much.

Eating out these days was more than just luxury, though. Nothing tickled Mama more than having dinner at a restaurant that had refused to serve her when she was young. She took great pride in sitting at a lunch counter in a place she once couldn't even step into without getting arrested and munching on food that white people said she couldn't have until the government forced them to treat her like a human being.

Her favorite place to eat was called Charlotte's Diner, right across from the mystery spot. For years, they'd had a sign on their window that said, "No Coloreds Allowed," but the government forced them to take it down. Mama liked to sit right by the window, where that sign had mocked her for so long, and stare out at the park, where every resident of Chandler could get a good look at her.

She would sit in that diner, sometimes all day, while I worked, just staring at that the mystery spot, which is exactly what she was doing when I entered the diner to the jingling of bells over the door. Mama never told me where she was going, but Chandler's a small town, and there weren't that many options.

"Mama!" I called to her from the entrance. She sat at a booth looking out the front window of the place through the big lettering that plastered CHARLOTTE'S on the front sign. Mama didn't look up as I sat down across from her.

"Didn't you hear me?" I asked.

Finally, she turned to me. Her wrinkled face cracked on its edges into a warm smile. "I heard you, but I was deep in thought. I'm glad you found me, even if you are late."

"Of course, I found you, Mama. You're always here."

She chuckled. "I'm not always here, my love. I'm just mostly here. And if I wasn't here, you would find me somewhere else. I do very much like that Chinese place around the corner, too."

A kindly, old woman named Martha came up to us. She was dressed in the powder blue waitress outfit common among all the wait staff, but she was different in her spirit. Martha was the only one who treated us like customers whose money was just as good as anybody else's and not a nuisance. It took me months to realize it, but she was the only person who would ever come to our table.

Everybody inside Charlotte's turned up their noses at us when we entered the place. Waitresses turned their backs and refused our calls for service. Patrons asked to move away from our table. Under their breath, of course, but there would suddenly be a chorus of shuffling tables and scampering feet whenever we sat down. Whenever I passed by the diner and Mama wasn't there, nobody ever sat in Mama's booth, as if we were contaminated with the plague.

Then, there was Martha, who smiled brightly at us just like we were any two other humans. "Good evening, Julia! What can I get for you?"

"Coke and a burger, please. Medium. You know how I like it." I returned her smile. Behind her, a couple scowled at me, but I didn't break my grin. You couldn't let them see you break, ever. "Mama, what do you want?"

"Oh, I already ordered."

Martha jotted my order down in her notebook. "Yes, she did. I'll have both your orders up right away."

She scooted away as the other patrons went about their business. Charlotte's wasn't a big place, and I could hear the animosity oozing from every table. Luckily, I got very good at drowning it out, though, and replacing it with idle chatter. Mama taught me that.

"How was your day?" she asked.

I just sighed. I opened my mouth to speak, but I just…couldn't get out the words. All I could do was grunt. Luckily, Mama knew exactly what that meant after hearing it every day since I came back.

"That bad, huh?" Mama asked in her most comforting voice.

"As bad as yesterday," I said, shaking my head. "Better than tomorrow, I'll bet."

"I told you I could put in a good word at Taft. Good people over there at Taft."

"No money over there at Taft, Mama," I said, exasperated.

"We don't need money, dear. We got the house free and clear."

"You still gotta eat." I gestured at the room. "This place ain't free."

She stared out to the park. The school loomed beyond the mystery spot. "I don't gotta eat here, my love, just like you don't gotta work there."

"Then why do you?" I asked.

"Same reason you do it, my love," she replied, knowingly.

I knew why I did it, and I knew why she did it, too. It was because we could, and because we could, we were compelled to do it. The rush was exhilarating, making everybody else in town uncomfortable, just like we made them uncomfortable when Dad went missing. It had been sixteen years since sheriffs found him hung from an oak tree in Mystery Spot Park.

"You know it's his birthday next week," Mama said.

"I know," I replied. "How did you know I was thinking about him?"

"Thinking about him all the time these days, aren't you?"

She was right. I thought about him often. I thought about him every time I passed by the park where he was snatched, and every time I stood under the tree where they hung him for the whole town to see for the high crime of being a loud, black man in a town full of quiet, black men.

"It's not his birthday, though, Mama. Birthdays are for people who are alive."

Mama nodded. "That's true, but he was still born then, my love. Nobody can take that away from him."

"No. They could just take away his life."

The whole diner stopped at that moment as if the needle on a record player skipped a beat. Waitresses stopped their deliveries as the patrons stared at us.

"Hush yourself," Mama said. "That's not polite. There's a line, baby."

She was right. My dad being lynched wasn't something you talked about in polite company, especially not during dinner.

It wasn't decent to talk about men stringing up your father. It wasn't proper to talk about how they watched his face turn purple as he struggled for breath or to discuss them cutting his throat and watching him bleed out. That wasn't proper conversation in Chandler.

The act wasn't decent, either, but talking about it was taboo. If you were black, you didn't talk about justice unless you wanted to wind up on a tree yourself, and when you can't talk about something, you can't convict somebody of it, either. Not that a white jury was going to convict good ole boys of killing a black man. So, we just had to move on and swallow our pain.

They didn't even talk about it on our side of the tracks. My dad's death sent a message to the whole community. *Shut your damned fool mouth.* They didn't just string him up, they cut his throat across the voice box to remind us not to say a word.

When I was growing up, there was a lynching like that just about every six months, for over a decade. Like clockwork. White folks needed to send a message every once in a while whenever we forgot our place. It could have been any other black man on any other day, but that day it was my father. It wasn't some other little girl who lost her daddy. It was me.

That kind of act, it built up a lot of resentment between black and white folks. Even though there hadn't been a lynching in ten years, the animosity never went away.

I looked out at the diner and saw a dozen hostile eyes staring back at me. There was no shame; they didn't even avert their gaze. Worse, they were disgusted that we weren't ashamed at interrupting their dinner with our insistence on existing. In that chorus of ugly, beady eyes, I lost my appetite.

"Can we go, Mama?" I asked.

"No. I'm hungry," she said, unaffected by their gaze. "And I'm gonna eat, damn it. You don't gotta eat, but don't go spoiling my appetite. You gonna keep spoiling my appetite?"

I shook my head. I knew the code. Shut your damn fool mouth. "No, Mama."

Martha smiled when she brought us our food, and the eyes of the other diners eventually turned away from me. The chatter of the diner drowned out my thoughts. Mama and I ate in silence, her staring out at the mystery spot and me staring at her, both watching with wonder.

CHAPTER 4

The only person who felt a bigger jolt at the mystery spot than me was my mother. She could have lived at that spot if they had let her. She could have pitched a big top tent over the spot and been quite happy for the rest of her days, but Chandler frowned on that kind of thing.

We tried to camp out there once when I was in seventh grade, but the security guards didn't think it was a good idea for two colored women to lie out all night like they were homeless. It wouldn't be good for tourism, they said. Still, they couldn't stop us from walking through a public park as often as we liked and dawdling a little and dancing around the spot.

After we finished our dinner, instead of turning right to walk back across the tracks to our house, Mama insisted on turning left and strolling through the park.

"It's a lovely night, Julia, and the fireflies will be out in full. It will be glorious."

"I'm not really that interested in seeing bugs, Mama," I replied. "I've been on my feet all day. All I want is a hot bath and sleep."

"Then, you can go on home. Leave your poor, old mother to her own devices. I'm going to stay, walk around the park, and enjoy the night air. I spent too many nights not doing that when I was bending over backward trying to raise you."

A mother's guilt trip transcended race, creed, and social status. It hit every child right in the cockles of their heart. When they wanted to, moms knew how to turn the screws and bend you to their will. My mother was no different, which is why, even though my feet were aching and my constitution was fried, I followed her around Mystery Spot Park in the late hours of the evening.

"Your father liked to walk me past this park, in our better days," Mama said.

"I know, Mama. He didn't like being hung here, though, so I'll bet all those good memories were drowned out by that bad one in his last moments."

"Memories don't work like that, honey."

"I guess we'll never know."

Mama looked up at the sky. Chandler was small and had very little light pollution, unlike Chicago. We could make out half the stars in the sky when we craned our necks skyward. "We might yet, child. We might yet."

I had nothing else to say to my mother. I just wanted to do my bit and walk her home, just like it was my bit to live in Chandler for as long as my mother saw fit to keep her house and hold onto her life. That could be five minutes or five hundred years for all I knew. Freeman women tended to live long, unnaturally healthy lives.

My hair stood on edge with the sparks of the mystery spot when I heard a man's voice. "Hey!" No Chuck Dixon this time. It was Duncan's deep growl. Now, every hair on my body stood at attention.

I whipped myself around to see Duncan and three of his thuggish friends stumbling through the park, drunk, as if they owned the place. Who am I kidding? They did own the place. Duncan's daddy had funded the mayoral and city council campaigns for every powerful person in town for the last twenty years. Duncan and his father, more than anybody, owned Chandler.

I put on my nicest face; the kind Mama taught me to plaster on myself at the first sign of trouble. "Good evening, boys. Nice to see you on this fine day."

"Don't talk to me, colored," Duncan sneered, taking a deep swig from a bottle of Jack Daniels. "We ain't in school no more. You ain't got no authority here."

The whiskey on his breath knocked me backward, and when he lurched forward, I stumbled into Mama. His flunkies hovered behind him like wolves waiting to strike. "I don't want no trouble, Duncan. I just want to make my way home in peace."

"It's Mr. Lewis to you."

"Excuse me?" I said, disgusted at the thought of showing him any deference.

Duncan strolled up to me, an ugly grin smeared across his face. He had the power, and he knew it. Plus, he had backup that egged him on with every step he took forward.

"You don't get to call me Duncan, do you understand me?" The words oozed out of his mouth. "It's Mr. Lewis to you from now on. I don't even wanna hear that you called me Duncan to your colored friends in the privacy of your colored home, got it?"

I wanted to shout out, but I knew the consequences. I looked down at the ground, just like Mama taught me. "Yes, sir. I sure do see your point."

He laughed and took another swig from his whiskey bottle. "That's what I thought, colored. You don't have no bones, and you don't have no spine. Like just like your mama."

I don't know where it came from inside of her, but Mama pulled back and slapped Duncan across the face. I'd never seen my mother so angry. She was the one who taught me to take it on the chin, and now, without warning, she exploded.

"Listen here, boy! I've been called a lotta things by a lotta white folks, but I ain't never gonna let you talk down to my daughter in front of me, you hear? Learn you some respect!"

But Duncan couldn't learn respect because nobody was willing to teach it to him. Even if they were, he was too dumb to comprehend the concept.

His baser instincts took over. I watched the humanity drain out of him, and a wild beast take its place, egged on by the chanting baboons behind him.

"I ain't never been hit by no colored," Duncan said, balling up his fist. "And I ain't ever gonna let no colored live who struck me."

Duncan charged at my mother. I leaped in front of her, holding my arms out wide to protect her. "Duncan! No! She doesn't know! She's old!"

Duncan threw me out of the way like I was a ragdoll and charged at my mother. "She won't have to worry about being old no more, cuz now she'll be dead!"

I rose to my feet and leaped on Duncan's back, holding back his arms as he tried to swing. He grabbed me under my shoulder and flung me. I crashed into Mama and sent us both onto the grass.

"Fine. I'll kill the both of you. It'll be a nice family plot up in Potter's Field with your daddy. And I'll come piss on it whenever I get drunk."

I clenched my fists. If I was gonna die, I wasn't going down without a fight. I might've looked like the meek girl who left Chandler, but I learned how to fight in Chicago, and I wasn't gonna let those karate classes my roommate dragged me to go to waste.

I pulled back my fist, but Mama stayed my hand. "No! I already done enough. If you hit that boy, they'll run you out of town for sure."

"So, you want me to let him kill us?" I shouted.

Mama looked Duncan in the eyes as he watched us on the ground. "Look at that boy. He's a coward. He won't kill us. It takes an ounce of courage to kill a person in cold blood, and he doesn't have it. His father might come for me, but he doesn't have the stones."

"I'll show you who has the stones!" Duncan shouted.

He charged us. I held onto Mama tight, trying to protect her from the savage beating sure to come. I had been beaten within an inch of my life before, back in high school, and I ended up in the hospital for a week. I wasn't looking forward to it happening again, but I would survive. A beating like that would destroy Mama's old, frail body.

I braced for the brunt of his assault as Duncan swung back his leg. His friends circled around, ready to join in on the violence…and then the whole world shook. Purple sparks fanned out in front of us, a bolt of light cracked where we lay, and we were gone, leaving Duncan to swing his leg at empty air and land on his behind in the wet, dewy grass.

CHAPTER 5

We reappeared in Mama's living room with a bright, purple flash, crashing through her antique, wooden coffee table in the living room and splintering every one of its legs. My hands shook uncontrollably, and my chest pounded like I'd taken ten shots of pure adrenaline.

"What the what?" I shouted, anxious and excited. "What just happened?"

The hair on the back of my neck stood on end. My eyes refused to focus, and when I looked at Mama, I saw three of her smiling back at me.

I thought I was having a stroke for a moment. Then, three mamas merged back into one, and my head stopped spinning. When I looked again at her on the ground, she seemed completely unfazed by the experience of transporting halfway across town in an instant.

"What are you talking about, dear?" Mama asked, pushing herself up to her knees.

"Are you kidding me?" I shouted from the floor. "We just…I don't know what just happened. One second we were in the park, and the next…we are here."

Mama pushed herself to her feet. "Oh, that. Well, sometimes it happens. Haven't you ever just ended up somewhere and didn't know how you got there?"

I tried to push myself up, but my head spun, and I lost my balance, sending me crashing back to the floor.

"This is not that, Mama. It's not like I just forgot where I was going and ended up somewhere. We…like…we teleported here like we were on *Star Trek* or some shit."

"I don't know what that means," Mama said, shaking her head at the broken table beneath her. "A damn shame. I had that table since before I met your father."

I shook my head at her quizzically. "Are you really more concerned with that stupid table than the fact we just…like, vanished from one place and appeared somewhere else?"

"Well, I loved that table. And as for the other thing, it happens. I don't see what the fuss is about."

"The fuss is because that's not normal. None of this is normal."

"Really? Seems normal to me. I don't know."

I rolled over to my stomach. "Are you saying that you make it a habit of teleporting all over the place? Do you have some special powers you haven't told me about yet?"

She shrugged. "I'm not saying it hasn't happened before. I can't remember an instance, but I'm saying that I'm old and lots of things have happened to me before. It takes a lot to make me take notice."

I gave up trying to stand and rolled back to my back, content to let my dizziness pass. "Alright, so what if I grew wings and started to fly? Would that be enough to grab your attention?"

"I think so. Yes, that would be something I've never seen before, I'm sure of it. This, well, I can't say that I have dealt with it before, but I can't say that I haven't. I've forgotten a lot in my life, kiddo. Probably more than you've ever learned."

"Doubtful. I'm very educated."

Mama walked toward the stairs. "And I am very old."

"Just so we are clear…you can neither confirm nor deny that this has happened to you before, and it's so uninteresting that it doesn't even warrant a couple of minutes of your attention?"

Mama thought for a second. "Yes. That sounds about right. Goodnight, my dear."

"You are the weirdest person I have ever known. Do you know that?"

She smiled at me, starting up the stairs. "Thank you."

I laid on the floor, listening to her amble up the stairs, trying to regain my balance and stand up. There was silence for a moment, save for the creak of wood under Mama's feet as she stepped. Finally, I called after her. "Can I ask you one more thing, Mama?"

She stopped. "It's not about this whole business, is it?"

"No," I said. "Well, not exactly. My whole life you taught me to behave and not act up to white folks…so why did you slap Duncan now?"

She smiled, creeping up the stairs. "Cuz I am old, dear, and while I've become quite accustomed to white people pushing me around, I am tired of letting little, white boys push you around. I let them disrespect me for sixty-seven years, and I just couldn't let them do it to you one more time—not tonight."

"I'm scared, Mama," I said. "I'm scared of what they're gonna do to you."

She chuckled. "I survived a whole lot worse than Duncan Lewis in my day. His father—now that's a real scumbag."

"And what if his father doesn't like what you did?"

"Then he can take it up with me if he wants," Mama said, continuing up the stairs. "Something tells me he's got better things to do than string up an old, black woman."

"What if you're wrong?"

She cackled from the top of the stairs. "Then I lived a good life, baby. A good, long life. And it sure felt good to smack that spoiled, young face. Really good."

***

My hands and feet shook for another hour as I tried to make sense of what happened to me. The panic I felt made it hard to concentrate on anything for too long. My rational brain wanted to make sense of transporting from one place to the other, and so I laid against the cold, hardwood floor and tried to force myself to calm down and focus.

I thought back on every single moment from the last hour, every single emotion I'd felt, and still, my mind wandered. I was hyper aware of every nuanced detail of my living room as I haven't been for my entire life. In the years since I'd left for Chicago, the ceiling had become warped. A crack split the room in half, winding its way from behind the rabbit-eared television and up the wall and ceiling until it disappeared behind our overstuffed brown couch. Another crack twisted on the wall next to our dusty grandfather clock in the corner. The whole house had fallen into disrepair. It had never been big or flashy, but Mama always took pride in keeping it spotless.

"This is our plot of land, baby girl," she told me when I was younger. "We don't have forty acres or a mule, but we got this place, and it's up to us to do with it the best we can and take pride in it."

When I was a child, she kept our house the most pristine on the block. She spent weekends pruning the garden and cutting the grass. Heck, she even bartered for better grass seed to make sure that our house looked as good as any on the other side of Chandler. Every week we cleaned the house spotless so that whenever somebody came over, they knew we did the best with what we had at our disposal.

But when I left for college, that all changed. It didn't happen at once, but the years wore on our house over time. The bright, fresh paint we spent every summer reapplying became chipped and dull; inside, the rooms were cluttered and dusty, with cracked ceilings and smudged walls, not to mention dust caked an inch thick on every surface.

I wondered if that was the reason Mama never liked being inside the house or if her never being inside the house was the reason it fell into disrepair. I knew better than to ask, though, because asking the question meant cleaning the house, and frankly, it never bothered me that it was dirty…just like it didn't seem to bother Mama that we transported across town in an instant.

My mind snapped back to the events of earlier tonight. How could teleporting across town not bother her? I mean, it *was* crazy that it didn't bother her. I wasn't just freaking out about something trivial, even if she tried to make me feel that way. No way. This was not normal.

And what did she mean when she said, 'Well, sometimes it happens'? Had it happened to her before? Would it happen to me again? I kicked myself for letting her go to bed without asking her more questions.

I struggled to stay awake and ponder answers to those questions, but the day's events caught up to me in a wave of exhaustion. I'd never been so tired. I made a vague attempt to get into bed, but my body simply refused to move. Eventually, I stopped fighting against it and drifted off into the silence of sleep, right there on the floor.

***

The next morning, I woke up to the sweet smell of scrapple cooking on the stove. "Get up!" Mama shouted. "You've been sleeping on the floor like a damn hobo too long."

My head throbbed as I sat up like it split down the center of my skull. I suffered from migraines as a child, but nothing compared to the pain I felt at that moment. I turned over to my knees to wretch at the pain, but nothing came out except a low, guttural heave.

"Don't you dare throw up on my floor like a damned fool!" Mama shouted from the kitchen.

I looked at the grandfather clock. 6:45! I was running late. I had twenty-five minutes to get to the school all the way across town. I sprang to my feet, fighting the headache smashing through my brain.

"Why did you let me sleep so long?" I yelled, bounding up the stairs toward my room.

"It seemed like you needed it!" Mama shouted back.

"What I need is not to get fired!"

There was no time for a shower. Luckily, I didn't have time to work out yesterday, so I didn't stink. I kicked off my shoes, peeled off my socks, then hopped out of my pants and threw on a pair of loose-fitting, stained blue jeans that I usually only wore on the weekends.

Scrambling through my drawers, I found a light green button-up shirt. It sagged off my chest and left me looking like an amorphous blob, which hopefully would appease the bitties gunning for my head. I threw a loose, argyle sweater over the top of the blouse and tied a black shawl around my shoulders. I couldn't stop my form from showing through my clothes, but I'd do my best to mask it.

A pair of boots under my arm, I lumbered into the bathroom and brushed my teeth before throwing on a half-gallon of perfume, just in case. I threw up into the sink as the pain of the headache overtook me, and the thick yellow bile stank enough to force me to brush my teeth again.

"Get down here, Julia!" Mama screamed. "Breakfast is ready!"

"I'll be right there!"

There was no time for makeup, save for a light foundation to cover up the bags under my eyes. Probably for the best. I wouldn't want the bitties from the PTA to think I was dressing too sexy *and* wearing enough makeup to make a whore blush. I looked a fright, but that's what they all wanted.

The pain pulsed against my skull with each hurried step I took toward the kitchen. I threw back four aspirin and chugged a glass of orange juice, then took a huge gulp of a sandwich that Mama left on the counter for me.

"You're going to choke, dear," Mama said.

"I'm going to get fired, Mama. They're looking for any excuse."

"Would that be so bad?"

Her sly grin belied the real reason why she let me sleep in. She didn't want me working at that school and thought I should be working at Taft. That was no secret. She told me that at least three times a week, but she'd never actively worked to get me fired.

Mama thought my talents should be used to help bring up the next generation of black men and women. I thought I should be paid as well as possible for all the work I put into getting my degrees, even if it meant rolling over for rich, white, entitled assholes.

"Yes, Mama," I said as I grabbed my purse. "It would be. I don't want to be fired."

Mama shrugged. "I'm just saying it wouldn't be the worst thing in the world."

"Few things are."

I wanted to ask Mama so many questions about last night and chide her for so blatantly working to get me fired, but there was no time. I threw on a leather coat and rushed out the door, boots squeezed in my hands.

I was halfway across the street before I slid on my boots and realized they didn't match. One of them had a three-inch heel and one laid flat on the ground. There was no time to turn back and change. I was barely able to make it on time as it was, so I just dealt with it, hobbling down the street like a pirate with a peg leg.

CHAPTER 6

I limped into the school at 7:05 after power-hobbling for the better part of a mile. I ran track in high school and was still quick on my feet, even in uneven boots. I held back vomiting three times on the way to school, and by the time I walked through the door, the aspirin had kicked in, and my head felt much better. Still, if I didn't look ragged before, I was a straight mess now—sweat dripping down my face, my bleached hair frayed at the edges, tottering to and fro as my boots clacked against the ground.

Principal Anderson called out after me when I passed by his office. "Everything alright, Julia?" he asked. "Almost late today…"

"Nothing is fine, Bob, but we're all getting through the best we can."

I hobbled into the office and came face to face with a smiling secretary named Mrs. Blick. True to form, she was grinning from ear to ear.

"Good morning, dear!" she said through her bright teeth. "Anything I can help you with?"

I eyed her up and down. "You're a size seven, right?"

She nodded. "Sure am. Almost my whole life."

"Do you happen to have any shoes back there I can use for the day? I seem to be…out of sorts today."

Without hesitation, she dove under her desk and pulled out a pair of moccasins. "Sure do! I use them when my feet hurt too much in these danged heels. Just around the office, though, never out."

I unzipped my boots and kicked them off. I slipped on Mrs. Blick's shoes, and they fit perfectly. However, my mismatched socks did them no favors. "Do you mind if I…don't wear the socks?"

Mrs. Blick shrugged. "Of course, dear. In fact, you can just have those old things. I need a new pair anyway, and this gives me a reason to bug Charles."

"Oh no. I couldn't."

She smiled wider. "I insist."

There was a kindness in her eyes that I didn't often see in Chandler. There was a reason she worked with Principal Anderson for so long. They were both decent people in a place with a severe lack of them.

"Thank you," I said, picking up my boots. "There is one other thing. I hate to ask…"

"Anything, deary."

I pointed to the thick ponytail jutting out the back of her head. "Do you have another ponytail holder? I'm sorry. I'm just all out of sorts today."

Mrs. Blick dug into her desk and pulled out a thick blue hair tie. "It's yours, too."

I heaved a sigh of relief and took the hair tie. "You are a lifesaver."

"Women have to stick together, right?"

I flashed her a huge smile as I walked out into the hallway. "That's right."

***

Clad in my new shoes and throwing my boots back under my arm, I walked down the hallway of George Washington High School with a renewed sense of spirit. I didn't feel like a new woman, but I felt more confident than I had hobbling into school. A quick stop at the bathroom to splash some water on my face and pop a breath mint revived me, and a stop at the teacher's lounge to grab a tall cup of coffee put me in better spirits.

When I left the teacher's lounge, I noticed that more students than usual were glaring at me; their facial expressions ranged from disgusted to horrified. I was used to getting the side-eye from people in town, but usually, the students were more respectful, with exceptions like Duncan sprinkled into the mix. Today, though, every other student murmured about me under their breath.

As if materialized by my thoughts, Duncan turned onto the hallway from behind a locker and pointed at me. "That's the one. The freak who vanished last night."

I grumbled as he stepped toward me. "Good morning, Duncan."

Duncan lunged at me. "What did I tell you about that, freak? You don't get to say my first name. Show some respect to people better'n you."

"Respect will be given when respect is shown, Duncan," I replied. "We are not in a darkened park anymore, and we are not alone. Now, we are in school, and in school, you show teachers respect." I took a step toward him until we stood nose to nose. "Is that clear, Duncan?"

His muscles quivered from what I assumed was so much misplaced rage. "This isn't over."

"It will never be over, Duncan, and yet I go on anyway, just like I've always done. Now, if you'll excuse me, I have to get to class."

The disgusted stares of the children turned to tittering voices as I walked away. The tardy bell rang, and for the first time since the previous day, I felt in control of my life. It wouldn't last, but I relished the moment.

***

Tales of last night spread around the school like wildfire, and the only talk all day was about me suddenly vanishing in the park, mostly jokes about how awesome it would be if suddenly I was gone.

I would be lying if I said their barbs didn't sting. I tried so hard to be a good teacher and make them passionate about learning, and here all they could talk about was how much they wished I would vanish off the face of the Earth.

By lunch, I needed a break from my room. I usually ate by myself there, away from the students that treated me like a pariah. Today, though, my room suffocated me. So, I walked out into the courtyard, where the students ate. It was cold, but not the kind of cold that kept kids inside, at least not in Colorado. The courtyard was filled with students chatting away. I grabbed a lonely seat on a picnic bench away from the students, under a big oak tree with gnarled branches that spun sinuously into the heavens.

People in Chandler called oaks "hanging trees." Towns across Colorado used them for hangings back in the 1800s. Ignorant folks still used them for hanging black folks when they wanted to send a message. They found my daddy in a tree just like it. It took them half an hour to cut him down. Stank something fierce after being left up all night. Mama barely recognized him when she went to identify the body.

In the shade of the tree in the corner of the courtyard, I couldn't help but think about my father. His memory clung to me in Chandler like it never did in Chicago. He always told me times were changing, that one day Chandler wouldn't look the same or feel the same as it did in the 50s, and he was right on one count. Times had changed, but Chandler still felt the same as it always did, full of the same types of people. People like Duncan Lewis.

I watched Duncan walk out of the school. He passed up sitting with his cronies, instead making a beeline for the edge of the school. There stood a group of men all in matching brown leather coats. I didn't notice them before because they clung to the shadows, but they emerged when Duncan came closer.

On the back of each of their jackets was a patch showing a bloody dagger dripping on a red star. As I focused on the leader, I recognized "Big Jim" Ellis, Duncan's father and proprietor of Big Jim's Used Car Emporium, the biggest car dealership in the tri-county area for over twenty years.

Behind him stood Sheriff Nick Taylor, and two city council members, George Wallace and Tom Seaver. Big Jim had got them all elected into office, and in return, they jumped when he called. Behind them, three men I didn't recognize stood in the shadows, silent.

Big Jim's expression turned from a frown to a scowl as Duncan spoke. He muttered a few words and pointed right at me as if I couldn't see him. The whole cabal craned their necks to look at me. Their dead eyes pierced into my soul, and my half-digested sandwich leaped back into my throat. It was one thing to deal with a bunch of punk children. It was quite another to have the most powerful men in town stare menacingly at you.

I should have averted my gaze, but something inside of me decided I wouldn't let them see my fear. I left my lunch on the bench and walked over to the group with the biggest smile I could muster. "Good afternoon, fellas. Can I help you with something?"

They scattered into the wind faster than I could reach them, like cockroaches when you turned on a light. Even Duncan, usually so cocksure, headed back into the school with some speed in his gait. As I walked back to my table

under the hanging tree, I wondered why they would fear
little old me. I had no power in Chandler while they had all
of it.

CHAPTER 7

I was elated that Duncan decided not to show up for my last class of the day, but with all the whispers, he was still an overwhelming presence in the room. Tales of my vanishing act infiltrated every crevice of the school to the point that students couldn't concentrate on their work. Instead, they just leered at me, gape-jawed through my lesson.

When the final bell rang, I watched the students fly out of my classroom. Once the room was clear, the loudspeaker crackled to life. "Ms. Freeman to the principal's office. Ms. Freeman to the principal's office."

The students' eyes burned into me as I trudged to the principal's office for the second time in as many days.

***

"I'm not going to respond to unsubstantiated rumors," I told Principal Anderson when I sat down. I was sick of being polite.

He ignored me. "Julia, this is a very troubling rumor. You vanishing at will like a witch, creating Satanic voodoo in the park at night. Is there any truth to these rumors?"

"Bob, I told you I'm not going to respond to rumors, especially ones as stupid as these. Are you telling me you believe I can vanish at will like a witch? I'm black, Bob, not supernatural."

Principal Anderson leaned back in his chair, trying to feign a level of cool I knew he didn't possess. "I know this sounds crazy, but I have to identify every possible problem and suss it out thoroughly. That's my job."

I leaned forward, trying to drive home my point. "Do you though, Bob? This sounds like the kind of thing you could just let go."

"It's scaring the children and causing them to talk, Julia. It's affecting their learning."

"So now, if I get this straight, I not only have to pull back my hair and dress more conservatively, but I gotta prevent children from spreading rumors about me, or I could wind up back here again. That's a lot of rules, Bob. It's too many rules. Children gossip. I thought my third-grade teacher was a troll because she had long fingernails and a mustache. But you know what, Bob?"

"She wasn't?"

"That's right, Bob, she wasn't. But that didn't stop me from telling everybody she was one. Do you think she got sent to the principal's office for some crap her student said?"

"I would suppose not, but you are in a different situation."

"Yes, I'm black, so clearly that means I'm a witch."

"I didn't say that."

I stood up. "Fire me or don't Bob, but enough with this literal witch hunt."

***

Without another word, I stormed out of Principal Anderson's office. Ripping the hair tie out of my hair, I left it on Mrs. Blick's desk, right beside the moccasins. I didn't want to be beholden to her kindness. I couldn't afford to owe anybody favors. I decided to walk home barefoot, with my boots tucked under my arm.

I knew the game that Bob was playing. It was thoroughly explained to me in four years at Northwestern just how disruptive and insidious racial injustice could be and how hard it was to break. Bob wouldn't outright fire me, but it was clear that he was going to make my job uncomfortable until I quit or until he could build up enough of a case to fire me for incompetence and win when I sued him for wrongful termination.

I could call my union rep and tell her that they were hassling me, but she didn't like me any more than the bitties in the PTA. I was a pariah for the color of my skin, plain and simple. Teaching was all I ever wanted to do, and now I had to tiptoe on eggshells just to walk through the door.

Maybe Mama was right. Maybe I should just get a job at Taft. I would make less money, but it would be less of a hassle, too. They would appreciate me and my years of schooling instead of looking to fire me at every turn.

I visibly shook with anger when I stomped out of the school and made my way toward the park. I was so upset that I almost didn't see the white van following behind me. Luckily, Mama taught me to keep my head on a swivel no matter how I felt and always look for anything suspicious out of the corner of my eye.

I lifted my arm, and "oops," my boots dropped to the ground. When I turned around to pick them up, I got a good look at the driver before he ducked behind the steering wheel. I recognized him as one of the nondescript men standing in the shadows behind Big Jim and his cronies earlier in the day.

I'd heard the stories before. I knew what would come next. They would wait until I was in a secluded area and snatch me. If I avoided them this time, they would wait. They knew who I was and where I lived. It was only a matter of time until I let down my guard enough for them to capture me.

Taking a deep breath, I continued walking. If I could make them believe they hadn't been spotted, I could lull them into a false sense of security. Then, when the moment was right, I could bolt, leaving them in the dust.

That was my plan until Duncan, and his gang walked around the corner in front of me and spotted me. My breath went shallow, and the hair on my neck stood on edge. I was about to die. I knew it. *Was this how my father felt when they got him?*

What I needed was a place to hide, a place to be safe, but I didn't trust any of the shop owners, not in Chandler. They were all white and in good with Big Jim since he was president of the Chamber of Commerce, among all his other illustrious titles. Any shop owner would surely rat on me, especially if they knew the richest man in town wanted me dead.

Wait, I thought. That wasn't true.

They weren't all white. I forgot the tea and curiosities shop across from the park was owned by a black woman. If I could make it there, I had a shot at staying alive. It was my best shot. I turned down the nearest alley and ran until I burst out the other side. The boys turned with me as the van sped up to catch me.

They didn't know I was fast. Even in my bare feet, I was faster than them—for a short burst, at least. Sprints were my specialty in school, and with the added adrenaline of running for my life, I made it through the alley in record time. The asphalt cut my feet something fierce, but by the time I turned the corner at the other end of the alley, I'd put some distance between Duncan and myself.

I needed to make it around the block to get to the tea shop. It was just one block, but I had to do it without being spotted. Quickly, I cut another corner before Duncan and his boys made it down the alley, but the white van saw me and sped up to close the distance. Luckily, the light turned red right as I rounded the bend, and I sped away.

They didn't need to break the law by running the red light. They knew where I lived. All they had to do was be patient and wait. This block was longer than the last, and Duncan got a glimpse of me before I turned the last corner before the tea shop.

I was across from the park now, and the tea shop was in front of me. The old woman often left for the day while my mother and I ate at Charlotte's. She seemed nice enough, even if I had no interest in teas. She must have been quite pleasant—and pretty darn savvy—to get approved for a business license in Chandler as a black woman.

Summoning every ounce of my strength, I churned my legs as fast as I could go until I reached the doorknob. The door jingled as I flung it open and lunged inside.

The old woman sat quietly behind the counter. She jumped a bit when I entered the door as if she wasn't expecting customers. Thank god, she was the only person in the place. She turned to me with a puzzled look across her wrinkled face.

"What are you—"

"*Shhhhh,*" I whispered. "They're after me."

"Who?" she asked.

I ducked down under the window as the old woman walked over and peered out. Soon enough, she saw the boys run past, followed by the white van. The old woman shook her head. "Damn fools."

She turned the "open" sign on her window to closed and flipped off the lights. Only the dim illumination from a dozen or so candles remained. "You must have had quite a fright, huh?"

"Please…don't talk…"

The old woman shuffled back behind the counter and picked up a ceramic teapot adorned with tiny, pink fairies. She poured a cup of piping hot tea into a matching teacup and shuffled back over to me. "This will help. Chamomile calms the nerves. Drink up."

She bent down and handed the cup to me. I didn't want to drink it, but she had just saved my life, so I was inclined to oblige her. The hot tea coated my throat as it went down, and my labored breathing returned to normal.

"Feel better?" she asked.

I nodded, finishing the last of the tea. "Yes, actually. Much."

"I thought it might do the trick."

I stood up, careful to avoid the blinds. "Why are you not more freaked out to see me run into your store?"

The old woman sat back down on the stool behind her register and leaned against a wall of jars, each labeled with a different variety of tea. Some I recognized, like Earl Grey and English Breakfast and Green Herbal, but there were hundreds I had never heard of before, like Oolong, Matcha, and Darjeeling. There must have been a hundred, maybe a thousand, different varieties. She followed my eyes to the teas and asked, "Do you like tea?"

"I'm more a coffee girl. I drink green tea sometimes when they give you tea at that Chinese restaurant Dim Sum, but it's not really my thing."

The old woman smiled, grabbing a pinch of tea from a jar labeled Oolong. "I would think that you haven't had the right tea, then. There's tea from all over the world, in every smell, taste, and look imaginable."

"Yeah, coffee really has, like, one flavor. It's a great flavor, though."

The old woman placed the tea leaves in a bright pink pot. "To each their own. I love tea. Every day I wake up to a different flavor, and smell, and taste."

I walked over to the register. Its big metal keys looked out of place around the delicate doilies and pastels around it. In the middle of the room stood a circular, wooden table. All sorts of rocks, mirrors, and crystal balls rested upon it.

"I'll stick with coffee," I replied, watching her fill the pot with hot water from a kettle. "Coffee is utilitarian. You get an injection of caffeine, and it lets you suffer through your day."

"Suffer? *Tsk tsk tsk.* I don't think I've suffered through one day in my whole, ancient life."

I chuckled, shaking my head. "Then you've been charmed, especially looking like that and living in Chandler."

The old woman poured the tea from the pink pot into a matching cup. "No, it hasn't been easy. I never said it was. It's never easy for people like me…or your mother."

"You know my mother then."

She nodded, taking a sip of the tea. "I have known her most of her life. There are not so many of us anymore."

"That's for sure. Black people are leaving Chandler by the bucket load every chance they get."

The old woman placed the teacup down on her register. "That's not what I'm talking about."

I picked up a purple geode from the counter. There was no price on it. "You talk in a lot of riddles. Did you know that?"

"I have been told it's part of my charm."

"I wouldn't call it that," I said, placing the geode back down. "Charm, that is."

"Tell me, Julia, are you a reader?"

I spun to her. "How do you know my name?"

"I told you that I know your mother, but even without that, this is a small town, and I am very nosey. I was disappointed that you never stepped through my door before. I've waited a long time, but I am happy you are here now."

"You've been waiting for me?" I asked, confused.

She nodded. "Just like I waited for your mother. Though she took far less time than you. I suppose we all have to appreciate tea in our own time."

"I'm not here for tea, lady. I'm here because I don't want to get lynched."

"Of course. We all come for our own reasons, but you did have a reason to be here, and that is what matters."

"I just want to go home."

"Home will not be safe for you. Not anymore. The people after you are relentless. After what happened last night, there is no hiding."

My eyes went big as saucers as my voice cracked with fear. "You know what happened last night?"

She smiled. "Of course. I see all and hear all. There is a reason I picked this location, besides the fabulous weekend foot traffic."

"And…you aren't freaked out by…what I did?"

The old woman reached under her table and pulled up a large book with the words "Pixie Dust" embossed in gold leaf on the red leather cover. The book itself was thick enough to be a weapon.

"I offer this to you," she told me, tapping the cover. "Take it home. Read it. Study it. It will help you understand what happened to you. Come back once you've read it, and I will answer all your questions about why you can disappear."

"Can't you just tell me now?" I replied. "I'm not really interested in a study session. I have a lot on my mind."

She shook her head. "I'm afraid not. This is how it must be. First read, and then we talk."

I sighed, picking up the heavy book. "And if I read all of this, you'll stop being a weird, cryptic lady and tell me what's going on?"

"I promise." The woman stood up and walked toward the door. She peered out the window for a moment, craning her neck in either direction. Then, she turned to me. "I don't see them. I believe it's safe to go but promise me that you will read it."

I nodded my head. "You saved my life tonight, so I promise. I promise I'll read it."

She smiled. "Good. Now, hurry home."

CHAPTER 8

I lugged that stupid book all the way home under one arm while I held my boots in the other. It must have been three hundred pounds, and the trip took forever because I wandered the back roads and alleyways to avoid any white vans or racist students looking for me.

I knew Chandler like the back of my hand. In order to avoid racist scumbags and stay safe growing up, I'd learned every shortcut and back alley junction in town. If anybody could get home from the park without being seen by Big Jim Lewis and his ilk, it was me.

When I finally made it home, the house was eerily dark. I was supposed to meet Mama for dinner but decided just to come home. She wouldn't wait for me to eat anyway, and I just couldn't deal with any more sideways looks.

Besides, I had work to do. The old woman's book was at least seven hundred pages, and I was determined to finish it before morning. I'd often binge-read textbooks in college, and this was no different.

I made myself a peanut butter sandwich and sat cross-legged on the floor with the massive tome sprawled out in front of me. Dust had settled into the grooves of the red leather cover and latched on tightly. No matter how hard I scrubbed my fingers into the nooks of the leather, the dust wouldn't budge. It had likely been there for generations, and the idea that a simple scrub from my icky fingers would clean it was insulting to dust of all kinds.

There was no author listed, either on the cover or inside pages, which felt like they'd been soaked in coffee and left to dry for a quarter-century. Each of the chapters—there were a hundred or so—chronicled the life of a different person: Argus, Zabina, Rasmus, Akta, Bilal, Grok, and dozens of others. The text itself looked handwritten with ornate images drawn into margins every bit as ornate as *The Book of Kells*. Every few chapters, the writing changed slightly, as if a new person had taken over transcription after the last one gave up or died.

I turned back to the beginning and started at the first chapter, entitled "Obren, the First Pixie."

Back in the days before time, in the lands of milk and honey, the gods toiled creating life. They molded amoeba that turned into fish. When those fish matured, they turned into rats, who turned into cats, who turned into bats, and eventually into all the creatures known throughout the world today.

But the world of governance was a slow one, filled with doldrum at every turn. Mostly, the gods just watched their creations mature over the years. It took generation upon generation for single-celled organisms to grow into humans.

While they waited, the gods built more entertaining creatures. In this way, they made the first monsters of legend. They created goblins and orcs, trolls and ghouls, giants and satyrs. Among the other monsters, they created the most beautiful creature ever to walk on Earth, one who could fly and disappear at will and who could govern all other monsters with pride and love.

These they called pixies, and the first was called Obren. Cast from one rib each from the goddess Aphrodite and the god Apollo, the great pixie Obren was immortal like a god, but full of free will like a human, able to mix between the two.

The creation of such a creature infuriated the cherubs of Mount Olympus, who were designed as servants to the gods. They lacked the free will given to Obren and envied him for it.

It took little time for the gods to become enamored with Obren. They loved him best because he chose to serve the gods where the cherubs were forced into servitude, and for that, Obren was rewarded with a wife, Lymeria, and children, Boatus, Yilar, Galertus, and Molvin, and their children begot more children, who begot more children.

For a time, the pixie race flourished across the land. They oversaw monsters from dinosaurs to minotaurs and down to the smallest sprite. Then, humans emerged, children of the evolution of monkeys. Humans were the last evolution of Earth before the gods could leave to begin another civilization across the stars, and for that reason, the gods' affection turned from pixies to humanity.

Obren, great steward of the gods, did not like humans any more than the cherubs liked him, as they curried the favors of the gods above all others, but the gods demanded he live among the humans and help them grow into a sustainable race capable of ruling the planet.

Obren would not allow an inferior species like man to rule over him, so he and his kin plotted to overthrow the humans at their nascent stages. As powerful as the pixies were, it wouldn't take much to destroy the entire race.

However, Obren's plan was thwarted by Cercopes, god of monkeys and overseer of the great evolution from monkeys to humans. For his treachery, Obren was sentenced to mortality, and his children were cursed to live amongst humanity for the rest of their days lest they have their powers taken away from them.

While the story wasn't without its moments, how did a magical story about fairies relate to my life?

I was incensed and didn't want to continue, but I wanted to know why I could disappear from one place and reappear in another. The old woman told me she had the knowledge I needed, and the confidence that accompanied her words convinced me she told the truth.

And I'd promised her I would read the book before I returned to her, so I flipped through to another story toward the back. This one had a beautifully calligraphed title, with flowers adorning the margins: Zabina.

The pixie race dwindled over the centuries since the days of Obren, until they were little more than a memory by the time of Zabina, one of a small band of true blood pixies that remained.

Zabina grew up in the Kingdom of Renault, named after the first king to conquer it. Before his conquest, Zabina's people flourished on the land, in complete harmony with the monsters and people who called it home.

However, peace with nature did not satisfy King Renault, who forced his will on the people of his kingdom and resented the monsters for their incredible power. He turned his subjects against them, sending heralds to warn of the great power monsters possessed, claiming they could destroy humanity if not contained.

Previously content to live in peace, the people of Renault's kingdom grew frightened of monsters. At the heart of Renault's hatred was the race of pixies. They were human-like but more powerful than a human could ever hope to become, with a longer life than King Renault could hope to live.

By the time Zabina was grown, the tension between Renault and the monsters in his land was a raging fire. No longer could monsters work with humans or trade with them. Instead, they were relegated to a place called The Veil. Beyond it, monsters were unable to travel without being viciously attacked, imprisoned, and in the worst instances, killed.

Zabina and her pixie brethren were a formidable fighting force, though they were few in numbers, they were strong-willed. They did not take kindly to the world of men encroaching on their land, so they took up arms against their oppressors, fighting through the forests and sweeping through towns.

For a time, they seemed to be winning their fight. While the king lived in a mighty castle which was easily attacked and fought with knights who wore bulky armor, the pixies lived in a secret town in the trees which the king could not find and fought in the shadows where the knights were not effective. But the gods are cruel, and they did not forget the fate of Obren, and they took their revenge on poor Zabina.

Zabina's job was to patrol the woods for intruders. It was on one of these journeys that she met a young man, a human named Sir Reginald, with whom she instantly bonded. Over the months, their bond grew into lust, and that lust grew until they consummated it. From her womb, two children came forth: Akta and Rasmus, firstborn of a hybrid race of human and pixie, and two of the last pixies born before their race faded into memory.

Zabina hoped that her loving mixed-race children would be enough to stop the war, but Sir Reginald had other plans. He could not be associated with a lowly pixie, as he was meant to be king.

Yes, Zabina realized all too late that her lover was none other than Prince Odgeir, crown prince of the kingdom. He never loved her at all. Instead, he used his wiles to trick Zabina and sought information from her about the location of her pixie stronghold. In trusting him, she had doomed her people.

In the dead of night, Prince Odgeir stormed the great pixie city of Shangri La and murdered their best soldiers. The pixie army crumbled, and Zabina was left with nothing except the guilt of her betrayal.

She was captured and brought to the castle with her daughter Akta, who would learn to become a great hunter of the same monsters that were also her kin, while Rasmus escaped into the forest in the arms of Ylfinger, who led a group of trolls and orcs. They were the end of the great pixie race, decimated by love and destroyed by hate.

I slammed the book closed, furious that somebody was trying to pass it off as history. If magical creatures were real, where were the bones of pixies? Where was the historical record of the magical beasts spoken about in folklore? It was all too convenient that the only people who "knew" they existed were crackpots and crazies?

No. I couldn't believe anything in the book. I set it down on the broken coffee table I didn't have time to fix and rose to my feet to take my plate back to the kitchen. While I washed and dried it, along with a few other dishes in the sink, I considered my game plan.

The next morning, I would go to the shop and return the book, thank the old lady for her time, and never see her again. I had hoped *Pixie Dust* might reveal who I was, or why I could disappear, or possibly why Big Jim and his cronies were suddenly after me with such fervor.

I was making my way back toward the couch in the living room when I saw the two bright lights shining through the front window. Instinctively, I hit the floor. Creeping to the window, I peeked out. Parked across the street was the same white van that had followed me earlier.

I couldn't make out the driver through the light, but I knew who was in the car waiting for me. It was the Shadow Men who flanked Jim Bob earlier in the day.

I locked the front door and shoved the lumpy, brown couch in front of it. I knew what they were doing. They were telling me they knew where I lived, and there was nowhere to hide. They didn't have to be coy about it, either. Eventually, they would get me.

And right now, Mama was still out getting food, and I didn't know when she would be back. She could be anywhere, maybe even walking up the street right now, completely oblivious. They could just snatch her. After all, one uppity, black woman is as good as another. She did slap Duncan, and in another time, that would have been enough to warrant a death sentence.

I ran over to the phone and called Charlotte's. After a few rings, Martha, the kindly waitress who served us every time we went, picked up the receiver.

"Hello? Yes, this is Julia Freeman. Is my mother there?"

"Sorry, I haven't seen her," Martha replied.

There was that little Chinese restaurant just off from the park, Dim Sum. I flipped through the phone book until I found the number and dialed it. Again, the phone rang. The owner's wife picked up.

"Hi. This is Julia Freeman. My mother eats there a lot. She's a lovely, older, black woman. Have you seen her?"

A pause. "No. Sorry. She's not here today."

I hung up the phone again. My knees buckled from under me, and I collapsed on the ground, crying so hard my whole body heaved.

That's when the upstairs light clicked on, and I heard footsteps above me. "What damn fool thing are you doing down there?"

"Mama!" I shouted, jumping to my feet.

She peeked her head down from the stairs. "Yeah, it's me. What kind of fool racket are you making?"

"Mama! I thought you were out."

"I was out. And then I was back. I was very tired today, so I laid down. Must've lost track of time. Did you eat?"

I hopped up the stairs and squeezed her tight. "I love you. Did you know that?"

A smile crept across her face. "I love you, too, baby, even when you're being a damn fool. Now, can you tell me what's going on?"

I nuzzled in closer to her. I didn't have the heart to tell her what had happened to me. "In a minute."

CHAPTER 9

The next morning, I decided to call off work. I got precious few sick days a year as a teacher, but I just couldn't imagine sitting in class again today, watching Duncan stare at me like a coyote eyeing his prey. The thought made me violently ill. It also made me violent.

Of course, that's exactly what Duncan wanted. He wanted me to call off, shirk my duties, and get fired. This kind of disgusting tactic was popular with awful racists who wanted to push forward their horrible agendas at the expense of people like me.

More than that, I had a special power that scared them. I could disappear like magic. If they didn't like me before I showed freakish power, they surely hated me now.

The white van was idling across the street. I could see it from my bedroom window as I rifled through my things and found my ratty, purple backpack from high school. I put on my darkest hoodie and blackest slacks and stuffed my bleached hair into a beanie before I made my way downstairs.

"Mama!" I shouted, rushing down the stairs.

She turned from the front window. "Did you know there's a white van across the street with some white men in it?"

"Yes, Mama. I know."

"And why is my favorite couch pushed up against the door like there's a tornado coming?"

"Because there is," I replied solemnly. "Don't go outside today, okay? Lock all the doors and windows. They aren't after you. They want me."

"Damned fool, just like your father. You know, there was a big ole white van like that when he up and vanished too."

I sighed. "He didn't vanish, Mama. He was abducted."

"Oh yes, he did vanish. Don't you forget that. Right after a white van like that followed him around for days."

I kissed her on the forehead. "That's not gonna happen to me."

"That's what he said, too."

I grabbed the *Pixie Dust* book from the broken coffee table and stuffed it into my old backpack. Its edges bulged out as I struggled to zip it up. "Promise me you aren't gonna leave until I get back, okay?"

She stared at me, steely-eyed. "And what if you don't come back? What then?"

"I'll be back," I told her with all the confidence I could muster, which wasn't much.

***

I couldn't take the front door without alerting Big Jim's goons, so I fled through the back door, jumping over the wooden fence that separated it from the alley behind our house. I'd watched the back of our house from Mama's window for half an hour before I left just to make sure there was nothing suspicious and I didn't see anything out of the ordinary.

Apparently, the people following me had plenty of time to wait for me to screw up, but not enough manpower to risk guarding the front and the back of my house. Perhaps they didn't think I was smart enough to use the back door or too poor to afford a backyard. Maybe they assumed they'd snatch me at school and devoted their energies to capturing me there.

Whatever the reason, I ran through the unguarded back alley and into the neighbor's yard without being chased and used a circuitous route back to the center of town. It took longer than necessary for me to weave through the tight streets and make my way across the train tracks, but the advantage was I didn't see one person on my way.

After an hour of carefully plodding along, I ended up in the alleyway behind the tea shop. It was still early in the day. In fact, I'd left the same time I left for school, forgetting that most of Chandler doesn't open at seven in the morning. I doubted the old woman who ran it would be around yet, so I leaned against a big, green dumpster, determined to wait until she showed up.

"The hell are you doing?" I heard from behind me. I turned to see the old woman, holding open the back door to her shop, shaking her head at me.

"I was waiting for you. I thought you would be in later."

"For what?" She looked me up and down. "To rob me?"

"No! What do you think, just cuz I'm black and dressed in a hoodie, I'm gonna rob you?"

"Well, I don't much care about that first thing, but as for the second thing, yeah. I think a creepy-looking person lurking in my alley might be reason to worry."

"I'm not trying to rob you," I said, pulling *Pixie Dust* out of my backpack. "I'm trying to give you this."

The old woman gestured toward the back door, rolling her eyes. "Why don't you come inside and have some tea and get your burglar-looking self out of this alley?"

***

In the cramped corridors behind the storefront, boxes were stacked haphazardly along every surface. Uneven wooden shelves held boxes of teas, rare stones, cartons of "magic" mirrors, and porcelain dolls. The floors were littered with stamped crates from Morocco, Burma, Mongolia, and a dozen other exotic places I had only read about in books, places I longed to visit one day.

Beyond the crates sat a small cot with a ruffled pillow and disheveled blanket. It looked recently slept in. That must have been how she got here so early. She lived at the store.

"Be careful not to touch anything," the old woman said as I snaked my way between the precarious boxes.

"Why? Is it dangerous?"

"Well, yes. I am not very good at stacking things, and these shelves are bound to fall with even the lightest touch. I wouldn't want you breaking your foot…or, more importantly, my merchandise."

"No, we wouldn't want that," I scoffed.

"Do you know how hard it is to find a legitimate source of magic mirrors and voodoo dolls? Trust me, it's dreadfully hard."

"Oh, is that what these are?" I said, chuckling at a straw figure, loosely bound together with a drawstring.

The old woman pushed through the beaded curtain into the main showroom of the store. "Not all of them, of course. The real things are much too expensive for your average person, and they wouldn't know how to handle them, anyway. Most of this is just designer garbage meant to look good, but I've been known to catch the attention of a mage or two in my day, and when they come in, I must be prepared. I can make a year's wage with the money they spend in one visit." She gave me a wry look. "A black woman running a tea shop in small-town Colorado? How else am I going to make money?"

I pushed through the beads behind her. "You realize what you're saying is crazy, right? I mean, there's no such thing as magic."

The old woman walked behind her register and picked up a teapot. I realized then that there was no burner or hot plate behind the register, yet the teapot in the old woman's hand steamed and smoked. "Oh, my dear, how naïve you are."

"How are you doing that?" I asked as she poured one cup of tea for me and another for her.

"Magic, of course." She looked me up and down. "You would know that if you read the book I gave you."

I set the book on the counter, worried that its weight would crack the glass case filled with assorted porcelain tea sets. "You mean this? Yeah, I read some of it. It's full of stories about fairies, but I never much cared for fantasy."

"No. Of course not," the old woman said. "Your degree is in history, is it not?"

"Yes, it is. How do you know that?"

She sipped her tea. "I make it a habit to know everything I can about the magical beings I come across."

I laughed so hard I snorted. "Now I know you're crazy, lady. I am not a magical being. I'm just a school teacher from Chandler."

The old woman handed me tea in a cup. It had two jousting knights painted on it. "One who can disappear at will."

I took the cup and a sip of tea. It was delicious. "Not at will."

"Splitting hairs," she said, shrugging her shoulders as she sipped her tea. "You can disappear in one place and appear in another, is that not correct? In its simplest form?"

"In its simplest form, I suppose that is correct."

"That makes you a magical creature. Of course, I've always known that since the day I first saw you. We always recognize our own kind."

"It doesn't mean I'm magic. There are plenty of logical reasons why a person might disappear at will."

The old woman leaned back with a smile. "Name one."

"Well, I don't have an example offhand, but it's not magic, which means this book is gibberish. It doesn't say anything of value. It's just a bunch of tall tales and folk stories."

"Of course, it does. As a student of history, I thought you would appreciate the history of your people."

I snorted again. "My people? So now you're saying that I'm not only a magical creature but a fairy?"

"A pixie, actually. Fairies are much smaller."

"Of course," I said snidely. "How callous of me to insult such a noble race."

"Well, you wouldn't call a black person a Caucasian or a horse a goat, would you? This is no different."

"Okay. The next time I see a pixie, I'll be sure to apologize to them."

The old woman placed her tea down and smiled at me. She rose from her stool and unwrapped the shawl around her shoulders. "Could you be a dear and lock the front door for me and make sure that the window is closed?"

I furrowed my brow. "Are you going to murder me?"

"No, dear. If I wanted you dead, then I would have told those white fellows yesterday that you were in my shop."

I clicked the deadbolt on the front door then drew the shades for the windows until all that remained was the faint glow of the candles. "Okay. It's done."

"And blow out the candles, my dear, if you please," she said.

"You're sure you don't want to murder me?" I asked, blowing out the first candle of many.

"I never said I didn't want to," the old woman said sweetly. "I just said I wouldn't."

"Splitting hairs," I replied with a smile.

I walked around and blew out a dozen or so candles throughout the shop. The smell of burnt wick filled my nostrils and calmed my spirit. I always enjoyed fire and especially the smoky smell left behind after a candle went out.

Before long, I stood in near-complete darkness. The old woman hadn't moved from behind the register as I worked, except to follow my progress with the slightest tilt of her head.

"Are you ready?" she asked me.

"I don't know," I replied hesitantly. "I have no idea what's going on."

The old woman took one deep breath, then another. A faint, golden glow emanated from behind the register. Two wings grew out of the old woman's back and filled the room with bright, blue light. She lifted into the air and floated there before landing delicately on the counter.

"My name is Elka, of the forest people, one in a long line of pixies descended from the last of our kind, Zabina, Akta, and Rasmus. And I await your apology."

That's when the room started spinning. My eyes rolled back in my head, and I fainted.

CHAPTER 10

I woke up to Elka fanning me with an exotic, black fan covered in images of peacocks and cranes. It took a moment for my eyes to refocus on the tearoom and on the old woman who owned it, whose wings still lit the whole shop aglow.

"Are you alright, sweetheart?" Elka asked me.

I nodded my woozy head. "I think so. This is just a lot to take in."

"I understand. It's not every day you're presented with indisputable proof that something you believed to be fiction is in fact as real as the nose on your face."

"I think that's an understatement," I said, bracing my hands under me. "If you suddenly find out that Nixon wasn't a corrupt bastard, that's a fact which you thought was fiction. What you're talking about is lunacy. Magic—real magic—exists in the world? That's a mind screw of the highest order. I suppose I owe you that apology now."

"Don't worry about it." Elka reached into her pocket and pulled out a chocolate-covered cookie. "Here. Eat this. You'll feel better."

"What is it? Some sort of magic biscuit?"

She shook her head. "No. It's just chocolate. Your blood sugar is low, and I thought you could use a nosh."

I took the biscuit from Elka, skeptical that I would start floating around the room at the tiniest bite. Still, who could resist chocolate? I ate the biscuit in a single gulp and quickly became ravenous for more.

Sensing my hunger, Elka pulled a box of chocolates from the shelf and handed them to me. Her bright, blue wings still illuminated the room. "Here. On the house."

***

I spent the next several minutes shoveling chocolates into my mouth until my head stopped spinning, and my stomach began to ache.

"Feel better?" Elka asked.

"Yes. I do, but can I ask you a favor?"

"Anything."

I pointed to her wings. "Can you put those away? It's still a little much for me to take in, you know."

Elka smiled sweetly. If I offended her, she didn't show it. "Of course, dear." She closed her eyes and hummed to herself. The room darkened as her wings receded into her back. I sat in darkness until she opened the window and lit the candles throughout the store. Soon, the room smelled like a forest.

I took my time making my way to my feet. "Thank you."

"I know this makes you uncomfortable," Elka said. "But there is something we must discuss."

"And what is that?"

"I can help you unlock your powers, Julia. You'll never have to worry about people chasing you again. You could be anywhere you want—Istanbul, Paris, London, New York—in the blink of an eye."

I laughed at the ridiculousness of her statement. "I appreciate that, but with all your powers, you still ended up *here*. I can't imagine how my powers would get me much further. And so far, they've given me nothing but trouble."

"I take it that is a no."

I scrunched my nose. "I'm sure you are disappointed."

"Not disappointed. Life is long, especially for our kind, and I will be here, should you ever change your mind." She gave a sigh and started wiping down the countertop with a cloth.

"I think I've had quite enough excitement for one day," I said, walking toward the door. "Thank you for the tea and the chocolate. I'm sorry for the mess."

"No need to apologize, my child. You have a lot to digest. Are you sure you want to risk going outside?"

I nodded. "I can't stay in this shop my whole life."

***

Daylight only protected you so much in Chandler and then only against people who felt shame or feared repercussions for their actions. The men who hunted me had neither shame nor fear. If they wanted to take me, they would take me. It was a risk I was willing to take.

Elka gave me much to think about as I crossed the street and walked away from her tea shop. I would be lying if I said the thought of disappearing at will wasn't intriguing; being anywhere in the world whenever you wanted held a certain appeal for somebody that hated Chandler and missed Chicago.

I could work in the city and still be home by nightfall to take care of Mama, then make visits to Gettysburg, the Kremlin, and the Louvre on weekends. While I could never leave Chandler, I would be able to visit anywhere in the world I wanted.

But the thought of that much power also scared me. The sensations I felt after disappearing were as frightening as they were exhilarating—my head buzzed, and my body filled with manic energy. The ability to do that at will and harness that kind of power, I wondered if I would lose myself to it.

Plus, I mean…I was crazy, right?

No matter what Elka said, the idea that magic existed was cuckoo banana pants. Up until this morning, magic was the furthest thing from my mind. Now, an old woman in a tea shop showed me her wings, told me magic was real, and I was just going to believe her? How do I really know that wasn't just smoke and mirrors? Maybe she had a pulley tucked behind that register which helped her fool naïve women.

Then again, that sounded even more crazy.

My logical brain couldn't comprehend something so fantastical, no matter what my eyes had seen. It would be like saying a fire-breathing dragon could walk right through downtown Chandler and stroll out of town.

Could it happen? Sure. I can't disprove the existence of dragons, but every bone in my body said that believing in dragons was for naïve idiots.

I stepped into Mystery Spot Park ruminating on the knowledge Elka gave me. I had avoided the park last night and this morning, but something about meeting Elka bolstered my confidence. I wanted to feel the energy of the mystery spot coursing through my veins.

Every inch I moved toward town, the hole at the center of the park made my heart beat faster until I could hear the thump in my ears as I stepped up to the spot and looked down into it. What wonders fell down that hole and never came back up? What horrors are buried in there?

"Well, well, well, if it ain't Ms. Colored," Duncan sneered from behind me. "You don't look sick, Ms. Colored Bitch."

Duncan and three other men were standing behind me. They were there to take me, I knew, but they had all the time in the world. And so, they inched forward slowly, confidently. Duncan smiled with a smugness only a seventeen-year-old boy who'd never felt pain could muster.

"You're supposed to be in school, Duncan," I said to him, inching backward in panic.

"So are you, Ms. Colored," he responded. "But my dad says finding you is more important than school. It's more important than anything in the world. He has big plans for you."

I decided to stop backing up. I dug my feet into the ground. If I was going down, I was going down swinging. "I know all about your Daddy's plans. I've seen them strung up all over town."

"I'll bet you have. He has a thing for uppity, black folk, but he's got a special place for ones who can disappear in the blink of an eye. He's seen a lot of things, but he ain't never seen that before. In fact, he almost didn't believe me when I told him 'bout you, but I was real specific. I told him every little detail. When I finished, his eyes went wide, and his mouth started waterin'. He's been looking for you a real long time. Yeah, he's got big plans for you, girlie."

"Hey!" I heard from behind me. It was good ole Chuck Dixon, last good man in all of Chandler. "What do you folks think yer doing?"

"Back up, old man," Duncan said. "My daddy pays your salary, so just turn the other way."

"The town pays me," Chuck said. "To look after this park, and everybody in it, including Ms. Freeman here."

"You wouldn't be sayin' that if you knew what she was," Duncan replied, fire in his eyes.

"I know enough about Ms. Freeman to know she deserves protecting, just like everybody else."

Duncan pulled back his jacket to reveal a pistol in his waistband. "Is this the hill you want to die on, Chuck? I know about you. Too weak to make it in the Army. They wouldn't even use you as cannon fodder."

Chuck flipped the lock on his own holster and grabbed the handle of his gun. "It's not the hill I want to die on, Duncan, but it's a hill I will die on if that's what it takes."

Without another syllable spoken, a gunshot rang out. Blood poured from Chuck Dixon's mouth as he collapsed on the ground.

"Chuck!" I shouted.

One of the men behind Duncan held a smoking gun in front of him without an ounce of fear on his face. "Goddamn it, Frank!" Duncan shouted. "We're not supposed to kill anybody."

"It was a life or death situation," Frank replied, shrugging. "He was about to draw on me."

Duncan turned to Frank, and I took the distraction to run to Chuck. He coughed blood on my pants as he turned to me. "You're a damned fool. Get out of here."

"I'm not gonna leave you."

"Then you're gonna die, too. Don't be an idiot. Run."

"Don't you die on me, Chuck," I moaned, tears filling my eyes.

He smiled. "Don't tell me what to do, Ms. Freeman. I'll do as I damned well please."

By the time I looked up, the Shadow Men surrounded me with guns drawn. There was nowhere to go. There was nowhere to hide.

"He's right, Ms. Freeman," Duncan said to me. "You should have run."

My body started to vibrate faster and faster, numbing my hands and feet and setting my chest to tingle. Everything turned to a purple so bright I couldn't see anything but the color. I grabbed Chuck's hand, and together—we vanished.

CHAPTER 11

I reappeared with Chuck at Elka's tea shop, hovering over an antique table that held a collection of collectibles, from magic mirrors to crystal balls and crystals of all colors and sizes. For an instant, I hovered in midair, suspended in space. Then, we fell. Chuck and I crashed onto the table, and our weight smashed the table into pieces. Mirrors broke, and crystal balls rolled every which way.

Elka rushed to my side from her place behind the register, gasping the question, "Oh my god. Are you okay?"

My adrenaline shot me upright. "I'm fine, but Chuck…I thought I could get him to the hospital, but I ended up here. Please, you have to help him."

Elka looked at Chuck, bleeding out onto the table. "There's nothing I can do."

"Yes, there is—you can get him to the hospital."

"I don't do that," Elka said, shaking her head. "Not in public."

"Then now is the time to start," I shouted at her, pounding my fist into my palm.

"It's too dangerous!" Elka hissed. "What if somebody sees me?"

I grabbed her by the shoulders. "If you don't do this, he's going to die."

Elka turned her eyes to Chuck and sighed. "Fine. Stand back."

I crept behind the register. A bright, purple light filled the room, and Elka and Chuck were gone. It looked like the sun erupted on Earth for a moment and then vanished from sight.

For a long time, all I could do was stare at the spot where Chuck's blood soaked into the floor. Watching the bloodstain on the carpet wasn't going to accomplish anything, but I couldn't stop myself from thinking about the fleeting nature of life. If I had just turned away from the park, Chuck wouldn't have gotten shot. I made a stupid mistake, and it might cost a good man his life.

I should never have walked across the park. I was always so careful, so precise. Elka got me in a tizzy with her talk of magic, and I forgot myself and the real terror I faced in Chandler.

Elka, the magic pixie. There was no denying it now. She was for real, which means everything she told me was real.

For the first time, I took a real look around Elka's store. It was full of hooky collectibles and weird "medicines" from around the world. There were bottles labeled with handwritten names like Love Potion, Draft of Sleep, and Luck Potion.

I wondered how many of the potions she sold were actual magic and not just flavored water. I suspected she kept the real stuff in the back, where discerning eyes would be able to take a better look.

Walking behind the beaded curtain, I stepped into the back room. The shelves lining the hallway were filled mostly with clean, new bottles and charms. However, mixed in with them were dusty old bottles—their labels almost completely faded with time. I picked one up and brushed off the dust. It read: *Elixir of aging. Add one drop for every year you want to grow older. Use potion of de-aging to reverse effects.*

I put down the bottle. The last thing I wanted to do was grow older or younger. I could barely deal with my current age. I kept walking down the hallway. Crystal balls and magic rocks speckled the shelves. A large blue pouch, adorned with moons and stars, seemed to call to me. I reached out my hand to pick it up.

"That was Zabina's," Elka said from behind me. "She was carelessly struck down by her daughter, Akta, one of the last pixies."

I turned to her. "Akta…I saw her in that book. She was a great monster hunter, yes?"

"Hunting monsters does not make one great, but she was the best there ever was until she was betrayed. Inside that pouch is the last of the pixie dust in the known world. I have kept it safe for as long as I've been able."

"Then why is it sitting on a shelf in the back of a tea shop?"

Elka let out a laugh. "That is a good question. It, like many things in this shop, are best left hidden in plain sight."

"What does it do?"

"It helps pixies disappear at will."

"But…I didn't need it, and you didn't, either."

She turned toward the front of the store and gestured for me to follow. "No. In the end, pixies relied on it because we'd forgotten the old ways. The dust was only a crutch that prevented us from embracing our true power. Some pixies were even powerful enough to use other people's thoughts to let them teleport."

I didn't care much about pixies just then. My mind was consumed with thoughts of my friend. "And Chuck? Will he live?"

"I don't know," Elka said, pursing her lips. "I am not a doctor. I left him in the front of the hospital and watched as they wheeled him inside. I did all I could. You did all you could as well."

"I should go to him," I said, heading for the door.

Elka grabbed my arm. "He'll be in surgery at least a few hours. If you go, the men who did this will find you. That I can guarantee."

"The men hunting me," I said, ripping my arm away. "They won't stop. They told me they were after me because I could disappear."

Elka nodded. "That makes sense. Tell me. Did you see a patch with a bloody dagger on it dripping onto a red star?"

I thought back to the school, and the leather jacket Big Jim and his cronies wore. "Yes. I did see a patch like that. The men in the park had jackets with that symbol on them."

"I thought so. You see, they're part of an ancient order called the Cult of the Bloody Dagger. They're trying to bring magic back to the world."

"That doesn't sound so bad," I replied.

"Yes, that is the kind version. Unfortunately, they're trying to use that magic for their own means, by opening a portal to Hell and unleashing the damned upon Earth."

"Why do they need me for that?"

"Long ago, all creatures had a spark of magic in them. Then came humans. In their jealousy of our powers, they hunted our kind until, over time, too few of us remained. We had the power, but humanity had the numbers, and they overwhelmed us. As our kind faded from this world, magic left the world as well…leaving only tiny traces behind, like the ones at the mystery spot or in our blood."

"Still not sure why they want to kill me."

"Magic, in its rawest form, exists only in Hell. Or what you know as Hell. Back when monsters roamed, it was just called the underworld. There was no Heaven or Hell back then, just the underworld and Mount Olympus. All monsters were sent there upon their death, and they reside there to this day."

"And that's what these men want to open? A portal to Hell?"

"Yes. That is their aim, but to open the portal to Hell, they need two things: a place on Earth with an unnaturally deep connection to magic, like our mystery spot, and a spark of magical energy to bridge the gap between our worlds and act as a catalyst to open it, which lives in our blood. That's why I have been hiding for so long."

"We're all drawn here, all magical creatures…" I took a deep breath, enraptured by this new understanding.

"Not only here," Elka replied. "There are many spots around the world, and we are drawn to them all."

"I want to learn from you."

Elka rubbed her hands together. "Then we should begin. Pick up Zabina's pouch."

"Are you sure?"

"Lesson one: don't question me. Now, pick it up."

I put my hands on the pouch and felt its weight in both hands. Time and debris hid the blue of the pouch under a layer of gray. I stuck my hand inside, mostly grabbing at air, but finally found a layer of pixie dust at the bottom.

"There's not much in here," I said, peering into the bag.

Elka nodded. "Then we must make it count."

CHAPTER 12

Elka closed her shop early. Not much she could sell with a bloodstain on the floor. We tried to clean it up as best we could, but no matter how hard we scrubbed, the blood would not come out. Until she got a brand-new carpet, I doubted she would be able to open the shop for customers. I think there was some sort of health code against that somewhere.

I had been on the phone with the hospital for over an hour. The nurses bounced me around from department to department, but none of them could find a Chuck Dixon listed in their paperwork.

"Yes," I said, holding the receiver of a phone up to my ear. "That's correct. I'm trying to get any information you have on Chuck Dixon. I'm a family friend."

"I'm sorry, ma'am," the latest nurse said. "I don't see that name."

I tried to contain my anger, but it wasn't easy. The adrenaline from everything that happened in the past day still ran through me. "What about John Doe? Do you have any John Does who came in with a bullet wound earlier today?"

"Hang on," the nurse said. I could hear her flipping through her registry. "Yes, I do have one John Doe who fits that description. He's out of surgery, in critical but stable condition."

I let out a long sigh of relief as if all the fear built in my body released at once. "Thank you."

I placed down the receiver and turned to Elka, who sat on the floor near the front of her store, as far away from the bloodstain as she could manage without being outside the store. "Is he okay?" she asked.

"As well as can be expected, given the circumstances." It was all my fault, but at least he would be okay...eventually.

She smiled, patting the floor next to her. "Good. Now, we can begin."

I walked over and sat down next to her, cross-legged. "Yes, now I can focus."

"Listen to your breath," Elka told me. "It is your best guide. You must see where you are going in your mind's eye, and for that, you need control and focus. Tell me about your last disappearance."

"I tried to get Chuck to the hospital, and it didn't work. I ended up here."

"That's because you couldn't see it. Not really. You had an idea of a hospital, but in your fear, you couldn't make it real. That's the secret to disappearing. It's why you have only appeared in places you already knew, your house and my shop. You could see them in your mind's eye. If you can see the place you want to go, really see it as clear as day, getting there is as simple as opening your eyes."

"So, I need to think of a place I want to go and…make it real?"

"Yes. You need to see every square inch of the place. You need to reach out and touch it, and then you can use your mind to pull you there."

"The only one place I know that well is Mama's house."

"Then that is the place you must imagine."

I took a deep breath. I pictured the kitchen where I made peanut butter sandwiches. I imagined the cracks on the roof of the ceiling and the stairwell where I hugged Mama after I found her alive the night before. I placed our ugly couch in the middle of the room.

"Do you have it?" Elka asked. "Can you picture it in your mind's eye?"

I nodded. "Yes."

Elka grabbed my hand. "Then take me there. Take a pinch of the dust, reach out with your mind, and throw. Then, let your mind pull yourself there."

I grabbed a pinch of the precious pixie dust. I breathed deeply. "Are you sure?"

"No, but I trust you."

I reached out with my mind's eye as I threw the pixie dust on the ground. A bright purple light engulfed us both, and then we were gone.

***

I let my mind pull me into Mama's living room, and we reappeared there in an instant. We hovered again in midair and then crashed upon the ground, this time avoiding any tables or other obstacles between us and the hard wood.

"I did it!" I shouted. "I did it! I did it! Mama! You won't believe what I did!"

But my excitement was short-lived. When my eyes focused again, I saw our living room in shambles, and the front door busted wide open. The couch was no longer propped against the door but flipped over in the middle of the room.

"Mama!" I turned to Elka. "What happened here?"

"The Cult of the Bloody Dagger," Elka said through gritted teeth. I had never seen her angry before, and it scared me. Her jaw locked tight, and her eyes burned like fiery embers. "They couldn't find you, so they took your mother. I thought it would take them longer to figure out the connection."

"What connection?"

"If you are a pixie, then your blood came from somewhere."

"My mother! My mother is a pixie?"

"Yes. And the Cult of the Bloody Dagger took her, just like they took your father so many years ago. They thought he had the spark of magic in him, but they were wrong. His blood didn't open the portal, so they strung him up to make it look like a lynching, just like they've done so many times."

"You knew that this would happen!"

"That's why I'm here, in Chandler. I have protected pixies from the Cult of the Bloody Dagger for decades, but for each one I saved, another was lost. Luckily, they didn't have the complete spell until most of our kind was gone, but now, I fear they can unleash Hell on Earth."

"That makes you a terrible protector."

"Since your mother has fallen into their hands," Elka said, cracking her knuckles and readying for a fight. "I can't disagree with you."

"We have to save her. Where is she?"

Elka looked out the window. It was pitch black. We had worked through the day and into the night. "They will take her to the mystery spot and bleed her dry to open the portal."

I rushed toward the door. "Then that's where we're going."

Elka grabbed my arm. "We're too late to go that way. You must picture it in your mind's eye."

"I don't know the park that well."

"Yes, you do."

I closed my eyes and tried to focus, but my mind raced in front of me. Images of mother strung up on a tree tormented me. "I can't—I can't—"

"I can," Elka said. "I can be your eyes. Place your hand on my forehead."

I did as I was told. "What am I supposed to see?"

"Just wait. I am reconstructing the park in my mind's eye. You should see it in your mind, too. Just focus. Focus on my thoughts."

"I can't—It's too much—"

"You can do this. You must. For your mother."

She was right. I took a deep breath and calmed myself. After a few seconds, the details of the park filtered in. Daddy's hanging tree, the grassy knoll where Duncan and his ilk first attacked me, and finally the mystery spot itself. Soon I could feel every blade of grass under my feet.

"Do you have it?"

I grabbed a pinch of pixie dust. "I have it."

"Then take me there."

I threw the pixie dust on the ground and we were gone in a sea of purple, leaving the disheveled mess of Mama's home in our wake.

CHAPTER 13

We rematerialized with a flash under my father's hanging tree. It was my most vivid memory of the park and the easiest to reach out and latch on to when I needed to pull myself forward.

"Good work," Elka said. "I figured there was a fifty-fifty chance we'd make it here."

"Fifty-fifty? Those are terrible odds."

"Using my mind to see where you want to go is very powerful magic. There are not many who can do it, but you did it. I'm very proud. Do you see anybody?"

"Not yet."

Elka pointed to a tree closer to the mystery spot. "I'm going to that tree over there to get a better view. If you see your mother, whistle for me."

"How can you disappear so fast and confident?" I asked. "And don't tell me it's about your mind's eye or the fact you're an old crone. It's more than that, and we both know it."

Elka pressed her hand against my heart. "The secret is inside of you. It's only your mind that blocks you. The dust was never important. It focused our energy, this is true, but it made us lazy as we relied more and more on it. Soon, we forgot that the power was always in us, not in the dust. The blood surging through your veins is more powerful than you can ever imagine. No matter what happens, remember that."

In another instant, Elka vanished. I saw a flash of purple light and her silhouette appeared in front of the tree she'd pointed out. Her magic was strong. The thought of gaining control of my powers like that one day exhilarated me.

I knelt on the roots of the old oak tree, in the silence, waiting for something to happen. On a normal night, old Chuck Dixon would be here to shoo me away or gab away for a spell, but this was not a normal night. This was the night I could have used Chuck by my side. This was the kind of night the city could use somebody protecting the mystery spot. I guess that responsibility fell to me now.

I scanned the horizon for the white van, but it wasn't the first car I saw. The sheriff's police cruiser was parked across the street from the park. Strolling away from it was the sheriff, Duncan, and Big Jim Lewis. They were not dressed in their normal clothes, but black robes with a bright red, bloody dagger.

Behind them, a half-dozen cars drove up and lined the park. If I didn't know better, I would have thought Big Jim was opening a new lot in the middle of town. Every one of the cars sparkled like it was just driven off the lot.

People I talked to every day filed out of those cars: Martha, the sweet waitress who served my mother at Charlotte's Diner, Mrs. Blick and her doddering husband Charles, and even Principal Anderson waddled out of his car and threw on a black robe. There were no pleasantries between them, only solemn acknowledgment as they walked toward the mystery spot.

These weren't vile racists like Big Jim or Duncan. These people were nice to me. They treated me with kindness. More than that, they treated my mother with kindness, and now they were going to kill her. Martha, the woman fed my Mama every day, damn near every meal, and she was going to help slit her throat. Principal Anderson worked with me every day since before school started, and still he's fine with killing my mother. For what? So they can open a portal to Hell to curry favor with some big, bad monster on the other side?

My heart leaped into my chest as I realized that even the people that I thought were friends, or at least allies, were nothing more than cultists bent on my destruction. I knew this town was filled with horrible people, but I had no idea they were "open a portal to Hell and plunge us all into darkness" horrible.

A limousine rounded the corner, and city councilors Tom Seaver and George Wallace stepped out of it. I hadn't seen them since they came to my school with Big Jim a couple of days ago. In their robes, the men looked even more intimidating. I was frightened in a way I'd never been before. Their low guttural chants joined in with the others gathered around. Once the group of two dozen surrounded the mystery spot, the sheriff brought a walkie-talkie to his mouth and spoke a few words into it.

Moments later, the white van pulled around a corner, hopped the curb, and drove onto the park grass. Seven sheriff's cruisers sped into the square and blocked every intersection, flashing their lights as a warning for the whole town to stay away. Deputies filed out of their cars and drew their weapons.

The back door of the white van swung open, and two of the Shadow Men, now dressed in the same robes as the rest, pulled a metal gurney out of the van. On the gurney, my mother struggled to break free from the leather restraints that bound her. She screamed bloody murder, but nobody listened. Nobody cared. She was nothing but a means to an end for them.

My mother would call me a damned fool for trying to save her. The odds against us succeeding were astronomical, but I had to try. They were going to bleed her dry, and I couldn't lose both my parents to cultists. More than that, I couldn't allow them to open a portal to Hell. No matter how little I cared about Chandler, even the worst of them didn't deserve that fate.

I rushed forward, balled up my fists, and hoped that the element of surprise would work in my favor. I wasn't two hundred feet from the cultists before a flash of purple light stole me away.

***

Elka rematerialized with me behind Dad's hanging tree. She squeezed my shoulders tight as she hissed at me. "You're gonna get yourself killed!"

I wanted to fight her, but I knew she was right. "Well, I don't see you having a better plan."

"That's because you didn't ask!"

"You're right," I sighed. "How do you want to play this, then?"

"I want you to run up to them and cause a distraction, a really big one. Make sure all eyes are on you. Then, duck."

"That's it? Cause a distraction and duck? How is that better than my plan?"

"Because I came up with it. I trusted you. Now, will you trust me?"

I wanted to argue, but I had no reason not to trust her. "Fine, but you're gonna get me killed."

"Maybe, but then you'd be in the same place you were a few minutes ago. Now go. And remember, make it a *big* distraction."

I stomped away from Elka and toward the cultists. "Oh, I'll make it huge."

***

Mama kicked and squirmed, but the leather restraints held her tight. The Shadow Men stopped the gurney and locked it in place, then one of them compressed the front legs and tilted it down, so Mama's head rested over the mystery spot. If they slit her throat, her blood would drain right into it, killing her and opening the portal.

The cultists chanted. With every repetition, their voices grew louder until their chorus thundered through the square and into the heavens.

"Dealus Mylarus Zilarus. Dealus Mylarus Zilarus. Dealus Mylarus Zilarus. Dealus Mylarus Zilarus. Dealus Mylarus Zilarus. Dealus Mylarus Zilarus."

Big Jim Lewis held up his arms and the cultists went silent. He reached into his robe and pulled out a golden dagger.

"This magical blood will bring forward the great Aziolith, god among monsters. He shall heap untold wealth and power upon us, and those who oppose us will bow before his might and tremble at his will! You, pixie, are the catalyst to a great new age of enlightenment. Take solace that your death shall not be in vain."

"Wait, wait, wait," I shouted, strolling up to the cabal. "You have the wrong person. This must be very embarrassing for you. I know my mama looks young for her age, but I'm offended you mistook her for me."

"Julia!" Mama shouted. "You damned fool. Get out of here!"

"Shut up, Mama. You are in no position to talk. Look at what you've got yourself into this time."

"Shut up?" she screamed. "How dare you talk to me like that! I taught you better than to give me lip. If I get out of this, you are gonna get smacked so hard upside your head you'll wish these damned fools killed you."

"Excuse me!" Duncan said. "Are we opening this portal or not?"

Duncan's father reached back and slapped Duncan so hard he fell to the ground in a heap. Then he turned to me. "Thank you for showing up. In case your mother doesn't have enough magic running through her blood to open this portal, it's always nice to have a backup."

"If she doesn't, you would have killed another one of my parents for no reason."

"Oh, there are reasons to kill your mother beyond her being a pixie," Big Jim said, pointing his dagger at me. "It also rids the world of another uppity, colored woman. It's like killing two birds with one stone, pardon the pun."

"Is that why you killed my father, too?"

"Partially," Big Jim said with a smile. "Your father didn't know his place, either, but when I slid this dagger across his throat, I really thought he was a pixie. To think, all this time I was in the right family, but the wrong parent."

And that's when Duncan's father lost his head.

I don't mean metaphorically either. I mean, his head severed from his body and rolled toward me. It was gross.

Blood spurted up into the air as Big Jim's lifeless body fell to the ground to reveal Elka holding two daggers behind him, drenched in the blood of her kill.

Elka looked at me for a moment, then disappeared once more, reappearing behind Martha and stabbing her through the gut with a dagger while slicing her husband with the other. In a frenzy of purple lights, Elka disappeared and reappeared at will, cutting through the gut of cultist after cultist in her path of destruction.

"Get your mom!" she shouted.

She didn't have to tell me twice. I ran over to the gurney and loosened the leather straps from my mother's arms. "Stay still, Mama."

"You are a damned fool, do you know that?"

I pulled off the leather restraints around her legs. "A damned fool that saved your life, thank you very much."

She held back the tears filling her eyes. "A damned fool nonetheless."

I helped Mama off the gurney while Elka made quick work of her tenth cultist. We were halfway back to Daddy's hanging tree when the gunshots rang out. I turned around, and Elka had stopped cold. Blood filled her eyes and soaked down her shirt. Two bullets had pierced her neck, another went through her chest. She fell backward toward the mystery spot.

"No!"

But it was too late. From where she collapsed, her blood seeped into the mystery spot. The dark black hole exploded into a bright red portal that spiraled and swirled fifty feet into the air, creating morning where there used to be night.

CHAPTER 14

The cultists that remained after Elka butchered their ranks stared up at the massive portal, which emitted a pulse as it spun clockwise in an oblong, red oval. The blood of their comrades spread over their feet, but the glee on their faces was unmistakable. They had succeeded in their mission after who knew how many years trying or how many innocents were killed.

There were a lot of disappearances during my childhood—at least a dozen I can remember off hand. I'm ashamed to say that after a while, they all blended together. If somebody asked, that's what I would tell them—there were enough disappearances that they blended together, and that's too damn many.

I pulled Mama off the gurney and dragged her to Dad's hanging tree. "Stay here!"

"Where are you going?"

"Back for Elka."

I rushed back toward Elka's body but stopped in my tracks when a giant roar escaped the portal. It curdled my blood and dropped my stomach into my knees. The ground quaked until a scaly, black head emerged from the blood-red portal, roaring upwards into Chandler.

With another tremor, the monster's scaly foot stomped through the portal and into the park. Long, white horns pointed in the night air as its yellow, snake-like eyes blinked against the sky. It was—I rubbed my eyes to be sure—a dragon, walking right through the middle of Chandler.

The cultists knelt at the sight of the great dragon and began to chant rhythmically. Wondrous Aziolith. We are not worthy of your greatness. Bestow on us your grace so we might be your shepherds in the new world order.

Another quake and a second front foot crashed into the human world. The dragon's muscles rippled under the weight of each step, and two dark, black wings fell to the ground on both of its leathery sides. Another ear-splitting roar and a great plume of fire escaped from Aziolith's mouth, boiling the night air.

"What is that?" my mother asked.

"That's a dragon, Mama," I said, struggling to believe my own words.

Yesterday, I never would have believed magic existed or that I descended from a long line of pixies. Today, I knew magic was real, and it had been used to open a portal straight to Hell. Any doubt I had vanished as I looked up at the enormous dragon in front of me.

"Who has summoned me, the great Aziolith?"

The cultists didn't look up. They only chanted. Bestow on us your grace so we might be your shepherds in the new world order…

The dragon bristled at the slight of being ignored. "Yes, yes. That is all well and good, but *why* have you summoned me?"

Again, the cultists did not move except to chant. They trembled under their cloaks. Being in a cult seemed fun in theory, but I don't think many were aware of what kind of horror they would let loose on the world. Staring at a forty-foot-tall monster rendered them useless. They chanted mindlessly. *Bestow on us your grace so we might be your shepherds in the new world order.*

"You!" Aziolith lifted his great claw and pointed at Duncan. "Answer my question. "Why have you summoned me?"

I took the dragon's distraction to sneak toward Elka. She quivered at the base of the mystery spot, blood pooling under her, the color drained from her face. I stepped quietly and gingerly, using what darkness I could find to move undetected, but the bright light from the portal provided little cover. Luckily, nobody seemed to notice. Their attention was focused on the great beast in front of them.

Duncan stood, knees knocking and voice shaking. "Oh…g-great Aziolith. I am not worthy of being in your presence."

The side of Aziolith's mouth curled up in a sinister smile. "This is most likely true. Still, since you are the one I called upon, I demand an answer. Why have you summoned me?"

Duncan looked up at Aziolith's great glowing eyes and then shot his gaze down at the ground. "I'm sorry, great dragon, I did not mean to make contact with your eyes. I am unworthy to be in your presence."

The great dragon sighed. Without another word, he stabbed Duncan through the chest with one of his claws, lifted him into the air and swallowed him whole. I winced as Duncan's agonized screams were silenced. Even though he'd been terrible to me, I took no pleasure in the death of a misguided child.

"Now," Aziolith sneered, "is there anyone who has not pissed their pants that can explain to me what I am doing here?"

I inched forward, careful not to draw the dragon's gaze until I kneeled over Elka's body.

"Come, Elka. I have to get you out of here."

She spit blood and shook in pain. "My time is done. I have lived all I could, for as long as I could."

"Don't say that. You can still—"

"Don't lie to me, Julia. Here, take these. Protection of our kind falls on you now." She handed me the two daggers she clutched tightly in her hands. "Go find the book in my shop; the one I gave you to read. In it, there is a tale of the great battle Akta had where she defeated Aziolith. It will tell you what you need to know."

"Don't go. I'm so sorry I—"

She gave a shaky smile. "It is my time. We all have a time to live and a time to die. This is your time to fight. My time is over."

"I can't do this, Elka. It's too hard."

Her smile dropped. "It is always hard, and it is never the right time. I spent a hundred years protecting pixie folk, only to die today. That was my charge. This is yours. If you cannot defeat this evil, then nothing can."

"I can't. I can't—"

"Then we are all doomed."

With that, the last of her breath left her, and the light faded from her eyes. I shook her awake, but her limp body weighed heavily in my arms.

"No…no! Don't leave me," I stammered like a baby, babbling through my panicked tears. "I can't do this. You don't understand, I can't."

I wanted to cry there on Elka's chest forever, but I couldn't, lest I alert the great dragon and the cultists to my presence. It was time to pull myself together. Sniffling, I dug through Elka's pockets until I found the keys to her shop, then turned to flee, her daggers clutched tightly in my arm.

Aziolith sighed again as the cultists stayed silent in fear. "Perhaps you do not understand how this works," he said. "I am the great dragon Aziolith. You have summoned me, I assume for a reason, and now I would like to know what it is. Your silence is both rude and infuriating."

Finally, Tom Allen walked toward the dragon. He was a black-haired, slick-talking city councilor with a golden smile that could charm the pants off any voter he came across. Hell, Mama voted for him repeatedly, even though he never showed anything but contempt for her, because at least he was the devil she knew. He ran against an outright racist that wanted to desegregate the school and run all the black people out of town.

At least Tom Allen's racism bubbled below the surface, so he was elected over and over in overwhelming fashion. If the voters knew he planned to unleash Hell on Earth, perhaps that would have been enough to kick him out of office. I don't know, though. Even given these new facts, they might have still voted for him.

"Great dragon Aziolith," Tom Allen said. "We, the Cult of the Bloody Dagger, have worked long to bring you back to the world so that you might take your rightful place as ruler of this land and bestow your countenance upon us."

Aziolith chuckled. "My countenance? Those are very fancy words, but I need you to speak in much smaller ones. What do you mean by countenance? And be very clear and deliberate, or I will devour you as I devoured your friend."

Tom Allen gulped. "Why…I mean your treasure, Aziolith. Everybody knows you hoarded the most amazing collection of magical artifacts in all of history. Those who know of your greatness have searched for it, but to no avail.

Even the pixie that slew you had no idea where your treasure was hidden."

Aziolith cleared his throat. "So, you have freed me from Hell so that I can take over the world and give you money? Is that right?"

Tom Allen shifted his eyes from left to right. "Yes, well, when you put it like that, it sounds a bit silly, doesn't it?"

The dragon nodded. "Yes, it sounds a bit silly. You have the power of a dragon at your command, and you would use it to make yourself richer. There must be an easier way to make money."

"And to collect power," Tom Allen added. "We would also like power."

"Ah yes, and you wish to gain power." The great dragon sighed. "I am so disappointed in you." With another great quake, Aziolith lumbered forward until its spiked tail whipped out of the portal.

Tom Allen rushed after the dragon. "Now, see here," he shouted. "We have worked to free you for a century and have finally done so. That, at least, is worthy of some compensation for services rendered. We demand–"

Aziolith swung back around. His great yellow eyes narrowed and turned a dark maroon. "You dare demand from me, human? Have you any idea what I've gone through, brooding in Hell, waiting for my moment to return to Earth, eager to meet those who would rescue me? The thought of returning to Earth was all-consuming, and now, after waiting thousands of years, I find those who freed me utterly lacking. This is not the great army I expected, but a pathetic, sniveling group of vermin unworthy of my time. Have you any idea how disappointing that is for me?"

Tom Allen gulped. "Given that as it may be, we have suffered long and lost much to return you to the world, with the expectation of reward once we did…"

"And who, may I ask, offered you this reward?"

"Well…you did."

"I did no such thing!" the dragon bellowed. "You have been deceived, and now you will know the true power of the dragon Aziolith, destroyer of men and monster alike, and doom to all those who cross my path!"

I ran away from the mystery spot back toward my mother. Aziolith unhinged his jaw and spewed fire from his nose so bright that it evaporated poor Tom Allen in an instant. Then, he turned his breath on the rest of the cultists, who drew guns to return fire.

Their bullets bounced off the dragon's hide as his breath set them ablaze. They screamed and rolled helplessly on the ground to put out the fire, but it was no use. The fire from the dragon's belly was too powerful. I like to think that in their last moments, their last words were "Aw, hell."

No sooner did Aziolith close his mouth, a great rumble came from the other side of the portal. Dozens of bright red demons, clad in human flesh armor and wielding great, obsidian swords, rushed through the portal and scattered in every direction.

CHAPTER 15

The cultist's dying screams echoed in my skull as I watched an actual dragon saunter across Mystery Spot Park and onto Main Street. The sheriff's deputies fired their pistols in vain at Aziolith, who stomped his meaty claws onto their cars on his way down the street toward the outskirts of town. His wings casually smashed into buildings along his path.

Honestly, Aziolith didn't seem angry at the many people trying to kill him. If anything, he looked bored with all the attention. I often felt that way walking through town, but then I wasn't a dragon, and when I walked, people didn't try to kill me. At least not until the last couple of days.

I finally reached Dad's hanging tree on the edge of the park and saw my mother cowering behind it. In front of me, the monsters of Hell sliced through police officers like deli meat. One day ago, I would have cowered in fear like my mother, but now I was a different person, literally baptized in blood.

"Mama!" I shouted. "We have to go!"

"What is happening here, baby?" Mama grabbed my hand.

I pulled her to her feet. "This is Hell on Earth, Mama."

"How? Why?"

"It's a long story," I said, wrapping my arm around her waist with my free hand. "The short version: You are a pixie. I am a pixie. Cultists wanted to open a portal to Hell, so they needed our blood. They succeeded, and now we have to deal with it."

I pulled a pinch of pixie dust from my bag. *Concentrate*, I told myself. *See where you want to go in your mind's eye.*

I took a deep breath, and then another, but the sounds of bullets ringing through the air and monsters howling made it impossible to think, which meant I couldn't teleport. If I couldn't teleport, then I would just have to walk. I propped Mama up on my shoulder and headed toward the edge of the park. "Don't look back, Mama. Just keep walking forward."

***

I laid Mama at the entrance to the tea shop while I dug Elka's keys out of my pocket. When I got the door open, I tossed Mama inside before following her and locking the door behind me. The battle raged outside, but there was an eerie calm inside the shop.

In that quiet, the weight of my task came crashing down upon me. The adrenaline faded, and all I was left with was the cold hard truth: Elka wanted me to battle a dragon, and that was impossible. No amount of artillery could take down that dragon. What good could I do?

I slid down the length of the door and onto the floor, and my eyes fell to the bloodstain Chuck Dixon created yesterday, and I bitterly wondered whether he was still alive. God help me; I wished that he wasn't. I hoped he did not live to see these times. The guilt of that thought overwhelmed me, and I began to cry. I couldn't protect him. I couldn't protect one human against a group of cultists. How was I going to beat a dragon?

"I can't do this…I can't do it," I muttered to myself.

"Can't do what, angel?" Mama asked, crawling toward me.

I looked down at the bloody daggers in my hand. "Mama, I can't do it. Don't make me do it. I can't—"

Mama cupped my face with her hands. "Breathe, baby. Breathe."

I closed my eyes and took a deep breath. Then another. And another. When I finally opened my eyes, tears poured down my face. "Elka, the woman who owned this shop. She told me I had to defeat this dragon, right before she died. I can't do it, Mama. It's too much."

"That's crazy, baby," Mama said. "Nobody would ask you to battle these monsters. We have to go home and wait for the police to fix this whole thing up."

I shook my head. "They are not going to fix this, Mama. Elka said that if I don't fix it, nobody could."

"And do you believe her?"

"I do. She never steered me wrong before."

Mama wrapped me in her bosom. "Then, I think you can do it. You can do anything, baby. You've done so much. You got a degree from Northwestern, right?"

I wiped tears from my cheek and sniffed. "Two, actually."

"That's something special. You have always been special, way before you could disappear yourself."

"No. No," I said, wiping the tears from my eyes. "You're right. We have to get out of here, Mama. We have to leave now. Get out of Chandler for good."

Mama pulled back from me. "Oh, baby. You can leave if you want, but I'm not going anywhere."

"Yes, you are. You have to come with me out of town."

"Baby, I love you, but I don't have to do anything." She took a step away from me.

I grabbed Mama's arm and pulled her toward me. "This is insane, Mama. There's a dragon destroying downtown and demons running amok on every street corner. If we stay here, then we're as good as dead."

Mama yanked her arm from me. "I'm old, baby. I'm already as good as dead. You can go, but I'm staying."

"That's crazy!" I stomped through the store, throwing angry looks at her. "This place killed my father and tried to kill you. How can you still defend it?"

"True. This town did try to kill me," Mama said. "But it's also the place I fell in love, and had you, and helped raise hundreds of kids. It's the place that took us in and fed us after your father died. It's the only place I've ever felt at peace."

I flung my arm toward the door, pointing at the park. "That's because of the mystical energy from the mystery spot."

"I don't care what it's from, baby," Mama said, shaking her head furiously. "It's where I want to be. I've never felt so sure of that."

I jumped up and down, frantically trying to make Mama see reason. "There is a giant portal to Hell in the middle of town! It doesn't matter where you want to be, this place is literally going to Hell."

"Then I'll go with it."

"You love this town that much?" I scoffed.

She folded her arms. "Yes."

"You and I must be living in two different towns, then. Everybody who lives here wants us dead. Some for being black. Others for being pixies, but they all want us dead. The principal at my school, for Christ's sake. Martha, the only person who served us at Charlotte's. Two city councilors! This town is full of awful people, mother, people that just brought about the end of times."

"It's full of good people, too, sweetheart. Full of children I used to watch, and who could use your help. People that will lose everything if they have to evacuate this place. You think my house is protected from demon attacks?"

"They can build again! They can't live again."

"Well, I think that portal to Hell is proof of the opposite, my dear. I think this shows, if anything, that we do live again, and if we do live again, what do you have to fear from death?"

"How about being burned alive in fire and brimstone? Is that enough for you?"

"I survived worse than this," Mama told me.

"Worse than Hell on Earth?"

"Yes, worse than this. I know you don't believe this, but losing your father devastated me. It changed everything I knew about the world. I was young and stupid, and I wasn't ready to take care of a kid myself, but I did, and I raised you right for twenty-five years."

"You raised me to keep my head down and survive."

"And you did that, baby. You survived, and now you could do something great. I don't know what that is, but I do know that if we run away, well, I'll never be able to live with myself."

"So, you're saying you want me to fight an unstoppable group of demons and a dragon, to save a bunch of ungrateful suckers who couldn't care less if we live or die?"

Mama shook her head. "No, baby. I'm saying we can't leave because there are people worth protecting."

"Name one."

"How about all those kids at Taft High School or George Washington? Those kids whose families might've done some terrible things, but they didn't do anything wrong. They don't deserve to die in a slaughter, do they?"

I grumbled to myself. "No."

"Or how about that nice man who guarded the mystery spot? What was his name?"

"Chuck Dixon."

"Yes, that's it. Is he worth saving?"

I pointed to the bloodstain on the floor. "That's his blood. He's probably dead."

Mama looked down at it, then back to me. "Even if he is, what about all the others like him? Isn't there anybody worth fighting for?"

"Maybe a couple."

Mama squeezed my hand. Her voice lost its edge. "That's enough, I think."

"Is it? You want me to risk my life because one person isn't a jerk?"

"Yes."

"Why?"

"Because we are better, Julia. We have to be better. It's the only way things are gonna change—if we are better than everybody else for longer than anybody thinks possible."

We were having a moment. In a better time, it would have led to a warm embrace. This was not that time, however, because we were rudely interrupted by a spiky-horned demon crashing through the door of the tea shop.

Snarling, razor-sharp teeth chomped together as it rushed toward me, pulling back its curved, black sword, ready to strike. On instinct, I spun Elka's daggers in my hand. I dodged the demon's sword, and in one swift motion, dug them deep into its throat.

The daggers penetrated to the hilt, and dark green blood oozed out of its mouth as the demon fell to my feet. I stepped on its chest and yanked them out of his body. My hands and clothes were covered in green blood that mixed with Elka's.

"I've never done anything like that before." I turned to Mama, trying to catch my breath. "How did I do that?"

"I have no idea," Mama said, visibly shaking. She beamed with pride. "But it was very special."

The adrenaline coursed through my veins, and I felt different. It was like when I had vanished, except even more amped up. I didn't just want to fight, I *needed* to fight. Confidence surged inside of me. For once, I wasn't just reacting. I needed to take action, not for the town, but for me.

I turned to Mama. "Alright, if I'm going to do this, you have to be safe. I can't keep thinking about your safety every moment while I'm fighting monsters and demons, alright?"

Mama put her hands on her hips and scowled at me. "I'm not leaving town."

I smiled at her. "I have an idea, but you have to trust me."

"I have always trusted you," Mama said softly, and I believed her.

I grabbed the Pixie Dust book from the shelf and stuffed it in a leather satchel I'd found under the register. I placed the daggers inside the satchel as well. Then, I took Mama's hand. "This is going to feel weird."

I closed my eyes, focused, and grabbed a pinch of pixie dust. My mind pulled me to where I wanted to go. Confident and calm, I threw the pixie dust and vanished with Mama into the ether.

CHAPTER 16

My father's cemetery plot. I envisioned it in my mind's eye and let it pull me toward my vision. A crack of purple light, and we were there. We snapped out of the void and landed in the cemetery. The grass was dewy under my hands and knees. Mama stood next to me, hunched over and gasping. I rose to my feet in front of my father's grave.

"That—I didn't like that."

I rubbed her back. "I know, mama, but we're here."

"You brought me here?" she asked, looking up at the cemetery.

I grabbed Mama's hand gently. "It was the safest place I could think of. Daddy will keep you safe."

"That was never his strength, baby, even in life."

I turned back to watch the giant, red portal swirling around Chandler. It somehow felt more ominous from miles away than standing next to it. Close up, I didn't understand its sheer magnitude, but from here, I could see it towering twenty feet above the church tower, the tallest building in town.

It was night again. Near the portal, it had been bright as day, but here in the cemetery, the stars were coming out. Crisp air filled my nostrils, and I took a deep inhale of the night air, my first breath since leaving the tea shop. I turned to my father's grave. Mama touched the headstone.

"They killed him because they thought he was a pixie," I said. "They drained him into the mystery spot just like they were gonna drain you. That's why his neck was slit. When that didn't work, they hung him to cover it up."

Mama smiled. "That actually makes me feel better in a way. The thought that he wasn't killed just for the color of his skin—I could never leave this place because of that. Leaving meant they won." She choked back her tears. "But they did win, didn't they?"

I shook my head. "No. They didn't win yet."

The rhythmic thud of a helicopter passed by overhead. Then another, and finally a third. Three military choppers, armed with missiles, flew past us. The national guard was here, and that couldn't be good.

From the top of the hill, I watched a string of Humvees drive into the town, shining their bright lights for all to see.

"This will not end well," Mama said. "The national guard never made anything better."

The Kent State shooting was still raw in my mind. I was supposed to be at the protests that day, but I decided not to join the carpool because I had too much work to do. It wasn't until later that night that my roommate told me to turn on the radio, and I heard what had happened.

And now, on top of a town full of monsters, the national guard was swarming the town as well.

The helicopters fired four rockets that exploded onto the dragon's scaly skin but didn't even cause enough damage for Aziolith to break stride. Instead, he turned back and spat fire at the choppers until they careened into the church tower, sending the steeple crashing into the street below.

"I have to go before it gets worse," I said to Mama.

"Be careful, baby."

I didn't know if she was warning me about the monsters or the military, but either way, her warnings fell on deaf ears. There was nothing careful about what I was about to do. I pulled a pinch of pixie dust out of my bag and kissed Mama on the head. Then, I closed my eyes, let my mind reach forward, and vanished.

***

I reappeared inside my classroom. Without students or teachers inside, I didn't have to worry about being interrupted as I read through Elka's book.

Three more explosions outside my window. No doubt the military trying to destroy the dragon, but I couldn't focus on any of that now. I had work to do. I was about to fight a dragon, and without a plan, I would be dead in the water.

Elka told me that there was a weakness in Aziolith, which I could find by looking through *Pixie Dust* and reading the exploits of Akta. I turned on the lights to my classroom and pulled out the book.

When I thought that the book was simply the foolish ramblings of an old woman, I had little respect for it, but now, as a historical document, I wanted to comb back over every page and take in every exquisite hand-painted image. No longer was this the fevered dream or fantastical story. Every page was brimming with vibrant colors and sacred texts; these were illustrations of my people, in full relief, depicting significant moments in time that I wanted to relive.

If I got through this ordeal, I promised myself I would devote the whole summer to studying its pages. Right now, there was work to do. Elka told me that the answer to killing the dragon could be found within the stories of Akta, one of the last pixies of memory.

I flipped open the book and turned toward the back. There was no table of contents, but I assumed the histories of each pixie were in chronological order, and I was correct because I found Akta's tales in the last pages of the book.

Pixies lived a nomadic life, apparently, and their traditions were passed down orally, which is why it was harder to find information about them. Most of the pixies would be lucky to have a single page, but Akta's story filled several. There were dozens of stories about monsters she killed and battles she won. She was an expert warrior, but her exploits were also well documented by virtue of time and place—she was a monster hunter for King Odgeir's kingdom, and written tales of the time were very thorough.

I skimmed through Akta's stories until I found a page with a giant dragon emblazoned on the page. The artwork depicted a great battle between Akta and the black-scaled dragon, Aziolith.

Many hundreds of knights from around the world fell by the claw of Aziolith. Men with great steel and brawn, with the smarts of King Arthur and the bravery of Lancelot, fought Aziolith to their death. Most never landed a blow on the beast before the great black dragon sent them to Velaska and the underworld below.

It was only after a decade of sending knights to their doom that King Odgeir, second of his name, called upon the greatest monster hunter in the land, Akta of the Forest People, friend to men and foe of monsters, to finally stop the scourge.

After six dozen days, Akta came upon the great dragon Aziolith on the battlefield. It had just laid waste to the town of Orelle and stolen all its treasures for itself.

The battle lasted for three days and nights, with no rest for either dragon or pixie. Akta never worked so hard felling a beast, and the great dragon never toiled so long battling one of its prey. Every attack Akta threw at the great beast clanked off its impenetrable armor, and with every attack from the great dragon, Akta disappeared, safe from harm.

It wasn't until the end of the third day when Aziolith made his grave mistake. After spitting fire at Akta for an entire morning with no success, the great dragon reared up to stomp Akta. She sliced Aziolith across the stomach, and two scales fell off its belly.

The dragon tried to cover up its new weakness, but Akta was too fast. She appeared at the monster's stomach and jammed her daggers into its hide. She plunged in her blades again and again until the great menace Aziolith fell to the ground with a great scream and departed from this world.

It was a prodigious victory, but with its death, so also was buried the secret of its immense horde of treasure.

I closed the book and sighed loudly. Elka was right. Akta's story gave me the means to kill the dragon, even if it would be nearly impossible to make my way to the great dragon's stomach and stab it in just the right spot using only the two tiny daggers. Yet, that was the only way to kill the beast, which meant that's exactly what I had to do.

I opened the bottom drawer of my desk and placed *Pixie Dust* inside it. I hoped it would be safe until I returned, if I returned, which was wholly unlikely. If not, I hoped it fell into the right hands and not one who would destroy it—or mock it.

Then, I pulled Elka's daggers out of the satchel and gripped them tightly in my hands. I left the satchel on my chair, pushed open the door to my classroom, and ran out into the hallway, ready to face my destiny, knowing that I had almost no chance of making it out of this alive.

CHAPTER 17

I walked out of George Washington High School into the hellfire of Chandler. The town burned from the dragon's breath, and demons ran amok, ripping people in half like it was nothing. Once they'd finished with the sheriffs, they started to pull people out of shops and homes, slaughtering them for fun. I always hated the people of Chandler, but they did not deserve this fate.

"What have I done? What have I done?"

The murmuring was coming from the corner of the school. I tipped my head around the side of the building to see Principal Anderson curled up in a ball, rocking back and forth against the side of the school, his black cape singed at the edges.

"I thought you were dead," I said, walking down the stairs.

"Oh god!" Principal Anderson shouted and looked like he might jump out of his skin. His eyes and face were swollen with tears. He noticed the daggers in my hand, caked with demon blood. "Don't kill me."

"I'm not going to kill you, Bob. I'll let the demons do that."

He shook his head and started rocking again. "No, no, no, no, no."

"You should be happy, Bob," I sneered at him. "Demons slaughtering you in the street is a far better fate than you deserve and much better than a dragon burning you alive. How did you survive that, anyway?"

"I-I-I hid under the burning corpses until they stopped smoldering."

"And then you ran to the school?" I asked, folding my arms across my chest.

"I thought I could hide here. It was big and empty. The demons, they wouldn't look here, at least not first. But it was locked, and I forgot my key."

I scoffed at him. "They didn't fit into your robes, huh?"

Bob shook his head and then began sobbing again. His head fell into his hands. I almost felt sorry for him until I remembered that he brought this on himself. And I thought of Elka.

"What did you think would happen, Bob, when you opened a rift to Hell and unleashed a massive dragon?"

Bob rocked back and forth. "Jim told me they could control him. That the dragon would make me rich beyond my wildest dreams. That I would have power and money. Do you know what I could do with that kind of thing? How many people I could help?"

I lunged toward him, unfurling my arms. "So, you were okay with killing me and my mother just to get power for yourself?"

He jumped back, but there was nowhere for him to go. "What is one life when weighed against millions?"

I pointed the dagger at his face. "And how did you think this dragon was going to get power—you know what? I don't care. I don't care, Bob. I only have one question for you—" I pointed the knife squarely at his heart. "Did you help kill my father?"

Bob shook his head. "No, no. I only joined three years ago. They recruited me when I became principal, said their society helped people become powerful. It was like a club. I had never been in a club."

"How many people did you kill, Bob?"

Bob threw up his hands. "None! I swear. I just went to the meetings. I never killed anybody."

"Until tonight, when you were willing to kill my mother."

He dropped his head again. "Yes."

"You are pathetic, Bob."

I wanted to kill him, but jowls soaked in that much sick made him even more pathetic than usual. Besides, even if I was learning a lot of things about myself and my abilities, I still wasn't a murderer. I didn't have to help him, though, and without my help, the demons would do the job for me.

***

The main road through town was infested with demons busy destroying the town, so I made my way behind the school and started on foot through the alleyways.

It wasn't hard to spot the dragon when it reared its ugly head, and when it stayed low to the ground, the constant barrage of bullets let me echolocate toward his location. All I had to do was follow the explosions from the tanks as they bounced uselessly on the dragon's impenetrable hide.

"Help me!" I heard a shrill voice as I wound through the alley. A hairy demon with long tusks chased after a young mother and her baby in the street. *Don't be a hero, Julia*, I said to myself, but it was too late. I had already decided to be a hero, and heroes help people.

I swung the daggers around in my hands and took off after the demon. When it raised its sword to strike at the mother, I stabbed it through the sides. The demon howled in pain and turned toward me. Bleeding from the sides, it gave chase, swinging its sword and stumbling forward. I ducked its blade and spun around to its back. From there, I raised my daggers over my head and plunged them deep into its neck.

The demon struggled to stay upright, choking on its blood. When it raised its sword to strike again, it fell on its knees instead—dead. I jerked my dagger out of the demon's neck and turned to the mother. "Get inside. It's not safe here. Do you understand?"

She nodded and ran off, whimpering and cradling her baby in her arms. It was more than likely she would die before she reached safety, but I'd done everything I could to give her a chance. The demon's blood-soaked through my shirt and smelled of raw sewage, but I couldn't help feeling proud of myself for killing my second demon.

Two days ago, I couldn't fight a punk kid, and now I had killed two demons in the past hour. I could only explain my newfound prowess with the power surging through my veins. I never felt anything like it. If the mystery spot made my head tingle with exhilaration, the portal to Hell made me throb all over. Every molecule of my body sparked as if I were the reincarnation of the great monster hunter, Akta. I longed for more demon blood to feel the cold steel of my blades.

For the first time in a long time, I felt confident. I felt powerful. I felt as though I could do anything. Then, five demons turned the corner and saw that I had mutilated their friend. Confident badassery devolved to fear as I bolted down the street away from them.

Even at my top speed, those monsters were faster than me. Their powerful legs churned against the ground and closed in on me almost instantly. They swung their swords and cut at my clothes. I tried to breathe and focus so I could disappear, but there was no chance of that. I was too amped up and in no position to calm myself. I was going to die.

Then, I felt myself rising into the air as a purple aura lit around me. The demons rushed around harmlessly under me as I floated into the air.

"What is happening to me?" I screamed, kicking against the wind. I spun myself uncontrollably until I caught my reflection in the window of an apartment building. Two bright purple wings protruded from my back and fluttered fast.

I had wings! I had *wings*! Just like Elka. I really was a pixie. I was so excited by the thought of having wings it didn't occur to me that I couldn't control them. Soon, I hovered above the building, kicking and screaming, trying to drop to the ground.

"I appreciate this, but I really must be going!" I shouted to the wings on my back.

They didn't retract. Instead, they fluttered faster into the air. How did Elka make her wings go away? She closed her eyes and meditated, just like she taught me to do when I teleported using the pixie dust.

With my eyes closed, I imagined myself without wings, walking on the ground. I opened my eyes and felt my back and shoulders. The purple aura engulfing me was gone, and sure enough, so were the wings. I was giddy…until I realized I was fifteen feet above the roof of the building. The last thought that went through my head before I slammed into the ground was *crap*.

I protected my head with my hands to prevent myself from cracking open my skull, and they slammed into the ground with a mighty thud. After a moment of catching my breath, I stood up. My fingers were bruised and battered, and I was sore and stiff, but I didn't seem to have broken any bones.

A mighty roar came from the distance. I looked out over the building and saw Aziolith on the horizon. A squad of helicopters and tanks battered him while soldiers took shots with their automatic weapons.

The dragon let out another mighty bellow that blanketed the sky with fireballs. The helicopters crashed into each other and fell to the ground, leaving nothing but a heap of smoldering wreckage. Screams of agony rose from the street when the dragon opened his mouth and engulfed the soldiers in a stream of fire.

Aziolith took another step forward, picking up a tank in its incredible claw and flinging it into the distance like some toy truck. Meanwhile, another set of soldiers rushed forward to take the place of their fallen comrades. I'll give it to them, the national guard may not be the best our country has to offer, but they were brave.

Blood-curdling screams caught my attention, and I turned toward the portal. A bearded demon with long dreadlocks picked up an old woman and ripped off her head. The demons were a menace. I realized then that while the dragon needed to be stopped, the national guard could keep it busy for a while. The true terror to Chandler were the demons murdering people for sport.

More and more of them funneled out of the portal with every passing minute. If I wanted to protect the people of this city, I had to close that portal first. Perhaps doing so would force the dragon back through it as well.

I knew what I had to do. I had to find Principal Anderson, the only cultist who had survived the dragon's fire. I just hoped the coward wasn't dead yet. I took a deep breath, imagined the front of the school, and, with a pinch of pixie dust, vanished.

CHAPTER 18

I reappeared in front of the school, exactly where I'd left Principal Anderson, except that he wasn't there. All that remained was a bloody drag mark leading down the sidewalk.

"Help!" I heard. I'd recognize the jowly scream anywhere.

I ran toward the sniveling cries and found Principal Anderson surrounded by three demons. Blood streamed down his head.

I held the grip on my daggers tight. "Hey!" I shouted, bracing myself. I felt even more powerful here, nearer to the portal.

The demons turned, and I smiled at them. I don't know what had come over me, but for some reason, I knew I could defeat them. Maybe it was the surge of power from the mystery spot or sheer stupidity. I grabbed a pinch of my pixie dust and closed my eyes. My wings sprouted behind me, bigger than they were before.

Two of the demons ran toward me just as I evaporated. I reappeared behind them and sliced at their legs. One of them swung its sword at me. With another pinch of the dust, I was gone, rematerializing to ram my dagger through its back. In another instant, I was in the wind, then back again with a stab through the neck. Green blood spurted out as it fell to the ground, revealing its companion whirling a sword at me. It turned to swing, and I stabbed it through the chest. It dropped in its tracks with a gasp.

The final demon grinned at me with razor-sharp teeth. I beckoned it to come closer, but the monster didn't move. Instead, it flipped its sword around and sliced Principal

Anderson across the stomach. Bob screamed, watching his intestines drop onto the sidewalk.

"That's it!" I shouted.

Another pinch of pixie dust let me appear right next to the demon. It swung at me, but I met its claw with one dagger and dug the other one into its side. Slicing through its hand with the first dagger, I stuck it through its chin. The demon dropped instantly, bathing me in sticky, green blood. With the demons finally dead, I ran over to Principal Anderson.

"Why? Why?" he blubbered to himself. "Why did this happen? Why? Why?"

I knelt next to him. He didn't look good. His small intestine had leaked out onto the ground. "Bob, you're going to die. There's no doubt about that."

"Why? I don't—Why?"

"Bob, listen. You can die a coward or a hero." I snapped my fingers to get his attention. "Listen to me. Okay? How do you close the portal?"

"I don't—I don't—"

"This isn't the time, Bob. You'll be dead any second. If you don't tell me how to close the portal, all this will have been in vain. You will die for no reason. No power. No money. Not a hero, just a sad man who brought about the end of the world. Think!"

The color faded from Bob's eyes. "The blood will open, and the blood will close. It will open and close. Close and open." That was the last thing Bob said before he faded from this world. Luckily, it was enough to give me an idea. If Elka's blood could open the portal, then mine could close it.

I knew what that meant. It meant I had to make the ultimate sacrifice—my life for this town. Damn, I hated being a hero.

I wasn't ready to die. I'd just got this incredible power, and now I had to return it for the greater good—even if that good was objectively pretty terrible. Still, I listened to the screams coming from the town. I thought of Chuck and my mother. They did not deserve this fate.

Bob, it turned out, was right. What is one life exchanged for a million?

I kicked my feet into the air and hovered above the ground. I wanted one last feeling of triumph before I went into the great abyss. When I could control it, floating above the ground was an incredible feeling. I wanted one last incredible feeling in my life.

Once I died, I would end up on the other side of that hole, with no way back. I would be in Hell, a damned soul. God didn't like people that killed themselves. I knew that for sure.

***

I flew toward the mystery spot as if fighting an incredible headwind. My feet hovered above the ground, but just barely. Demons broke before me like a great ocean, and I slit the throats of those that dared confront me. I was a stone-cold butcher.

It's not an easy thing, facing your own death. You always think it will happen in the distant future, but the truth is that whenever death comes for you, it comes in the right now.

Even as I made my way closer to the mystery spot, I wanted to believe that something would come along, some supernatural force that would save the day. Right?

Something had to stop me from spilling my own blood to save the lives of everybody else.

I thought of my mother. She loved this town. I thought back to Chuck Dixon, who protected this spot with his life. And now, I would do the same. I always knew I would die in this town. I just never thought it would be by my own hand.

I looked down at the daggers in my hands. They shook as I raised them into the air. *Blood will open. Blood will close,* I said to myself. In one swift motion, I plunged the daggers deep into my gut.

The air left my lungs, and I felt a warmth ooze down my legs. Blood—my blood—poured onto the ground and snaked like a river toward the mystery spot, still visible at the center of the giant portal.

My knees wobbled, and I dropped to the ground. Lying there, I felt my warm blood pooling underneath me, and I struggled for every breath. It was working, though. My blood was flowing into the mystery spot like a waterfall. At least my death would close the portal.

Except—it didn't.

More and more of my blood fell into the mystery spot, but still, it stayed open, and more monsters flooded out from it.

I had failed.

As my eyes closed, I thought about what a waste my life had turned out to be. What a pity.

CHAPTER 19

When my eyes opened again, my wound no longer throbbed. In fact, nothing hurt at all. I felt nothing except the jagged rocks under me and wet dewiness coating my body.

Everything around me was tinged red and orange, and it was hotter than the surface of the sun. I sat up too quickly, and my head felt dizzy. I was on a cliff, overlooking a great city in the distance.

I looked down at my stomach. Two holes punctured it, but the wounds didn't bleed, though dried blood caked my pants and shirt. My clothes were wet, but not from blood. It was from something that smelled of sulfur.

In front of me, a river of molten lava flowed down a rocky embankment toward a great black gate in the distance. Thousands of bodies filled it; the people screamed out from the river, swimming with all their might to make their way to shore, but the current was too strong.

Along the riverbed, I saw demons, like the ones invading Chandler, busy stacking bodies on top of each other. Corpses covered every inch of the rocky terrain for as far as the eye could see.

"You should be down there," I heard behind me. I turned to see a dark-skinned woman in a green tunic, with leather bracers on her arms and legs. She wore a red bandana around her forehead, and her pointed ears stuck out from her head. She sharpened my daggers with a rock as she stared at me with deep, emerald eyes.

"I almost didn't find you before the current swept you away," she said. "If you made it to the black gate, I wouldn't have been able to save you in time."

"And who are you?" I asked, pushing myself to my feet.

She pointed at me with the tip of the dagger's blade and chuckled. "You really are my descendent, aren't you?"

The woman closed her eyes. A pair of blue wings grew out of her back and illuminated my face with a soft glow.

"Akta?" I asked.

She nodded. "That is my name, Julia."

"You know me?"

"Elka told me enough to get me by," Akta said, scraping a smooth rock down my blade that sparked every time she reached the tip. "Said you might do something stupid and asked me to look out for you."

Akta's dark face cracked from years in the Hellish heat, but under those grooves, she could have been my age, save for the clothing which looked straight out of an epic fantasy book.

"And where is Elka?"

"She is in another place," Akta responded, straightening her headband.

"Heaven?" I said, confused.

"I can't say, but she's not here. That's for sure."

"Why are you here?"

Akta didn't look up from her work, sharpening the blades with long, deliberate strokes. "I made a deal with the wrong goddess a long time ago, before Lucifer, and I can't leave until I honor my debt to her."

"I'm sorry."

"It's not that bad down here," the wizened pixie said with a sad smile. "Especially if you can avoid Aziolith.

He's cranky most of the time, and he's never forgiven me for killing him."

I took a step toward her. Even though she was family, her presence scared me. "He's destroying Chandler right now."

"I know," Akta replied, stopping her sharpening for a moment. "He should never have been allowed to escape, but Lucifer can't keep track of anything. He's a horrible bureaucrat. Hell is a shell of its former greatness ever since Velaska ran off to live among the stars. Luckily, his incompetence affords me the ability to do what I want, so I can't complain. Sometimes, when the moans stop, it's downright peaceful here."

I looked out over the valley of damned souls. Their bodies rose to the tip of the giant cavern like a great mountain range that stretched over the horizon. "Is that what I have to look forward to?"

Akta stood, my daggers now razor-sharp in her hand. "Not unless you want it to be. You can go back, still. There is time to fix your mistake, kill Aziolith, and send him back beyond the gates of Hell, but time is of the essence."

"Go back? But I'm dead, right?"

"Your soul is dead, but your body is alive, at least for a couple more moments. Right now, you are in limbo. Luckily, you are bleeding out slowly. A stomach wound takes a long time to cause death," Akta said, twirling the daggers in her hand. "I've missed these over the centuries."

"They are yours?" I asked.

She nodded. "They were mine, enchanted by the first pixies. They passed through my family for generations until they made their way to you. Now, you must use them to destroy Aziolith again."

"I can't." I shook my head. "I've already failed."

Akta grabbed my chin. "No. My family are not failures. We do not leave things undone. There is still time for you to return, reunite with your body, and save yourself. Look behind you."

Akta spun me around until I saw the portal to Earth. From the cliff where we stood, it only looked like a few feet tall. Hundreds of demons sat on its edges, waiting for their chance to pour through and wreak havoc.

"That's so far away," I said.

"It is the only way." Akta let go of my head. "You can stay here and take your chances with Charon. Or you can return and take your chances with the dragon."

"What's the point of going back? I don't know how to close the portal. I don't know how to stop this."

"That's not what's important," Akta said, handing me back the daggers. "What's important is trying. You'd know how to close it if you thought for a moment. Unfortunately, we don't have a moment, so I'll just tell you how to stop this horrible mess. Only Aziolith's blood can close the portal. Elka's opened it with her magical blood to summon him, and only his can close it. Now, will you help?"

I didn't have to think about it. I grabbed Akta's daggers from her outstretched hand. "Yes. I will. But I don't stand a chance against Aziolith. He's shaking off guns and missiles like they are nothing. I'll be eaten in a second."

"He has a fatal flaw," Akta said.

"The lining of his stomach, I know."

"Not only his stomach. His wing is also his weakness. He used to be able to fly across the world in a matter of minutes, but I clipped his right wing during our fight. He cannot fly. He can only walk, and he lumbers slowly. In the sky, Aziolith is unbeatable, but on the ground, he can be killed."

My skin was turning a pale white hue. "I don't feel well."

"Your death is imminent. We must hurry. There is not much time."

Akta grabbed me by the shoulders, and we both lifted into the air. I closed my eyes and grew out my own pair of wings. They fluttered as fast as I could manage, right alongside Akta's. Together, we bolted across the plains of Hell, kicking up dust in our wake. Millions of damned souls moaned in agony as demons tortured them beneath us. Every moment Hell packed fuller with the damned. There were piles of souls, a thousand high, for as far as the eye could see.

"Soon, Satan won't be able to fit all these souls in Hell," Akta said. "I wonder what he will do with them."

"Unleash them on the world, maybe?" I replied.

"Perhaps. There is plenty of room on Earth, and it's rife for an Apocalypse. The demons will have a field day with humanity, doughy and soft as they've become. Your kind has clearly lost their warrior spirit."

I gripped my dagger tightly. "We can get it back."

"I hope so."

We neared the portal to Hell. The demons groaned as they mulled around the entrance to our world.

"When you get to the other side, don't waste time," Akta told me. "Pull out the daggers in your stomach. This will be the most painful part. Then, use the pixie dust to close your wound. Imagine yourself healthy, let your mind pull yourself toward it, and you will recover quickly. Then, swallow the last of what is in your pouch. Your body will do the rest. A fact I wish I knew when I was alive."

"Shouldn't I go to the hospital?"

We were only a couple of feet away from the portal now. "They are only good for the dying. Trust me."

"Thank you."

Akta let me go. "Good luck to you."

I flew as fast as I could into the portal, and it sucked me right in. I tumbled through, experiencing every color imaginable—some I didn't know existed—until I woke up back in my body, bloody and broken. I watched the ghost of Atka's daggers spin forward and mold perfectly with those protruding from my stomach.

My arms were weak, but I focused my mind to lift them. I wrapped my fingers around the hilts and yanked the daggers out of my abdomen. I screamed bloody murder. The blood gushed out onto the ground as I pulled the pixie dust from my pocket and sprinkled it over the wound.

I closed my eyes. It was hard not to fall asleep and dream again forever, but I imagined myself healthy. I reconstructed every molecule of my body, and then I let my mind pull myself toward it. A blue light flashed around me, and I suddenly felt better. I touched my stomach, and it no longer bled. It no longer ached. There were no wounds or scars, either.

I was ready to carry out my mission. If the blood of Aziolith was the only thing that would close the portal, then I would make him bleed. I rubbed what remained of the pixie dust on my gums and swallowed. It gave me a surge of energy, and I found myself in a thousand places at once, fighting every demon in front of me with ease.

The blue light was me, and I was the blue light. We were one and the same. I watched the blue light dance in front of me. I closed my eyes, and I was there. The world moved forward but in slow motion.

Monsters swung their swords like sloths as I disappeared and reappeared at will in front of them. I sliced one across the throat and stabbed another through the brain before they'd even moved an inch. My wings fluttered into the air as I stole the sword from one demon and stabbed it in the eye of another effortlessly. They didn't stand a chance. I existed on another level.

I saw the dragon Aziolith in the distance, and I flapped my wings harder to reach him, killing every demon I came across along the way.

CHAPTER 20

I didn't even have to close my eyes anymore to make myself disappear or reappear. I saw Aziolith in front of me, and in just a blink, I appeared in front of him. The bullets from the military whizzed by my head as I floated inches from his face.

Suddenly, I no longer saw the world in slow motion. Everything sped up, and a dozen bullets clanged off the great dragon around me. An RPG exploded against his neck. He wasn't even fazed.

Aziolith looked even more imposing up close. His shimmering scales jutted out from his body, each one a little shield that protected him from all harm. He stomped down on the tank that had fired a missile at him. I gathered my wits about me and flew out of the way as the dragon's breath destroyed three Humvees, and his tail whacked over the last tank in his path. Only a small contingent of guards still stood against him, and they cowered as he walked forward.

"Now, humans," Aziolith said. "I give you a choice. Leave now. Run and never look back, and I will spare you. Stay, and you shall feel my wrath."

One of the soldiers pissed himself. He looked at his fellow soldiers, then stowed his gun and ran away as fast as his feet could carry him. The others watched him flee, took a second, and ran after him.

The dragon watched them go and turned his gaze toward the horizon as if summoned by a force beyond his control. "I hear you there, pixie," he said. "Or do you not remember that my hearing is impeccable? I seem to remember you commented on it on the second day of our battle."

I floated toward him. "I have no idea what you are talking about, Aziolith."

Aziolith turned its lumbering head toward me. "Ah. My apologies. I mistook you for another of your ilk. You smell the same. A combination of magic and sulfur."

"I know who you're speaking of. I just ran into your nemesis Akta in the pits of Hell," I said, holding up my daggers. "She helped me sharpen my blades to defeat you."

"Is that all you people think about, destruction? My entire life, all your kind did was try to defeat me. Such violence."

I floated up toward the head of the great black dragon until I settled near his great eyes. "We're violent? You massacred towns for sport!"

"Ah, you have been reading the wrong history books. I was always provoked," Aziolith said, indignant. "That is the curse of great power. Many will try to take it from you. If you do not protect yourself, you are seen as weak and invite attack. If you defend yourself, then you are labeled a monster."

"So, this was all what? You protecting yourself? You destroyed my town!"

"No! I have not destroyed anything that did not provoke me first."

"You burned a group of cultists for fun!"

"First, it was not *just* for fun. My enjoyment was but a small part of it. Second, they were horrible people, as you recall. I mean, they demanded blood for their loyalty. Those are not the kinds of people I associate with if I can help it. Their bloodlust is never satisfied. I did the world a favor by ridding it of them."

"You also let demons roam the world and started Hell on Earth!" I yelled.

"You are mistaken. All I did was walk through a portal, and toward the edge of town, content to be left alone. Whatever happened with that portal afterward was out of my control. Frankly, those demons are just awful. I wish I could have left them in Hell, but unfortunately, the portal only has one way to close it."

I rested on the ground in front of Aziolith. "Yes, only your blood will close it."

Aziolith lowered his head until he was at my level. "I am aware of that fact."

"If you really aren't evil, why would you allow this massacre to continue, especially if you could stop it?"

Aziolith gave a heavy sigh, and hot smoke poured from his nostrils. "I do not want to go back, little one."

I walked slowly down the length of Aziolith's neck. "You must know you'll be hunted across the sea. There is no place you can go that people will not attack you."

"That was the nice part about Hell. Nobody bothered me. Finally, I was just another monster. Unfortunately, that was the only nice part about it."

"You can't fly. Akta made sure of that, which means that you will never be free. You might defeat individual humans, or even whole nations, but never humanity as a whole. How far do you think you'll get before somebody else finds your weakness and kills you again?"

"I just want to find peace."

I moved toward the fleshy weakness of his stomach and placed my hand on it. His breath moved the stomach up and down, just like any other creature. He was alive, as much as

I was alive. We had both seen Hell and lived to tell about it. "I can help you find peace."

"I am not stupid, pixie. I know what you are doing. You would not have got so far if I didn't will it." Aziolith pulled away his right wing to reveal a patch of pink skin near his heart. "Make it quick. Akta, for all her faults, made my death painless. Do not hesitate. Dig the dagger in deep."

"Not here," I said. "I need you to bleed into the mystery spot. Will you come with me there?"

"Why should I do humanity any favors?"

"You shouldn't. You should do one for me."

"I have never done a favor for a pixie before," Aziolith grumbled. "Especially not one who is ready to kill me."

"Please," I said, pressing against his pink belly.

Aziolith nodded his head down to me. "I will do you this favor if it allows me to find peace once again."

I put my hand on him and closed my eyes. I pictured the mystery spot, not as it was before, but as it stood now, spinning portal and all. My wings started to vibrate faster than I could see, and then purple light flashed.

***

We reappeared in front of the mystery spot where the red portal spun six stories into the air. This close to the portal, my whole body trembled with its power, and my mind focused sharper.

"Mmm," Aziolith said, looking up at the great portal. "I just spent the whole evening walking away from this place only to end up where I started."

"Isn't that the truth?" I nodded. "I just died here."

"Ah, then you will be coming back with me."

I hadn't thought of that. Closing the portal might just send us all back to Hell, and then we'd be stuck there for all eternity. What if I could never escape?

No. I couldn't think like that. I was willing to sacrifice myself once. I must be willing to do it again.

I looked up at the great dragon. "Are you ready?"

"I have died before." Aziolith nodded. "I can die again."

I swung my daggers across the breast of the great beast and nicked open his chest, but I didn't stab through it.

Instead, I allowed the blood to seep onto the ground slowly. I opened my nearly empty bag of pixie dust and let the blood pool inside it. When the bag was full, I walked it over to the mystery spot and poured it in.

The portal stopped moving and turned from a bright to dark red, and eventually a sackcloth black. It expanded a hundred feet into the air and then shrunk back to nothing before a great red shockwave blew through the town and flung me away from the mystery spot until I landed at the edge of the park and rolled to a stop.

CHAPTER 21

I came back into consciousness with a great ringing in my ears. The sky was pitch black, and every light in the town was on. Car alarms blared in my ears, and the screams of men and women filled the air. Demons and monsters still roamed the streets, and the smell of sulfur lingered, but when my eyes regained their focus, I wasn't in Hell—at least not in the literal sense.

The light from the portal was gone, and night descended back on Chandler. The portal was closed, and with it, no more monsters could break free from Hell. However, it must not have removed the beasts that were already here, which meant Aziolith was still here, too.

It didn't take me long to confirm that thought. As I stood, a scaly tail wrapped around my waist. I looked up to see the great dragon Aziolith grinning at me, flames shooting out of his nose. "So, pixie. It appears that I now have the upper hand in our encounter," he said. "What to do with you now?"

His tail squeezed tightly around my waist until I couldn't breathe. I tried to vanish, but the incredible pain coursing through my body made it impossible to concentrate. Even if I could concentrate, I no longer felt the deep connection with the magic. It must have dissipated when the portal was closed, and with it, my connection to the power that flowed from it.

"Please, stop," was all I could muster.

Aziolith's sharp teeth grew larger and larger as he moved me closer to his mouth. "Your ancestor sent me to Hell, little one, and you…you have set me free," he said, laughing. "I suppose your blood debt is paid." He let go of me, and I dropped to the ground. I tried to flap my wings to break my fall, but they weren't there.

"That was a good one," I said, woozy.

I stood and walked toward the mystery spot. Before, being close to the spot made the hairs on my neck stand on edge, but now I felt nothing. There was no power within it. All that remained was a deep hole. My powers had come from the portal, and my ability to control them came from its massive magical power influx. Now, I had nothing. I cried.

"Please don't cry," Aziolith said to me. "I just hate it when beings like you cry. It looks so pathetic."

"I miss my powers already," I said, wiping my tears.

"Listen here, I am a massive magical beast, and I still exist. I can still breathe fire. Those demons are magical too, and they still wreak havoc. Which means your powers are still there, even if they are buried deep inside of you."

I looked down to see my daggers lying on the ground, covered in demon blood. I was covered in demon blood. Aziolith was right. The portal hadn't destroyed them—I had destroyed them. Yes, the portal amplified my strength, but it did not swing the daggers. It did not disappear throughout the city. It did not stand up to a great dragon. I did that myself.

"There is something we must do, dragon," I said, standing tall. "And we must do it together."

"There is nothing I must do, little one." Aziolith turned up his chin slightly.

"If you help me in this, I will make sure that you make it wherever you want to go, unharmed and unmolested. You have my word."

"Heroes often make promises to powerful beings. On what authority do you make these promises?"

"I just fought a dragon and saved the world. If you don't believe I can do anything, then what will it take?"

The dragon thought for a moment. "If you can guarantee this, then I will help you. What must we do?"

"We need to kill the demons remaining in town—you with your fire and me with my daggers. I can't do it alone. The magic from this place has drained, and I'm not as powerful. Together we can clear this town of monsters, and then I swear you will have peace."

The dragon nodded. "Then I will help you."

***

Life is much easier with a dragon by your side. It's so much easier, y'all. Demons that would have taken me months—if not years—to kill by myself, and probably would have killed me, were burned up in a second with the help of Aziolith. I cleaned up anything he left behind with a slice here and a stab in the gut there, but he did most of the heavy lifting, eating and setting fire to one demon after another.

Often, I would run in front of the lumbering dragon to lure demons toward his mouth. Aziolith had trouble moving fast, and I knew that before long, more tanks and helicopters would come for him. The portal was closed, but the national guard still had work to do.

We cleaned up as many demons as we could find until we heard choppers cutting through the air. The national guard was close, and the attacks on Aziolith would start again.

The great dragon had performed admirably. It was time to fulfill my end of the bargain. If there were one or two demons left, the military could figure out what to do with them.

"Wait here for a moment," I told Aziolith as we walked in front of the school back toward the mystery spot.

"Do not flee, pixie," Aziolith said to me.

"I won't."

I ran inside, breaking through the front door as I went, and grabbed the book I had stored in the bottom drawer of my desk. I took one final look at my classroom. I would never be back. I would never come back to this town again if I could help it, not after what I had seen and done. Not now that the mystery spot was gone.

I ran back outside, where Aziolith was waiting for me. "I told you I wasn't going anywhere."

"I was prepared to chase you to the ends of the world should you have vanished."

"Then it's a good thing I came back," I said, smiling. I was surprised at how much I liked this dragon. I felt more kinship to him in just a couple of hours than I did to people I'd known my whole life.

We continued walking toward the mystery spot, where I picked up my bag of pixie dust. I hoped I was right that there was still some residue left in the bag. I made a promise to a dragon, and if I couldn't fulfill it, I would be burned alive for sure.

The bag was coated in blood when I turned it inside out, but luckily there were still remnants of the dust clinging to the inside of the sack. I scraped the flecks of dust into my hand. It was time to fulfill my promise.

"Imagine where you want to go," I told Aziolith. "Picture it in your mind's eye. Make it real. Make it perfect. Remember every last detail. Do you have it?"

Aziolith closed his eyes. The sound of the Humvees echoed in the distance. In a few moments, they would come into view and attack Aziolith.

"Yes, I have it," the dragon said.

"We only have one shot at this. Make it real. Reach out with your mind and let it pull you toward it."

I rubbed the last remnants of the pixie dust on my gums. Aziolith's blood was bitter and reeked of sulfur. "Come down here."

Aziolith dropped his head, and I touched his forehead. I saw where he wanted to take me, and we vanished from sight.

CHAPTER 22

We were on the top of a mountain, and I trembled at the immense cold of the snow hitting my face. I was used to the bitter winds of Colorado, but the raw cold that hit me when I rematerialized made even me ache for relief. It felt as if a million needles were piercing me at once, all over my body.

Still, the view was astounding. I looked out over a thousand mountains disappearing into the distance. Wherever we were, it was atop the highest peak for miles.

"Come, little one," Aziolith's gruff voice called to me. I turned around as he lit a great fire from his nose and burned through the mountains of accumulated snow in front of him. The fire from his blast warmed me, and I ran over to gather as much of the heat as possible. When the smoke cleared, a great cave stood before us.

"Is this your home?" I asked. "Explorers have searched for this cave a long time, but they never found it."

Aziolith smiled. "They must not have looked very hard." He strolled into the cave, his nostrils lighting the way for me to follow. We walked through the cave and then down a narrow passage filled with frosted stalactites and stalagmites. The tunnel dead-ended at a ledge overlooking an immense cavern. Gold coins were stacked from floor to ceiling, and gems sparkled throughout the cave.

Aziolith made his way down a set of stairs next to the ledge and toward the base of the cavern, lighting lanterns with his breath along the way to guide us. With every lantern, I felt my body temperature rise.

When we reached the ground level, I craned my neck up to the ceiling and still couldn't see the top of the gold stacks in front of me. As we walked, I nearly tripped over a pile of jewel-encrusted swords strewn about the cavern floor.

In fact, everything was strewn about like a child's room, except that the combined wealth in this room was more than all the wealth in Fort Knox and the Federal Reserve combined times a million.

He made his way to a clearing in the middle of the room, where there was a great pile of kindling set up for a bonfire. With another blast from his nose, the dragon lit a bonfire which stretched twenty feet into the air. Then, he curled up under it.

"Would you do me a favor, pixie?" he asked.

"If it is within my power."

"In the chest across the room, there is a green potion in a glass vial. Please, bring it to me."

I walked over to the chest, adorned with gold and jewels, and lifted it open. Inside were a hundred different vials, all filled with iridescent liquid in every color I could imagine. I sifted through the vials until I found one that glowed green and brought it to the dragon.

"Yes," Aziolith said. "That is the one. Will you please pour it onto my tongue?"

The dragon stuck out his forked tongue, and I poured the liquid on it until it was empty. When it was done, he pulled his tongue back into his mouth and closed his eyes.

"What does that do?" I asked.

"It will heal my wounded wing, given time."

"How much time?"

"Days. Weeks. Months. I am not sure. I will sleep until my wing is mended. Meanwhile, you are welcome to anything you can carry down the mountain, as long as you promise never to tell another soul about this place."

"What about my mother? I can't lie to her if she asks where I've been."

"Is she discrete?"

I nodded. "Very."

Aziolith thought for a moment. "Then I suppose two pixies knowing about this place won't hurt much more than one."

I nodded. "Then I promise, but I doubt I can carry much. Besides that, I don't know where we are."

"The Alps of Switzerland, of course. The only place worthy of a dragon's lair. Take a handful of gold. Once you are down the mountain, it will afford you safe passage to anywhere you would like."

I looked down at the ground. I only wanted a handful of my pixie dust, and then I could go anywhere I wanted. I would have given anything for it, but I dared not say that and seem ungrateful for the dragon's great gift.

"What has got you so down?" Aziolith said. "You are rich beyond measure now."

"I—Nothing."

"Hmm…I see it in your eyes, pixie. I know what you seek. I believe you will find it three mounds over on the left, assuming the mountain hasn't shifted it over the years."

His statement confused me, but I counted three mounds and turned to the left. I walked around the large heap of armor and weapons until I saw it—a jeweled pouch covered in moons and stars. My eyes lit up, and I dove to retrieve it. I opened the pouch and found it full of pixie dust.

I screamed loud enough to shake the stalactites from their slumber. "Oh my god!"

"Quiet!" Aziolith said sleepily.

"How did you get this?" I shouted, rushing toward him.

"Akta was not the only pixie to chase me. She was just the one that defeated me. I've collected a dozen or so similar pouches from pixies of all types."

My eyes grew even wider. "That. That is what I want. Those pouches."

"Unfortunately, I only remember where that one is. Pixies were never much of a bother to me until the last couple." Aziolith yawned. "An inconsequential species, really. Except for two."

I walked toward him excitedly. "Would it be possible to come look for it again when I'm able?"

"You may return any time you wish and take anything you wish when you do, as long as you only take what you need."

"And my mother?"

"She is welcome as well," Aziolith groaned with a contented sigh.

"Why are you being so generous to me?" I asked.

Aziolith let out a long, contented sigh. "You brought me home, which is all I ever wanted. It is the least I could do."

I nodded to him as he drifted off to sleep. "Then I promise."

My pockets filled with gold, I rubbed a pinch of pixie dust in my hands and vanished.

***

I reappeared in the cemetery in front of my father's grave. My mother was lying down next to it. When she saw the flash of purple light, she jumped up to wrap her arms around me.

"Oh, thank the Lord," she said, her voice full of grateful joy. "I thought you were dead, child!"

"Are you okay?" I asked, hugging her.

She nodded, her face still pressed into my shoulder. "I'm fine, child. Nothing from that town ever came for me here, but I saw it all from a distance. Did you kill that dragon and close the portal? It was quite a sight. I was sure you were dead."

"Aziolith is not dead. I returned him to his lair."

Mama pulled away from me. "After all he did, you didn't kill…him?"

"No. I took pity on him," I said, pulling a gold coin out of my pocket. "And I was rewarded for my mercy."

I handed the coin to Mama, and she looked at it with wonder. "Oh my...that is a pretty sight."

"And that's not all." I pulled a whole handful of gold coins out of my pocket.

Mama started to cry. "This is wonderful, baby."

Gunshots rang out behind us. "What are they fighting now?"

"I don't know. Military men have been funneling through for a long time now. I don't think it's safe here anymore."

"We don't have to stay here, Mama," I said. "We can go anywhere we want."

Mama looked out at the town, then back at Daddy's grave. "It's funny. Suddenly, I don't feel as connected to this place as I once did. It feels different to me, cold even. Like I have nothing holding me here."

I nodded. "I know, Mama. It's because the magic is gone from this place."

"Your daddy will understand…if I leave—won't he?"

"He will," I said solemnly. "He wouldn't want you to be bound to this place."

Mama reached for my hand. "Then I think I'm ready for a new adventure."

I clasped my hand in hers. "Me too. Where should we go?"

Mama thought for a minute. "Paris always sounded nice. I loved that postcard your daddy bought for me one Christmas—the one with the Eiffel tower on it. He always wanted to take me there. I would love to see it."

"Is that the picture that you kept on your bedside?"

She nodded. "That's the same one. I could never get up the nerve to see it for myself, but I studied it almost every night."

"Imagine that card, Mama. Every detail of it. See where you want to go in your mind's eye. Let your mind pull yourself toward it." I grabbed a pinch of pixie dust. "Do you see it?"

"I see it, baby."

I dropped a pinch of pixie dust onto the ground, and we disappeared, hand in hand.

BOOK 2

"Into Hell"

PROLOGUE

I want to go home. I want to go home. I want to go home. I want to go home now. Please let me go home. God, just let me go home. I should never have left. I know that now. I know that now, but it's too late. I ran too far and too fast after I crawled out of my window into the cold, dark night, and now I don't know where I am.

I had never been so far from home. Mom always told me to stay in the yard, especially on rainy nights, but I wanted to show her that I was a big girl who knew what she was doing. I was eight years old, not a baby, and I would show her. I would run away and hide, and she wouldn't be able to find me.

She would worry. She would cry, and then I would come back home. She would realize I was right, and she would stop yelling at me so much. Except it didn't work like that, exactly.

Who am I kidding? It didn't work like that at all. It started out fine. I ran past Old Man Magill's house and crossed the rusted, old train tracks that hadn't worked in years. Mom told me never to cross the train tracks, not ever ever ever, but I didn't care. She wasn't the boss of me.

It started to rain when I crossed the tracks—almost exactly when I stepped onto the other side. It was like God telling me to turn back…but I couldn't turn back, not until Mom learned her lesson. She can't raise her voice to me. She can't tell me what to do. Not anymore.

The rain came down harder, and I hugged close to Teddy, my stuffed bear. I squeezed him tighter with each step I took past the train tracks. Teddy would keep me safe.

He always had before, even in the worst of times. Even when Daddy got loud and scary.

The thunder cracked behind me, and I leaped into the air. My palms were sweaty, and my heart thumped in my ears. It was time to go back home . . . except I didn't know how to go back. I had turned into one alley and then another until I lost the train tracks, and now I didn't know what to do or where to go.

What did Mom tell me to do when I was lost? Find a police officer. They would help. What did a police officer look like? They were tall, with blue suits and badges. Yes, I would look for one of them, and they would take me home to mom.

"Hi, little girl," a grating, female voice said behind me. Her throat sounded like she rubbed it with sandpaper. "You are out late, aren't you?"

I didn't want to respond, but my mouth opened despite itself. "Who—who are you?"

The woman stepped from the darkness of the alley into the street. Her eyes were bloodshot, but not in the way Mom's were when she came home late from work. No, this woman's eyeballs weren't red, her pupils were, and they seemed to glow at me, sending chills up my already cold, wet spine.

"I'm a friend, now aren't I?" the woman said, inching toward me. Her cloak was so long it covered her feet, and she moved so gracefully toward me it seemed as if she floated through the air—but she couldn't do that, could she? Mom specifically told me magic wasn't real. She made sure I knew that magic wasn't real.

It felt real, though. Once, when I was two years old, I swore I floated into the air to reach a cookie jar on top of a high counter. Mom told me that was impossible, though, and I believed her, about that at least. Now, I was starting to see she was right about everything.

"Mom told me not to talk to strangers," I said, backing up from her until I reached the edge of the alley.

"Your mother is very smart, and she's right. You should never talk to strangers, but what if we weren't strangers? Could you talk to me then?"

"I—I—I don't know."

"Well. Let's try it. I am Imogen." She held out her pale, bony hand toward me. It shook in the cold night air as it neared me. "And now, if you tell me your name, we won't be strangers."

I didn't trust her. She didn't sound like a nice person. I turned from her and ran out of the alley and across the street. I just wanted to go home. If I could just go home, I would never cause problems again. I would never say anything bad again. I would be a perfect, little girl and Mom would be proud of me and never yell again. I would do whatever she said if I could just go home.

Except I couldn't go home because now I was even more lost than before. I ran for two more streets—or was it three—trying to escape that horrible Imogen woman. I was confused and drenched in rain.

When I finally made it to a main street, I ended up in front of a row of stores. I stopped in front of one with a candy-striped overhang that protected me from the rain. In the darkness, I started to cry. I might have already been crying and didn't realize it with the rain pounding down all around me.

I closed my eyes and squeezed Teddy close. Morning. By morning the shops would open, and I would be safe. Somebody would find me then. All I had to do was make it until morning.

"Where is your mother?" a voice said. It sent chills down my spine. I thought Imogen had come back, but then I realized it wasn't the same voice as before. This voice was deep, gruff, and manly. I looked up to see a smiling man with a beard, dressed in a blue police officer's uniform and hat, smiling at me.

"Are—are you a policeman?" I asked hesitantly.

He smiled. "Yes, little girl. I'm a policeman. Now, where did you run off from?"

I wiped my face from the tears and rain. "I ran away from home."

"You did? Well, that's not a very smart thing to do. Why would you do that?"

"I got in a fight with my mom."

The police officer knelt next to me. "Hmmm…I get in fights with my children, too."

My eyes went wide. "You do?"

He nodded. "I do, and sometimes, we get so angry we want to run away, but you know what?"

"What?"

"Once we calm down, we always realize we would miss our family something terrible if we left, right?"

I wiped away another tear. "I just want to go home."

"Then let's get you home." He held his hand out.

I hesitated to take his hand. "How do I know you'll take me to my house?"

"Cuz that's my job, little lady." He pointed to his badge. "I'm an officer of the law, don't you know. Our job is to protect and serve."

He gestured to a blue car with a rack of lights on the top of it. Mom pointed them out to me every time we went into town. It was a police car, and the thought of getting into his warm car and being driven home put me at ease.

I smiled, reaching out my hand. "Okay."

"You will leave this place," a slithering, growling Imogen groaned from behind the officer. The pupils on the cop's eyes narrowed, and his face went slack. The color drained from his face as I stepped back from him.

"Leave me alone!" I shouted to Imogen, but I knew she would never listen to me.

The police officer rose and turned to her. "I—I—can't leave—the girl—"

"She is of no concern to you," Imogen said. "Leave, and forget you ever found her."

Her voice was deeper and smoother than it was when she talked to me. She sounded like the snake from *The Jungle Book,* and the officer was under her spell.

The officer nodded. "Yes, ma'am." He walked off in a daze, leaving me alone with Imogen.

She turned to me. "Men are so easily seduced."

"What—What do you want?"

"I told you. I want to be your friend. Don't you want to be friends with me? Most little girls want to be friends with me, and you are a very special little girl, aren't you? I smell it on you."

The sides of Imogen's mouth curled up, but they did not stop where normal mouths ended. No, her mouth opened all the way to the far side of her cheeks and touched the edge of her hair. When she unhinged her jaw to smile, her mouth was filled with hundreds of spiked teeth like a shark.

"I—I—I don't want to be friends with you!" I screamed and sprinted out into the rain, anything to get away from her.

Slowly, gracefully, she floated after me. She must have known I had nowhere to go and would eventually tire out, so she didn't bother rushing. All she had to do was follow me close enough until I couldn't run anymore.

"You can't escape me, girl. I have caught your smell and can follow you anywhere. The sweet smell of magic. You will be a prize like no other—a prize for my prince!"

I wanted to scream out that there was no such thing as magic but couldn't spare an ounce of energy. Not that she would care. She would never believe me, just like I didn't believe Mom.

I didn't stop to see where she was or whether she was still following me at all. I just kept running down the street as fast as my feet could go.

In front of me loomed a monstrous mansion. It was the Colburn estate. It was big and scary, and nobody went in there, not even Mom. People said they heard screams at night coming from the mansion, even though it had been abandoned for years. It was just my luck that of all the places in town, my feet led me there.

Then I realized something. I knew how to get home from the Colburn house! In three more blocks were the train tracks, and five blocks after that, I would see Mr. Magill's house. Then I would just have to cross the street, and I would be home free.

I smiled for the first time all night. I would be home soon enough. Mom would make me hot chocolate and bundle me up until I was nothing but a face and two little arms. She would tell me she loved me, and then I would be safe. If I pumped my legs fast enough, I could be home in less than ten minutes.

"Interesting," Imogen hissed, making her way up the sidewalk in front of me. "That you would end up here."

"Just—let me go home," I said to her.

"I can't do that, my precious," Imogen said with a crooked smile. "You are too important. I have been looking for you for a long time. You are the key to everything. Don't you see that?"

I shook my head. "I'm just a girl."

"No, my love. You are so much more." Imogen moved toward me, this time with the speed of a cheetah, and pounced on me. She pulled open her coat and wrapped me into it. A drowsy feeling came over me, and I knew I would never see my mother's face again.

In my last moment of consciousness, Teddy fell out of my hands. He could not protect me. I was not safe from the nightmares that skulked in the darkness. I was not safe from anything, not anymore.

CHAPTER 1

I hadn't been back to Chandler for two years. Not since the Cult of the Bloody Dagger opened a portal to Hell and released the dragon Aziolith onto the Earth so he could run amok. It turned out Aziolith was a pretty chill dragon, but the cult didn't know that. And the demons that invaded Earth with him certainly weren't chill. They were the anti-chill.

Luckily, I was able to close that portal and destroy all the demons—with Aziolith's help, no less—and escape the city with my mother before the military descended on us.

My poor mother.

That's the reason I'm back in Chandler. She died just a couple of days ago. For the past six months, she was only staying alive to see Bob Marley sing at the Smile Jamaica concert. When somebody shot him a few months ago, I thought Mama was gonna die on the spot, but that beautiful man came out and delivered one hell of a performance. He sang on and on forever, and Mama was ecstatic the whole time, enraptured by his words, and alive in a way she hadn't been since her struggles with cancer zapped all her strength.

It's true the blood of pixies ran through our veins, and thus we were blessed with long life, but we were still mortal in the end and susceptible to the same diseases as humanity. Cancer could take us at any moment, and it took Mama right before Christmas. She told me she wanted to die in Chandler; she wanted to be buried in Chandler, and I had to make that happen for her, even if I hated the place.

The doctors at Chandler General Hospital told me that the US government swarmed the town after the portal closed, and they killed the last of the demons. They interviewed everybody in town, took soil samples, cleaned up dead bodies, and threatened the whole town to keep their goddamn mouths shut if they didn't want to be a science experiment. It was brutal for that first year, but after eighteen months, the government abandoned Chandler in the dead of night to track down some other horrible thing, and life kind of returned to normal.

Chandler was always good at sticking its head in the sand when it came to the big, important things—like my father's lynching, along with those of dozens of other black men and women during my childhood—and this was just another secret in a long line that stretched back well into the Jim Crow era.

That's why I tried my best to stay away from Colorado and America as a whole. Since I could disappear and reappear at will, Mama and I traveled the world. We could flash to Switzerland for hot chocolate and then head down to Jamaica to see Bob Marley before having dinner in Egypt overlooking the pyramids.

When I first learned about my powers, I needed special pixie dust to move between places, but after enough practice, I learned to move with just my mind alone. As my mentor Elka once said, pixie dust was a crutch. With enough effort, we could travel the world in the blink of an eye without using it. It was a great power, and my old mentor Elka would be furious at me for using it to tour around the world instead of helping our people.

Our people. As if I had any idea what that meant. Elka taught me how to unlock my powers as a pixie, but she didn't tell me anything about helping the last of our kind. During her life, she was the great protector of monster kind. I had no interest in following in her footsteps, though, and risk dying young. I just wanted to see the world and live a quiet life.

When I first left, I thought I would get bored of traveling eventually and return to Chicago, my first love, but the more of the world I saw, the more America looked small and cold. I preferred Asia, or Europe, or Africa to America.

Still, time made fools of us all. My mother's health took a turn for the worse, and then she dwindled away until she lay dead before me in the same hospital where I was born, leaving me to pick up the pieces and figure out how to carry on without her.

***

"Will she be cremated?" was the question the funeral director asked when I first entered the funeral home. Not even a hello; he just went straight to business, which part of me appreciated since I didn't want to stay in Chandler any longer than necessary. Still, it was a funny question, especially if you knew my mother's idea of the afterlife.

"No. She bought a plot next to my father. She wants to be buried."

"Are you sure? Cremation is much less expensive."

I nodded, gritting my teeth. "I'm sure that's what my mother wants, Norbert."

"It's Norman," he said.

"I'm sorry about getting your name wrong, but it doesn't change my mother's wishes."

Mom believed that you couldn't get to Heaven if you were cremated. After I came back from Hell—I died briefly when the portal opened—her views were only strengthened. Mama believed in Heaven from the depths of her soul. No matter where we went, she needed to be in church every Sunday and pray the rosary twice a day. She believed those small acts paved her a pathway to Heaven as if God was keeping a mental tally of how many people idolized him.

"He is, believe me. It's the first two commandments," she would say to me. "So, he probably takes them pretty seriously."

My views, on the other hand, had never been more in question. I wasn't an atheist because I knew there was something after death, though I didn't know what waited for me. And even if there was an afterlife, I still wasn't convinced there was a God. In any case, I refused to worship a God that would send so many of his people to be tortured in Hell.

"Very good," Norman said. "I have already placed an obituary in the paper for her. I kept it tasteful but short to save on costs."

"Okay," I said, furrowing my brow. That was the second slight about money he'd made since I arrived, and I was getting tired of it. This man was lucky Mama already bought a funeral plot on his land since it meant I was stuck working with him.

"And what kind of casket would you prefer?" Norman asked.

."Your most expensive option, please."

"Are you sure? We have a very nice bargain casket that—"

I cocked my head. "Excuse me? Why would you think I needed a bargain casket?"

The only reason he could have thought I needed a bargain casket was because I was black, which must mean I was poor. But I wasn't poor. Aziolith, after I returned him to his dragon cave, allowed me to take as much gold as I wanted from his mountains of treasure, whenever I wanted, to use however I wished, and so I lived the high life.

I wore expensive clothes—the dress I wore to meet with Norman cost five hundred dollars—and I pampered myself with diamond earrings, manicures, and every new skin care product that hit the market. I looked fly as Hell, and yet I still couldn't catch a break from racists like the one across from me.

"I—I—I don't know. I just thought—"

I pulled out a single gold coin from my purse full of them and placed it on the table between us. "My mother gets the best this gold coin can get her. I would love to stand up and walk out on you, but I can't. My mother had a detailed will, and part of it was to be buried in your cemetery, so I'm stuck working with you. Just know, I have a purse full of coins like this one. You could have retired from overcharging me for this funeral because money literally doesn't matter to me. I have mountains of it lying around. I'm like Richie Rich, but you assumed I was poor, just cuz of the color of my skin."

"That's not why—"

"Don't interrupt me," I said. "It's rude to interrupt people."

"Sorry," he replied softly.

"Yeah, and you should be. Cuz instead of retiring, you are going to live the rest of your life kicking yourself for making an assumption about me. Now, let's wrap this up. Then, I don't want to hear another word out of you, got it?"

Norman dropped his eyes to the floor and gulped loudly. "Yes, ma'am."

***

After finishing with the funeral home, I decided to walk through town. I hadn't been back since the night of the portal opening, and I figured it would be my last chance to see the old town before I left it forever. There was nothing holding me to Chandler anymore.

I had nothing but bad memories here. I had no friends. I had no lovers. I had nothing that I wanted to burn into my memory forever, except for the mystery spot, which was the start of all this. It was the beginning and the end of everything good—and bad—that happened to me over the last two years. Maybe my entire life.

I had always thought the mystery spot was just a hole in the middle of a park that made my hair stand on end. After all, that's what it had been doing since before I was even born. The town was built around the mystery spot. It was quite literally the hub of everything we did. Stores, schools, and churches lined the square around the mystery spot, and people bustled between them all day and night.

People from all over the world came to our little corner of Colorado to witness the spectacle for themselves. The mystery spot drew over a million visitors a year in its heyday and brought prosperity to the town. Nobody knew what it was until the night it opened a portal to Hell. Now, the streets were deserted, and the buildings lay fallow and desolate, their windows boarded up and their facades cracked and chipped.

Of course, I knew why. I destroyed it when I closed the portal to Hell. The mystery spot no longer had any spark in it; it didn't have any power left, which meant there was no reason for people to travel here. What used to be a unique attraction was merely a hole in the ground. No reason to drive a thousand miles just to see that.

Crossing the street to Mystery Spot Park, I turned back to see Elka's old shop, once full of teas and curiosities, now abandoned to time. The windows were boarded shut, just like the shops on the right and left of it. I never thought I would see something so sad in Chandler. Those shops seemed like they would outlive all of us, and yet in just a few short years, they were gone.

"I didn't think I'd ever see you again," I heard as I walked toward the center of the park. I knew the voice well, even if I hadn't seen the man behind it for more than two years.

It was Chuck Dixon, the park's security guard. The last time I saw Chuck, he was bleeding from a pair of gunshot wounds to the chest. He walked with a cane now, but he had the same big, warm smile as ever.

"It's good to see you, Chuck," I said, walking toward him.

He wrapped his arms around me. He was big, strong, and handsome as ever, even if he was doughier than I remember him. "I'm sorry to hear about your mama."

Seeing Chuck again and thinking about Mama made my eyes well up with tears, but I knew Mama wouldn't have wanted that. She didn't want me to mourn her. She made her choices and lived with them, with no regrets. She didn't want chemo to spend her last months getting violently ill. Hell, she didn't want to be stuck in one place for long enough to receive treatment. Mama lived as best she could with the time she had, and she wanted me to do the same.

"Thank you." I unlatched myself from Chuck's hug. "I'm glad to see you're alive."

"Me too." Chuck nodded. He was looking at me hard like he wasn't sure if he should say something. "That night—what happened that night?"

I smiled. "Do you really wanna know, Chuck? Or should we just chalk it up to one of those Chandler secrets?"

He laughed. "You know, I think I'd rather not know. I was unconscious when it happened, clinging to life, and then I came to, and they told me some fantastical stories. Last thing I remember was you . . . you bringing me to that store and that nice, old woman bringing me to the hospital."

"That's all you remember?"

Chuck shook his head. "I was just trying to stay alive, Julia. I barely remember anything."

I walked toward the hole in the ground that was once the Mystery Spot. "That's for the best."

"Maybe," he said, following behind me. "But when I got back up, I was out of a job, and the city was overrun by the national guard. That's a pretty rude awakening."

I sighed. "And the mystery spot wasn't special anymore."

"No," he said, looking down at the hole. "No, it wasn't."

I don't know what I hoped for when I walked to the mystery spot. Some piece of me hoped my hair would stand on end and my toes would curl like the best memories from my childhood, but that wasn't possible now. Intellectually, I knew it would be that way, but I still couldn't comprehend it until I felt it for myself. The stark reality was that there was no magic left in Chandler anymore.

CHAPTER 2

After moseying around the park, I considered touring the old high school where I used to work but decided against it. Principal Anderson was long dead—eviscerated by demons right in front of me—and no doubt some other racist lackey took his place. There would be another token black teacher hired after me, and that teacher would be bearing the brunt of the PTA's not-so-subtle prejudices perpetrated against her for the heinous crime of existing while black.

I didn't need any of that in my life. So instead of walking southeast from the park in the direction of the school, I headed northwest across the train tracks toward my old house. Even though it had been years since I traversed the streets of Chandler, I remembered the route like I had never left.

While downtown Chandler looked dilapidated, my street looked better than ever, and with good reason. I had been paying not only my mortgage since we left but the mortgage of everybody on my block. The extra money allowed the street to thrive, grow, and repair itself. Every house had pretty, white picket fences, new paint, and the makings of fine gardens, which must have smelled wonderful in the summer. It was some real *Leave it to Beaver* type crap.

I didn't owe anybody a dime after I came into Aziolith's treasure, but the truth was that the people on that block helped us along when we needed it most. When Mama didn't have enough daycare clients to make her mortgage, two more kids from the block magically enrolled. When Mama got sick while I was in graduate school, and I couldn't drive home to help her, there was always somebody willing to check in on her for me.

None of those sons of bitches from the "good" side of the tracks helped us along when we needed it, but my neighbors did, and they deserved some repayment when I got up in the world. A rising tide, after all, should raise all ships.

It was a nice day in Chandler, unseasonably warm even in December. When I turned up the street to my house, all of my old neighbors were on their porches, sitting in their rocking chairs and waving to me as I passed. Even though I looked completely different, they all recognized me immediately. Gone was the blond hair that the high school forced upon me. Now, I kept my hair natural. I wore it in a tight afro, well-manicured from weekly trips to the finest salons in Paris and London.

"Is that you, Julia?" one of the old, black women shouted from her rocking chair.

"Nice to see you, Miss Gilbert." I waved, walking toward her picket fence.

She hobbled down the stairs to shake my hand. "Well, well. It's nice to see you in the flesh. The only time I heard from you in the past two years was when you sent those checks."

I laughed. "Yes, it looks like you've been able to do some mighty fine work on your houses with it."

Miss Gilbert nodded. "And we've been keeping up with yours, too, Julia. Even with that new tenant you got. We been keepin' an eye on her. Seems like a nice lady, though."

My brow furrowed of its own volition. I kept the house more for my mother's sake than mine, but I didn't rent it out. Why would I? I didn't need the money.

"What do you mean, tenant?" I asked.

"Don't you know? She moved in a couple of days ago. Said she was waiting for you to come back. I told her she would be waiting a long while, but she didn't seem to mind. I guess it's her lucky day."

"Excuse me, Miss Gilbert. I need to go. It's nice to see you." I turned away from her and headed toward my house at a quicker pace.

She nodded. "And you. I saw the obituary in the paper. We're all sorry to hear about your mama. She was good people. We'll be at that funeral tonight. You believe that."

"Thank you." I smiled and waved as I walked away from Miss Gilbert, but inside my head, I wasn't happy. I was furious. Somebody was squatting in my house and waiting to see me?

When I stepped up onto the curb and looked at my old house, I barely recognized it. Gone were the ramshackle shutters and high grass, replaced with beautiful white paint and new red shutters, along with a perfectly manicured lawn. The front gate no longer wobbled and creaked. Mama had always wanted to fix it something fierce but never had the money when she lived here. I wished she had a chance to see it before she died. It would have made her so happy.

I was halfway up the stairs to the front door before I realized that I didn't have a key. I didn't have a key to my own house and didn't feel like going back to Aziolith's cave to find it. I would just have to knock and hope whoever this tenant was answered it.

I banged on the door, harder with each rap, until I was slamming on it violently again and again. The door shook on its hinges, but still, nobody answered.

"What do you want?" I heard behind me.

I turned to see a young, black woman at the bottom of the stairs, holding a paper bag of groceries. At the sight of me, she dropped the bag and started to stutter. "You—It's—It's you—"

"I seem to be at a disadvantage," I told her, "because you know me, and I have no idea who you are."

The woman reached into her pocket and pulled out a picture. "I'm Adelaide Stevens. My daughter—" She pointed to a picture of her with her arms wrapped around an adorable, little, black girl, laughing big with pigtails and a bright pink dress. "—her name is Kimberly. She was . . . she was taken from me."

I stepped down the stairs. "That is a tragic story, but I don't see what it has to do with me."

"She was—" Adelaide said, carefully looking down the street on either side before leaning toward me. "She was one of you."

"Excuse me?" I said in a huff. "You're black, too."

"No. Not black. That's not what I meant. Well, she was that. She was—we are—pixies—just like you."

"Oh," I said, calming myself. "Well, that's different. I still don't know what that has to do with me."

"Elka was a great friend of ours," Adelaide replied. "Right before—well, right before she died, she told me to find you if we ever needed anything."

"Find me?" I said, furrowing my brow further. "We barely knew each other."

"Be that as it may, that's what she said, and I need your help, so that's what I'm doing."

"Your kid is adorable," I said, "but this is a police matter."

"It doesn't matter to the police!" Adelaide screamed too loudly, and the whole street gasped as they watched us argue. "Look, we both know a little, black kid in Colorado ain't top priority to nobody, but Kim is special. She barely started unlocking her powers. The police wouldn't even know what to do with her if they found her."

I swallowed hard and looked down at my watch. The funeral was starting soon. I had to get back to the parlor. "I'm sorry. I can't help you."

"No," she said, tears streaming down her face. She grabbed at me as I walked past her. "Please! She's my only baby. Please!"

But I didn't stop. I weaved around her hands and walked straight past the picket fence. The woman broke down screaming into her busted groceries as I walked away, but I couldn't be caught in some damn foolish chase for a child. That wasn't my business.

***

When I got back to the funeral home, Norman met me at the entrance, stuttering and dry-mouthed. "I have done everything I could. I spared no expense. The body is ready for examination, and we can start whenever you are ready."

"Thank you," I told him. "You aren't getting paid one cent more, though. Just remember that. Where is the body?"

Norman pulled open a set of thick, red curtains to reveal a big room filled with flowers. An oak casket sat on a platform, with four dozen chairs placed in rows in front of it. Mama didn't know four dozen people when she was alive. What were the chances they would come to her funeral?

"There are too many chairs," I said.

"It's the standard number, Miss Freeman. Mourners tend to come out to pay respects, even if they didn't know the deceased that well in life. You will be surprised."

"Oh," I said absently. Being in the funeral home was making me feel somber. "I guess it's fine then. I went to my old house, and my neighbor said she saw the obituary, so maybe there will be a lot of people here. Thank you for that."

I walked through the curtains onto the hideous, plaid carpet lining the chamber. Honestly, it looked more like a swingers club than a funeral home—bright red wallpaper with purple birds wrapped around the room.

The top of the casket was open, and inside, my mother lay peaceful and smiling, as if she were having a pleasant dream. "Well, Mama," I said, walking slowly toward the platform, "this is everything you wanted. I did what you asked. I made the announcement. I came back to Chandler. You're being buried next to Dad."

I bit my lip. "It didn't have to be like this. You didn't have to go so soon. Why didn't you do chemo? Why didn't you try to save yourself? Why did you leave me all alone?" I was crying now.

The coffin smelled of lilacs and honey. Mama—I couldn't get over how happy she looked. She rarely looked that way in life, and certainly not with so many people looking at her.

"What am I supposed to do now, Mama?" I said, looking down at her. "I don't have anybody else. I didn't want anybody else. And now, I'm alone. Am I just supposed to carry on like life's worth livin' now, Mama? Cuz I gotta say, it ain't worth livin' now."

I took a long moment of silence and dropped my head down to the casket. After a full minute of silence, I heard a throat clear behind me.

"I know what you mean," somebody behind me said. I knew it was Adelaide, even though we only talked once. "I can't say life's worth living for me, either."

I wheeled around. "You don't give up, do you?"

"Well, if you didn't want to be found," she said, holding up the paper. "You shouldn't have announced where you would be in the paper."

"In all fairness, I didn't think I would have a stalker following my every move when I ran it."

"I'm not a stalker, Ms. Freeman—"

"Please, you are living in my house, call me Julia."

"I don't wanna live in your house, ma'am. I want to go home and be with my family, with my Kim—but that ain't gonna happen unless you help me."

"Why me?"

"Because Elka said—"

"Elka said a lot of things!" I shouted. "She didn't tell me anything about how to help you."

"She said you were good people," Adelaide replied calmly, inching toward me. "I'm sorry, but I don't have nobody else to turn to. It's not like there's a Rolodex of fairy folk—"

I leaped down from the platform toward her. "Hush up now. People are gonna think you are crazy, talking about fairies."

"Fine. But you know. And I don't have anyone else. All I know is you and Elka."

I beckoned her forward. "Let me see the picture again."

Adelaide reached into her back pocket and pulled out the picture of her and Kim laughing together. Adelaide had her hands wrapped around Kim's chest. They both looked so happy. Like at least a half dozen pictures of Mama and me.

I grabbed the picture and stared at it intently. "I don't know if I can help you, you know that, right?"

"I don't have any other choice. Without you, it's either pray the police start caring or figure it out myself. And I swear I've tried to do it myself, but I can't get anywhere, Julia. You are my last hope. Maybe you can find her when everybody else has failed."

"How long has she been gone?"

"Two weeks."

I nodded. "All right. It's not like I have anything else to do. Let me get through this funeral, and then I'll help you."

"Thank you."

"Don't thank me yet. You don't know just how incompetent I am at this kind of thing."

CHAPTER 3

"Many of you knew my mother," I started after the pastor finished his initial blessing. I didn't want to give the eulogy, but Mama put it in her will, so I didn't have a choice. "If you knew her back when I was a child, then you knew she didn't like a fuss being made about her."

I looked back on the casket, and my mother's smile, finally at peace. "Which is funny because since we left Chandler, all she wanted was a fuss being made about her. She became quite the diva in her last years—but I loved her for it. She spent decades watching out for others, caring for others, and making others the center of her world. For her first six decades, she pinched every penny and squeezed every dollar. It was nice to see her get everything she deserved in the end, even if it was only for a short while.

"She didn't deserve to die like she did, but that is life, I suppose. That's what she told me anyway, any time I got bitter about her refusing treatment. 'God wanted me around for a while, and I stayed around just as long as he thought necessary,' she would say to me. I don't like the idea of that kinda God, personally, but it brought Mama comfort."

I gulped loudly and glanced down at my notes, but I could barely read them through my tears. I looked out on the audience, which filled every chair just like Norman told me they would, but they were deadpan. They didn't care what I said. They just wanted it to be over, so they could pay respects and go home.

My stomach churned into knots. I didn't want to keep talking even if I could see what I wrote down. I crumpled the pages up and tossed them aside. It didn't matter anyway.

"I will miss you, very much, with every waking breath. I hope you were right, and Heaven is more than just a place on Earth."

I walked over to the casket, kissed my hand, and placed it gently on my mother's cold forehead.

***

I stayed at the funeral home for another hour, greeting and thanking all the mourners. They were pleasant and polite, full of kind words and nice stories, but it was more draining than anything, and I felt a great weight lift off me when the last of them left, and I could be alone with my mother.

"Mom," I said. "I don't know what to do now, and I need your help. I promised this woman I would help her find her daughter, but I have no idea how to do that. I'm just a teacher from Colorado who somehow saved the world once, but you know I'm not a hero. I just want a simple life."

As I looked down at my mother, I felt two eyes burning into the back of my head. I knew it was Adelaide without her saying a word. "I told you to wait for me outside."

"It's the middle of December outside. I'm cold."

I gripped the edges of the coffin. "I'm starting to see why your daughter ran away."

The breath went out of the room. I crossed a line and I wasn't sorry about it. I hoped that my cruelty would send her away, but she didn't move. "My daughter and I had our differences, just like you and your mother, but she would never run away, not for long."

"Plenty of times I wanted to run away as a kid—hell, I did run away to Chicago for a few years."

"I'll bet you always came back, though."

"I always did."

"So would my Kim if nothing happened to her. That's why I'm so worried."

I dropped my head down to my mother's and touched her forehead with mine. "I love you."

After a moment of silence, I picked my head up and turned to Adelaide. "All right. Let's go."

***

Adelaide didn't live in Chandler. Something I found out only after we got in her car and started driving. I hadn't been in a car since before I unlocked my powers.

"Where are we going?" I asked.

"Stubbins," Adelaide replied. "I've lived there all my life."

"Except for when you were living in my house."

"I wouldn't say living. I can't say I'm living anymore, at least not really. Besides, I was only there a couple of days."

"You would have been there for the duration, though, yes?"

She sighed. "Unless my little one came home or until I had a better idea, yes."

"What about your husband? Your kids?"

"I never much liked my husband, Miss Freeman. And as for other kids, well, Kimberly was the only one. She was the glue that held our house together, and I want to get her back. I need to get her back."

"I get it," I said, looking out the car window as Adelaide drove.

Kimberly wasn't the only child I knew who was born to parents that didn't get along. I was the product of parents that didn't get along, after all—the product of an ill-fated scheme to force love where it didn't belong—but I was the exception. After I was born, my parents found love for each other. Usually, it goes the other way and heaps scorn on the child for forcing the parents to stay together in a loveless house.

"How far until we hit the town?"

"Hour or so."

I watched the scenery drifting by. There was probably something I should have said, but I doubted there was anything I could say to make her feel better, and I knew there was nothing she could say to me to fill the gaping hole in my chest. Neither of us could help the other.

***

Chandler always had the mystery spot to drive traffic and funnel money into local businesses, propping up an otherwise destitute town. Stubbins reminded me of what Chandler would have become if we hadn't been so lucky for all those years—and what Chandler was turning into now that the allure of our biggest attraction had disappeared.

The roads into Stubbins were cracked and riddled with potholes. The businesses were mostly shuttered, with boarded windows housed in derelict buildings. Even with the sun out, there was a gray haze that covered the town as if all hope had drained from it. The whole town reeked of piteous desperation. Just like Adelaide.

Adelaide parked her car outside a rundown, ranch-style house, more a shipping container than a house, and stepped out of the car. I followed as she walked toward the front door.

"Tommy ain't very nice, and he definitely ain't sweet, but I figure you wanna see Kim's room before you start looking around and get a sense of her, so we gotta deal with him."

"I don't know what I should be doing, Adelaide," I replied, and that was the truest statement I've said in a long list of recent truths, "but I guess that makes sense."

I smelled the pungent odor of vodka before I stepped into the house. Every surface reeked of it, from the walls down to the carpet on the floor. Beer bottles and pizza boxes littered the ground. In the middle of the room, a black and white TV blared onto the face of a fat, slovenly, unkempt pile of a person that only vaguely resembled what would happen if a human had mated with a container of Play-Doh.

"The hell have you been?" the amorphous blob slurred. "I've been hungry!"

"I was out, Tommy. You know I was out."

Tommy wobbled to his feet and stomped over to Adelaide. "Does it look like I knew that?"

Without thinking about it, I sprang between Adelaide and Tommy in a puff of blue smoke. "Whoa now! Easy there, tiger."

"Who the hell are you?" Tommy shouted, rushing me, completely unfazed by my powers.

I disappeared again and reappeared behind him. I grabbed his hair and slammed him into a wall. "I'm not here to fight you, but I can't have you punching my friend here, can I?"

Tommy fell to the floor, and I knelt on his stomach. "Can I?"

Tommy shook his head. "No . . . no."

"Good, now sit down and shut up. You can last a little while longer without food." I squeezed a layer of fat oozing out of his stained shirt. "Probably more like a year or so, huh?"

I stood up and kicked him in the stomach. I hadn't needed my fighting skills for a while, but they were still there under the surface, and that was nice to know, especially if I ever got into a fight with whatever or whomever I was chasing.

***

Kimberly's room was every eight-year-old girl's fantasy. While the rest of the trailer looked like it'd been hit by a hurricane that deposited cheap bullcrap and trash in its wake, Kim's room was filled with dozens of stuffed animals and matching pink furniture. There were posters of Donny and Marie, David Cassidy, and the Beatles on every wall. There were Barbie dolls and toys everywhere. It looked like a Toys 'R Us threw up in there.

"I know what you're thinking," Adelaide said. "And yes, we spoiled her."

"You spoil her, you mean. She ain't dead yet."

"Of course," Adelaide replied, crying again. "I can't believe—I'm just saying we loved her."

"I get it," I said after a long pause. "What was the fight about?"

"What makes you think it was a fight?"

"Guilt. It's written all over your face. What was the fight about?"

"She wanted to get her ears pierced. I told her no. She freaked out and locked herself in her room. I wanted to go after her, but I work three jobs to support this family."

"And you didn't know until she was—"

"Until the end of my shift."

"That is a stupid reason to run away. Still, it's never about the reason, is it?"

"I don't know."

"I lived in a poor house too, where my mama worked too much for too long to get by, and I know Kim's type, at least, so that's something going in your favor. Is anything gone from the room?"

"Just her teddy bear."

"Teddy bear?"

Adelaide nodded. "Yeah. She never went anywhere without that teddy bear. Teddy was his name."

"There's a hundred stuffed animals in this room, and she only brought Teddy?"

"I guess. That's what I'm saying. She loved that bear more than anything."

"Maybe that's a good thing. Since she didn't take a bag, she probably wasn't planning to be gone for long, like you said—course, that also means something might've happened to her, like you feared."

"What is it you are looking for exactly?"

I wanted to give her some good news, but the truth was I was just doing my best Joe Friday. I had no idea what to look for in a crime scene except what I saw on TV. "Clues, ma'am. And I'm afraid I'm not finding many."

"You sound just like the cops," she replied.

She was right, and it was just about time to figure out what they knew. I was wasting my time already. I might as well waste time at the police station.

***

The boys at *Dragnet* would laugh if they saw what Stubbins considered a police station. It was a single wood-paneled room with four metal desks. Even Chandler had a more impressive police station—though most of its deputies were burned alive by Aziolith, so who knew what it was like now.

A fat officer with a receding hairline and thin mustache waddled over to me after I waited an hour for him to finish his lunch. He brought me back to his desk, where he had hundreds of manila file folders stacked around him.

"So, you see, Miss Freeman," he said with a sigh, "it's like I said on the phone. We don't have time to go through all these cases. There are literally dozens of them from the last six months alone, and your friend's kid is just not a top priority."

"Can you tell me who is a top priority?"

"They are all equal priority."

"I'll bet it's a little, blond girl, isn't it? It's always a little, blond girl."

"What are you trying to say?"

"I'm asking you if Kimberly is not your top priority, who is? Somebody must be top priority."

He leaned forward over his desk. "It's the one who goes missing last, Miss Freeman. Your friend has been missing for weeks. Do you know what the chances of finding a kid after they've been gone for forty-eight hours are?"

"I would assume—"

"They're zero, Miss Freeman. They are effectively zero. All these children on my desk. They are gone in the wind. They might be dead, or they might show up tomorrow, but as far as we're concerned, they're not a priority. The only ones we have a chance to find are the ones that just went missing. It's not a black thing or a white thing. It's just a time thing."

I leaned forward. "I don't accept that."

"You don't have to accept it for it to be true."

"Where is her case file?"

The doughy detective held up a file. "It's right here. See, Miss Freeman. I keep it close to me because it matters."

"Bob!" a tall woman shouted from the front desk. "You didn't chip in for food again! Gimme my money!"

Bob pushed up from his desk with a groan. "I'll be right back."

Detective Bob waddled through the bullpen. The other detectives were busy behind their own desks. Nobody was paying attention to me. When Bob ducked out of sight, I scooped up Kim's file, and as many others I could carry. Then, I thought of Mama's house and vanished in the wind.

CHAPTER 4

I read police report after police report for the rest of the night, sitting on the floor of Mama's living room. There was one thing I knew for sure by the end of it: police reports were boring as hell. Seriously, I couldn't believe there were people who wanted to be in the police force since it meant writing—and reading—such boring bull all day.

By the time I reached the end of the pile, I had read three dozen reports. The abductions had happened all over Stubbins, a city of just a few thousand people. There seemed to be no consistency, rhyme, or reason to the abductions except that they were concentrated heavily in the last six months. I figured there shouldn't be more than a couple of disappearances a year, and there were several dozen in just a couple of months.

The only consistent things that I saw in them were that all the abductions happened at night, and they all involved girls between eight and ten, just like Kimberly. Other than that, there were little white girls, black girls, Asians, and Hispanic girls all the same. They came from rich homes and poor homes, broken homes and intact ones.

Around three am, the front door creaked open. I stood up from my place on the living room floor and readied myself for a fight, but it was just Adelaide.

"You gave me a fright, girl," I yelled at her as she crept inside. "What happened? I thought you would be at home now that—"

And that's when she turned to me and revealed her black eye, so swollen that she could barely see out of it. She tried to give me a smile, even if it was a fake one, but winced at the effort.

"I'll kill him!"

"No!" Adelaide grabbed me as I rushed for the door. "That's what he wants. That's what he wants!"

I spun around and gripped her by the shoulders. "You can't let him do this to you. I won't let him do this to you."

"It's not your choice! If you fight him, he'll take it out on me. Every time somebody stands up for me, it just gets worse."

"Then why don't you leave him?"

"He's a good father." Adelaide looked at the ground, shrugging my hands off her. "He's a terrible husband, but he's a good father, and a girl needs her father."

She was lying to herself, of course, but I didn't know the situation enough to comment on it. Instead, the best thing I could do was just be a friendly ear. "Sit down." I pulled an ice tray out of the freezer and poured some ice onto the towel that had been hanging from the stove.

"You don't have to do that," Adelaide said. "I'll be fine."

"I know," I said, handing her the towel. "After all, it's not the first time, is it?"

She sighed. "It won't be the last, either."

"It's not my place, but—"

"You're right. It's not your place." She grimaced as she placed the ice-filled towel over her eye. "What did you find out?"

"I went through over thirty reports of girls that have been abducted in the past six months. Who knows how many more there are, but even thirty, in a town like Stubbins, is really high, right? Like, really high?"

"Is it? It's been a way of life for us for a while, but yes. I think it's high. 'Course, I think one is too high."

"It can't just be coincidence. There must be a person, or a string of people, orchestrating these abductions. Is there anyone—anywhere—that's particularly freaky in Stubbins?"

Adelaide tensed up. "Since I was a kid, there was a weird house, the Colburn house. Guy murdered his whole family back in the fifties and then turned the gun on himself. It's been abandoned for years cuz nobody will buy it, so it's even creepier now. People still say they hear screaming in there from time to time, but police say it's just the wind."

"How well do you know it?"

"It's haunted my nightmares since I was a child."

"That's as good a place as any to start. Close your eyes. Think about it. Really concentrate. You need to remember every single brick. Do you have it?"

Adelaide winced again as she closed her eyes for a moment. "Yes, I have it."

I placed my hand on Adelaide's forehead. "Good. Good. I see it. All right, stay here. Get some rest. Lock the door. Don't let anybody in. Do you understand me?"

"I understand," Adelaide replied without opening her eyes.

I took a deep breath, and then, in a second, I was gone, leaving Adelaide to deal with the broken pieces of her life by herself, just as she must have done a hundred nights before.

***

It was pouring down rain where I reappeared in an alley across the street from an old, abandoned mansion that looked like it was owned by a Scooby-Doo villain. When I took a step forward, the toe of my boots dragged across a doughy lump on the ground. I bent down to investigate and found a teddy bear, soaking wet and worn to pieces. It looked like the kind a little girl would lovingly wear to the felt.

If nothing else, I was on the right track. I didn't know if I wanted to be, though. Frankly, I hadn't fought anybody scarier than Adelaide's drunken blob of a husband since the portal to Hell opened. I wasn't ready to handle a kidnapper, but I pressed forward anyway. Lightning cracked across the sky, and a booming rumble of thunder followed it.

The house was guarded by an old, rusted gate, which opened to the lightest touch. I pushed through it on my way toward the house. The whole thing was falling apart. The bowed roof over the front porch looked like it would collapse at any moment, with any one of the drops of rain that fell on it. Holes rotted through the wooden skeleton, and rain swamped the house's interior.

Drenched and cold, I knocked on the front door, and it swung open for me. "Hello?" I called down the echoing hallway. The house responded with a loud, creaking sound and the whole frame shifted, almost moaning for me to run away.

But I didn't run away. I stepped another foot forward on the loose floorboards and made my way into the house. If I were in a scary movie, the door would have shut and locked behind me, but instead, it just blew in the wind, rapping against the doorjamb.

An eerie emptiness filled every room. There were no chairs or any other furniture. Somebody had taken great pains to write words in a foreign language on every wall of the house in what I hoped was paint but could have easily been dried blood. I recognized three of the words from my time fighting the Cult of the Bloody Dagger: *Dealus Mylarus Zilarus.*

The rest were foreign to me, but I remember the cult kept saying those words to open the portal to Hell. Was it happening again? Was somebody searching for the blood of a pixie to open another portal to Hell?

It stood to reason that more people than just the Cult of the Bloody Dagger wanted to use the beasts of Hell to do their bidding, and it appeared I had just stumbled onto another one of these horrific cults.

"Hello!" I shouted again. I knew I was acting like I was the dumb person in a horror movie, but if Kimberly was here, she needed to know I was coming for her.

The only sound that responded, though, aside from the house settling, came from underneath me. Faint at first, it grew louder when I knelt on the ground to listen. A scratching sound was coming from the basement.

A bolt of lightning flashed through the rotted holes in the ceiling and illuminated the door in front of me. It was a stupid idea to enter the basement, every horror movie ever made told me that, but I couldn't stop now. A little girl's life was on the line—a little pixie girl's life at that— and I wasn't going to let her become a victim. Not if I could save her.

I pulled open the cellar door and peered down. Nothing to see but the dark. I closed my eyes and pressed out from my shoulder blades until my wings sprouted from me. They glowed blue and shimmered, lighting my way. The steps were old and creaky, so I chose to float down them instead. The scratching intensified as I made my way to the bottom of the staircase, and I knew I was headed in the right direction.

"Maybe it's just a bunch of rats," I said to myself. "A bunch of disgusting rats, like a rat king."

Of course, I didn't believe that at all. Rats kings were just the stuff of urban legend. Of course, but so was Hell, and I had seen it with my own eyes, so I could never rule out any possibility. I would have loved it to be a rat king. That wouldn't have been scary at all, not compared to the other horrors that lived in the dark.

I turned the corner once I reached the bottom of the stairs. The unfinished basement reeked of mold. The wooden pillars holding up the house were bowed and nearly gnawed through, and dozens of boxes littered the floor, sagging and waterlogged. At the far end of the basement sat a large, iron door. That's where the scratching was coming from.

"Kimberly?"

But it couldn't be just Kimberly. There was too much noise for just one small set of hands. It sounded like dozens and dozens of hands. My fear turned to excitement when I realized it must have been all the girls—at least those that were alive.

"Watch out, girls! I'm coming!" A metal bar crossed the door, locking it from the outside. I pushed the crossbar into the air and threw it across the room, then dropped my feet onto the ground for better leverage. I pulled the door open and peered inside, expecting to see a group of little girls…and I got them. Except they didn't look like little girls in anything but stature.

Their eyes were bloodshot—no, not bloodshot—their eyeballs were red. When they smiled at me in unison, their mouths curved out behind the reaches of their cheeks. They shrieked at me all at once, and the sound was so painful I grew dizzy, fighting not to pass out.

The girls charged at me in the enclosed basement, screaming their horrid sound and unhinging their jaws to reveal row after row of pointed teeth. I was too scared to raise my hands to defend myself. All I could do was close my eyes and think of the safest place I could imagine, and then I vanished.

CHAPTER 5

Over the past two years, I hadn't had anywhere to call a proper home. It didn't make sense to keep up a house or an apartment when I was just going to leave the next day for another country halfway around the world. It's not that I couldn't afford it, either. I could have afforded a hundred houses if I wanted them, but I didn't think that would be a good use of Aziolith's money. He had more money than Queen Elizabeth, but I still tried to use it wisely. Aside from Mama's house and the block around it, which I kept up more for sentimental reasons than anything, there was no reason to keep a home anywhere.

But I needed a place to rest, and whenever I needed to rest, I returned to Aziolith's cave. After rescuing him from an eternity in Hell, he had taken me there. Travelers and explorers had tried to find it for generations with no luck. Rumor was that it was filled with enough gold and treasure to rival a small country.

The rumors were mistaken. They so undervalued the amount of treasure locked inside Aziolith's cave that it was laughable. Gold mountains stacked to the ceiling like Richie Rich, but with coffers so vast, it makes that rich, little, white boy look like a pauper. If Aziolith were a country, his wealth would dwarf all of the richest kingdoms on Earth several times over.

I reappeared inside the walls of the cavern to the loud sounds of the slumbering dragon. Aziolith had been asleep—for the full two years since the day I brought him here—after drinking a potion to repair his broken wing and overcome the effects of Hell. No matter how loud I was, it never disturbed his slumber. I never saw him twitch, adjust, or move in any way, aside from the rising and falling of his chest and the flaring of his nostrils as he snored.

Mama and I bought beds from Paris and placed them along the back wall of the cavern. Often, we would spend days cataloging and rearranging Aziolith's wealth as we recovered from extravagant trips across the globe.

Aziolith didn't seem to care about what kind of wealth he had, just that he had a vast collection of shiny things. Golden armor lay in the same piles as rubies and gold. Deeds were stuffed inside priceless books. Once I found the property rights to the country of Iceland carelessly tossed onto a mound of gems.

My favorite things to scour for, though, were the ancient, leather-bound books that Aziolith collected. First edition leather-bound books from thousands of years ago were worth a small fortune, and yet I read through them as if they were mass-market paperbacks from the grocery store. Among those ancient tomes was one filled with illustrations about different types of monsters, and one picture reminded me of the shrill children I encountered.

Before I could find it, though, I had to check on Aziolith. He was curled up in the center of the room, just like always. His once thick, robust frame was frailer now; his body had eaten much of the fat that was stored around him, like a bear in hibernation, and bones poked through his scaly skin.

I placed my ear onto his chest and listened for a beat. His strong heart thumped loudly, and his chest rose rhythmically up and down. It was weird that I had grown so close to the dragon over the past two years, and he probably wouldn't even remember me. Aziolith had only known me for one night before he fell asleep.

Satisfied that the dragon was alive and healthy, I walked toward the back of the cave. All around me were mounds of gold and treasure. I lived very well with only a handful of gold at a time. A few coins could sustain me for months. I had taken a couple of hundred coins over the last two years and hadn't even begun to make a dent in a single stack of Aziolith's gold, let alone the entire cavern.

"Where did I put that book?" I said to myself as I neared my bed. Stacks of books littered the floor around my mattress. Hand-woven tapestries rested on top of my sheets. I'd found them in the cavern's riches. They were warmer and more comfortable than the designer duvet I'd bought in Paris. Mama still preferred the fancy sheet, even though it wasn't nearly as warm, because it looked newer than my tattered ones.

Her bed stood next to mine. The sight of it brought memories of her flooding back, and the tears came. I missed her so much. Especially her wisdom. She would never approve of me risking my life to find Kimberly. Truth be told, if she were alive, I would never have agreed to help Adelaide, but without her, there was no reason to refuse. If I didn't have something to take my mind off the pain of her death, I would lie catatonic in bed all day until I withered away.

I couldn't live like that. Mama wanted me to embrace the long life ahead of me. That meant moving on, not wallowing in pain. I let the tears flow for a few more seconds before I wiped them away.

I knelt on the edge of my bed and flipped through my collection of books. They were ancient and fragile, some of them so old they were scrolls and not bound books as we know them now. It wasn't as if I could sift through covers on the shelf until I found what I was looking for. I had to open each one until I found the right one. I went through some early manuscripts of *Gilgamesh* and *Beowulf* and assorted fairy tales. While I enjoyed those books, they couldn't help me now.

The next was a journal of recipes. I promised myself that I would cook more, but I never did. When you have more money than god, it's hard to get into cooking for yourself. Finally, I opened a book and found the title *Monsters, Where to Find Them, and How to Avoid Them.*

It was filled with facts, figures, drawings, and measurements from monsters of all types, from water nymphs to trolls. Somebody who cared deeply about monsters put a lot of love into its pages, and I turned them delicately as I searched for answers.

I flipped through the book, looking for any information on the sharp-toothed screechers I'd found in that basement. It took a few turns of the page before I realized the book was the only sound in the cavern—that and my own breathing. I froze. A low growl, like that of a tiger stalking its prey, emanated from the center of the cave. I turned to see the great dragon Aziolith stomping toward me.

"Who are you?" he shouted.

I stood up. "Easy, Aziolith. I'm just—"

"What? Here to steal my gold?"

"That's not—no! Aziolith," I said, walking toward him with my hands up in the air, "it's me."

The dragon shot a fireball out of his nose. I had no choice but to vanish, abandoning my beloved collection of books to escape the fire.

I reappeared on the other side of the cavern. "Stop it, buddy! It's me? Don't you remember?"

Aziolith's fire breath plumed across the cavern as he turned in my direction. I ducked behind a pile of gold coins.

"I remember fighting you, pixie! You will not win a second time!"

I let my wings flutter out behind me and rose into the air. "I didn't beat you. We did fight, but then I saved you from Hell. Don't you remember?"

The dragon shot another fireball, and it exploded on the pile of coins, which cascaded into the air and rained down on me as I fluttered away. "I remember your ilk and your brethren killing me."

"That was thousands of years ago! Listen, you have to remember. We were in Chandler, Colorado. You came through a portal to Hell. The national guard wanted to kill you, and I brought you here."

A glint of recognition filled Aziolith's eyes for a moment but fizzled out before it could take hold. "Lies! You are taking advantage of me!"

I disappeared to avoid yet another fireball and reappeared on the ceiling. "Damn it, Aziolith! I've been taking care of you these past two years, making sure you were okay and generally being nice. Snap out of it! I am Julia Freeman. I saved your life."

Another glint of recognition, longer this time, as the dragon's eyes settled on me. The dragon's angry lip dropped, and his furrowed brow calmed. "Julia…that name…it sounds familiar."

"It should," I said, touching back down onto the ground. "That's because it is familiar. Look at my face. I was the person who brought you the healing potion." I placed my hand on the dragon's wing. "How are you feeling?"

"Mmmmm…better," the dragon grumbled. "I was never very good upon waking up. I tend to forget things when I sleep."

"Is there . . . coffee—or something like, dragon coffee that I can get you to bring you back to the land of the living?"

"No," he said, shaking his head. "It just takes time. Perhaps…you can tell me what happened over the last years while I get my head together."

I smiled. "Gladly."

***

I filled Aziolith in on the last two years of my life, from the moment he went to sleep until the moment he woke up and fought me. I left no detail out that I could remember, and when I finished, he looked back to my bed and the ashes of the books he burned.

"A banshee," Aziolith said. "That is what you saw. They are nasty business."

"There were dozens of them. Little girls."

"That is what they do. They turn little girls into new versions of them. They cannot reproduce, except by corrupting others."

"What do you think she wants with Kimberly?" I asked.

"You say you didn't see her in the brood of children?"

"I didn't have a chance to check them all, but I didn't see her there. No."

"Then there is only one option. She is using that little pixie to get back into Hell."

"How can she do that? We closed the mystery spot."

Aziolith laughed. "Certainly. But there are dozens more around the world."

"Really?"

"Yes, you did not truly think your little town so special, did you?"

I was too ashamed to tell him the truth. "So, you think this is where she's going? To another mystery spot?"

Aziolith shook his head. "I have no idea."

"That's not good enough! Think harder!"

"I don't know!" Aziolith screamed so loudly that fire blazed out of his nose.

"If she's trying to open a gate to Hell, we have to stop her."

"We? That's very funny, we."

"If she opens a portal, you might be sucked back inside for all I know. If you care about that at all, then yes, we have to work together."

"Fine," Aziolith grumbled. "I might know a place we can get an answer, but I can't go looking like this. Get me a yellow-tinged potion from the same chest as you found the one to repair my wing."

I rushed off and came back with the potion he requested. It smelled of urine, and from the look on Aziolith's face, he was none too happy to drink the concoction down. Still, he tilted back his head and took a big swig.

For a moment, nothing happened. Then, Aziolith's skin bubbled and oozed. His twenty-foot-high frame shrank and contorted until he was no bigger than a normal-sized man. In fact, he was exactly an average man once it was all done, with black hair and dark, shiny skin—and completely naked.

"Bring me clothes," he demanded.

I sifted through some gigantic piles of clothing and brought back a medieval tunic and pauper's pants. He grabbed them from me and put them over his muscular, naked frame. He looked every bit the man everywhere but his eyes, which were still yellow and reptilian.

"What did you do?" I asked.

"Draft of transformation," he replied. "It will last until I break the spell. I used it often in my youth to outsmart dragon slayers."

"Are you ready to go, then?"

Aziolith nodded. "In a moment. I must put myself together, and you should change out of that dress."

He was right. I was still wearing the dress from the funeral. It was not appropriate for investigating old houses, nor for whatever tasks we had in front of us. Luckily, I had more rugged clothes from when I hiked the Rockies with Mama. I ran off to put them on, leaving Aziolith to collect his things in a leather satchel.

Ten minutes later, I returned, clothed in jeans, leather boots, a t-shirt, and a brown leather coat. I hooked two sheathes around my belt and slid Akta's magical daggers into them. I once used her daggers to kill demons and save Chandler from the gates of Hell, and if I was going to fight a banshee, my gut told me I would need them again. I also strapped a switchblade to my shin on the inside of my right boot. It couldn't help me with demons, but in a pinch, a hidden switchblade had a thousand uses.

When I returned to the middle of the cave, Aziolith slung the satchel over his head and turned to me. He looked exactly as he had when I left him—muscular, stoic, and very much human.

"Are you ready to go?"

"I am," he said.

I placed my hand on his forehead and closed my eyes. "Think of the place you want me to take us. Picture it in your mind's eye. Make it real, down to the last detail."

I saw the image of a house from Aziolith's mind, and a moment later, we disappeared in a flash of blue light and a puff of smoke.

CHAPTER 6

We reappeared in front of an unassuming house on an unassuming street, like my mama's. It could have been my street or any other street in any other suburb in all the world. Inside, the lights were on, and a dozen shadows danced across the room.

"What are we doing here?" I asked.

Aziolith walked toward the house without answering. A dim light flickered in the sky, and for a moment, an electric purple dome illuminated the property as he walked through the dome to the other side of it. Once he was through, it disappeared.

"Let's go. Don't stop. Just walk straight—don't stop, no matter what."

His instructions worried me, but that made me determined to follow them. As I neared the house, though, his warning became clear. The illuminated dome became visible once again, and this time I saw blue and red runes floating throughout it, each of them depicting flames, dragons, or pentagrams. I stopped, fascinated and terrified of what would happen if I took another step.

"I told you not to stop!" Aziolith shouted.

"What's going to happen to me if I walk through?" I asked.

"Nothing. They are simple wards to keep out humans. Since you have already been to Hell, and pixie blood flows through your veins, there is nothing to be worried about; I don't think."

"You don't think? That's not very reassuring!"

"Just step back, and then walk forward at full speed. It can sense fear and hesitation. You'll be fine."

I looked Aziolith in his yellow, reptilian eyes as he stared at me from the other side of the bubble. The purple glow of the dome danced in his eyeballs.

He wasn't lying to me, but the timbre of his voice made it clear that he didn't know what was going to happen if I tried to step through the hexes. However, if I wanted his help, I had no choice but to continue despite my uncertainty.

I took a deep breath and walked forward at a brisk pace. The closer I came to the bubble, the more I wanted to turn away, but I didn't. I willed myself forward, and with one final step, the bubble absorbed me. For a moment, the bubble held me back like a rubber band, but then the tension all released at once and flung me through to the other side, unharmed.

Aziolith caught me in his arms and steadied me. "See? I knew you would be okay."

"And yet, it sounds like you are as surprised as me I made it through."

Aziolith lifted his hands, palms up. "Fine. I didn't know for sure. I just thought I knew. This place was made for angels and demons, but once I made it through, I knew you were going to be fine. Or at least I thought so, and look at that, I was right."

"Oh, that makes me feel loads better."

Aziolith climbed up the wooden stairs toward the front door. "Well, the other option was to die a horrible death, so I would agree with you. This is better." He pounded once on the door, then twice, then four times, and finally once again. The door clicked open, and Aziolith let himself in.

I followed behind him. Once inside, I found myself surrounded by a dozen demons with spiked horns and red faces and a cadre of ethereal, androgynous humans, tinged with blue, with long wings protruding out of their backs like eagles.

"This," Aziolith said, "is what's called a safe zone. It's the first of its kind. Think of it like a way station between Heaven and Hell for angels and demons alike."

A bar was situated along the back of the house. Angels and demons crowded next to each other, laughing and drinking as though they weren't locked in eternal conflict. Long, wooden tables seated more unearthly creatures chugging beer and singing.

"So, Heaven is real?" I asked.

"Well, yeah," Aziolith said. "In a way, at least. I'm not sure how it works because I've never been there myself, but it's real. I assure you of that."

I smiled. It meant that my mother might be there after all. She was right all this time. She led a wonderful life, went to church, prayed to God, and if anybody deserved Heaven, it was her.

"I don't understand," I said. "How can we be looking at demons if they're all contained on the other side of the mystery spots in Hell?"

"Because they're not. Demons do the Devil's bidding, and some of them are assigned to Earth for various tasks, like retrieving monsters that escaped Hell and making deals on behalf of Satan—just like some angels are assigned to Earth to fulfill God's purposes, whatever that may be these days. They're all errand runners."

"How, though?" I said, taking a seat next to Aziolith at the bar. "How is this place even possible—angels and demons drinking together?"

"The way I hear it," Aziolith paused to take a dramatic look up and down the bar, "is that it started with a pastry. Right, Frank?"

The burly bartender laughed. "That's what they say," he said in a thick, Scottish accent. "They say my father's grandpappy was eating a muffin and accidentally summoned a demon with a stick of butter."

"How do you accidentally summon a demon?" I said, chuckling.

"It was a rune he made spreading the butter that brought about the accursed creature. Of course, he didn't know it was a rune. My grandpappy's pappy was just hungry. He offered the demon a homemade muffin, and they got to chatting. The muffin must've been good, cuz the next night another demon came, and then another, until a couple dozen demons showed up every night."

"So, it was a demon bar?" I asked.

"For a short spell. Then the angels got into the mix, and well, since then, angels and demons come and go as they please. No fighting. No hexing. No yelling. The barriers outside prevent that."

"And this has been going on for—"

"Oh, be a hundred and fifty years in a couple more. Don't really know when it started exactly. Nobody knows, but it's been a while, ya see."

"All right," Aziolith cut in. "Do you want to get a history lesson, or do you want to find the girl?"

I knew the right answer, but the truth was I wanted the lesson much more than I wanted to find the girl. "The girl. I guess."

"All right then," Aziolith said. "Have you seen Fritz?"

"The imp? Called back to Hell. He owes me money. If I see him again—"

"All right, all right," Aziolith said, laying his hands out in front of him. "How about Charlie?"

Frank pointed his finger to a long table on the other side of the house, where a shifty-looking imp in a tattered vest sat alone, talking to his own tail. "He's even worse. Good luck with that."

"Hey, Charlie!" Aziolith said, walking over to him. The little demon leaped in his skin. He calmed down when he turned and saw Aziolith.

"Oh, thank god. I thought you was a dragon. You sound just like one I used to—" At that moment, Charlie got a look at Aziolith's eyes and knew he was talking to the very dragon he feared. "Oh crap—"

"You stole something from me, Charlie, back in Hell."

"I didn't steal it. I just borrowed it for an eternity or so. You'll get it back."

Aziolith sat down on a chair across from the little imp. "Forget it. It's done. You keep it."

"Really? You really mean that? Wow, thanks. Cuz honestly, I pawned it in Dis, and I dunno how to get it back."

Aziolith smiled a long, toothy smile at Charlie. "That means you owe me one, and since I need a favor, it works out perfectly."

"Oh. Is that all our relationship means to you?"

"Yes."

"Fine, then." Charlie crossed his arms. "But that hurts, though, ya know? It hurts real bad."

"I'm sure you'll get over it. Julia, please sit."

I sat down next to Aziolith. "Who is this?"

"This is the guy who is going to help us find your girl. Isn't that right, Charlie?"

Charlie nodded. "Yeah, yeah. That's right. I'm real helpful. I don't know if I can help, but I can be helpful for sure. You're looking for a—what was it again? A succubus?"

"A banshee." Aziolith gave Charlie a long look. "One who lived in Colorado. Turned quite a few little girls."

"Stubbins, Colorado," I added.

"You're being specific there, huh?" Charlie said. "I didn't think you were gonna be so specific."

"Do you know the banshee or not?" Aziolith asked with a curt tone.

"Yeah, yeah. Imogen, She's a crazy one, all right. She wants to get back into Hell. Who tries to get back into Hell, ya know? She got out now she wants back in? That's a crazy broad if you ask me."

"Where is she going?" I asked. "Why hasn't she tried to open a portal yet?"

"Oh, she tried. She was in here a couple of weeks ago trying to get a ride into Hell for her and that brat she was with."

"Brat?" I replied. "Was it a little, black girl?"

"That's the one."

"So, she's still alive."

"Let's not get our hopes up," Aziolith said. "All we know is that she was alive a couple of weeks ago."

"Yeah, yeah," Charlie nodded furiously. "I'll bet she's still alive, though, cuz nobody would help her. You can't just bring a soul with a body into Hell, and nobody was willing to risk being sent back to Hell to help her. A couple demons told her they were gonna let Lucifer know, and if she tried to open a portal…well, she would be up Shit Creek, I'll tell you what."

"So, where did she go?"

"That information, I'm afraid," Charlie said, "is gonna cost you."

"You said you would help me," Aziolith growled.

"And I helped you as much as that little trinket was worth. You want any more, you'll have to pay."

Aziolith's lips curled up on him. "What is your price?"

"The Mirror of Yilir. I know you have it, and I want it."

"That is worth more than one little girl," Aziolith replied, choosing his words slowly.

Charlie shrugged. "Then find her without me, but if you want to know where she went, that's my price."

"I'll be back," Aziolith slammed his hands on the table and stood.

***

Aziolith stormed out of the bar and across the street. I followed behind him, barely able to keep up. "What is wrong with you?"

"That mirror…it is priceless. I can't just give it away for a pittance."

"It's not a pittance. It's a little girl's life. And what do you care anyway? It's just one of a million treasures you have in your possession. What's one less?"

"This is different. This one is special."

"So is that little girl."

Aziolith growled again. "Very well, but now Charlie's debt passes to you. Take me to my cavern."

He grabbed my hand, and we vanished together, rematerializing inside his cave. He stomped toward the middle of his lair, where he had rested for the past two years.

"This girl had better be worth it," he said.

"It's less the girl and more the Apocalypse I'm trying to avoid," I said behind him. "Who knows what would happen if a live body made it into Hell?"

Aziolith reached behind the chest which kept his potions, and pulled out a shining, silver mirror just big enough to fit inside his hand. "The mirror of Yilir. It can see anybody on Earth at any time if you can imagine them in your mind's eye."

"Wait," I said. "Anybody? What about magical creatures?"

"I suppose," Aziolith replied.

I snatched the mirror from Aziolith. "That little sneak. He wasn't going to help us. He was going to trick us and use the mirror to find Imogen."

"Yes, but you don't know what Imogen looks like."

"No," I replied. "But I know what the girl looks like. How does this thing work?"

"You just imagine the person you wish to see, and then you will see them. If they are alive, they will be seen in the reflection. If they are dead, you will only see black."

I closed my eyes and remembered the photo of Kimberly. I pictured every hair on her head, her smile, her cheeks, her hands, and when she was real in my mind, I opened my eyes.

For a moment, the mirror didn't do anything but reflect me back to myself. I thought it was broken, but before I could ask Aziolith what to do next, the image clouded, and a blue light swirled around like a whirlpool. When the mirror settled into focus again, it showed Kimberly sitting in a dark forest, crying.

"That's her!" I shouted.

"Yes, but where is she?" Aziolith asked, peering over my shoulder.

"I don't know, but I know who would know."

I didn't have to tell him. He already knew what we had to do. We had to go back to Frank's house and see if Charlie knew anything about those woods.

CHAPTER 7

There was a strict "no fighting" policy inside Frank's house. That much was drilled into me by Aziolith for thirty minutes while we sat outside in the cold, waiting for the shifty imp to leave the place and walk away into the night.

"Technically," Aziolith said, "it's not against the rules to beat up a demon outside of Frank's house, but it is frowned upon."

"How frowned upon?"

"Medium, I guess. Like, it won't damn you to Hell, but it won't send you to Heaven either."

I thought about it for a second. "I can deal with that."

And so, we hatched a cockeyed plan to torture Charlie until he told us what we wanted to know. Aziolith knew Charlie well from his time in the bowels of Hell.

"Charlie isn't much of a fighter. He's got a silver tongue but a glass jaw. Plus, he's pissed off nearly every demon and angel on Earth. Nobody's going to give it a second thought if he turns up tomorrow with a busted face."

I brought along the Mirror of Yilir for good measure, just in case we ever lost sight of Charlie, but even if he cooperated completely, something in my gut screamed that I would need it eventually. After all, you can't go wrong keeping a mirror like that around. Snow White taught me that.

Stakeouts were boring, but Aziolith passed the time by regaling me with stories of his younger days. "I shouldn't brag," he told me, "but more than twenty towns worshiped me as a deity."

"Was that so you wouldn't burn them down?"

"Of course," Aziolith said with a proud smile. "I was a vengeful deity who needed to be appeased with gold and food often. That is how I acquired the mirror to begin with, as an offering so that my countenance would shine down upon a town. If they didn't appease me, I would eat their livestock."

"Speaking of, you haven't eaten since you woke up. Aren't you hungry?"

Aziolith laughed. "Two years? I've gone ten without eating. Hunger is a weakness, and dragons are not saddled with a need for it often."

"No, just a lust for treasure."

"We all have our vices, little one."

Charlie exited Frank's house and turned up the street. Aziolith crawled out of the bramble first, and I floated behind him.

"Get down here," Aziolith said, pulling me toward the ground. "Do you want those bright blue wings to give us away?"

He was right. I hid my wings and landed on the ground, inching forward on the balls of my feet. Aziolith lumbered more than I did, uneasy with his new form. It didn't matter much since Charlie was too drunk to notice us even if Aziolith was twenty feet high.

The imp turned down a dark alley, and we followed behind. He hummed to himself and flipped a coin into the air, blissfully unaware that he was about to get trounced.

"Hey, Charlie!" Aziolith said, balling up his fist. Charlie turned around, and Aziolith socked him in the gut, sending him crashing into a brick wall.

"You have quite a punch," I said.

"Matter cannot be created or destroyed, little one, so I have the same mass as a lumbering dragon, compacted into this form."

Aziolith picked up Charlie before he could scurry away. "I think you have something to tell us."

Aziolith lifted Charlie high into the air. The imp squirmed, trying to break free, but Aziolith had him well in hand. "You can't do this. There are rules, man!"

"There are rules for demons and angels, but as you have pointed out on more than one occasion, I am neither. Now talk!"

"The mirror!" Charlie asked, fumbling over his words. "Where's the mirror?"

I pulled the Mirror of Yilir out of my back pocket. "Here. I have it with me. And I'll give it to you once we're done here and not a second sooner. Where is Imogen?"

"Make it fast," Aziolith added. "As my colleague correctly pointed out, I haven't eaten in two years, and I'm happy to make you my first meal."

Charlie wanted to lie. I could see it in his face, but he thought better of it. "Romania."

"Why Romania?" I asked.

"She wanted a portal to Hell close to Dis."

"Why?" I replied.

Charlie kicked and squirmed under Aziolith's strong hands. "You don't know much about Hell, do you sister?"

"Enough to know there are plenty of portals to Hell all around the world. Why that one?"

"Cuz they all lead to different places in Hell. If you wanna go somewhere specific, you gotta find the right portal to get you close enough. You think Imogen's gonna get far in Hell with a meatbag? No way. She's powerful up here, but down there, she's just another banshee, baby."

I thought of Kimberly, and in a second, she appeared in the mirror, still very much alive, being dragged through the same woods I saw earlier. "Is this where the mystery spot is in Romania?"

I showed the image to him, and he cowered with a shudder. "Hoia Baciu Forest. They call it the most haunted woods in the world. There are things that go on there you don't want to even think about, honey. Things that left Hell long ago before we got civilized. The portal is at the center of the woods, but trust me, you don't wanna go in there."

Aziolith dropped Charlie, who scooted back against a wall. "Thanks, Charlie, you've been a big help."

"The mirror! What about the mirror? You owe it to me!"

"We're gonna keep it," I replied. "Instead, we'll pay you in not beating you up anymore, all right?"

Charlie didn't like that deal. It was written all over his face, but there was nothing he could do about it. "You aren't really gonna go there, are ya?"

I raised an eyebrow at him. "What could possibly be in there that scares you so much?"

"Something lurks there Satan himself don't even want back into Hell. Archangel Michael trapped it in the woods, but even he couldn't destroy it."

A crash sounded behind me, but when I whipped around, I only saw a cat sashaying across the lid of a dumpster. There was a tug on my hand, and when I turned back around, the mirror was gone. Charlie hobbled down the street before he snapped his fingers and vanished.

"That little jerk!" I shouted, chasing after him.

Aziolith tugged me back. "It's okay. We know what we have to do. Do you remember the woods?"

"I . . . think so," I replied. I really wasn't sure.

"Do better than that," Aziolith said with a snarl.

"I remember, okay?" I replied. "I remember!"

Aziolith grabbed my hand. "Take me there, then."

And we vanished.

***

We reappeared in a forest so dense the sun's light couldn't penetrate the dark canopy. I couldn't see my own feet for the fog that covered the ground. The place was suffocating.

I turned around to Aziolith, barely able to make out his face in the darkness. "Are you okay?"

"I'm fine," he said. "It's just some trees."

I knew that was true but still couldn't shake the creeping dread in my bones. The forest was noisy. Crows cawed and flapped their wings across the branches. The wind moaned through the trees, whose gnarled trunks looked like shrieking horrors from beyond, contorted and wrapped around each other.

"I don't like it here," I said to Aziolith, letting my wings grow long to illuminate the ground in front of us. I didn't like having a beacon on my back, but without my wings, I couldn't see more than a few feet in front of me.

"Is this the place you saw?" Aziolith asked. "Is this where Imogen took the girl?"

I looked around at the trees. I remembered them, and their haunting shapes, from the mirror's image of Imogen pulling Kimberly through the woods.

"Yes, it looks like the place." I nodded, cupping my hands around my mouth. "KIMBERLY!"

Aziolith quickly covered my mouth. "Don't shout. It will give away our position. We have the element of surprise now."

"You're right, sorry." I hovered above the ground and started to make my way forward through the verve. "Charlie said the portal was in the middle of the forest."

"Then that's where we go."

"Perfect," I replied. "Except where is that? Where are we? Which way toward the center of the forest?"

"Hmmm…I can feel the portal call to me. It's pulling me toward it as if it was sucking at my bones toward Hell, pulling me home."

"That's not home," I said, grabbing him by the chest. "Remember that."

He nodded. "I do, Julia. I do."

"Which way is it telling you to go?" I asked.

Aziolith pointed forward. "This way. I'll bet Imogen feels the same pull as I do. We are both supposed to be in Hell."

"I won't tell you again to stop talking like that. You belong up here. This is your home."

"Follow me," Aziolith said, lacking any of his trademark confidence.

Aziolith slumped forward, his arms swinging below him. He seemed to be led by an invisible string that pulled him forward. Every hundred meters or so, he stopped and changed directions until, after thirty minutes of wandering, we were back to where we started.

"Shit!" I shouted. "We're lost."

"We're not lost," Aziolith replied. "We just don't know where we are."

"That's the same thing."

"The portal is around here somewhere; I can feel it."

"Maybe, but I'm sick of cluelessly circling around. I'm going to break through the canopy and try to find the portal from above."

I spread open my wings and rose higher into the air. A strange howling noise emanated from the canopy, and as I neared the top, dozens of vines shot out and entwined me in their clutches before I could twist to avoid them.

"Get off me!" I struggled against them in vain.

I dragged Akta's daggers out of my belt and slashed at the branches until I broke free. I wasn't free for long before a torrent of new, sinewy vines attacked me. No matter how many I destroyed, twice as many shot back at me until they had me by the throat and arms and pulled me tighter and closer to the branches of the old gnarled trees. On either side of me, I saw old bones poking out from the underbrush. Tree branches wrapped around rusted armor and broken weapons. The more I struggled against them, the tighter the branches clung to me until my vision clouded.

"Help!" I shouted with the last of my breath.

I had nearly blacked out from the vine's tight hold around my neck when Aziolith's breath seared the branches around me. The trees let out a screech and released me into Aziolith's talons. No longer was he a human. He had reassumed his true form, and with his fiery dragon's breath, the trees caught fire, and the canopy parted for us. We rose high into the air above it.

"Thanks," I said, rubbing my throat.

"Don't mention it."

I climbed out from Aziolith's talons and floated onto his back, expecting to watch the fire consume the trees. Instead, the flames dissipated as quickly as they came, and the canopy expanded again to cover itself as if it had never been burned—except for a streak of bright red light rising into the Heavens, against the far horizon.

"There!" I pointed. "That must be where Imogen is going!"

"Then it is where we must go as well."

Aziolith flew us toward the bright light. Its presence there could only mean that Imogen had opened the portal to Hell. I only hoped we weren't too late to stop her from bringing Kimberly into Hell with her or draining her blood and leaving her dead on the floor of the forest. I wasn't sure which was worse.

CHAPTER 8

We landed in a forest clearing, where I witnessed a sight that I had only seen once before: a massive portal, fifty feet high, circling atop a big hole in the ground. This was Romania's mystery spot. It hovered ten feet off the ground and glowed the same deep red as the one I remembered.

In front of it stood Imogen, surrounded by a hundred shadow-like wraiths grabbing at the child she held in her arms. Blue light cracked through the darkness of the wraiths like sunlight peeking through the cracks of a house. Imogen batted them away, but they seemed to pay her no mind.

"No!" Imogen shouted. "You cannot have her. This soul is mine! It is my birthright!"

"Lay down some cover fire," I shouted to Aziolith.

I leaped off his back and flew forward. The last time I was in front of a portal to Hell, I was the most powerful I had ever been, and I felt the same power now. Time slowed down, just as it had the last time.

I could see Imogen's every move in detail. Again and again, Aziolith burned a path through the wraiths, and I jumped toward the banshee. Each time I charged, a hundred tortured arms clawed at my face, but I didn't worry about them. They were inconsequential to my mission. All I cared about was Kimberly.

Several times I disappeared, then reappeared slightly closer to my target, until I finally arrived at Imogen's side. I pried Kimberly free of the banshee's long, bony fingers, though I couldn't stop the monsters clawing at her. Finally, I managed to wrestle her into my arms.

"Come with me," I said to Kimberly.

"No! No! She is mine!" Imogen shouted.

But she couldn't stop me. I had Kimberly safe in my grasp, and I jumped backward, away from the shadows, toward the searing dragon fire.

The banshee screamed with delight as the shadow wraiths ran away from her and toward us. "Yes. Yes! Attack them and take their souls! They are the ones you want!"

I looked at Aziolith. "We need to get out of here."

I lifted Kimberly onto Aziolith's back, but we were too late. The wraiths descended upon us as the canopy closed to prevent our escape. Vines shot out from every direction and weighed down Aziolith's wings until he couldn't lift off the ground. The entire forest went dark, except for my wings and the glow of the portal.

"You know not what lurks in the shadows, do you?" Imogen said. "Otherwise, you would not have been so foolish as to come here."

"I came for the girl," I replied, grunting as I fought back the shadow wraiths. They broke on me like waves. I stood firm between Kimberly and the wraiths, slashing at anything that came for her. "What did you do to her? Did you hurt her?"

"Of course not! She is a gift—a fresh soul, a pixie soul, unspoiled by time, to lead his army to victory on Earth!"

"Satan doesn't want you back!" Aziolith shouted, fending off the shadow wraiths.

"You do not know! You cannot know!" Imogen rushed toward me and the girl. "The wraiths are hungry for souls, and yours will be a delicacy for them."

The wraiths pulled me by the arms and pressed me against the ground until I couldn't move. I felt as though I was inside the canopy again, about to be taken into the darkness. Meanwhile, Imogen floated through the wraiths, unhurt or untouched by them.

"Why don't they go for you?" I asked.

"I have no soul. I am born of Hell, after the rise of the demons. We are not blessed with souls. The wraiths care not for me."

Imogen picked up Kimberly while the wraiths kept their attention on me. "She will make a wonderful present."

"What are you going to do to her?"

"I will do nothing. My love—he will decide what to do."

Imogen flew higher into the sky as the shadow wraiths crashed through me. I felt the cold of each wraith as it passed through my body, stealing the warmth from me with each new attack. "Stop!"

"I really must thank you," Imogen said, floating into the air. "I could never have survived their onslaught alone. You have a more seasoned soul than the child, so they hanker for you. They care only for you now, not this child. Wonderful. Enjoy having your soul ripped from your body and devoured before your very eyes."

And with that, Imogen disappeared into Hell with Kimberly, leaving Aziolith and me to struggle against the might of the shadow wraiths.

"NO!" I shouted, but it was too late. I could feel myself disappearing. My strength had left me, and all that remained was death. What had I done? I had delivered Kimberly into Hell and gotten myself killed in the process. Was there a fate worse than this?

I was ready to fade into unconsciousness when a hideous screech echoed through the forest. The wraiths heard it too and let out an accursed moan before they left us alone and slithered into the forest.

"What was that?" I asked.

"I don't know, but I don't want to stick around to find out. Let's go." Aziolith shouted.

"I can't go. I have to save Kimberly. There's still time to bring her back."

"That means venturing into Hell, and that's crazy. You barely survived the last time."

"Yes, but you can—"

"I'm not going anywhere. I've already been to Hell once, and I don't plan on going back again."

"I can't do it alone," I said, pleading quietly.

"Then you can't do it," Aziolith replied.

Just then, a massive wolf crashed through a pair of twisted trees and snarled at us. Its fangs hung from either side of its jaw, oozing green bile onto the ground below it. Its black body, drenched in shadows and covered in flames, pressed itself into the ground, ready to pounce. It howled into the air as it sneered at us, its haunting, yellow eyes searing into us deeper and deeper with every second that passed.

"That does not look good," Aziolith said.

"That looks like a monster too hideous for Hell."

The beast charged at us, and I rose into the air to dodge out of the way. Aziolith wasn't so lucky and locked horns with the beast, sliding across the forest floor with it. Aziolith's fire breath didn't hurt the beast in the slightest. Really, the dragon seemed to stoke its flames.

"Go!" Aziolith shouted. "I'll hold it off and make sure nothing else comes out onto Earth."

"He'll kill you!"

"I can take care of myself!" Aziolith grunted, pushing the beast back with all his might. "Go! Bring the girl back and figure out how to close this blasted portal!"

He was right. I looked back at him one last time, then flew up into the air. Hell was the last place I wanted to be. Honestly, I just wanted to go home, but that wasn't in the cards for me. I took a deep breath, one last breath of fresh air not full of sulfur—and flew into the blood-red portal.

***

Falling through the portal into Hell wasn't unlike pressing your hand through a bowl of jelly or falling through a lava lamp. The red goop clung to me as I fell and allowed me to move through slowly. Painfully slowly. I spun around to look where I was going. Hell rose below my feet until it filled my entire field of vision. With one final tug, I dropped through the goop and landed on a large boulder with a thump.

I stood up and cracked my back into place. All around me, demons shoveled damned souls into large pits. The ground was covered in lost souls, except for small pathways for the monsters to walk.

In every direction as far as the eye could see, human bodies were stacked from the lowest point of Hell until they touched the top of Hell's cavern, creating a sprawling mountain range of moaning humans. The great skyline of a walled city loomed in the distance.

"Hey!" a nasal voice said from the path below me. "Did you really come here? Are you really here?" A tiny, impish head poked out from behind a mound of bodies. "Holy crap. You really are here!" It was Charlie, and he was laughing at me. "I can't believe you came here. I mean, I was watching the whole thing in the mirror back on Earth. Honestly, it's better than cable."

"Charlie! I'm gonna kill you!"

The demon workers on either side of me turned, and the heat from their eyes bored into me for a moment. Then, they resumed their work, consumed with the heinous task of torturing human souls.

"Ah ah ah," Charlie said, wagging his finger. "You can't talk to me like that here."

"Why not?"

"Cuz humans don't talk here, sweetheart. Least not dead ones." Charlie snapped his fingers and appeared in front of me. "If anybody finds out you're here and that you have a soul, oh man. You don't even know what they'll do to you. No, you gotta play it cool."

I grabbed Charlie by his vest and pulled him toward me. "I'm in Hell, Charlie. The last thing I'm going to be while I'm here is cool. Now, where is Imogen?"

"I dunno," Charlie replied, holding up the Mirror of Yilir. "This thing only works on the surface. I've been watching you, though. I just came down here just in time to see the epic conclusion."

I snarled and let him go. "So, you're useless, then?"

"I wouldn't call me useless. I'm just not helpful in the traditional sense. I can take you to a place where you can find answers, though."

I didn't want his help, but I didn't have much of a choice in the matter. It's not like I had a lot of friends in Hell. I only knew one person in Hell, my ancestor Akta, the great pixie who hunted monsters and who knew where she was right now. Charlie, unfortunately, was my only choice.

"Fine. Lead the way."

And with that, I was on my way to wherever the imp would take me, to save Kimberly, and get back to Earth.

CHAPTER 9

"You can stay down here as long as you like," Charlie told me. We were walking down one of the roads carved out between the piles of human souls on either side of us. Charlie balanced on the rows of the moaning corpses like a child would along a balance beam. "Course, the heat will take a toll on your physical body as time goes on. In case you were wondering."

"I wasn't," I replied. "And I didn't ask."

"I know you didn't," Charlie said with a spring in his step. "But you had to be thinking it. I heard you've been down here before, but sans body, which means your body was rotting on Earth. That won't happen this time since you brought your body with you, so you don't have to worry about it. Of course, your magic won't work."

"What are you talking about?" I said, snapping my fingers to try and vanish, but nothing happened. "What the hell? My magic worked last time I was here…at least my wings did."

"You were just a soul last time, honey, and your wings would work this time too if you were just a soul. 'Course, you have a body this time, so they won't work, either."

I focused my energy, trying to push my wings out through my back, but they wouldn't come. I tried again and again, but all it did was make me light-headed.

"Don't do that. It looks like you're taking a dump."

"It will work! I know it will."

"You don't know Hell at all, huh? It doesn't work like the surface. Magic don't work down here. But at least you don't have to worry about rotting on the surface or dying unless, of course, you die down here. Then I don't know what will happen to you. Might destroy the whole system for all I know."

"Let's hope," I said.

"Yup. You really don't know how Hell works. We're as necessary down here as God is up there."

"I doubt that. Your job is to corrupt men's souls. His is to save them."

Charlie hopped down off the moaning bodies and back onto the road. He held in a chuckle as he craned his neck up to me. "Wait, say that again. I don't think I heard you right."

"You have no purpose but to turn men evil."

Charlie rolled onto the ground, laughing, and kicking his feet into the air. "That's what I thought you said. I can't believe—oh my god—that's—well, that's so naive is what it is, isn't it?"

I grabbed Charlie by the ear and brought him to his feet. "I don't like being made fun of, imp."

Charlie held up his hands. "I'm very sorry, miss. I didn't mean to offend; it's just that I didn't think people held such backward beliefs anymore, truth be told."

"What's so backward about it?"

Charlie slapped my hand away from his ear. "Well, let me ask you. What did you do up there on Earth?"

"Dicked around mostly, with my mama."

"No," Charlie said, wagging his finger. "I mean before that. What did you do for work when you worked?"

"I was a teacher," I replied proudly.

"Liked it, did you?"

"It was all right," I said, pulling back my enthusiasm.

"Yeah, but it was a job, right? One of the many offered to you? I suppose you coulda been a nurse or an office manager, too?"

I nodded. "That's right. It was one of many careers I had to choose from."

Charlie pointed to a burly demon with thick black horns shoveling humans into a big pile. "And what do you think he's doing?"

"His jo—no, come on, that's different."

"Is it, though?" Charlie said to the burly demon. "Hey, buddy! Yeah, you. What's your name?"

The demon growled for a good fifteen seconds at Charlie. For a moment, I thought he offended the great beast and would be eaten—and for a moment, I would have been happy to see it—but Charlie looked unconcerned about his potential death. "Yeah, but that's your demon name. Can you put it in plain English, though? Some of us don't speak the old tongue."

The demon growled softly under his breath. "Na-uthal."

"I heard Nathanial, so for the sake of argument, I'm gonna call you Nate, all right?"

"Call me what you will," the demon said, heaping another shovelful of bodies onto the pile. "I care not."

"Nate, how long have you worked this job?"

Nate leaned against his shovel. Underneath him, the weight of his body snapped off somebody's head, which rolled onto the street. "Three hundred and seventeen years."

Charlie wiped his brow. "Damn, that's a long time."

I bent down to pick up the head in front of me, which moaned and screamed in my hands. "Please, kill me. Let me die. Let me die!"

"I have bad news for you," I said to the head. "You're already dead."

Nate scooped the screaming head from my arms and gave me a suspicious look. "I smell something different about you, human."

"I'm not a human. I'm a pixie."

"Hmmm," the demon said. "That must be it."

Charlie snapped his fingers. "Hey, hey, hey! Over here. I'm asking you a question. Why do you have this job?"

Charlie's annoyance grabbed Nate's attention. He looked away from me and over to Charlie. "I have had this job since I lost my other one, and I must work."

"And what were you doing before this?"

"For ten thousand years, I was a bookkeeper in the Tower of Babel, in Dis. It was a good job with normal hours. But then layoffs—"

"Say no more, buddy!" Charlie said, waving his arms. "I get layoffs. I got laid off a dozen times in the last century."

"Yes, well, you are very annoying. I can see that." Nate turned back to his work without another word, and I walked away with Charlie.

When we were out of earshot of the demon, Charlie shook his head. "See what I'm saying to you?"

"That it's just a job?" I asked, confused.

"It's just a job, my friend," Charlie said, wagging his finger. "It's not all we are. It's just a part of it, just like you weren't always a teacher."

"I was a teacher—"

"For a time," Charlie said, hopping back up on the row of bodies. "And then you weren't, but you didn't vanish when you stopped being a teacher, did you?"

"Of course n—"

"Of course not. Exactly. And these guys all have lives outside of torturing people."

"Yeah, but part of their job is torturing people, right?"

"Well, sure it is, but I'm just saying there's a lot more to them than that."

I was sick of arguing with him. "Sure."

***

"How much further?" I asked Charlie as we marched down the dirt road toward the walled city in the distance.

"Almost there. You know you're close to Dis after you pass all the refuse. They try to keep the smell out of the city. We hate that smell."

"Those are humans," I replied. "Not refuse."

"Whatever. Do you know what powers a fourth of Dis? Burning human souls in the pits."

"See? That's what I mean. You can't be good if you are going around burning human souls."

"Who said anything about good? I certainly never said we were good. You said we were evil. I like to think there is a big ole gray area between a goodie-goodie angel and something like Imogen."

"Imogen is one of you, though, isn't she?"

Charlie turned around, more serious than I had ever seen him. "Imogen is nothing like us. She is an abomination, as are her kin."

"Wow, so there's something too disgusting even for demons to touch."

"And you use that word. I'm not a demon. I'm an imp. I don't go around calling you a fairy, do I?"

"I wouldn't care if you did."

"Well, I do. Demons were created from big, muscular, ugly angels. Imps were made from cute, cuddly cherubs, ya dig? Ugly to ugly. Cute to adorable."

I looked Charlie up and down. He was half goat and half demon, covered in red hair, with tiny spiral horns coming out of his head. His voice was harsh and coarse, but he was right. There was something slightly adorable about him.

"Sorry. I didn't mean to offend you."

"Well, all right then. Just try to be more respectful next time."

***

"You hungry?" Charlie asked.

A walled city rose in front of us. We were still a half day's walk away, but I could no longer hear the screaming souls in the distance behind us.

"I hadn't thought about it much, but yeah, a little."

Charlie snatched a lizard off a nearby rock and broiled it in his hand. Then, he sat down and handed it to me. "You'll need your strength if you want to find Imogen. The soul, it can stay up for eternity down here, but if you aren't careful, your body will give out on you, ya hear?"

"I thought magic didn't work down here," I said to him.

"Yours doesn't, but mine does," Charlie said, pulling a necklace out of his pocket. "Which reminds me, put this on."

I grasped the necklace out of his hand and looked it over. The leather string held a black talon on it. "What is it?"

"I took it when I realized you were coming down here for real. It will help with the heat. It can't protect you completely, but it will help a lot."

I placed the necklace around my neck. "Thanks."

"Don't mention it," Charlie replied. "Now quit yapping and eat. You need your strength."

I nodded, taking a big bite of the lizard. "This is actually pretty good."

"Yeah, I know. I can cook. We got all sorts of skills. My friend Bernie used to sing opera. It's like we're three-dimensional beings if you get to know us."

"That's not what I meant," I said, taking another bite of the lizard.

"I know it's not, but you got me all riled up with that demon comment earlier. You know that's our word. You shouldn't even be saying it."

"Are you really offended by something I said?"

"I'm allowed, aren't I?"

I chuckled. "Yeah, but it's usually me being offended by something somebody else says, so it's just—different, I guess."

"Well, don't say that demon nonsense when we get into Dis."

"Is that where we're going? Dis?"

Charlie pointed to the walled city that dominated the horizon. "That's right. It's the biggest city in Hell, and it's our best shot to find Imogen. Every monster in Hell passes through there at some point."

"You think we'll find her there?"

"Hopefully. If nothing else, we'll find somebody that knows something. It's going to be weird enough walking the streets looking like you do, but I have a plan. We're gonna have to say you're a wraith or something."

"What's a wraith?"

"It's like a zombie with a conscience or a ghost with a personality. Look, don't worry about it, just eat your lizard, all right. I'll handle it. Don't you trust me?"

I had to admit, from the moment I met Charlie, I didn't trust him, but he was being cool to me, certainly cooler than I was to him. I would have been completely lost if he hadn't helped me. "Why are you helping me?"

"Helping you? I'm not helping you. I'm helping Charlie. What do you think is gonna happen if monsters like Imogen are coming in and out of hell whenever they please? Charlie's cushy job ain't gonna be so cushy no more, ya got me?"

"What is your job?"

"I'm supposed to find beings that escaped Hell and bring them back. When it's just one or two a month, the job's easy. Lucifer doesn't ask questions as long as the monsters return. Once they're back, I can dick around for a few weeks before I come back here. If somebody gets their hands on a pixie, though, and they can open a portal to Earth, I'm suddenly working night and day. No, thank you.

That's work. I didn't get into this racket to work for a living."

I took another bite of lizard. "How did you get into this 'racket' or whatever?"

"I knew a guy who knew a guy in Retrievals. It's not an easy gig to get. There's only one opening a century cuz the job's so cushy. After all, most demons escape Hell because they were summoned by teenagers. Not that hard to track them down. They aren't usually like Imogen."

"You knew her."

"Yeah, I knew her. She was one of my friend's assignments, Bernie—"

"The opera singer?"

"He ain't singin' opera no more. Imogen ripped his throat out and burned what was left. She is a cold-hearted bitch, and that's comin' from an imp."

"If she was one of your assignments, why isn't she back here?"

"I dunno," Charlie replied. "One day, I get a message that Lucifer called off the contract. She was a bit of a star chaser, and Lucifer is the biggest star of all down here."

***

The walled city of Dis reminded me of a medieval castle from the height of the middle ages. I had seen them all over Europe, but it reminded me most of the ones in England and Ireland, with its pointed towers and parapets and gray bricks towering into the sky. Its black walls were higher, though, easily rising a hundred feet into the air.

"Now," Charlie said, walking toward a ghostly apparition guarding the front gates, "when we get to the front, I do the talking, got it? You don't say nothing."

"Fine," I replied. "I'll keep my mouth shut."

"Sure you can do that, sweetheart?"

I gritted my teeth and glared menacingly at him for a moment, but I bit my tongue before speaking. If there's one thing I could do well, it was keep my goddamn mouth shut.

"State your business," the ghastly apparition spat at us, glowing a neon blue that pulsated with every word. It was holding a clipboard, "if you wish to pass."

"We just gotta stock up at the old homestead, Gil," Charlie replied with a wry smile.

 Gil looked down at his paperwork. "Name."

"Charlie."

"Real name."

A low grumble escaped Charlie's throat that lasted for ninety seconds. If I didn't know better, I would have thought it a long burp.

"Ah yes," the apparition replied. "And your guest?"

"She's nobody," Charlie said. "Seriously. I would appreciate it if we could keep it under the radar. My wife—"

"Name."

Charlie turned to me. "Run."

"Excuse me?" I replied.

"Run!"

I bolted down the edge of the castle wall as Charlie sprinted behind me. His short legs were making him fall behind more and more with every stride I took. Then, with a snap of his fingers, he appeared in front of me.

He slid down a hill and opened a sewer grate. "Get in."

I rolled down after him and, once I'd dropped into the sewer, Charlie jumped in and covered the hole. We watched as the apparition rose over the hill and continued his slow, pulsating float past us.

"Why didn't you just snap us into the city?" I whispered.

"You don't know how our magic works, do you?" Charlie said, waddling down the sewer pipe. "We can't just bring other people with us when we vanish. That's against the rules. If we could do that, then I could just snap people out of hell all the time. Unless you got a contract on your head, I can't transport you."

The stench was foul and rotten in the sewers. I wretched with every step I took. "This is revolting."

"Yeah, we smell pretty bad on the outside, but our insides smell even worse. Human noses weren't meant for this level of disgusting. They're too sensitive. That's why I was trying to get us through the walls legit."

"But you couldn't do that…because of the rules."

"Different set of rules, but basically that's right, sweetheart. You think we are all ruthless savages, but we have rules too. Lots of rules. Hell is nothin' if not rules." Charlie doddered forward and pushed up another sewer grate, peeking around. "We're good. Hurry up."

He poked up out of the sewer and pulled me up with him. We rose onto the cobblestoned streets of Dis. I felt like we had accomplished something, but in truth, we hadn't done anything yet. I still had no idea where to find Imogen.

CHAPTER 10

After an hour of walking around the outer edges of the walled city, I became skeptical Charlie was leading me in the right direction. After all, it was a little too convenient that he would just happen upon me exactly when I came out of the portal and be my guide into Dis to find Imogen. Who knew if Imogen was even in Dis? It was hard enough to get me, a willing adult, through the gates. How did she manage with a scared child?

Admittedly, I was too overwhelmed with the thought of being lost in Hell to think straight, which is why I latched onto Charlie to begin with, but at least I could think straight enough to know I couldn't think straight. I came through the portal hot-blooded, without any forethought, and having a familiar face to look upon eased my fears before they crippled me.

However, as I walked through the streets behind Charlie, my overwhelming fear subsided into a manageable one, and my natural skepticism blared loudly in my ears. I started to question every step the little imp took, especially after he led me into the bowels—literally—of Dis, through its sewer. Everything he did felt like a stall technique.

It was still only a feeling that I couldn't confirm. I didn't know anything about Hell, so it was either go off alone and try to find Imogen myself or trust that Charlie was helping me even though I doubted it. Neither were appealing options, but the latter seemed like the only reasonable one for the time being until I had confirmation that my suspicions were more than a gut feeling.

After another hour, my feet ached in my boots. They were literally made for walking, but my feet had limits.

Luckily, after a third hour of walking, Charlie stopped in front of a small clothes shop.

"You need new clothes, honey. You stick out like a sore thumb down here."

Apparently, the dress code for the city was drab, loosely draped clothes layered on top of each other, so Charlie swathed me in tattered cloth until I could barely move. When we were finished, he led me toward the inner gate of the city. He was right. The monsters that once turned their heads as I passed no longer took notice of me—and there were so many different monsters in Dis, it was like something out of the Lord of the Rings.

What amazed me about the city was how normal it felt the longer I walked through it. There were cobblers and blacksmiths, butchers and bookstores. The only difference between this town and the hundreds of others I'd read about and visited was that its inhabitants, the denizens of Hell, were monsters of all types instead of humans.

"Why are there so many ogres and orcs and goblins down here?" I asked Charlie as we walked. "I figured it would all be demons and imps like you."

"Centuries ago, they lived on the surface, just like Aziolith, back when the gods roamed the earth."

"Gods? Like, multiple gods?"

"Of course, multiple gods. That's what I'm saying. There used to be hundreds of gods on Earth, trying to move things along and make sure you didn't destroy yourselves. But then most of the gods left Earth until only one guy remained."

"Who was that?"

"Bacchus, of course. The drunk. Didn't you ever wonder why everything was so messed up on Earth? It's because he doesn't care, man. He's busy drinking himself into oblivion."

"That sounds unlikely."

"And yet, it's true. Back in the old days, some of the gods looked out for monsters, but Bacchus didn't care about that. He had a boner for humanity. Which meant humanity had carte blanche to hunt monsters to the brink of extinction, and they ended up here. Not like Bacchus was gonna let them into Heaven, and Lucifer seized an opportunity to put them to work."

"What do they do?" I asked.

"Some of 'em torture people, but they usually don't have the stomach for that kind of stuff—"

I smirked. "Because it's gross."

"I'm not saying it ain't," Charlie sighed. "I'm saying that it's a job. You wanna hear this or not?"

"Yeah, I do."

"So, they don't torture people, but there's all sorts of jobs you can do in Hell without torture. You can shovel shit. You can make shoes. You can carry messages between cities. I mean, the opportunities are endless, almost more than they had on Earth. Plus, we don't look down on monsters down here."

We had chitted and chatted our way through the inner walls without issue and into the main city. While the outer wall had a small collection of medieval-looking shops and markets, the inner wall made it seem like the modern world encroached on the cobblestone streets of the ancient one. Mixed among the thatched roofs sat buildings with high, white-washed walls, shingled roofs, and sleek, tinted windows that would not have been out of place in New York or Chicago in the 1940s.

"Where are we going?" I asked as we moved through the streets.

"I have a friend in the constable's office. He owes me a favor, sweetheart."

"Constable? There's law and order in Hell?"

He turned to me and stopped. "You gotta get it out of your head that we're just a bunch of ruffians down here. We got jobs. We got families. I have two kids that I gotta get through high school."

"You are married?"

"I didn't say that. I just said I had two kids. Now, if you act like this around monsters with feelings, they're gonna get offended, maybe even find you out. So, if you want to keep your head, just keep the prejudices to yourself, all right?"

"Fine, but we need to hurry this up. I don't have all day. Imogen—"

"Do you trust me?" Charlie asked.

"That's a loaded question. You're an imp from Hell, so no, not really. But you are the best choice I have if I want to get things done, so I guess I have no other option."

He nodded. "That's as good a reason as any. Now, let's go."

***

The constable's office wasn't much of an office at all. It was more like a warehouse with desks. There were no visible jail cells, and the monsters inside didn't wear uniforms, just a little gold badge pinned to their ragged shirts. The constables were some of the biggest monsters I had seen in Hell yet. Even sitting behind their desks, they were seven feet tall and wider than a Cadillac.

Before we stepped into the station's bullpen, Charlie pulled me against the wall. "So, you are not supposed to be here, clearly. The foul stench from the sewer masks any human smell from you, but if they find you in here, then they'll—well, I can't protect you from what they'll do, got it?"

"Got it."

Charlie led the way through the bullpen toward a lime green ogre poking keys on a typewriter. Smoke steamed out of his nostrils as he tried to navigate a keyboard too small for his fingers.

"Gorgin! My man!" Charlie said, strolling up and leaning on the desk.

The ogre did not look impressed or happy to see him. "Go away."

"So, what?" Charlie said. "You only talk to me when you want something?"

"That is exactly it."

"That's not much of a friendship."

Gorgin looked up from his typewriter. "This is not a friendship. You are my informant. Thus, I come to you when I need information and pay you handsomely for it. When I do not, you cease to exist."

"Wait," I said, "you are the informant, and you need information? How is that—"

"Don't worry about it, toots," Charlie said, holding up his hand, a nervous grin plastered upon his face.

"So, you need something from me. This should be good," Gorgin said, loosening his fingers from the keys. "What can I do for you?"

"There's a banshee, Gorgin, real bad news. Brought a kid, body and all, into Hell. I need to know if you've heard anything."

"Hmmm…there has been some rumbling in the streets about it, but I thought it was a fairy tale. In fact, I have heard a great many things about it just today. But why should I tell you anything?"

"Can you imagine what would happen if somebody found that baby, or what she could do with it in Hell? It would be bedlam. Every deviant in Hell would kill their mother for a chance back to Earth."

"Hmmm. I'm not sure I care, but I will tell you the Old Hat has been a hotbed of gossip about this kind of stuff lately. Do with that information what you will."

Charlie smiled. "Got it. Thanks, Gorgin."

"Now, you owe me one."

Charlie gulped. "I'll remember that, and I'm sure you'll come to collect."

"Oh, I will. And soon."

***

Charlie led me higher and higher up a set of wooden stairs in a tall building that looked out over all of Dis. We had climbed six flights, and there were at least a dozen flights more to the top.

"Where are we going?" I asked.

"The Old Hat is not a nice place. If we're gonna go, you gotta be at the top of your game. I mean, look at you. You're tired. You're weak. You're hungry."

"I am not."

But even as he said those words, I wobbled to stay upright. I could barely hang onto the banister, and when Charlie opened the door at the next landing, I audibly squealed with glee since I wouldn't have to climb any more stairs.

"Yeah, you are," Charlie said, walking out into a hallway lined with doors. "It's the heat. That's what'll zap your strength. Even that necklace I gave you can't help completely. The Old Hat starts jumping around eight. We'll go then and figure out what Imogen is up to, but right now, you need to sleep."

Charlie opened a door halfway down the hall and walked inside. My brain was too muddled to fight him. I should have, probably, but every bone in my body wanted a warm bed and a slice of pizza. I didn't even like pizza all that much, but just then, my body craved it.

When I walked inside, I realized the door led into Charlie's apartment. An imp had an apartment, and it looked a lot like an apartment on Earth. There was a couch, table, chairs, bookcase, kitchen, and even a little balcony with a set of chairs on it.

"Here," Charlie said, handing me a glass. "It's vodka. You can't drink the water down here, but this is the next best thing."

I took the drink in one swig. Almost immediately, my eyes started to blur. "What's happening to me?"

"I told you, sweetheart, you're tired. Lie down on the couch and get some sleep. You're no good to me tired."

"Maybe," I said, stumbling to the couch, "just for a minute."

The second my head hit the pillow, I was out like a light. If I had time to think, I would have questioned

Charlie's hospitality, but he'd done right by me. Maybe there was no reason to worry.

CHAPTER 11

I woke up groggy and with my wrists burning. I tried to jerk my hands forward, but they were bound with rope behind my back. The rope was tight against my skin, rubbing it raw. Charlie had made me his prisoner.

"Yeah, I got her here." His voice carried from the other room. "Don't worry. You have my word she won't be harmed…unless that's what you want…no?...didn't think so."

My eyes came into focus on the little imp, confidently kicking his feet up on the kitchen table, back turned to me as if I couldn't possibly escape. He must not have any faith in humanity, or at least in me.

"Nah. It went down just like I said," Charlie continued. "Flawlessly. You gotta have a little more faith."

So, he was working against me after all. I had been an idiot to believe him, but I didn't have much choice. I was scared of Hell—I would be an idiot not to be—and Charlie eased that fear. He was so cool and confident that I glommed onto his confidence and made it my own. He was at such ease that it put me at ease.

"By the time you get there, she'll be ready for transport."

Charlie didn't know, though, that I kept a switchblade knife inside my right boot just in case I needed it. For a second, I worried he had taken it, but when I shifted my feet, I felt the steel strapped against my shin.

Charlie had tied my hands behind my back, and my feet were tied to my thigh like I was a prized hog. Luckily, that made it easier to reach my weapon. I inched my hands slowly into my boot.

"Nah, it was easy," Charlie said proudly. "She was like putty in my hands. Didn't even know what hit her."

Charlie was too stupid to think I was smart enough to keep up with him. His weakness was hubris, and I very much looked forward to making him look like a fool. I tilted my boot to the left, and the knife slid out into my hand.

"Hang on a second," he said. I could feel his eyes on me, looking over my face. It was all I could do not to scream at him, but I needed him to believe I was asleep.

"Never mind. She's good. I thought I heard something, but I shoulda known she was still asleep. She's ready for your boss, Ghul. Don't you worry."

Wait, Ghul? Who was Ghul? Wasn't Charlie working with Imogen? Of course, he wasn't because I was a body with a soul. Just like Kimberly, I could be used to open the portal to Earth and set about the Apocalypse. That was incredibly valuable, and he was selling me to the highest bidder.

I flipped open the knife and started cutting myself free. It wouldn't have been my first choice in a fight, but in a pinch, the little blade did a fine job fraying the ropes that bound my hands. After a minute of cutting, I was free and set about loosening the ropes on my feet.

"All right, I'll see you in ten. Bring cash."

Charlie slammed the phone down just as I finished unbinding my legs. When he turned around, he saw me rise to my feet, full height, and his eyes went wide.

"You little imp!"

"How did you—" Charlie started, but I didn't let him finish. I rushed toward him and slammed him into the wall.

"You weren't helping me at all, were you?" I shouted.

"What are you talking about? Of course, I was being helpful."

"You call tying me up helpful!" I screamed, squeezing his neck.

"Well, helpful. I was being helpful. I wasn't really helping, but you can't deny that I was being helpful."

As I questioned whether I should drag my knife across his throat or cut him in half, the front door creaked open, and two tiny imps walked in, a third the size of Charlie.

"Daddy!" one shouted. "We're home."

"Are you really home?" the other yelled.

"That's my kids," Charlie whispered. "You really want them to see you kill me?"

I dropped Charlie to the ground and stowed the knife behind my back. "Where are my daggers?"

Charlie pointed to the kitchen counter, and sure enough, both of Akta's daggers were lying there, next to the sink. I placed them back in their sheaths as Charlie ran to pick up his children.

"My boys!" he said, scooping them up. "How was school today?"

"Good," one of the boys said. "We learned fractions."

"You did?"

"Yeah," said the other, pointing at me. "Who's that?"

Charlie smiled at me. "That's—that's just one of Daddy's friends."

I put on my biggest, fakest smile. "That's right, and I was just leaving. Charlie, we'll talk about that thing later. I promise you'll be seeing me, and I'll give you what I owe you."

"Oh," he replied with a toothy grin, showing off all of his pointed teeth. "You can count on it."

I bent down to Charlie's ear and whispered into it. "They are lovely kids, Charlie. I hope they live long, healthy lives…unlike their father."

***

I was alone when I exited the building. I was free, but I was terribly alone. In Hell. And I had no idea what I was doing or where I was going. If anybody in Hell found out I had a body and a soul, it would be bad news, and I would be hunted mercilessly.

I would have to talk to somebody, though. Eventually. After all, there was only one lead I had to go on—the Constable told Charlie the Old Hat would provide him more information. Was that a bar? Was it a store? Was it even in Dis? I would have to be careful who I asked for help, and I couldn't just wander around aimlessly.

I set off down the street with only the name of the Old Hat on my lips. I worried every eye in Hell would be upon me as I moved. Luckily, the monsters of Hell kept to their own business. It was easy to navigate unseen between their lumbering bodies, as they weren't looking for me, or anything for that matter, except for what was in front of their face. Still, I was careful to keep my shabby rag clothing pulled closely around my face. There were not many humans in Dis and those that were tended to be zombies, succubae, or ghosts.

I turned from an alley onto a wide street. On either side of the road, vendors of all types screamed out for customers. Trolls, ogres, goblins, orcs, and ghosts hollered about food and wares every few feet on the side of the street. Some of the monsters ambling down the street stopped to browse, but for most, it was white noise.

These suckers were ugly, even by the standards of Dis. Except for one vendor. One little girl with pointy ears and a wide smile stood on top of a wooden stand, selling shoes with her father, an older man with even pointier ears. They were by far the most humanlike thing in the whole of Dis, and as such, they were passed over again and again by the monsters that walked past.

"Don't you even wanna look?" the girl said. "My daddy can make shoes for anybody! Troll! Orc! Ogre! Demons, even! He's not picky!"

She smiled wide as people passed, unfazed when they ignored her. I had not seen much smiling in Hell, and it was a welcome sight. I trudged through the cobblestone streets toward her.

"You, ma'am! Do you need shoes?" She pointed at me while she shouted.

"Actually," I said with a parched throat. "I have a question."

"What do I look like?" the girl barked. "An information booth? Take it to City Hall!"

"Please," I replied.

"Don't make me—"

The father looked up from his spectacles and frowned. "What did you just say?"

I cleared my throat before I spoke. "I have a question."

"We know!" the little girl said. "Get lost!"

"No," the old man said. "Not that. The other thing."

I said, please. I'll bet that's not something they hear in Hell. I'd only said five words since leaving Charlie, and already I was about to be found out and flayed alive.

"Nothing," I replied, turning away. "Never mind."

"Ask your question," the man said, standing behind his booth.

"The Old Hat," I said cautiously. "Do you know it?"

"He knows everything!" the girl replied.

"Quiet now, Beatrice. It's all right." The old man nodded, studying me. "Yes, I know it. Dodgy place, that. Not somewhere you go lightly."

"I go nowhere lightly, sir," I replied. "Please, do you know the way?"

"There is that word again," the man said with a wistful look. "I haven't heard it in a long time. I have been trying to teach Beatrice, but she refuses to learn manners."

"I have lost everything, sir. I use that word to remind me where I came from."

"And where did you come from?" the old man asked.

I shook my head slightly. "I don't recall. I don't recall much, except that word."

The man flapped his hands and shooed off the gathered bystanders, who went about their business, grumbling to themselves. "Very well, miss. Come closer. Come closer."

I took a hesitant step closer to him, and he said, "I don't know who you are, miss, and I don't much care, but if you plan to stay alive down here, you best stop using that word."

"Why are you being so kind to me?" I asked. "The last time somebody showed me kindness—it wasn't pleasant, in the end."

He looked at me for a moment, then the sides of his mouth curled ever so slightly. "I remember that word.

Please. I have not heard it in some time. It is a good word. Keep it close.”

“All of that, because of a word?”

He nodded. “Beatrice, show this woman to the Old Hat, but do not go in. Run back right after, okay? I need you here. Chop chop!”

“Yes, Daddy!” Beatrice said, hopping down from the stand. “Come on, idiot, follow me.”

I ducked my head and followed the little girl down the street. Maybe it was too soon to trust again, but I wanted to believe there was goodness, even in Hell, so I let her lead me forward. Besides, how bad could a little girl be?

***

“Don’t look anybody in their eyes,” Beatrice stated confidently as we walked down the street toward a dark alley on our left. “And don’t go into any dark alleys. You’re just asking for trouble if you do.”

“It was the same on Earth,” I replied.

“Was it? I guess so. I was murdered in a dark alley, so I have a thing about them.”

“You were murdered?”

“Course,” she said, turning around. “You don’t think I died of natural causes, do you? I’m too tough for that!” Beatrice yanked up her shirt and revealed a jagged hole through her chest where her heart would be, and I could see the street on the other side of it.

“Gross,” I said, my nose scrunching up at the sight of it.

“Yeah. You can touch it if you want. People like to touch it.”

I shook my head. “That’s okay.”

Beatrice pulled down her shirt. "That's your loss. So, how did you die?"

I didn't have a lie on the tip of my tongue. I didn't expect people to ask, but she said it like it was the most normal question in Hell. I wasn't prepared, honestly, to have so many conversations with the dead, just as if I was in Cleveland or Lisbon.

"I choked on a ham sandwich," was the first thing I blurted out. Mama Cass just died a couple of months ago, and her death had been all over the news for a while, so it stuck with me.

"That's not a fun story. Kind of depressing. Daddy always taught me to chew."

"How did he die?"

"A long time after me, actually. Heart attack. Old age. Whatever you call it. He was one of the lucky ones."

"Lucky ones?" I asked. We turned the corner down another long, cobblestone street.

"Yeah, most of us were hunted to extinction for sport by humans. Daddy was able to outlive almost all of us."

"How long have you been dead?"

"About four thousand years, or so. Daddy says we went extinct soon after that."

"So, you're not a human, then?" I asked.

"Duh?" she said, pointing to her ears. "I'm an elf. And you're a pixie."

I was taken aback. "How can you tell?"

"I dunno. You can just tell these things. Like, how can you tell an ogre is an ogre. You just look and say, 'damn, that's an ogre,' ya know?"

"I must say," I said, continuing behind her down the street. "You are taking your death quite well."

"I was only alive for a few years, pixie. I've been dead for thousands. I don't really remember what it's like to be alive."

My jaw unclenched when she said those words. I had worried she would be able to smell the stench of my body even through the layers of feces, but since she died so young, I doubted it. She probably didn't even remember what a body smelled like after so long in the bowels of Hell.

"How much further?" I asked.

She pointed to the sign at the end of the street. It was a wooden crest, with a beat-up top hat carved into it. "That's the one, right there."

"It doesn't look like much, does it?"

She shook her head. "It's not much inside. Just a bunch of drunks and hooligans. Daddy says it's the worst bar in Dis, but I think Mallory's worse. You don't wanna go in either one, though."

I sighed. "And yet, that's exactly where I'm going."

"Well, I hope you find it, dumbass. Don't die again, or whatever."

Beatrice skipped down the street away from me as if she were skipping down any street in any town on Earth. She didn't have a care in the world, and she didn't seem to mind Hell, either.

A loud bell chimed over my head eight times. Above me, an old clock tower read 8:00. Charlie said we would check out the Old Hat at eight, and I had no doubt he would come to find me there.

I had no choice but to enter, though. I couldn't wait. I only had one lead, and this was it. If I wanted to find Kimberly, I needed more to go on, so I opened the door. My fate waited for me inside, but I was already in Hell. How much worse could it get?

CHAPTER 12

The musk of death hit me when I pulled open the door of the Old Hat and walked inside. The place was packed with all manner of sweaty, disgusting monsters. I squeezed between their burly frames and sat down at the bar between a fat ogre and a waifish goblin. They drank from beer steins in silence and stared forward at the liquor behind the bar. I knew the look well. It was the look I had after a hard day teaching when all I wanted to do was have a drink and turn off my brain.

"What'll you have?" The surly demon bartender with a thick beard and thicker muscles was cleaning glasses at the other end of the bar.

"She'll have a vodka." I heard a voice I recognized over my shoulder. I spun on my stool to see Charlie grinning at me maniacally. Behind him stood four of the biggest trolls I'd seen in Hell, cracking their knuckles.

"I was hoping they would kill you," I replied. "So I wouldn't have to."

Charlie shrugged. "I can't die, sweetheart. I have nine thousand lives."

The demon slammed a shot of vodka down on the table. "That'll be—"

"Just put it on my tab," Charlie grunted, pushing the shot to me. "Least I can do is give you one last drink before I sell you off."

I picked up the vodka and gripped it tight in my hand. "You know, I really appreciate you showing me that Hell is worse than I ever imagined."

"We all gotta make a living, hon. This ain't personal. It's business."

I smirked. "Well, this is personal."

I threw the vodka into Charlie's face and punted him into the far wall. It was worth it, booting Charlie, but it only gave me a reprieve of a couple of seconds. The four trolls bore down on me as I slid off the stool.

"Fight!" a voice shouted from the back of the room. The whole bar stood up, just like in a John Wayne western, and started throwing punches at each other.

Out of nowhere, a dagger flew into one of the troll's heads, and he dropped to the ground dead—or as dead as somebody can be in Hell. Another of my attackers slammed into the bar as a demon hit him with a chair. With only two trolls left, I saw an opening between them and took it. I ducked under their massive hands and sprinted toward the door.

Before I could reach it, a hand grabbed me around the shoulder. "Not that way."

I spun around. A figure cloaked in darkness pulled me by the hand toward Charlie, who was just coming to.

"Grab him!" a voice shouted.

I stuck Charlie under my arm without breaking stride as we rushed past. A bottle of whiskey flew over my head, and I swerved to avoid it.

"What's happening?" Charlie said in a daze.

"Shut up, or I'll knock you out again," I growled.

Two ogres pummeled a centaur as we rushed toward a door in the furthest corner of the bar. The centaur spun around and kicked the ogres with her back legs, sending them through the front window.

"How is this better?" I asked the cloaked figure as we rushed past the bucking centaur.

"If there are four trolls in here, there are double that waiting outside just in case you make it out alive." The hooded figure pushed me into the kitchen. Imps and goblins shrieked as we sprinted past them and slammed through the back door into an alley full of dumpsters.

Two orcs ran into one end of the alley, and a demon hobbled into the other. "Man," the figure said, "they really want to capture you."

"If you only knew."

My rescuer reached into its cape, pulled out two daggers, and sent them flying toward the orcs, who dropped to the ground. We hopped over their bodies and broke into a crowded street. Monsters of all types halted their gait for us to cross in front of them. As we made our way into the next alleyway, a gang of orcs chased after us. The figure slammed a ball onto the ground, and a giant plume of smoke rose into the air, shrouding our exit.

"Who are you?" I asked as we rushed into another dark alley.

The figure pulled off her hood and smiled at me. Her dark skin and long ears were familiar to me, but I never thought I would see them again, at least not in my lifetime.

"Akta?"

She raised an eyebrow. "I wish I could say it was good to see you again. Now come on, before you get caught like the fool you are."

***

After three more blocks, Akta stuck a wad of cloth in Charlie's mouth to shut him up. He kept kicking, screaming, and putting up a fight, so after two more blocks, she knocked him out with the butt of her knife. Charlie wasn't big, but he wasn't light either. After thirty minutes of dragging him through the city and into dark passages to avoid detection, I was tired. Still, I didn't mind. It was nice to be with somebody I could trust.

This was the second time I'd seen Akta in the last two years. The first was when I ended up in the Underworld after I died fighting demons back in Chandler. Akta found me and pulled me out of the River Styx, where souls floated to be judged for their crimes. She also returned me to my body so that I could kick the crap out of the demons who made it through the portal.

She was my great, great, great, great—well, she had been in Hell for thousands of years, so let's just say that she was my ancestor on my mother's side, which meant we were bonded by blood. Unlike Charlie, I had every reason to trust Akta, as she literally saved my life before, and her blood flowed through my veins.

Akta poked her head out of a dark alley and held up her hand. "When I say, run across the street and into the door on the other side. Ready?"

"Ready."

"Go."

I bolted across the street as fast as my legs would allow me—still dragging Charlie along—and dove into the door on the other side. A few seconds later, Akta joined me, giggling. "Well done. I liked the diving part most of all."

"You said quickly."

She shook her head. "No, I didn't."

"Well, you implied it."

Akta pulled the unconscious Charlie out of my hands and climbed the stairs to the second floor of the dimly lit staircase. Feet stomped overhead. When Akta burst into the room, two voices shouted excitedly to greet her.

"Get up here!" Akta shouted, and I climbed the stairs. When I reached the top, I was greeted by a bustling kitchen where Beatrice and her father were making food.

"Julia!" Beatrice said, running to me. "You're here! See, Daddy! I told you that dumb lady wouldn't die."

Her father nodded. "I suppose I owe you a treat, then."

Beatrice wrapped her hands around my legs. "I'm glad you aren't dead."

I patted her on the head. "Me too."

Beatrice's father brushed the food off his hands and walked over to me. "I feel like I was a bit rude earlier. I didn't even give you my name. It's Clovis."

"No need to apologize, Clovis. You did right by me." I shook his outstretched hand.

"You have no idea," Beatrice said. "You'd be dead if Daddy didn't call Akta."

"Whoa now," I replied with a laugh. "I might've survived on my own."

She shook her head. "No, you wouldn't."

Akta pulled Charlie through the kitchen and around a corner. Even with her gone, there was plenty to watch in the kitchen as Clovis chopped meat, and Beatrice threw vegetables into a stew.

"What are you making?" I asked, walking to the pot. I waved the smell toward my nose. "It smells like chicken noodle soup."

"Well, I suppose there are noodles and the closest thing to chicken down here as well, so it wouldn't be out of line to call it that."

It didn't matter to me, the fact of the matter was that I was starving, and my body ached for nutrients. All the running around took the last of my strength out of me, so the prospect of a hearty soup made my mouth water and stomach churn.

I picked a spoon lying on the counter and dipped it in the soup. "So, you called Akta for me?"

He nodded. "I thought you could use some backup. Guess I was right."

I took a sip of the soup. It tasted awful, but my body didn't care. "Needs more salt."

"Well, that we have plenty of," he said, turning around and scraping some salt off a rock on his counter. "You know, you really are the spitting image of her."

"Except for the ears, of course," Beatrice replied, mimicking my tasting of the soup. She wanted to taste what I tasted, but she didn't react at all when she put it in her mouth. "What does this taste like?"

"It tastes delicious…" I lied through my teeth. "Savory and…garlicy…and chickeny at the same time."

"Oh," Beatrice said. "I guess I haven't tasted things in a while."

"Julia!" Akta screamed at me from the other room. "Quit messing around and come in here."

"That's my cue," I said, walking toward a doorway across the room. "Thank you. For everything."

He smiled. "It's my pleasure. There's not a lot of reason to smile down here, and you gave me one today, so thank you."

***

I walked into a dark room. Akta had moved all the furniture against one wall and draped a blanket over the window. All that was left within the stucco walls was a chair. Sitting in that chair was Charlie, drooped over, still unconscious, his hands and feet bound tightly with rope.

"Is he supposed to be unconscious like that?" I said. "Seems like he's been out for a long time."

"I hit him harder than usual." Akta shrugged. She was holding a bucket of water in her hand. "Have you ever interrogated somebody before?"

I shook my head. "No, but I've seen plenty of people in pain and enough movies to know the gist."

"Getting information doesn't matter. If you care about any old information, then you'll get sent on wild goose chases. What matters is getting the right information. That's the key. It's the only thing that's going to move us in the right direction."

"How do you know what's right and what's wrong?"

"You just know. Once you break somebody, they will tell you anything you want to know."

"Do you even know what we're searching for?" I asked.

"No," Akta replied. "This is where you fill me in. Then we'll get started."

I told Akta the whole story, starting with Mama's death. I was careful not to leave out a single detail and hoped Charlie wouldn't wake up before I was finished.

CHAPTER 13

"That's quite a story," Akta said after I finished speaking. "And you went into just…all the detail…so much unnecessary detail."

"Sorry. I thought you wanted to know everything before we started interrogating Charlie."

"I did want to know everything—or at least I thought I did." Akta paused, noticing a groggy Charlie looking around. "It doesn't matter now. What's important is figuring out what Charlie knows about Imogen as soon as possible."

"Right." I nodded.

Akta picked up her bucket of water and splashed it over the imp's face. "Wake up!"

Charlie regained consciousness in a hurry and shook his head back and forth, trying to shake off the dripping water. "Where am I? What am I doing? What's going on?" Then, he saw my face. "Oh, it's you. Hello again."

I crossed my arms. "We have to stop meeting like this."

"We could stop meeting at all if you would just let me finish kidnapping you!"

"And what? Become a slave? Get flayed alive?" I took a step toward him and got in his face.

"Yeah," he said, bobbing his head emphatically. "That's the plan, and it would be nice if you were in on it."

I swung back to clock him in the jaw, but Akta caught my hand. "I like hitting monsters as much as the next person, but it's not going to help us right now."

Charlie swung his head toward Akta. "You ain't foolin' me, sweet cheeks. I know you aren't the good guy. You are a bad pixie, and I ain't dealing with you again."

"Again?" I asked.

Akta grumbled. "I may have crossed paths with this imp a time or two before, much to my chagrin."

"And you weren't going to tell me about this?"

Akta shrugged. "It didn't seem relevant at the time."

"Relevant?" Charlie snorted. "That's a laugh as if that ever stopped you from doing anything nasty before."

"I never said I did," Akta snarled. "I particularly like doing nasty things to demons, and I'll take special pleasure in torturing you."

"Then it's torture, is it?"

"As much as you can stand until you give us the information we need."

"Oh, so it's information you want, huh?"

"Obviously," I snorted. "And you're gonna give it to us."

"I can see that," Charlie said, chuckling. "Yeah. Charlie Two Bits screws over demons to help a coupla nothings rescue a nobody. Yup, that sounds like me. Take a hike."

Akta pulled her blade out of her belt. "I have ways of making you talk."

"You can't do nothin' to me that Hell can't do ten times better."

"No. I don't expect I can torture you better than the demons of Hell. I can come close, I think, but I'd rather it not come to that. All I want to know is where Imogen is taking the child, and you can go free."

"You broads are one note and booooring."

Akta snarled at Charlie. "This isn't working. You are clearly too smart for your own good."

Beatrice called from the other room, "Dinner's ready!".

"Go eat," Akta said. "When you come back, I will have the information we need."

"Pretty confident about that, toots," Charlie said with a giggle. "This I wanna see."

"Go," Akta said emphatically. "You do not want to be here for this."

I wanted to stay, but my body was shaking so hard from hunger that I could barely think straight. "Fine."

"You messed up now," Akta said as I walked away. "She was the good cop."

I smiled as I turned the corner into the kitchen, and Charlie started to scream. I might have been the good cop, but I took immense satisfaction in his pain.

***

Charlie screamed miserably as Beatrice and Clovis sat and watched me eat. Beatrice had her own soup, but after a couple of bites, the novelty of eating wore off, and she pushed her bowl to the center of the table.

"I know it's not like what you get on Earth," Clovis said, "but I hope it's edible at least. I followed the recipe, but I don't have the best sniffer anymore."

It wasn't great stew, but I was already on my third bowl, and I didn't plan to stop any time soon. I hadn't eaten a meal since coming to Hell, and my ravenous body didn't care if the soup tasted like gravel, which was good because it kind of did. I was just happy to shovel it in my gullet while Akta worked her magic in the other room.

"I'm sorry for the noise," I said after another hearty spoonful. "Won't the neighbors be mad or call somebody?"

"You haven't been in Hell for very long, have you?" Beatrice replied.

"Long enough to never want to come back."

"This is what I would call a mild annoyance compared to what we deal with on a regular basis," Clovis said.

"It must be horrible," I replied, shoveling another spoonful into my mouth. "Living down here."

"It's not so bad," Beatrice replied. "I mean, you get used to it."

"So, you two don't mind it, being in Hell?"

"We don't have any other option. I mean, Bacchus turned Mount Olympus into Heaven and started letting all the good boys and girls in after—well, after we died, so there was no other place for us to go."

"So, there are no monsters in Heaven?" I replied. "Not even one?"

"The way I heard it—" Beatrice looked over at her dad. "Can I tell it? Is it okay?"

Clovis nodded. "Go ahead."

"So, the way I heard it, a long time ago, gods roamed the world. I dunno. I never saw them."

"They did roam the world, little one," Clovis added. "They were everywhere, but then they abandoned us, leaving one god in charge, and that's when humans started getting a big head."

Beatrice stood up straight. "They hunted us to extinction. All of us. Some for sport. Some out of jealousy, but it wasn't long before we were all gone, and then after that, God decided to send down Jesus and open Heaven up to mortals."

"So, nobody was in Heaven before that?" I asked.

Clovis shook his head. "No. Only the gods. It used to be called Mount Olympus, you know. It's where the gods lived until they abandoned us. I have a theory that God—or Bacchus—became lonely by himself, and that's why he let people into Heaven, but it's just a theory. I have a lot of time to theorize down here."

Beatrice sulked down in her chair and folded her arms. "Harrumph."

"What's wrong?" I asked.

"Daddy said I could tell it."

Clovis reached over and kissed Beatrice on the forehead. "I'm sorry, sweetheart."

I scraped the bottom of the bowl. "You two are cute together."

"She keeps me sane," Clovis replied. "She's the only reason Hell is bearable. We all need something to hold onto, you know. Something that keeps us going."

My eyes went wide. He was right. Everybody has something to hold on to, something they care about, and while watching Beatrice and Clovis, I figured out the thing Charlie cared about. His children.

I abandoned the bowl and ran out of the room. "Thank you for the food. It was…food!" Akta's darkened torture chamber was filled with Charlie's screams of agony. She was busy filleting Charlie's arm, opening his bicep to the hot air of Hell.

"Stop!" I shouted.

Akta didn't look up. "If this makes you queasy, just go back into the other room and eat."

"No. It's not making me queasy. It's useless. Charlie doesn't care about his own body, do you, Charlie?"

"Of course I do!" he screamed. "Look what she's doing to me!"

"I don't buy it," I replied. "You're screaming, sure, but it's not real, is it? It sounds like a B-movie scream queen, trying to sound scared but failing miserably at it."

Charlie's scream stopped, and his tortured face turned up into a grin. He looked down at his arm without uttering so much as a dull moan. In fact, he seemed to get an odd satisfaction watching Akta's knife cut into his skin. When she noticed him admiring her work, Akta threw up her hands.

"Well, that was fun while it lasted, I guess," Charlie said. The wound on his arm healed instantly. "I suppose you have some other way of getting me to talk?"

"I do," I said, nodding slowly. "I know what you really care about—your kids."

"You only know what I want you to know," Charlie said in a huff. "I don't care about them."

"You're lying, Charlie," I replied. "I saw it in your eyes. You love your children as much as a demon could love anything. So, if you don't tell me what I want to know . . . I'll take your kids and bring them back to Earth with me—"

Charlie laughed. "So what? They're little bastards. Take 'em. Good riddance. Save me from dealing with their horrible mother ever again. You'll be doing me a favor."

"You didn't let me finish, Charlie," I replied. "It's rude to interrupt. As I was saying, I'll take them back to Earth, and when I get there, I'll feed them to Aziolith. He hasn't had a meal in two years, and I'll bet he would love fresh, demon blood."

Charlie gulped loudly. "You wouldn't—you're lying."

"Look into my pretty eyes and tell me if I'm lying. Not only will they die in agony, but I will also laugh as they suffer to their last breath."

Charlie couldn't do it. He couldn't look me in the eyes, and he didn't need to, either. He knew I was telling the truth.

"I will do anything to find that little girl," I continued. "Even if it means becoming a monster like you."

"Fine. I'll help you," Charlie said. "What choice do I have? Shake on it?"

"I don't like this," Akta said. "Something's not right."

I grabbed the dagger from my belt and cut through the rope on Charlie's left hand. "Maybe, but we're running out of time."

"It's too easy," Akta said. "It's never this easy."

"Easy?" I replied. "You call this easy? Why? Just because your way didn't work? This has been a nightmare for me!"

"That's not what I'm saying."

"We don't have time to examine every detail just because it doesn't go like you thought it would go. Sometimes, you gotta trust your gut, and mine is telling me this is the right move."

Akta grabbed my arm. "You're wrong."

"Then I'll suffer the consequences for it," I replied, pulling myself free. "But I'm doing it."

Charlie tapped his foot against the chair. "Do we have a deal or not?"

I looked back once more at Akta, who glared her disapproval, then stuck my hand out for Charlie to grab. "Deal."

"Your friend was right, you know," Charlie said, grabbing my hand tightly. "You shouldn't make deals with imps. We are known to be conniving tricksters."

And with that, Charlie's grin returned, and he snapped the fingers on his other hand, taking me with him as we vanished from Akta's sight.

CHAPTER 14

We reappeared in a derelict warehouse with high windows shining streaks of light into the otherwise darkened building. Charlie yanked me forward before I could fully catch my bearings. The sound of our footsteps bounced off every wall.

"No funny business this time, all right," Charlie growled. "I've had enough of that for one night. I just want to drop you off, pick up my reward, and go to bed."

"And leave me to suffer the consequences, right?" I struggled against him and failed miserably to slow his gait.

"There have to be winners and losers in life, toots, and today, you are the loser. Don't blame yourself, though. It could have been any idiot who decided to fall into Hell. Granted, most people wouldn't come here willingly, but if they did, I would've taken them, too. You are a lot squirmier than most, at least. You should take a little pride in that."

A light blinked on in the far corner of the warehouse, revealing a chain-link fence blocking off the furthest part of the warehouse. Two enormous trolls stood in front of the fence, stoically guarding its entrance.

"Take pride in becoming a sacrifice for the demons of Hell?"

"Who said anything about demons?" Charlie replied, walking past the two trolls as they turned to enclose around me.

"I assume that demons—"

"Most demons like it fine here, just fine. It's the other monsters that want to return to Earth. It's all they talk about—the trees, and the meadows and the, well, I don't think they really understand what Earth has become, truth be told. Man, are they going to be disappointed."

Charlie let go of my hand, and the two trolls grabbed me by the arms and lifted me into the air. Parked in front of me was a unicorn-led cart covered with a wrought-iron metal cage. A one-eyed goblin with broken teeth already sat shackled inside, looking down at his feet and crying. It didn't take a genius to figure out that was my destination.

A small army of goblins, orcs, and trolls loaded up horses with supplies. A large ogre with huge tusks rising from an underbite guided the monsters around from atop a small platform. He held a clipboard and barked orders to his troops. "Hurry up! I'm not paying you to loaf!"

Charlie sauntered over to the large ogre and raised his hand cautiously. "Morticai! Long time no—"

Morticai sighed. "What do you want, Charlie?"

Charlie pointed back toward me. "I brought her, just like I said I would. Ghul will have his prize. Now, it's time to hold up your end of the bargain."

Charlie pulled the Mirror of Yilir out of his belt. Morticai stared at me, then at the mirror, then back at me again. He looked down at his clipboard and jotted down a note.

"Very well," he said, snapping his fingers. "A deal is a deal."

A wraith, just like the one who guarded the gates of Dis—Hell, for all I know it could be the same one— appeared out of nowhere, glowing in the darkness.

"What is it, master?" the wraith screeched.

Morticai gestured to the mirror. "Unlock the true power of this mirror. Make it work even in the pits of Hell."

The wraith moved its hands in concentric circles until a great ball of blue burst forth and electrified the mirror. Once the electricity dimmed, the wraith dropped its arms, and the mirror glowed blue.

"Show me Monica!" Charlie said.

The mirror glowed blue and shone brightly in Charlie's face. He stared inside the hand mirror and smiled, jumping into the air. "Yes! It works! You cocky slut, you'll never get away from me again! Just try to find a new boyfriend now!"

The trolls tossed me in the back of the cart and shackled me to the floor, then slammed the door and locked me in the cage. The metal bracers cut into my arms and legs.

"All right!" Morticai shouted. "Move your asses out! We have a long way to go and a short time to get there!"

"I'll be going then," Charlie said.

"Not so fast," Morticai replied. "You leave when the portal opens."

"That's not part of the deal!"

Morticai grinned. "Deals change. She dies, you leave. It's as simple as that. Unless you want to feel the boss's wrath."

Charlie shook his head viciously. "No, no. I don't want that." He leaped up onto the cart and was soon joined by an ogre who took the leather reins. The ogre snapped the reins, and the unicorn whinnied forward, surrounded by four orcs on horseback.

***

We traveled along a burned desert road until the city of Dis was barely visible behind us, and a gnarled, black Gothic castle loomed ominously over the horizon.

"It's Lucifer's palace," the goblin across from me sniffled through his never-ending tears. His name was Glorbal in the common tongue, and he had been bumming me out since we left Dis, professing the fact that we were going to die on a non-stop loop.

Between him and Charlie, the din of annoying voices never stopped. Charlie hadn't stopped complaining the entire ride, either, feeling like he was being cheated. I took some satisfaction in that, actually.

"How much further?" he asked for the umpteenth time. "I have to torment Monica."

"I know," the ogre driving the cart said. "You have said that a million times. And as I have said in return, we will get there when we get th—"

The ogre was in mid-sentence when the arrow stuck in his neck, and he slumped over. Four orcs turned their horses around and surrounded the cart. After four more perfectly aimed arrows, each of them lay dead on the ground. A figure in a green cape leaped from a rock formation onto our cage. Throwing back her hood, Akta stood gloriously atop of us. She pulled out another arrow and aimed it at Charlie.

"Where is the key to the cage?" she growled at him.

"I dunno!" Charlie said, throwing up his hands. "Seriously! I dunno!"

"Search the driver's pockets. If you snap yourself away, I will find you and take you to the edge of death over and over again until you wish that you had never been born."

Charlie reached over and rummaged through the pockets of the ogre. He pulled out a rusted key. "Here. Here ya go!"

"Open the cart. Don't make any sudden movements."

Charlie jumped off the cart and walked around to the cage in the back. "Look, there's no hard feelings. I just had to do what I had to do, don't you know? We all gotta do that."

"No words," Akta replied, fitting her bow with another arrow. "Open it up."

Akta followed Charlie as he climbed up the cage and opened the lock. "Seriously, Julia. No hard feelings."

I slammed open the cart into Charlie's face, and he fell onto the hot, desert floor. I wanted to beat him senseless, but he had something valuable, and I knew that taking it would hurt him more than anything else. I reached into his pocket and pulled out the mirror. "I'm taking this as payment for my life. Now, leave, and never come back. If I see you again, I will kill you."

Charlie wanted to protest, but all he could do was snap his fingers and vanish, like the sniveling coward that he was.

"Why did you let him go?" Akta asked as I helped Glorbal down from the cage.

"Because he couldn't help us anymore. He didn't know anything." I turned to Glorbal. "You are free to go. Live a good life."

"Thank you," Glorbal said, wiping a tear from his eye. "I will try." The little monster ran off into the horizon without looking back.

"How did you know where I was?" I asked.

"Please," Akta replied. She leaped off the cage onto the ground, stowing her bow against her back and straightening her cape.

"The scent of adult human is overwhelming, even when you mask it with the sewers of Dis. If the child were slightly older, she would stink enough for me to track her too, but her scent is too mild to make an impact on my senses. I have been tracking you for several hours, waiting for the caravan to stop. When I realized it wouldn't until it reached its destination, I took action."

"Thank you for saving me."

"Don't thank me. We are still no closer to rescuing your friend."

I looked down at the mirror. "Yes, we are." I took a deep breath. "Show me Imogen."

The mirror glowed blue and swirled around. When the mirror stopped, it showed me Kimberly, alive and crying, as Imogen pulled her forward toward a set of black gates with a red, bejeweled eye in the center, shining down at them.

"Do you know this place?" I asked, pointing the mirror to Akta.

"I do," Akta replied with a nod. "Come. I know a shortcut. It will not be easy, but if we hurry, we can catch them."

Akta jumped onto the cart and took the reins. I followed her, giddy. I didn't know where we were going, but for the first time, I knew I was on the right path to save Kimberly and leave this accursed place.

CHAPTER 15

Akta didn't talk much as she guided the unicorn and our cart down the dirt road that curved along a serrated mountainside. Its sheer cliffs rose into the tips of Hell's cavern. I wanted to ask her many questions, but every time I looked over at her, she was staring at the horizon in front of us, focused and silent.

On the other side of us, a molten lake of lava cascaded into the distance. Alongside the road, demons shoveled souls into heaps high enough to rival the size of the mountains. They didn't take much notice of us, but the damned souls screamed out for us to grant them solace. Their outstretched arms grasped at our cart as we passed.

It was weird to think that one day, before long, it would be me in those piles. I hoped it was a long while, but with every damned monster in Hell trying to kill me, I doubted I would live long.

I turned away from the heaps of souls and again stared at Akta's face as she forced the unicorn into a trot. She wasn't old when she died, and even thousands of years in Hell couldn't age the smooth skin that only came with youth.

"Stop staring at me," Akta finally said. I don't know how long I studied her, but it was clearly a while.

"I'm sorry," I replied.

"If you have a question, ask it. I can't tolerate indecisiveness."

"How—old were you when you died?"

"Twenty-six. Why?"

I looked out over the piles of human souls, scared to ask the next question but needing to know the answer. "Why didn't you end up in those piles with the other souls—"

"Because I'm not a human," she replied.

"You look a lot like a human."

"True, but I am not one, and thus I am not judged like one."

"That doesn't sound so bad. I mean, the worst that happens to you is you have to live out your life here without being tortured."

"And yet, this feels like torture. I choose not to bother myself with such thoughts, though. I have accepted my lot, and there is no hope I might better it."

"Then why are you helping me? If there is no hope, why even try?"

"There is no hope left for me, Julia. There is still hope for you, and as long as there is, I will help you because we are kin."

That answer didn't satisfy me, but I could hear the curtness in her voice sharpened with each answer, so I decided to shelve my curiosity and change the topic.

"Where are we going?" I asked as the road turned closer to the molten lake of fire.

"The Gate of Ulthar, the one we saw in the Mirror of Yilir. It guards Lucifer's castle. It is the only way through to the lake of fire which surrounds his castle."

"You mean that lake?" I asked, pointing to the lava in front of us.

"Yes, but only one being can navigate the lava safely, and he lies beyond the gate."

"How do we get to it?"

"We must climb up the mountain. It's a few thousand feet, and the way is treacherous, but I am taking us to the easiest section of the rock face. Once we reach the top, we will be judged by the black gate. Bound inside is the soul of Ulthar, who guards this pass. If we are found wanting, Cerberus will rip us to shreds."

With that, Akta fell silent and returned her attention to driving the cart toward its destination.

***

A full hour passed before Akta stopped the cart along the sheer cliffs. They now surrounded us on two sides.

"Come on," she said, hopping out of the cart. "Time is wasting."

She latched on to the rock face and hoisted herself up. Two blue wings emerged from her back and fluttered behind her. She was nimble and quick on the rocks like a mountain goat. I, on the other hand, couldn't go so fast. I wasn't sure I could go at all. My hands weren't very strong, and I didn't have a lot of stamina left in the heat of Hell.

"I dunno about this," I shouted up to her.

"For the gods' sake, just open your wings, latch on, and climb!"

I closed my eyes and imagined my wings popping out of me as I had a thousand times before I entered Hell. However, no matter how hard I tried, my wings would not come. "I can't do it!"

"You can try to find another way into the castle if you want," Akta shouted down at me. "But you'll never catch Imogen going any other way!"

"Is there another way, though?"

"You have to backtrack twenty miles and start on the path from the base. It'll take you three days, and you'll face a dozen guards, at least! Or you can quit being a child and start climbing now!"

Akta's wings fluttered again, and she kept climbing. I wanted to follow her, but without my wings, I feared falling from a great height and breaking my neck. Nothing Akta said eased that fear.

I would have to find another way that didn't involve wasting three days of backtracking. It wouldn't be easy. The only egress from the rocks led to the molten river— unless I wanted to go back the way I came.

I unlatched the unicorn from its cart and pet its glittering mane. "You know, meeting a unicorn was a dream of mine when I was a kid. If that girl could see me now and what I had to do to find you, I wonder if she would have thought it was worth it."

I pressed my head against the base of the unicorn's horn and closed my eyes. The soft touch of the mane eased my restless mind, and the cool of the unicorn's horn on my forehead soothed me, cooling my skin. I didn't know what to do. I couldn't climb. I couldn't ford a molten lake. I just wanted to be in front of that gate when Akta reached the top, but I couldn't—

A cold breeze washed over me, and I couldn't feel the unicorn anymore. My hands that had wrapped around the unicorn's mane now grasped at the air. The coolness of its horn was gone from my brow. When I opened my eyes, I looked down from the cliff's summit a thousand feet in the air. The cliff's face descended below me, and Hell stretched for miles around in every direction. Behind me, a pack of dogs echoed in my ear.

I turned around, and a snarling, three-headed dog forty feet high snapped at me from a dozen feet away, snapping its chain with each lunge. I jumped back until I was at the edge of the cliff. The dog jumped at me again, but a metal chain yanked it backward. I was just far enough away to escape its wrath—for now.

Behind the snarling dog, a black gate rose into the sky. A giant, red jewel adorned the middle of its obsidian face, scanning the horizon like the great eye of Sauron.

I made it. I couldn't believe it, but I was at the summit of the cliff . . . but how? All I did was pet that unicorn and touch its horn—and then it hit me. Unicorn magic must still work in Hell. I filed that knowledge in the back of my brain, hoping I would never need it again.

Below me, Akta climbed the rock face at an incredible speed, using her wings as leverage to ascend faster with each leap. I watched her reach the top of the cliff and rise into the air, then smiled at her as she landed on the ground.

"It's about time you got here," I said.

"How did you—" Akta replied, confused.

"I prayed to a unicorn."

She paused for a moment, considering this, then shrugged. "Somehow, that makes sense to me. Well, let's go then, Ulthar doesn't have all day."

"Do we have to do that? Can't we just, I don't know, fly over it or around it? I mean, you can easily just fly around this place."

While at the base of the great cliff, the path surrounded every entrance to Satan's palace. At the top of the cliff, there was room on either side to fly around the gate. It was a pretty piss poor design, at the heart of it.

"Do you think the Devil is that stupid?" Akta asked.

"I don't know anything about the Devil, honestly. I guess he could be that stupid, though."

"The great eye watches everything. It can rise and stretch to infinity to defeat any foe. Fifty legions of angelic guards once tried to attack Satan's palace and were stopped cold by the Gate of Ulthar, incinerated and eviscerated in an instant as if they were children. The only way through the gate is if it allows you to pass."

Cerberus howled at Akta as she walked toward the gate. The pixie held up her hands and took out her weapons, lying them on the ground as an offering to the great dog. "You too, Julia. Get rid of all your weapons."

I walked forward slowly. The dog's great heads growled at me as I laid my daggers down on the ground. I pulled out the knife from inside my boot and put it on the ground as well. The dog took a great sniff into the air and ducked its heads, retreating into a nook on the side of the great gate.

Akta kept her hands high as she walked toward the gate. "Cerberus can smell any aggression before you strike. Make no sudden moves."

I followed behind her, painfully aware of Cerberus's three heads tracking my every movement. I kept my hands held high. When we got close enough, the glowing, red jewel took notice of us and turned its gaze toward us. The red beam emanating from it widened until we were both doused in its glow. It focused on us for several long moments until it finally went dark.

"What now?" I asked.

"Now it decides if we are worthy to continue or if we will be destroyed."

"Fun."

The gate moaned and creaked from the hinges, and for a second, there was silence. Then, the gates swung violently toward us. I was certain we'd be dead in an instant. I closed my eyes and tried not to picture myself as a sniveling soul in a mountainous pile of other souls, but heard the gate stop on its hinges before it reached us. With one eye open, I saw it swing the other way. The red eye lit the way for us toward the fire lake that surrounded Satan's castle.

CHAPTER 16

"Why can't I sprout wings?" I asked Akta on our way down the path toward the lake of fire. "I was able to do it last time I was in Hell, and that was just a couple of years ago."

"Perhaps it is because you still have a body, or because you have the soul of a human, or because Hell works in mysterious ways. I've been here for thousands of years, and I barely understand it most of the time."

"So, your answer is that Hell is weird?" I thought about it for a second. "I can buy that."

"Perhaps Lucifer has the answer, though I doubt it."

"Why not?"

"Lucifer is an outsider here as well. He isn't even a god."

"And gods are usually the rulers of Hell?"

"Yes. First, it was Anubis, who tricked Hades into taking over for him, then Hades tricked Velaska into taking over for him, and Velaska—desperate to leave Earth since the other gods had already left eons ago—she tricked Lucifer, a mere angel, to take her place."

"Velaska? I've never heard of her."

"Be glad. She was not the best god the Underworld ever had. Most demons and scholars write off her reign, choosing to move from Hades to Lucifer. Good riddance."

The venom entwined with Akta's words sounded personal. "Was she the god when you—when this happened to you?"

"When I was cursed, yes. I am here because Velaska wished it so, and Lucifer is incapable of changing the will of a god, no matter how powerful he might seem to humans. Truly, in the eyes of the cosmos, he is insignificant."

It was hard to believe that Lucifer was insignificant when his castle took up half of my line of vision. It was huge, a mountain of black rock twisting into the sky. A skull of black onyx stared out into the lake, its mouth made of a great black door that snuffed out all the light around it.

"This castle is at the furthest edge of Hell," Akta said, sliding down a hill toward a dock in front of us. "With nothing at its back, it is the perfect defensive position. It can resist attacks from the gods themselves for a thousand years before it crumbles."

"That doesn't seem very insignificant," I said to Akta as we neared the obsidian dock. "It feels pretty damn significant to me."

"It is one of the true seats of power on Earth. However, just because Lucifer sits on its throne does not make him powerful. He did not create the castle, Anubis did. The Devil is insignificant compared to the office. He is but a cockroach sitting on an abandoned throne after everything else more powerful than him has gone. If you found a dog sitting on the throne of the queen of England once the humans died off, would you bow to it?"

"Well, the queen doesn't have much power anymore, but yes, I see your point. The dog didn't construct Westminster Abbey."

"Precisely."

We had finally arrived on the dock. Mist rose from the lake, obscuring the castle behind it. Akta took a seat on the ground, but I refused to sit.

"What are we waiting for?" I asked.

"The ferryman, Charon, who will guide us along the lake."

"Why don't we just fly across? You've carried me before."

"It is not the way that it is done."

"Who cares if that's not the way it is done?" I said, pulling out the mirror from my back pocket. "Imogen is almost at the castle!"

"You do not have to live here after you are gone. I do. Life here is hard enough without being held in Lucifer's contempt."

"Whatever," I said, turning my attention to the mirror. "Show me Imogen."

The mirror glowed blue and swirled like a whirlpool. When it stopped, I saw Imogen climbing the great steps to Lucifer's castle, holding Kimberly in her arms.

"Look!" I shouted. "Imogen is at Lucifer's castle. We cannot wait another second or stand on ceremony, no matter how uncomfortable you might be later!"

"It won't be long now," Akta replied with a calm smile.

A long, black gondola floated out of the mist, ferried by what can only be described as a black cloak. There seemed to be nothing under it, except for two haunting orange eyes that glowed through the blackness under its hood. The cloak pushed its gondola through the molten liquid with a large oar.

"This is Charon. Pay him much deference. He holds your fate in his hands." Akta turned to the ferryman. "What ho, good Charon?"

The voice that oozed out of the cloak was caustic and low. "State your business, pixie."

"Must you be so cold," Akta replied. "We were friends once."

"That was some time ago. Now, I repeat. State your business, pixie."

"We have business with Lucifer."

"Did he request your presence?" Charon croaked. "He has not told me as much."

"He does not. However, I must see him. I have been a friend to him in the past and come with news in this great hour."

Akta snapped her fingers and pointed to the ground, indicating that I should come forward. When I hesitated, she gestured with her hand again and again until I was by her side. She cast an impatient glare and clucked her tongue at me.

"And who is this?" Charon asked.

"This is my . . . ancestor. She bears news for your master."

"I smell life on her. No body may pass."

"Pardon, sir," I said. "I mean no disrespect, but you just allowed a body to pass, not long ago, in fact." I held up the mirror, which showed Imogen ascending the great stairs with Kimberly under her arms. "That little girl is also alive."

"Is that—? The mirror Yilir . . . my love," Charon croaked, audibly upset.

"It is," I replied.

"But how—how did you come by it? How does it work when all magic fails in Hell? It still retains its power?"

"It was unlocked by a great witch in the bowels of Dis."

"And it is our gift to you, my friend," Akta added. "If you should see it fit to bring us to Lucifer, from an old friend to an old friend."

"This would be a gift unlike any other," Charon replied.

"Yes, I know Hades forbade you from leaving this lake for all eternity, which means you will never meet with Yilir, your love, again…but with this, you can be with her any time you choose."

Charon groaned for a moment, then let out a howl. "Very well, for the price of this mirror, I will ferry you across the lake of fire."

Akta looked at me and then at Charon. "Then it is an accord."

I didn't agree to give him my mirror, but it didn't seem I had a choice. I took a step forward, bowed my head, and presented it to him. His bony fingers reached out from the cloak and clasped the mirror tightly before they disappeared again.

"Please," Charon said. "Enter."

Akta and I stepped onto the boat. We sat down across from each other at the front of the boat as Charon pushed off from the dock and started across the lake.

***

Charon's gondola slid across the lava at a glacial pace. He was in no hurry, and Akta showed no reason to rush, but that didn't stop my anxious energy. I tapped my foot and bit my nails.

"You realize that by the time we get to Lucifer, he might have already split the child open and used her to exact his revenge on the world."

"I realize that," Akta conceded. "But I don't think it's likely."

"Why not?"

"Have you ever met the prince of darkness?" Akta asked, in the smug way somebody only uses if they know the answer to the question.

"You know I haven't."

"Well, I have, a couple of times, and I know the inner workings of Hell. If Lucifer were to accept Imogen's gift, he would need to gather an army before any attack. He wouldn't just willy-nilly open the gates to Hell. This isn't some stupid cult or even a banshee we're talking about. Lucifer is smarter than that."

"How do you know that?"

"The one thing we all have down here is plenty of time to think about what we've done and how to go about fixing it."

"And how would you fix what you've done?"

"Well, I certainly wouldn't have bargained my soul away to the Devil, that's for sure."

"You say that word, Devil, but doesn't that mean Lucifer?"

Akta shook her head. "No. The devil is a title, like king or czar. Whoever rules Hell is thus a devil, just like whoever rules a country is called a king. It's semantics, really, but people cling to their titles. That much hasn't changed in the millennia since I've been here."

"What has changed?" I asked.

"Not enough," Akta replied, pointing to the shore. "We'll be there any second."

***

Charon let us off the boat and departed back into the abyss. Before he faded back into the mist, a bright blue spark emanated from the boat. He must have called out to see his love. I hoped he liked what he saw.

I turned toward the steps in front of Lucifer's palace. There were hundreds, and Akta was already busy climbing them, leaping from step to step with her wings carrying her along. I didn't have such powers, so all I could do was climb the stairs, one gigantic step at a time. By the time I reached the top of the stairs, my thighs burned in agony. I wanted water, vodka, or anything to help ease the fire that burned in every muscle from the climb.

"When we get inside…you might not like what you see," Akta said. "I don't know what condition we will find the child. I'm warning you now, so you may make peace with it."

"I've been in Hell for over a day," I replied, hunched over and gasping for breath. "I think I can handle it."

"Suit yourself," Akta replied. "I hope you are as strong as you think you are."

"Me too."

I rose as straight as my weary body could muster. Only the knowledge that my quest was almost over kept me upright. A tall door covered in black bones towered over me. I pushed hard against it and prepared myself to face my destiny.

CHAPTER 17

Our footsteps echoed against the walls of the castle as we walked through the large door and into the foyer, which was lined on either side with full suits of armor made from blackened bones. The theme of black bones continued from the door, along the walls, and up into the rafters, which funneled into an arch far above us. The ceilings were painted with dancing skeletons and ghoulish monsters with demonic smiles. Candles along the walls accented the bones and mixed with gothic paintings of dead bodies.

Akta moved toward one of the knights and pulled a sword from its hands. I walked toward another and pulled down a spear.

"We'll need these to kill Imogen," Akta said. "The black weapons of Hell's army can destroy almost any monster, except the Devil, or a god."

"What was the point of leaving our weapons at the gate if we could just get more here?"

"Few weapons can hurt a devil, and these are assuredly unable to hurt him, while ours might not be. Besides, there used to be hundreds of demons inside these walls to guard Lucifer. However, they abandoned this castle some time ago."

"Why?"

"For reasons," Akta replied curtly.

"So, what, this castle is just—"

"I'm not a tour guide. Stop asking me questions and stay on your toes."

I shut my mouth and gripped the spear with both hands. The obsidian blade blended into the darkness, but I saw it glisten against the flickering candlelight.

"Up ahead is the throne room," Akta said. "That is where we should find Lucifer, especially if he is still entreating with the banshee."

"And if they are done entreating?"

"Lucifer likes to pontificate. They will not be done, especially if she just entered the castle when we set out with Charon across the molten lake."

As we neared the throne room, the sound of two people bickering grew louder and louder. A shrill, high-pitched voice argued with a deep, low one. I could hear the low voice grumble while the shrieking voice continued.

The hallway gave way to Lucifer's throne room, where torches illuminated the entirety of the room. It burned my retinas after the long corridor of near darkness. When my eyes focused again, I saw the banshee flailing her arms in front of the throne.

"Imogen!" I growled.

"And Lucifer," Akta added.

Unaware of our presence, Imogen continued her argument with the pot-bellied demon sitting atop a throne of yellowed bones. I expected Lucifer to be in a regal cape, dapper and dangerous in his kingliness, but instead, he wore a stained wife-beater and nothing else. Not even pants. His yellow eyes glowed brightly as he rested his chin on his taloned hands and stroked his thin beard.

"King of Darkness," Imogen squawked. "Lord of the Underworld, I have traveled far to bring you an offering so that you might retake Earth from our enemies and reclaim Heaven for your glory, and you deny me! How could you turn away such a gift, which I bring you to smite your enemies?"

Imogen pointed to the corner, where Kimberly rocked back and forth, crying. I wanted to rush toward her, but Akta pulled me back.

"We currently have the element of surprise," Akta whispered. "Best not to spoil it."

She was right. We inched toward Imogen. I gripped my spear tightly as the banshee frantically pleaded with the Prince of Darkness.

"Take up your birthright!" Imogen screeched. "Overthrow Bacchus!"

"That sounds like a lot of work," Lucifer replied with a sigh.

"My king, my love, it is your birthright to sit atop Bacchus's throne and rule the Heavens."

Lucifer groaned. "Yes, you've said that before, but I just don't agree with you. Technically, my birthright was to sit at Bacchus's right hand and do his bidding. Hell was my punishment, as was being turned into a hideous demon. So, I'm good for now."

"My king would never be so lazy!" Imogen shouted. "Perhaps you do not deserve such a gift!"

"This line of inquiry bores me," Lucifer said as his eyes rose from the ground to spot us. "Oh, look, more visitors."

Imogen whirled. "Spies! Sent to kill you, my lord! I will make short work of them."

Lucifer snapped his fingers, and the banshee exploded into a thousand pieces in front of us. Her viscera and blood exploded in every direction, ending up on the walls, the floor, and on Lucifer himself, but he didn't seem to mind one more stain on his shirt.

"Let's not do that," Lucifer replied. "She was annoying. I hope you bring more interesting tidings, Akta of the forest."

"I hope so, Lucifer. We come to entreat with you," Akta said, stowing her weapon.

Lucifer rolled his eyes and shifted on his throne. "There seems to be a lot of that going around today."

I gripped the spear tightly and moved forward. "We come for Kimberly. Give her to us, or we will have no choice but to destroy you."

The huge demon stayed quiet for a moment, staring at me, and then he burst out laughing. "My dear, do you know that only five weapons in all the solar system can defeat me? And a dull spear isn't one of them."

Akta nodded at me and dropped her sword. "It's true. I brought this weapon to fight Imogen, and now she's done for, which makes them useless."

"I do appreciate spunk, though," Lucifer said. He was still chuckling. "Come forward, drop the spear, and let's talk like two civilized beings."

"How do I know you aren't lying to me?" I said. "You are the prince of all lies, after all."

"That is a harsh nickname. I prefer Old Scratch. Reminds me of a loyal dog instead of some hideous beast out to destroy humanity. If I wanted you dead, you would be dead. Did you not see what I'm capable of just a few seconds ago? I thought it was very impressive, personally. I made it a show of power for you to see. I prefer imploding people to exploding them. Much less messy."

"Just put it down," Akta said, gesturing toward the spear.

I tossed down the spear and walked forward with her. "I come—"

"I know. You come for the girl. You mentioned it before."

"She needs to be returned to her family."

"Oh, I agree. I wouldn't dream of flaying a young girl to open the gates of Hell to Earth. I mean, monsters roaming Earth? Ugh, who wants that? Earth is abysmal already. Add some pissed-off monsters, and it could turn real ugly real fast."

I frowned. "You can't possibly prefer it down here."

"To Earth, and humanity? God yes. I liked Heaven, but Bacchus turned it into such a dull place. Still, it would have been nice if he didn't abandon me without a word. We're supposed to be working in tandem here, and he hasn't talked to me in years. Thousands of them! It's very annoying."

"Maybe because you tried to overthrow him," I said to him.

Lucifer held up his hands. "That was a misunderstanding…taken way out of context. It's easy to think I was in the wrong when the winner writes the narrative, but what you read and what you hear is not always the true account."

"What is the true account?" I said.

"Maybe another day," Akta said. "Let's finish the task at hand. This is no time for a history lesson."

"I'm a history teacher. Trust me, there's always time for a history lesson," I replied. "But I take your point. May I take the girl, then?"

Lucifer nodded. "Yes. And I will return you to the portal from whence you came."

"That was . . . easy," I said.

"Was it? It seems to me you had quite the difficult time down here. The least I can do as a gracious host is make this part easy."

"Thank you." I walked toward the child, half-expecting him to change his mind.

"And I know what you want, pixie," Lucifer said, his eye on Akta. "Alas, I cannot give you peace or rest. That curse was given to you by Velaska, and she alone can break it."

"And she will not."

"Even should she walk through the gates right now, I doubt it. She was cold and vindictive, and you made a fool of her."

"It was worth it."

I knelt in front of Kimberly. "Hey."

The poor little girl didn't look up; she was crying too hard. I reached forward to wipe away her tears, and she jumped back with a scream.

"Hey, it's okay. I'm going to take you home."

"H-h-h-home?" she stuttered.

I nodded with a big smile. "Yes, I'm going to take you home now. Would you like that?"

She nodded furiously as she took my hand, squeezing harder with each step we took toward Lucifer.

"Don't be scared, okay?"

Kimberly took a big, deep breath and another big step forward. Before long, we were standing in front of Lucifer, next to Akta.

"Are you ready?" Lucifer said.

"I have one more question," I said.

"About someone you lost recently."

I nodded. "My mother. Is she here?"

Lucifer sighed. "I cannot tell you that."

"Is she at peace?"

"I'm afraid you are out of questions, pixie." Lucifer averted his eyes. "Now, it is time. Before you go, please feel free to take any weapons you find lying around. I want to replace the ones taken from you. The Gate of Ulthar is just…a dreadful relic from a bygone era…and I know how hard it is to find good weapons."

I had so many questions, but I didn't want to incur the wrath of the Devil, so I shut up. His answers didn't give me comfort, but they didn't take any away, either. I would have to live in the ambiguity for the rest of my days until I saw my mother again in the afterlife.

I bent down and pulled an obsidian dagger out of an orc's skull and stuck it into my belt. It was longer and wider than my others, but it had a good weight to it.

"That's a nice piece," Lucifer said. "Good eye."

"Thanks," I said, grabbing onto Akta's hand. In my other, I held Kimberly tight. "Don't let go, okay?"

Kimberly nodded. "I won't."

"Me either," Akta added.

With a snap of his fingers, Lucifer sent us away.

CHAPTER 18

We reappeared underneath the portal that would return us to Earth. It swirled above us like a blood-red whirlpool, dozens of feet in the air. I held Kimberly's hand as tightly as Akta held mine. I let go of both and turned to Akta with a big smile.

"Thank you for everything," I said, wrapping my arms around her neck.

She was clearly uncomfortable, but I didn't care. I was so grateful to her, and the only way I could express my gratitude was by giving her a hug. "One day, I will get you out of Hell. I swear it."

Akta pushed me away from her. "Don't make such promises. Grab the child. I will fly you as close as I can to the portal before the weight of Velaska's curse pulls me back to Hell."

I lifted Kimberly into my arms and wrapped her tightly around my chest. Akta grabbed me around the shoulders and flapped her wings hard until we ascended into the air. She struggled with our weight, but she managed to lift us toward the portal.

"This is it!" Akta shouted when I could almost reach out and touch the whirlpool.

She flung us into the air with all of her might, and the pull of the portal's gravity sucked us inside. I threw one last look at Akta, watching her descend back down to Hell as if an invisible hand tugged on her. If I didn't know her better, I would have sworn I saw a tear escape her eye.

The portal pulled us through its red goop toward Earth, and my thoughts drifted toward Aziolith for the first time since I left Earth. He was locked in battle with a gigantic monster when I left him, and the great monster might have killed him, for all I knew.

A surge of guilt mixed with my relief. I was so caught up in my own battle that I never thought about him, not for even a second, since I entered Hell. He risked his life for mine, and I could not even take a moment to spare a thought for him. I had never felt more shame.

***

The portal spat us out above the haunted forest in Romania. We were several stories above the forest floor, just like the portal had been when I left for Hell—except that when I left for Hell, my wings worked. If they didn't work now, we were in for a nasty fall into the haunted forest.

Luckily, when I squeezed my shoulder blades tight and focused on pushing the wings out of my back, they protruded just as they had done a thousand times. With my wings fluttering as they should, we floated down from the portal and onto the ground with ease.

I expected to see at least one dead monster's body, maybe more, based on the viciousness of the fight when I left, but instead, I heard laughing, gregarious laughing. I walked toward it, hand-in-hand with Kimberly, hearing Aziolith's voice grow louder.

"And then, after I destroyed seven garrisons with just one breath, they sent another garrison at me, as if that would do anything! I burned them all in two minutes flat."

"Humans," another low, gruff voice growled.

Coming around to the other side of the portal, I saw the great dragon Aziolith, twenty feet high if he was an inch, sipping tea with a shaggy wolf of the same size. It held a large bone with one onyx paw, a pipe in the other.

"What the hell is going on here?" I asked, walking forward.

Kimberly pulled me back. She shook her head in fear. "No, I'm scared."

"There's nothing to be scared of, my love," I replied, cupping her face in my hand. "That dragon is my friend."

"You're friends with a dragon?" Kimberly said. There was wonder in her eyes.

"That's right. Pretty cool, right?"

The young girl smiled. "Pretty really cool!"

Watching Kimberly smile, a feeling of contentment overcame me. I wasn't sure how I would find meaning in my life again after Mama died. I'd had so much fun and learned so much traveling the world with her, but my life, for the last few years at least, lacked meaning. There was fun—a lot of fun—but there was no meaning. Helping Kimberly reminded me that a life without meaning is wasted.

"I wouldn't say we are friends necessarily," Aziolith said.

"Well, can you really ever be friends with a human?" The great wolf looked us over with a bored expression.

"I don't want to eat you, though, and I don't want to burn you to a crisp. Is that friendship?" Aziolith pondered out loud, taking a sip of tea.

The hairs on the back of my neck stood up as I watched Kimberly tense up in fear. She held her breath and her hand shook nervously in mine. I instinctively felt the need to protect her.

"There is a little girl here," I replied, feeling Kimberly's hand tighten around mine. "And she's already scared."

"Of course, and me without my manners," Aziolith replied, gesturing to the wolf. "This is Harold. Humans have been hunting him for ages, thinking him a monster, but he's truly the dearest creature."

I rolled my eyes. "And you've made friends with this creature?"

"My name is Harold," the wolf said, indignant. "Humans."

"I'm sorry," I replied. "You've made friends with this . . . Harold?"

"Well, we both spent time in Hell and are constantly beset with humans trying to kill us. So, yeah, we bonded a little bit."

I'd heard enough of their ridiculousness. I lifted Kimberly onto my shoulders. "Have any monsters come through the portal?"

Aziolith shook his head. "No. It's been a rather pleasant...how long has it been?"

Harold squinted, considering. "About a week, give or take."

"A week? I couldn't have been gone more than a day!"

"Yes," Harold said. "That happens. Time moves differently in Hell than up here. I wonder why."
Aziolith shrugged. "More time to torture people, I would guess."

"Yes, that makes sense," Harold said. "I wonder if it has something to do with its proximity to the earth's core and gravity or something."

"Does it matter, though, in the end?" Aziolith asked.

"Does anything?" Harold replied, chuckling.

"All right, while you two are blathering on, I'm going to close this portal now. Then, we can go, yes?"

Aziolith finished his tea and stood on his clawed feet. "I suppose so, yes. It has been a lovely visit, but I should be getting home."

Harold waved. "Come back any time!"

I walked toward the mystery spot and pulled out the obsidian knife I'd taken from Lucifer's castle. I knelt down and looked Kimberly in the eye. "This will only hurt for a moment, okay?"

The little girl nodded. I pulled her finger over the great portal and pricked it with the tip of my knife. Kimberly winced and dug her head into the nape of my neck. The blood drizzled down into the hole, but nothing happened. I drizzled a little bit more blood into the hole, but still, there was nothing.

"What . . . why is nothing happening?" I asked.

"Oh, silly me," Harold said. "I had forgotten how you went into Hell. You must think the little girl opened the portal, but it's been open for ages. I'm afraid I was the reason the portal was opened."

"It's been open for ages?"

"Yes, yes," Aziolith said. "That must be why Imogen came here. She couldn't open a new portal without alerting the demons, but she could go through an already open one."

"Of course!" Harold exclaimed. "I fear I may be the cause of all this trouble. Oh, bother."

He walked over to the mystery spot and bit down on his paw with his fangs. "A druid opened it some thousand or so years ago and pulled me through, so I ate him. I always thought I would go back, but...I doubt it now."

"Why wouldn't any other demons come out in all this time?"

"Well, they have, you see," Harold said. "But they get lost in the woods. I suppose over time, demons just gave up returning to Hell, or maybe they liked it here. It's very nice."

He dribbled his blue blood into the hole, and the ground quaked. With a thunderous roar, the portal creaked and shook and then imploded upon itself. In a moment, the portal was gone, leaving nothing but the dark forest around it.

"Thank you," I said to Harold.

"It was really no trouble. I should have closed it ages ago, but well, years went by, and I stopped caring, and then I plumb forgot."

I ripped off a piece of my shirt and tied it around Kimberly's fingers. "I'm sorry. All better now?"

Kimberly nodded. "Can we go home now?"

I didn't want to let go of Kimberly's hand, but I knew she had to go home. Life would not be easy for her in the future. Monsters knew she was special, and they would try to use her for their ends.

Then, it dawned on me—what Elka had tried to show me all those years ago. The world was hard for fairy folk. We were beset on all sides with challenges and obstacles, and there was nobody to look out for us. That wasn't okay. We needed a protector…I needed to be our protector.

It started with Kimberly. I wouldn't let Kimberly become a victim. I wouldn't let anyone become a victim, not ever again—not as long as I could help it. I hopped onto Aziolith's wing and climbed up onto his back, then held my hand out to Kimberly. "Hey," I said to her, "did you know you could fly?"

"No," Kimberly said as we climbed into the air. "I can do that?"

"You can do a lot more than that. How would you like me to teach you?"

"Can I take a nap first?"

I laughed. "Of course."

"Then I would like that very much. Once I get home."

It was nice that my life had purpose now. I would train Kimberly to be a pixie and take up Elka's mantle defending the rest of my people as best I could. That was a destiny I could live with for as long as I could stay alive.

BOOK 3

"Last Stand"

PROLOGUE

"Legnoe Lashufaka Timlir Itakla!" Bruce chanted from the altar. "Legnoe Lashufaka Timlir Itakla!"

"This is stupid!" Mark shouted from the termite-infested pews. "We've been doing this, dressed in these stupid robes, for an hour!"

It was Bruce's idea to come to this rotting, abandoned church and summon a demon dog from Hell to do our bidding. I thought it was a pretty stupid idea, and Mark thought it was a very stupid idea, but Bruce can be very persuasive. He even got us to dress in dark burgundy robes, so we looked like a real cult.

"And you're okay with Allen Templeton stuffing you in lockers until we're seniors?" he asked me when he told us about his plan. "Is that how you want the next four years of high school to be?"

I didn't, and neither did Mark, so we agreed to come, mostly because we were confident it wouldn't work, but also because, well, let's face it, there wasn't a lot else to do in Stubbins, Colorado on a Friday night.

"Come over here and help me," Bruce said, holding his hands in the air above him. "It's not working because we're not all doing it together."

"Piss off, Bruce." Mark slumped down in the church's vestibule where the carpeting was overrun with moss and twigs. "This was your thing, not mine."

"It's never gonna work if you don't help," Bruce said.

"I'm not really sure I want it to work," I replied, walking up the creaky steps to the altar. "I mean, did we really think this through? What happens if we do bring this dog back from the dead?"

"First of all, it's not back from the dead," Bruce said. "This is a demon born in Hell. It's never been on Earth before, and the book says that—"

"Of course, that's what the book says." Mark stood up, brushing leaves from his robe. "Where did you get this thing, anyway?"

"I . . . found it. Look, I don't have to tell you anything. If you don't wanna help, just go!"

"Oh no," Mark said, stomping up the stairs. "I'm not gonna let you get all pouty and hang this over my head forever. When this stupid spell doesn't work, I'm not gonna be the reason."

"Stand on one of the points of the pentagram and chant with me then," Bruce said, pointing to the floor where I'd used pig's blood to draw a pentagram within a circle.

"Tell me again, why pig's blood?" I asked, shuffling my feet along the circle's edge. I lined myself up with a point of the pentagram.

"Because that's what the book said." Bruce shrugged. "Most of these demons need pixie blood or demon blood or something crazy hard to find. This is a nice, simple spell that just needed pig's blood."

I laughed. "Pixie blood, like we're in Dungeons and Dragons."

Bruce smiled at me. "That's right, Greg. Just like that."

I liked Dungeons and Dragons, but not enough to obsess over it like Bruce did. He couldn't wait to turn sixteen, buy a car, and drive to Gary Gygax's house and

TSR Hobbies. I thought it was a stupid dream, but at least he had a dream.

"Grab hands," Bruce said, holding his palms up.

"Gay," Mark said.

"Don't be weird, Mark," I said, grabbing Mark's hand and taking Bruce's in the other.

"Now chant," Bruce said. "Legnoe Lashufaka Timlir Itakla!"

I added to the chorus. "Legnoe Lashufaka Timlir Itakla!"

"*Legnoe Lashufaka Timlir Itakla*!" Mark joined in after a long sigh.

After a couple of seconds of nothing happening, Mark tried to pull away. "See, I told you this was stupid."

Bruce held on tight. "Just a couple more seconds!"

"Fine!"

"Legnoe Lashufaka Timlir Itakla! Legnoe Lashufaka Timlir Itakla! Legnoe Lashufaka Timlir Itakla!"

The ground under us quaked, and a dim, red light emanated from inside the summoning circle. The more we chanted, the brighter the light grew.

"It's working! It's working!" Bruce shouted. "Don't stop!"

"Legnoe Lashufaka Timlir Itakla! Legnoe Lashufaka Timlir Itakla! Legnoe Lashufaka Timlir Itakla!"

The red light exploded in a flash and sent us tumbling backward against the walls of the church. I was blind for a moment, but I heard the snarling of a massive beast. When my eyes focused again, a growling, three-headed dog, wider than a Mack truck and uglier than Cujo, leaped through the air toward Mark.

Mark screamed as the dog ate him alive, ripping him into pieces and sending his head flying across the church into the pews.

"Mark!" I shouted. I wanted to run to help him, but I was too scared to move.

"Uhh…Stop that dog!" Bruce fell backward, cradling the summoning book in his hands. "Bad dog!"

"Make it stop!" I shouted.

"I don't know how!" Bruce said, crying through his words, flipping through the pages. "It's supposed to listen to my commands, but it's not!"

"Then send it back!" I said, running over to him to look at the book. "How do we send it back?"

"I don't know, I don't—"

"Think, Bruce! Think!" The dog's lips smacked loudly as it chewed on Mark's carcass. "Hurry up!"

"Here it is!" Bruce said, running his fingers across the pages. "All we have to do is kill the dog and speak the words backward to send it back."

"Kill it? How are we supposed to do that?"

"I don't know!"

"You didn't think this through, Bruce! You never think things through!" I screamed. "Just run!"

I ran toward the door of the church. I just wanted to smash through it and rush out into the night, away from this accursed church, and crawl into bed as if this never happened.

But it had happened. As if I needed more confirmation this was real, I stumbled on Mark's severed head and looked down to see his dead eyes staring up in horror, his mouth open, screaming out for help that would never come.

"What are we going do?" I shouted at Bruce when he caught up to me. "What are we gonna do?"

"I don't know," he said. "But pull it together. That dog—oh, no."

I looked over my shoulder and saw the bright, yellow eyes of the demon dog bearing down on us. It had finished its meal and wanted more. I turned toward the front door just as the dog leaped into the air and landed with a crash in front of us, sending us onto our asses. I scooted away toward the altar, but Bruce was frozen into place.

"Come on, man," I whispered to him, but he still didn't move, except to quake in his boots.

The dog stepped forward and sniffed Bruce with one of its heads, then another, and finally the third.

"I think it's—" Bruce started to speak before one of the dog's heads bit off his head, and another ripped off his arm. It stood there in front of the door, chewing and slurping.

A gurgling scream escaped my throat. There was no way out except for the front of the church. How the hell was I going to get out? I wouldn't. I was going to be dead in a matter of seconds, and I would go to Hell for pulling out that demon dog. Why couldn't we have just gone to the arcade?

The dog finished its meal and still looked hungry. The walls around me were soaked in the blood of my two best friends, but the dog wanted more. It stepped over Bruce's mangled body toward me slowly. I wasn't ready to die, but I closed my eyes and tried to resign myself to it.

Two flashes of blue light blinked in front of me. When the light dissipated, I saw two women standing with their backs to me, staring down the dog. They were each holding daggers, and both of them had bright blue wings between their shoulder blades.

"Shit," the tall one said. "We're too late."

The smaller one glanced back at me and smiled. "Not totally. This one's still alive."

"At least that's something. Take the front. Don't let it get out outside."

They leapt into the air and rushed for the dog, and that's when my knees went limp. I fell to the ground and blacked out.

CHAPTER 1

"Duck!" I shouted as the three-headed demon dog lunged at Kimberly.

Kimberly stooped down to avoid the dog's snarling heads and bloody paws. The dog wanted to get outside, which meant smashing through the front door that Kimberly guarded. It came close to slicing her arm, but she dropped a pinch of pixie dust just in time. She vanished into thin air and reappeared across the room, behind me.

"I told you to duck!"

"And I decided to try it another way, Julia!"

It had been eight years since I'd taken Kimberly under my wing. In that time, she'd grown to be quite the expert in martial arts and even better at fighting monsters. She was a natural fighter, intuitive and strong, way better than I was at that age. Hell, at that age, I didn't even know monsters existed outside of the vicious racists in my hometown.

Kimberly's mother didn't like it much that I took her little girl out at all hours of the day and night, but I needed help, and Kimberly was hungry to learn. She did everything I told her and was an asset in a battle . . . most of the time.

"Sure!" I pointed at the door. "But now there's nothing to stop that stupid dog from running out of here, is there?"

The dog turned toward the front door that Kimberly gave up guarding when she vanished away. It eyeballed both of us and then made a mad rush for the door.

"Damn it!" I couldn't let it escape. Who knew what would happen if I let it loose into the town? "I guess I'll have to do it."

"Don't hurt yourself!" Kimberly replied.

I closed my eyes and pictured the door in my mind's eye, recalling every detail. Then, with a flash, I disappeared from where I was standing and reappeared in front of the door.

One of the heads of the demon dog lunged at me and fell down limp when I stabbed it through the eye with one of my daggers. I kicked it away from me.

Demon dogs were one of the easier monsters to kill. They didn't require any special weapons or enchantments to take down. If you could avoid getting bitten by their three massive heads and got a clean shot, you could take their heads down one at a time.

The snarling dog chomped at me, and I swerved my body to avoid its jaws. I heard whimpering in the corner when I moved to a new position. "What did I do? What did I do?"

The poor teenager who summoned the dog must have woken up. We'd gotten here in time to save him, but his friends weren't so lucky. Flecks of the boy's comrades hung from the dog's teeth.

"Shut up, idiot!" Kimberly snapped. "We can't concentrate with all your blubbering."

"I c-c-can't," he stammered. "I'm just . . . I can't—"

"What's your name?" Kimberly asked.

"G-r-r-r-Greg."

"Shut the hell up, Greg. We're trying to save your life!"

Most of the monsters we dealt with these days were from idiots like Greg. Lonely high school losers who wanted people to pay for their rejection. They couldn't comprehend the harsh truth: the reason nobody liked them was because they were assholes.

The demon dog dove for me, and Kimberly flung herself onto its back. Another head lunged at her, and she kicked it in the face. That was one thing I loved about her; the girl had no fear. She was only sixteen years old. In her short life, she's already survived Hell and battled countless monsters. She might as well be invincible.

I gripped the jaws of the demon dog's head as it pinned me against the wall. Its hot breath inched closer to me with every second that passed, and my arms burned the longer I held tight.

"Little help!"

Kimberly jumped to avoid the clamping of the monster's jaws. She was having the time of her life, smiling broadly as she toyed with the monster. "Sorry!" she said, spinning her dagger in her hand and slamming it deep into the demon dog's brain through its ear canal.

The head fell limp, and my muscles relaxed gratefully. But I should have known better than to take a break, even for a second. In my momentary respite, the wounded dog batted me through the door of the church and into the crisp night air.

Once it hit the open outdoors, the dog lost interest in both of us and ran off. Kimberly was already flying after the beast by the time I rose to my feet. I chased after them. I hated showing my wings in public, but sometimes there was no choice. Luckily, the few people who ever saw us were quickly cast off as nutjobs: nutjobs and tabloid rags.

By the time I caught up with Kimberly, she was deep in battle with the dog. Two of its heads lay fallow at its side, but the final one had enough energy for three. It swiped at Kimberly until it smashed her across the face, and she fell down.

"Kimberly!"

I rematerialized between her and the great dog. It tried to bite down on her throat, but as the head gnashed down, I swung my dagger up and caught it in the throat. Dark green blood sprayed all over us. The dog let out a howl before it collapsed on top of us.

"Oh my god," I choked, trying to push the beast off me.

"I can barely breathe," Kimberly wheezed under me.

"On three, okay?" I said. "One, two . . . three! Heave!"

With one massive push, we rolled the demon dog off and let out a deep gasp of relief. I was lying there catching my breath beside the dead dog, covered in its blood when I saw Greg weasel out of the church.

"Oh no, you don't." I stalked toward the church. "Kimberly, get this thing back inside. I'll handle the idiot."

She let out a groan. "Why do I gotta carry the dead dog?"

"Cuz you're the apprentice."

"I hate this job."

***

It didn't take long to capture the little weasel and bring him back inside the church.

"I want you to look at what you've done," I said, holding him by the scruff of the neck.

His friends' blood splattered every wall of the church, and its rotten pews were covered in viscera. As we walked up to the altar where the summoning took place, I nudged his friend's disembodied head with my foot. "Is this how you thought tonight would go . . . what's your name again?"

"Greg, ma'am."

"And is this how you thought this night would go, Greg?"

Greg shook his head. "N-n-n-no, ma'am."

"Then what did you think would happen when you summoned a demon?"

"We—we didn't think anything would happen. We thought it was just a joke, you know?"

"It's a joke now to summon demons from Hell? Who were you trying to get killed?"

"What?" Greg shouted, indignant. "Nobody. We weren't—"

"Cut the crap, Greg," I said, squeezing his collar as we stepped up to the altar. "Who were you trying to kill?"

Greg sighed. "Allen Templeton. He's a dick."

"Ah. Beat you up, did he?"

"Beat us all up," Greg said. "Since fifth grade."

"Sit down," I said, pointing to the pentagram painted on the floor in pig's blood. "I'm going to tell you what happens now, Greg. Are you listening?"

Greg took a seat on the bloody floor. "Yes, ma'am."

"First, you are going to send that demon dog back to Hell. Then, you are going to jail."

"Jail! But I didn't do anything!"

"That's not true, Greg. You summoned that dog, right?"

"We all did!"

I nodded. "And you are the only one still alive. They are going to call you a butcher, Greg. Look at what you did to this place."

"Nuh-uh," Greg said, shaking his head vigorously. "I'll just tell them the truth!"

I laughed. "You think they are going to believe that a demon dog escaped Hell and rampaged around this church?"

The boy crossed his arms. "Then I won't send it back."

I pulled out my dagger and pressed it against his cheek. "Then I'll kill you for real and do it myself. Do I make myself clear?"

Greg gulped loudly. "Yes, ma'am."

I pulled my dagger away and slid it back into its sheath at my belt. "Good, Greg. That's real good. Now, your best defense is going to be temporary insanity. After all, your story doesn't make any sense. If you're lucky, you might even get out of the looney bin before you're fifty. Who knows? But that's your best bet, Greg. I'm telling you this because I want to help you, okay?"

"You got a funny way of showing it," he replied, crossing his arms.

"You're lucky we were here at all," I shouted. "Otherwise, you'd be dead. Down in Hell, floating down the river Styx, ready to be judged for your actions. Is that what you want? To end up in Hell?"

Greg shook his head. "No, ma'am."

"I didn't think so."

"Hey!" Kimberly shouted. "Can I get some help here?"

I watched her dragging the three-headed demon dog into the church. "Why didn't you just teleport it in here?"

"Damn!" she said, looking down at the massive beast. "I didn't even think about it."

"Let this be a learning moment, Kim. Go help her, Greg. We don't have much time."

***

It took ten more minutes to get the body positioned on the pentagram, so we could send it back to Hell. I counted my blessings that we were in the middle of nowhere. Otherwise, the cops would have been on us already. Of course, that's probably why idiots like Greg chose places like this because they were in the middle of nowhere.

Greg hadn't stopped crying since I talked to him. He probably wasn't a bad kid. I'll bet he did all right in school, and he seemed to like his friends, but when it comes to the dark arts, even the nicest kids get corrupted. They see riches, or power, or money, and it's just too much for them—a damn shame.

"All right," Greg said, holding a spell book in his hands. "I should just have to say the incantation backward and send this thing back to Hell, right?"

"I don't know, Greg," Kimberly said. "I don't summon monsters. I just fight them."

"Everybody needs to hold hands and chant."

"I don't want to hold hands with you," Kim said, making a face.

"Just do it," I said.

Greg paged through the book for a moment, then asked the two of us to lock hands. "Repeat after me. I think this is right. *Alkati Rilmit Akafuhsal Eongel!*"

Kimberly sighed. "Alkati Rilmit Akafuhsal Eongel!"

I joined in. "Alkati Rilmit Akafuhsal Eongel!"

The pentagram under the demon dog glowed red. Then a great light shot out from its center and dragged the monster back down to Hell. In a moment, it was over, and we stood in the church surrounded by nothing but the carnage.

"You hungry?" I asked Kim.

She shrugged. "I could eat."

The two of us walked away, leaving Greg to stare at the empty space where the dog had been and await the police and his doomed future.

CHAPTER 2

"Wipe your face off before you get up to the cashier, okay?" Kim said to me as we pulled up to the McDonald's drive-thru.

It was late, and all the late-night, sit-down places like Denny's were out because, well, we looked like death warmed over . . . quite literally. I felt the blood caked on my face, but I was too tired to do anything about it.

"Seriously," Kimberly said, emphasizing each syllable. "You're gonna freak her out."

"Fine," I grumbled.

Kimberly held up a rag, and I wiped my face with it. I flipped down the visor and looked at myself in the mirror. There were more flecks in my hair, but I'd managed to get enough off my face that the cashier probably wouldn't call the cops on us.

"You don't look too great yourself," I said, passing the towel over to Kimberly. "What do you want?"

"Big Mac with fries and a shake," Kimberly replied, wiping off her face.

"You are going to get fat with a diet like that."

"I don't worry about that. Fat is something old people like you have to deal with."

"Hey!" I said. "I resent that."

"It's not my fault you're old. What are you getting?"

I smiled. "Big Mac, fries, and a shake."

The drive-thru speaker crackled to life. "Welcome to McDonald's. How may I help you?"

***

I parked in an empty field on the outskirts of Stubbins, so we could eat our dinner in peace. I liked to lie out in the fields, on the roof of my car, looking up at the stars, and Kimberly humored me, so I wouldn't have to eat alone.

I hadn't driven much before I ended up in Hell to rescue Kimberly, but I started loving it when I got back. While Mama was alive, it was all zoom zoom all day, every day, but things with Kimberly were different. Kimberly had school, and soccer practice, and a hundred things that didn't allow me to fly away at a moment's notice. Besides, after my experience in the bowels of Hell, I had more appreciation for slowing down and enjoying life.

Kimberly's mother, Adelaide, was mighty happy with me when I first brought her beloved daughter home. Hell, she even welcomed me teaching Kim how to defend herself from attacks, but as Kimberly got older and wanted to work with me more and more, her mother stopped being so supportive. She hated that I put her daughter's life in danger every night; she especially hated that I brought her back so late after stuffing her full of junk food.

"Which one is that again?" Kimberly said, pointing up at the stars with a mouth full of Big Mac.

"Cassiopeia. She was a vain queen who boasted that she was more beautiful than the sea nymphs."

"That's cool. Are sea nymphs really that pretty?"

"I dunno," I said, shrugging. "I never met one."

"You've met ogres, orcs, trolls, banshees, demons, imps, and the Devil himself, but no nymphs?"

"I also met elves and pixies, but no nymphs. I guess there's not a lot of call for them in Hell since the only rivers are full of either dead bodies or molten lava."

"You mean magma." Kimberly took another bite of her Big Mac and washed it down with her shake. "Magma's when it's in the ground. Lava's when it's on the surface."

I swallowed a mouthful of fries. "Who cares? This isn't school. You'll never need that stuff anyway."

"Really? Weren't you a teacher?"

"I can't think of one reason, outside of school, that you would have to know the difference between lava and magma."

"Yeah, it's like algebra," Kimberly replied before wolfing down the rest of her burger.

"I use algebra all the time, actually."

"Screw off," Kimberly said, beaming me with a fry. "No, you don't."

I glanced down at my watch. I promised Kimberly's mother I would have her home by ten pm, but it was already past midnight.

"Come on," I said to her. "We need to get you home."

"Ugh," she replied, pushing herself up from the hood of my car. "Can't we stay a little longer? I'm not even tired yet."

"Your mother will be worried, which will make your father worry, and you know what happens when your father worries."

Kimberly slid into the front seat. "Fine!"

***

It was close to one am by the time I pulled into Kimberly's driveway. "You know, we could have just flashed home."

"I know," Kimberly replied. "I don't like to, though. I wanna keep some things normal, you know?"

I shook my head. "No. I don't know. There's nothing normal about us, but if that's what you want, then it's fine by me." I turned off the engine and walked Kimberly up to the door.

Before we even hit the steps, her front door swung open, and Adelaide stepped out onto the porch. "Where have you been, young lady?"

"Just . . . out." Kimberly looked down at the floor, so her mom wouldn't see the blood.

"And you're covered in blood," Adelaide said, tilting Kimberly's head back with one hand. "You're always covered in blood."

"It's not mine!" Kimberly scoffed and pushed her mother's hand away.

"Just go inside and wash up."

Kimberly disappeared into the house, and Adelaide shut the door behind her. When she turned to face me, a fresh black eye glinted in the porch light.

"I've been up for half the night worrying, and then you bring her home late, covered in blood and —what was that green stuff?"

"It was a demon dog. Three-headed. They gush green blood."

"I. don't. care. Stop taking my daughter out late at night. Stop disobeying my rules. I expect this from her," Adelaide said, pointing her finger at my chest, "but you are supposed to be an adult."

"I am an adult," I scoffed.

"Then act like it. You're gonna get her hurt. Or worse."

Big words from a woman that literally lived with a monster, one who beat her every time he had a bad thought in his brain. I could have said something, but I didn't. I let her keep her dignity and the high ground. "I'm sorry."

"Yeah, I'll bet you're real sorry. Sorry enough to do it again tomorrow. Look, I can't stop her from going. If I do that, I'll lose her forever. Just . . . please. Be careful. She's my only baby."

I nodded. "I'll be more careful."

It wasn't a promise I could keep, but it made Adelaide feel better to hear it. We were in a dangerous line of work, and that was the cold, hard truth of the matter. It's not like I didn't take care of them. I paid the mortgage and gave her daughter a good stipend for her troubles. Still, there's nothing like having your only daughter safe and sound.

I could see Adelaide's brain calculating every time I dropped her off, wondering if it was worth it, but she was right. She didn't have a choice. Kimberly wanted to train with me—work with me, even—and until she stopped wanting that, Adelaide was stuck accepting it, especially because she needed the money.

***

Since Aziolith the dragon woke up, I didn't feel comfortable staying in his cavern. I was fine staying there when he was asleep for two years—he actually needed me to make sure he wasn't dead then—but when he woke up, it felt like I was cramping his style. I still visited him often, but I decided to stay back at my mother's house in Chandler.

Chandler hadn't been the same since I closed its portal to Hell almost a decade ago, but my little block, the one where my mother used to live, was thriving. That's mostly because Aziolith let me keep using his treasure in any way I saw fit, and I decided to use a teeny, tiny fraction of it to pay off the debt of everybody on Mama's old street.

I didn't think I would want to come back to Chandler after Mama's death, but the more time passed after her funeral, the more I wanted to feel close to her. Staying in her house was the closest I could reasonably get to feeling her presence.

I usually kept my car in Stubbins, where Kimberly lived. There was no reason to use it without Kimberly around—after all, I was perfectly fine being different—but sometimes, after dropping her off, I needed the drive home to clear my head. Stubbins was about an hour from Chandler, and in the dead of night, you could make better time if you wanted. I chose to mosey home instead.

Tonight shook me more than I let Kimberly see, and part of the reason I kept her out so late was because I didn't want to be alone. In the past eight years, we had helped a lot of fairy folk, but rarely did we confront Hell beasts. Most of the calls I received were for domestic assaults, runaways, and the occasional robbery of a magical artifact. Once in a while, we dealt with murders and such, but mostly it was petty crimes.

In fact, for the first seven years of training Kimberly, we closed maybe a half dozen portals like the one tonight, but in the last six months, we'd closed more than twenty, and they were opening more frequently. Why? Were demons seeding spell books around the world so that idiots could summon more monsters?

I used to believe that portals to Hell only opened through mystery spots like the one that used to exist in Chandler before I closed it. How naïve I was. It turned out any moron could open a portal anywhere if they knew the right incantation and gathered the right ingredients.

Most of the portal openers Kimberly and I fought were like Greg, a little daft and naïve, but none too dangerous. They got their hands on a new book or a cool spell and wanted to take it for a spin. They couldn't summon anything dangerous, really, at least not dangerous enough to take over the world.

It was the cults that worried me, like the Cult of the Bloody Dagger, which had summoned the great dragon Aziolith, killed my mentor, and sent me on this path. They were the ones with the real ambition, and they were exceedingly dangerous. We hadn't faced one yet, but I feared for the day we would be up against real evil.

Adelaide was right, after all. It was a horrible risk I was taking with Kimberly, but one I thought was necessary. I needed help, and I needed somebody to take over when I died—preferably somebody with an intimate knowledge of Hell. Unfortunately, Kimberly fit the bill, and she was eager to learn.

***

When I came down the stairs the next morning, somebody was sitting on my stoop. This wasn't an unusual occurrence anymore. Adelaide was the first person to beg for my help on my front porch eight years ago, but since then, it had become a normal occurrence. The neighbors didn't think anything of it anymore.

I opened the front door and smiled at the black man rising to greet me. He was bald, with a thin beard and broad shoulders. He lumbered as he stuck out his thick hand for me to shake.

"Miss Freeman. Good to finally meet you."

I shook his hand. "You have me at a disadvantage because I don't know who you are."

He nodded. "I know. I know. I'm Gus, ma'am. Gus Harper. I got your name from a man, who got it from a woman, who got it from Adelaide, who I think you know. Kimberly's mother. You helped her a while ago."

I chuckled to myself. "Yes, I remember her."

"I'm afraid I need your help, ma'am. My daughter. She was kidnapped a couple of nights ago."

"You sure she didn't just run away?" I asked. "Usually, they just run away. Pretty much always, that is. Except for once. So, you better be sure."

Gus was absentmindedly wringing his hands. "Oh, yes, ma'am. Petunia and I had a good relationship. We didn't fight or nothin'. She ain't never not come home, you know? I just got a feeling in my bones something is wrong, and I need your help. Don't know who else to call who can help us kinda folk."

"Fairy folk, you mean?"

"Well, yeah. I mean, on her mother's side."

"Of course."

"Will you help me, ma'am?" Gus said, taking a small step forward. "Will you?"

"Of course, I will. Why don't you come in for some tea?"

I had come a long way from yelling at Adelaide on my porch and denying her help all those years ago to inviting strange people into my house, but that was the kind of person I was now and the kind of person I liked being. The kind of person who would make her mama proud.

CHAPTER 3

"Tell me a little bit about your daughter," I said to Gus as he took a seat on the leather couch in my living room.

I brought a cup of chamomile tea over to him, and he looked down at the cup for a moment. He watched the water swirl into eddies, evaporate into the air, and dance on the wind until it disappeared into the ether. He bit his lip as the tears formed in the corners of his eyes.

I grabbed a box of tissues from the coffee table and handed them to him. "It's okay."

"I'm sorry," he said, dabbing his eyes with a tissue. "I just . . . never thought it would happen to me, you know."

"Well," I replied, "we're not quite sure what happened to you, are we?"

He sniffled. "I suppose you're right. I should be positive, right?"

"Hope for the best. Expect the worst. And remember, I've literally gone into Hell and back to rescue little girls like yours before. If there's a way to get her back, I will find it."

When I traveled into Hell to find Kimberly eight years ago, I was a novice at tracking people. I was a novice about most things. I was only slightly better than Kimberly is now at using my powers. When I returned to the surface, I knew I needed more training.

So, I went back to school to become a private investigator—a real one this time, not a play one. I took every criminal justice and profiling class I could find. Eventually, I sat for my private investigator license and passed. Since then, I'd rescued over a dozen runaways from across the USA.

One thing was true about all parents . . . they never believed their child could run away. They always had a great relationship with their kid. Usually, it turned out they were wrong. I hoped Gus was wrong, too. The alternative was always worse.

***

I couldn't get any more out of Gus. He was a blubbering mess. I decided it was best for him to take me to his home, so I could search for clues. Cops were horrible about finding magical kids, mostly because they had no idea what they were looking for. Magical folks weren't like other humans, especially if they knew they were magical, and their powers were starting to develop.

Gus lived halfway between Chandler and Stubbins in a little town called Ginsberg. Fairy folk liked small towns and faraway places, away from cultists and monsters, where it was quiet. Ginsberg didn't show up on many maps.

"It's up here on the left," Gus said, pointing to a blue, two-story, colonial house with pale yellow shutters.

"Not bad," I said, pulling into the driveway.

I stepped out of the car and onto the lawn, bright green and manicured to perfection. Rose bushes sprouted across the front of the house and gave off a lovely aroma.

"We do what we can," Gus replied. "It's getting harder with the economy and all. Reagan said we would be seeing more money in our paychecks, but I haven't seen anything yet. Come on. Her room's upstairs."

***

Petunia's room was sparsely decorated and organized flawlessly. I sifted through the pressed clothes hanging nicely in the closet, and the crisp, folded clothing in the dresser, wondering if they had just been bought. It was hard to believe anybody actually lived there.

"Petunia was a bit . . . particular about things," Gus said, watching me. "I know it's weird. I just wanted her to be a kid, get messy, throw her stuff everywhere, but Petunia wouldn't have any of it. She needed things just so."

There were no posters on the walls or makeup on the vanity, but I did find a little notebook next to her bed, sealed with a tiny padlock.

"Do you know where this key is?"

"No idea," Gus replied, shaking his head.

I opened the dresser on her bedside table and found a single key lying in the otherwise-empty bottom drawer. The rest of the house was equally sparse. Each room contained only the essential furniture, and all of it looked untouched. No pictures on the walls . . . no pictures anywhere. I couldn't shake the feeling I was walking through the model home realtors showed to get people to buy into a new neighborhood.

"How long have you been here, Gus?" I asked, my curiosity piqued.

Gus sighed. "A month."

I snapped my neck toward him. "That all? Where were you before this?"

"My wife—well, my ex-wife . . . she got most everything, down to the picture albums." He rubbed the back of his neck. "This is all very new to me."

And immediately, it made sense to me. "Why didn't she get Petunia?"

"That's . . ." He let out another deep sigh. "She didn't want her."

I stood up, placing the notebook in my pocket. "Have you spoken with your ex about this? About Petunia disappearing?"

"No. My wife, she just vanished away one night. I don't even know where she went. When I came home, the house . . . it was just empty . . ." He trailed off, shaking his head and shoving his hands into his pockets. It was all pretty fresh, still.

"Do you think Petunia could have gone to look for her?"

Gus didn't look up. "No, she hated her mother. They didn't get along at all."

I frowned, scratching my head. "I'm not going to lie to you, Gus. This is all really weird. I've never seen a house this pristine before, especially not one with a kid living in it."

"Well, there's lots of people in this world, Miss Freeman, and I'll bet you haven't met all types yet. I keep tidy cuz this house is new, and my daughter, well, she is particular."

"All right," I said, holding up the notebook. "I'm going to keep this and go through it, okay?"

Gus nodded. "Anything you need."

***

I read through Petunia's diary twice after I got home, and I couldn't shake the feeling that I was missing something. The slang was just right, and the words were precise—nice and neat, just like the clothes in the closet. Something about the tone and inflection made it seem . . . off. I wasn't an expert in teenage slang, though, and there was only one person I trusted who could tell me if my hunch was right or not. I transported myself to Kimberly's school to talk to her once when the bell rang.

I didn't like to interrupt Kimberly at school. I held firm that she should have a life of her own outside of working with me, but some things were too important and—well, that's why I paid her the big bucks.

By the time I appeared at the school, most of the students had already left for the day. Only those serving detention or involved in extra-curricular activities remained. Kimberly was one of those overachieving types who seemed to live at school when she wasn't with me.

She sat on the student council and played clarinet in the marching band. She was fine at those things, but her real gift was sports. This time of year, it was soccer. I sat on the bleachers and watched Kimberly drill ball after ball into the goal. She was an excellent striker and, just a sophomore, led the team in goals. I'd been to most of her games, where she would burst down the field on a breakaway and score on an unsuspecting goalie. She was really going places, Kimberly. That is if she could live long enough.

I couldn't shake the feeling as I watched that I was doing her a disservice, mucking around with her and exposing her to dangerous situations, but she loved the work. I asked her all the time if she wanted to quit, but she just smiled and shook her head as if I was asking the stupidest question in the world.

Kimberly finished her drills and went to get water. That's when she looked into the stands and saw me waving at her. "I'll be right back," she said to her coach. He rolled his eyes at her and didn't look happy, but what could he do? Suspend his star player for missing a little bit of practice?

***

"This sounds like bullshit to me," Kimberly said after flipping through the diary for a few minutes. "Nobody talks like this. At least nobody I know."

"Well, the gal who wrote this lives about a half-hour away. Do you think somebody else could—"

"No way. Nobody would be so proper in their own diary. I mean, she uses perfect grammar and everything. Big words, too, like she had a thesaurus on her the whole time. And look at this," she said, pointing to inkblots on the pages. "It's like she's stopping mid-word to remember how to write. That's weird for anyone, not just a teenage girl. Humans don't do that."

"Wow," I replied, scratching my head. "How did I miss that?"

She patted me on the back. "You just haven't been a sixteen-year-old girl for a while."

"Thank god."

"So, what do we do now?" Kimberly asked.

"Finish practice," I said. "Your mom will kill me if you miss practice. Then, we'll go and tail this Gus fellow and see what he's playing at."

"Kim!" the coach shouted. "Get down here!"

Kimberly smiled at me. "Wait for me here. I'll be done in a bit."

***

After practice, Kimberly and I scarfed down a quick dinner and drove to Gus's house. By the time we got there, it was night. The house was pitch dark except for the porch light. We'd sat there for just a few minutes when the door squeaked open, and Gus pulled out of the driveway. I inched out of my spot across the street and followed behind him, keen on figuring out why he would lie to me.

CHAPTER 4

We tracked Gus to a big mansion on the outskirts of town. This wasn't like the big Holly-Hobbie homes that we saw everywhere else. No, this place was old and storied. You could tell thought and time went into its construction, unlike the cookie-cutter bull lining every other development.

The golden emblem of a Pegasus accented the wrought-iron gate enclosing the driveway. A ten-foot-high brick wall surrounded the rest of the property and made the mansion nearly impregnable—if you weren't a pixie, that is—and a dozen guards wandered the property between the wall and the house proper.

"Something's going on in there they don't want people to see," Kimberly said, staring through a pair of binoculars at the roof. "I count two more snipers up on the roof, too."

"Why would somebody kidnap Gus's daughter if this is what they were up against?" I asked.

"That's easy," Kimberly said. "They wouldn't."

"Exactly," I replied. "You wait out here. I'm going in to figure out what the hell is going on."

"Let me come with you." Kimberly stowed her binoculars. "I hate waiting in the car."

"It's too dangerous."

Kimberly laughed. "We just took down a dog from Hell last night. How could this be more dangerous?"

"Easy. It didn't have guns. If I'm not out in fifteen minutes, I'll meet you back at my house, okay? Don't follow me inside."

Kimberly nodded. "Okay."

"You remember what it looks like?"

"Yes."

"Remember every brick on every wall before you throw your dust, okay?"

"I remember, okay? Christ, I'm not a child."

I smiled at her. "No, you aren't, are you?"

***

In the past eight years, I'd learned how to dim my wings, so they made only the slightest glow when I pressed them out flat. Flapping them lightly, I peeked over the wall to make sure there were no guards looking my way before hovering over it and dropping into the bushes on the other side. I stowed my wings when I landed. Even though they weren't bright, they gave off too much light in the darkness of the yard.

"Area four clear!" one of the guards spoke into a walkie-talkie. "Over."

The guard passed in front of me and continued to walk in the other direction. I surveyed the rest of the property. Eleven more guards patrolled the grounds, and spotlights shone on the yard. I couldn't pass through without alerting them; I would have to find an access point and vanish to it.

After examining the house, I found a ledge above the porch overhang leading to a darkened, circular window that nobody guarded. It was the best way into the house. I studied every brick and beam before I closed my eyes and vanished in a flash of light, reappearing on the roof. There was a chance that the guards would see my flashes, but nobody noticed.

The ledge was slick and ivy-covered, but knowing I was pushing my luck on being spotted, I didn't dare use my wings to help me. When I ended up at the circular window, I pressed my hand against the frame, and it swung open for me. I hopped inside and found myself in the attic, surrounded by dusty books, antique trunks, and ornate trinkets.

Careful not to make a sound, I pushed my wings out of my shoulder blades and hovered over the floorboards. I floated to the bookshelves, looking for a clue as to what kind of humans lived inside this mansion.

The shelves were full of books on the metaphysical and the occult, explaining how to call forth demons and open a portal to Hell without the presence of a mystery spot. Of course, I knew how to do that already. All you needed were the right runes, a pentagram, and an appropriate blood sacrifice, depending on what creature you were trying to conjure. For a basic creature, you only needed something like pig's blood, but if you wanted something more exotic like a banshee, you needed a more exotic type of blood—the rarest of which was monster blood—namely, pixie blood. My blood.

***

I made my way into the hallway. The top floor of the house seemed empty, but I heard plenty of commotion below me. When I came around the corner, the hall opened into a giant atrium revealing the lower levels. Below me, two dozen hooded figures stood in a circle drawn in blood.

In the center of the circle was a familiar pentagram, along with some runes I didn't quite recognize. Different monsters had unique conjuring runes, and it was impossible to remember every single one. I knew they weren't summoning a demon or a dragon, but with over a hundred different runes combining to call forth a thousand different monsters from Hell, I could never keep them straight.

"Ah, Julia of the Freeman Clan," a voice said, wafting upwards. "So nice of you to join us."

I was found out. I closed my eyes to disappear, but I couldn't do it. I tried again and again. I failed.

"I'm afraid escape isn't an option," the voice continued. "This house has been, let's say, protected from your kind egressing by your 'special means.'"

I turned around to run for the door as two hired goons came out around the corner on either side of the hallway and closed in on me.

"I don't want to hurt you—" I started to say. "Oh, who am I kidding?" I pulled out my daggers and stabbed one of the goons in the leg, then flung my other dagger into his friend's neck. The first guy was still twitching, so I took my dagger out of his leg and jabbed it into his ear.

"*Ulago Mafilo Amchangio*," the voice boomed from the bottom of the stairwell, and suddenly I couldn't move. Worse, I floated backward. No matter how hard I fought, I was moving through the air and down to the circle below me.

"Ulago Mafilo Amchangio," the group chanted in unison. "Ulago Mafilo Amchangio. Ulago Mafilo Amchangio. Ulago Mafilo Amchangio."

When I reached the first floor, two old men shackled my wrists and legs. "What's happening to me?" I shouted.

"We have studied the dark arts for a long time, dear Julia," the voice said. It was coming from a hooded figure that moved closer to me and pulled off its cloak to reveal an old, shriveled man who could barely hold up the huge book in his hands. "A long, long time."

"And what, you sold your soul to Satan for money and power?"

The old man laughed. "Oh no, Miss Freeman. All the knowledge I used to entrap you was readily available without any of that sort of thing. You just have to know where to look . . . and have the money to seek it out."

I nodded. "I guess that's where everyone else went wrong. They didn't have the money."

"Perhaps, Miss Freeman. May I call you Julia?"

"You plan on killing me, don't you? Might as well get rid of the formalities."

"Ah, good. My name is Edgar. Edgar McNulty the Third. I am descended from Scottish royalty dating back four millennia."

"I'm descended from nobody and nothing."

"Not true, Julia," Edgar said, circling me. "You are descended from magic folk, and thus you are incredibly special to me. You can unlock everything I've ever desired."

"And what is that? Money, power . . ."

Again, Edgar guffawed. "No, my dear. You are too shortsighted in your views."

"Then what is it? What are you after?"

Edgar directed a nod at the hooded figures surrounding him, and they dropped their cowls, revealing old men and women, frail and weak. Some wore oxygen masks, and others wobbled against their canes.

"Immortality. Of course."

"There is only one being in all of Hell who can make us young, again and again forever. But it is very old magic.

Very old and powerful. In order to unleash it, we need a sacrifice and an offering."

"I'll never help you!" I struggled against my bindings.

"You don't have a choice."

Edgar snapped his fingers, and the large front door opened. Four men walked in carrying a kicking and sobbing Kimberly. One of the guards tossed her bag of pixie dust at Edgar's feet.

"Leave her out of this!" I shrieked.

Edgar smiled at me, giving another snap. A dozen of the elderly people shambled into the other room and came out a minute later, pushing a large marble slab.

"Throw her on the altar," Edgar said. "She will make a fine offering to our new pet."

"No!" I shouted. "Look, do anything you want with me, but let her go. Please just let her go."

I sobbed uncontrollably. My own death I could handle, but I was going to be responsible for Kimberly's. Why did I bring her here? I didn't have to. I just liked having her around. Now, she was going to die.

"I'm afraid I can't do that, Julia," Edgar sighed. "We need you both."

"No, you don't." I choked out the words. "With me, you can open a mystery spot. You can unleash anything you want. I know where they are. I can take you to one. You can unleash Hell itself."

Edgar turned to me, making a face. "That sounds horrible. I have no interest in Hell on Earth, just a small piece of immortality." He walked to the altar and squeezed Kimberly's cheeks. "Yes, you will be a fine offering to our new pet, won't you?"

Kimberly spat on his face. "You can go to Hell."

"Oh no." Edgar shook his head. "I'm quite sure that Hell will come to me. Bring him out!"

Two doors opened at the other end of the hallway, and two goons dragged an unconscious Gus to the center of the circle. He was pale, and his head lolled to the sides. He certainly didn't seem like the same person we'd followed just an hour before.

"Hold him up," Edgar said. "That's a good lad."

Edgar reached into his robe and pulled out a dagger. With one smooth motion, he plunged it deep into Gus's chest and started to carve. Gus moaned slightly and collapsed, blood gushing from his wound. Edgar dropped to the floor with him and finished digging into his chest until he pulled the heart from Gus's chest.

"Is that what you get for messing up?" I said. "Death?"

"Messed up?" Edgar repeated the words and looked over his shoulder at me. "Why would you think he messed up?"

"There was no way we would have believed that was actually a little girl's writing."

"Of course not, which is why you followed him here. Gus performed exactly as expected, and his sacrifice was willingly given, as is necessary for the ritual." Edgar made a slight grimace and a short tug, then popped Gus's heart from the hole in his chest cavity. The chanting began again when he raised the heart high above his head.

I pulled on my restraints as hard as possible, but they wouldn't budge. "You're crazy!"

"Great Birsharka, we beseech you. Come to us now. Do our bidding, and you shall be fed and happy. I, your humble servant, demand it!"

Edgar dropped the heart to his mouth and ripped off a big bite. The robed men and women rushed forward and devoured the heart with him.

"Julia!" Kimberly screamed. "Help me!"

"I'm trying! I'm trying!" I pulled uselessly at my restraints.

"Try harder!" she screamed back. "I don't want to die here!"

"Me either!"

But the harder I struggled, the tighter the restraints held me. There was nothing I could do but watch in horror as the cult consumed their meal. Once they were done, they returned to the circle and began to chant in unison, blood dripping down their faces.

"We have marked ourselves," Edgar continued. "You shall know who you serve now. With the blood of the first magic, I summon thee!"

"No!" I shouted as Edgar swiped at me with his dagger. "I—"

But that was all I could say because Edgar cut my throat open, severing my vocal cords. He tilted my neck forward and drained my blood onto the ground. I watched in horror as the blood seeped onto the floor, and then, when I could no longer hold onto life, my eyes closed, and death came upon me.

CHAPTER 5

I woke up in the mouth of a fast-flowing river, struggling to breathe as I fell under the black water. The rapid current dragged me forward, and I kicked my legs to fight against it and bobbed to the surface again. All around me, thousands of bodies struggled against the will of the water, gasping and choking.

"Help!" I shouted. Bilge from the murky water poured into my mouth. "Help!"

I slapped my hands against the cold water's surface again and again in my attempt to get to shore, but the bodies in the river fought me, preventing me from doing anything but following the raging watercourse.

I could not go quietly; I would not succumb to the waters. Placing my hand over the top of the nearest body, I heaved myself on top of it. Hands grasped at me as I splashed down into the river and climbed over the next body. Then another, and another, until I reached a short cliff at the mighty river's edge.

But the current flowed too quickly, and I couldn't latch onto the high cliff that kept me from reaching land. I pressed against my shoulders, and my wings popped out. They were too damp to raise me out of the water, no matter how viciously I flapped them.

I gripped the clay at the base of the cliff and dug my fingers as tightly as I could onto the edge of the cliff. Each time I found a decent handhold, another body battered me back into the river. Over and over again, I tried to rise out of the current with no use, but I was carried further down the river until it descended into a great waterfall. Down,

down I fell into the cavern below until I crashed upon the ground with a great thud.

Two demons pulled me to my feet and dragged me, soaking wet, toward a long line of humans who stared forward at the great gate in front of them, waiting to be judged. There was no doubt about it: I was in Hell. I reached up a hand to feel the jagged skin of my throat, which the cult leader Edgar had severed, and I hoped for redemption.

I had seen what happened to those who were judged unworthy in my previous trips to Hell, and I did not want that to happen to me. All around me, rising to the tops of the great caverns of Hell, countless bodies moaned and screamed in a great human wall that stretched as far as I could see.

I could not fathom an eternity in this place. Surely, Hell would break me quickly, then spend the rest of time stealing every last shred of my dignity, my humanity.

***

"Just tell them you were a good person. Just tell them you were a good person. Just tell them you were a good person. They'll believe you if you tell them you were a good person."

The young man behind me had been mumbling to himself for the past three hours. I tried to get his words out of my mind, but I just couldn't shut him out. I didn't like waiting in lines usually, but this one was moving too fast for my taste. Any minute I would be at the front and would be judged. I knew I would be judged wanting.

"Just tell them you're a good—"

"You're not a good person," I said to the man. "I hate to break it to you, but if you were a good person, you wouldn't be here."

"That's not true," he replied, face contorted and aghast. "Don't say that. How can you say that?"

"Because it's the truth. This isn't my first time here, and I know. I promise you I know. Everybody in this line thinks they're a good person, but none of us are. None of us were good in life. I'm not even sure you can be good in life."

"Sure, you can. I was good. Look at Mother Teresa—"

"Mother Teresa was a racist who didn't think black people could help themselves. Martin Luther King, Jr. was an adulterer. Gandhi beat his wife. We're all bad. I think that might be the point. There's no hope for any of us."

But the man wasn't listening. He stared through me. "Just tell them you're a good person. Just tell them you are a good person. Just tell them you are a good person."

I didn't blame him. I had been here twice before, and still, I wasn't ready to face my own punishment. I should have been a better person. I should have been nicer, tried harder. I should have just kept traveling around the world and avoided helping anybody. I should have abandoned Kimberly all those years ago. I should have . . .

***

When I got to the front of the line, there were several dozen pulpits lining the front of a black gate, and each one of them had a damned soul in front of them. Behind each pulpit, a bored monster listened to the men and women plead their cases. Wraiths and demons, ghouls, and imps wrote in their ledgers as the souls wept for clemency. A zombie holding its own head directed the souls to different lines.

"You," it shouted at me. "Line twenty-seven."

I walked down the line of pulpits, listening to the unheeded pleas of men and women. It was pretty disgusting, hearing them try to bargain away their lecherous and disgusting behavior.

"I know I beat her once or twice, but it wasn't like an everyday thing," one man in a cardigan said to a werewolf.

"It's not like I stole all their money," another scoffed at a ghoul. "They still have enough for a decent nursing home."

***

I queued up in line twenty-seven and waited my turn. I was behind an old man holding an IV bag and in front of a fat, soggy man who was electrocuted in his bathtub.

"Next!" an old, shrill harpy with bad teeth shouted, and the old man stepped up to her. The harpy pulled out her glasses and looked down at a large, ornate book on her pulpit. She ran her hands along it slowly and carefully, studying each line closely.

"I'm afraid it doesn't look good for you, Reginald. No, it doesn't look good for you at all."

It didn't last long, and when it was over, two flying demons carried the old man off to his final destination. He would spend eternity having his pride tortured out of him by having his face boiled off and eaten by maggots.

"Next!" the harpy shouted.

Now it was my turn to be judged.

I didn't want to move forward, but the man behind me bumped me forward with his soggy stomach. I didn't know what his big hurry was—it wasn't like he was going to be spared. At least let me have a couple more seconds before wallowing in agony forever.

"Name?" the harpy snapped at me when I stumbled in front of the pulpit.

"Julia. Freeman."

She looked down at her notes. "Ah yes. Here we are. Oh my. That's a terrible way to go. Just terrible."

"Yes, well, I think there has been a mistake. You see," I said, pointing to my wings, "I'm not really a human at all. It's a common mistake. I'm a pixie. So, you can just . . . let me go into Dis, or whatever."

It was a desperate play, but pixies were considered monsters in Hell, and monsters weren't tortured in fiery pits of agony. They could live out their afterlives in Dis, Hell's biggest city. While it wasn't a great life, it was a far sight better than getting tortured in the pits of Hell for all eternity. Since that was my fate otherwise, I was willing to try anything, even if it was a long shot.

"There haven't been fairy folk in many centuries, at least not any that qualify as fairies." The harpy pulled out her reading glasses and looked at her notes. "Ah yes. You are . . . three one millionths fairy. Hmmm. That's not very much, is it?"

My eyes widened. "No. It's not. But look at the wings."

"Well, I just don't know what to do. I will remand your case to the appellate court to review your case. If they deem you truly are a fairy, you will be set free from your eternal damnation. You should have a ruling within six million years or so."

"Six million years! That's too long!"

"But sooner than eternity, yes? Now, let us see. What to do with you until then . . ." The harpy looked down at her book. "Oh, this isn't very good. You are very violent, aren't you?"

"Only against monsters."

The harpy looked over her glasses at me with a raised eyebrow, and I became very aware that she was considered a monster.

"Yes, quite. And also quite vain, I see."

"I have been doing better."

"Hmm. Not much, though. I sentence you to the pits of wrath, where you shall be burned alive every day, flesh melted from your skin, only for it to reform every night so you may do it again. Once you are sufficiently broken, you will be thrown in the coals of agony. Next!"

"That's horrible," I said. "Isn't there some other way?"

The harpy gave me a bored look. "Frankly, I'm being quite lenient on you. Now go! Guards!"

Two demons scooped me up with their talons and tossed me in the back of a cart bound for the pits of wrath. Around me, dozens of other tortured souls stared solemnly at the floor, resigned to their fate. Some of them cried, others wailed, none had hope.

CHAPTER 6

The road to the pits was a long one, and with every turn of the wheels, we passed more demons shoveling souls into heaps on either side of the road. The last time I was in Hell, the bodies stacked like mountains into the tips of Hell, but it was even worse now. Now, the body piles blotted out the fires all around us.

I had seen the agonized souls before—twice, in fact—but I wasn't ready to be one. Not yet. Part of me thought that I was in a worse position than anyone else in my caravan. At least they didn't know what they were about to experience. They could deny, lie to themselves. They could hope for reprieve even though there would be no reprieve for them.

I was holding out the slimmest of hopes that Akta would find me, and I couldn't let that go, no matter how bad it got. Even if it took a thousand years or a million. Even if it took an eternity.

***

"Once, I was a baker," the man next to me said.

"Why are you telling me this?" I asked, furrowing my brow in confusion.

"I thought somebody should know. You are the last human I will likely talk to for the rest of eternity, and I thought you should know."

I nodded. "Once I was a teacher."

"And then you weren't," he said.

"And then I wasn't."

"I would like to say I tried to be good," the man replied. "But that would be a lie. I was angry. So angry all the time."

I stayed silent for a moment, taking in the last words a human would likely say to me. "What is your name?"

"Reeves. Kyle Reeves."

I held out my hand. "I am Julia Freeman."

He shook my hand. "I would like to say that it is nice to meet you. However, we both know that is not true."

"It can be nice to meet somebody even if the circumstances are horrible."

He nodded. "Yes, that is true."

"What was your favorite thing to bake?" I asked Kyle after another long silence.

"Wedding cakes. I was a sucker for watching a couple get hitched. Plus, it was a great way to get tail. I slept with so many bridesmaids."

"Isn't that a bit cliché?"

"Yes," he said, almost snickering before the weight of endless torment fell on him again. "But one that works. It nearly killed my poor wife."

"I'm surprised you didn't end up in the pit with the adulterers."

"Me too, honestly. I guess my violent tendencies outweighed my lecherous ones. I don't suppose it matters much, though, in the grand scheme of things. Torture is torture."

"That it is."

We sat in silence for another few minutes, listening to the moans from the great wall around us beg for mercy. I didn't much like talking, but it was a far sight better than listening to the moaning of a human wall.

"What about you?" I asked a husky woman with blond pigtails across from me. "What did you do?"

Her neck muscles rippled as she looked up at me. "Wrestler. Fifty-six and zero."

"That's a good record."

"Never lost. Never taken down. I was a champion until the day I died. I take pride in that."

"Did you die . . . in the ring?"

She shook her head. "Steroids. I knew they weakened the heart and the brain, but I needed an edge. I was on the bench, lifting, struggling to finish a set, and then black. That's the last thing I remember before I ended up here."

"I'm sorry."

I studied at her hardened face as she wept and said. "I was a good person. I did charity work. I visited sick children at hospitals. Why am I here? Why am I here?"

It's a question I couldn't answer. I'm not sure there was an answer. Even if I had one, there was no way it would be acceptable to her. There's no way it would be worth hearing.

"I'm sorry," I said, and then I fell silent. The pain of the moans outside of the carriage was unbearable, but it was nothing compared to the desolate emptiness of those inside the cart.

***

Demons shoveled more bodies onto the great wall of souls with every turn of the wheel. Their job horrified me, but I knew it was just a job. Charlie taught me that. Charlie, the imp from Hell who tried to sell my soul to the highest bidder. He found me when I first entered Hell the last time and pretended to help lead me to Dis, Hell's biggest and, as far as I knew, only city.

On our way through Hell's countryside, we had stopped and talked to one of the demons shoveling endless bodies onto the mountain. The demon was actually not a bad guy for a demon. He really was just doing his job, like the ogre who pulled our cart or the harpy who gave me my punishment. It was hard not to hate them because their jobs were so horrendous, but at the end of the day, they were only jobs. You can work a job you hate, or you can be hated for a job you love. Just look at meter maids and lawyers. Universally despised, but I'm sure some of them like what they do.

"Halt!" the ogre leading our caravan shouted. I rose to my feet and looked out in front of the cart. Unlike the great wall which hid the other fires of Hell, the flames in front of us burned brightly, scalding my face until I turned away. If that was as hot as it was from a distance, I couldn't imagine what it was like up close. Of course, I wouldn't have to imagine. Soon, I would know for sure.

***

We finally came to a stop in front of a giant pit, and a collection of ogres took their time pulling us out of the cart one at a time and lining us all up. In front of the pits, a single desk sat with what looked like a goblin behind it, though I couldn't see him well through the backlighting of the flames.

I was lucky enough to be pulled out last, so I could watch every other person get processed through the line before it was my turn. It was a horrific process. Once the goblin crossed a name off his list, two demons, ten feet tall and rippling with muscles, pulled that person from the line and tossed them into the pits.

The line wasn't long, only a dozen or so deep, so it wasn't long until I was next. When the ogre pushed Kyle up to the front of the line, I mourned for him as if he were myself. In our short time together, I learned he was more than just a pile of meat and bones. He was living and breathing. He had hopes. He had dreams. And now, they would be burned off him in the fires of Hell.

"No! No! No!" Kyle screamed as the demons picked him up. "Please, don't do this. You don't have to do this. I am a good person. I am a good person! I am goooood!"

But it didn't matter to the demons. They just had a job to do, and with one heave, they tossed Kyle high into the air until the flames licked his face and melted away his skin. I gulped. In just a couple of moments, that would be me.

"Next!" the goblin said in a squeaky voice.

I summoned all my strength and moved forward. This was my lot in life—or death—and I was going to deal with it with as much dignity as possible.

"Name," the goblin said, looking down at his paper.

"Julia. Julia Freeman."

The goblin's ears twitched, and he looked up at me. "Holy heck! Julia! Is it really you?"

I cocked my head to the side. "Yes. It's me. That's why I said my name."

The goblin smiled a wide smile. "Don't you remember me? It's Glorbal. You saved me from being used as bait not that long ago. I mean, it wasn't that long ago, was it?"

"Glorbal."

"Yeah! I work here now, and it's all thanks to you."

The last time I was in Hell, I was kidnapped by Charlie and sold to a dark lord who was going to use me to open a portal to Earth. They locked me in a cage with one other sad goblin, and when Akta rescued us both, I set him free. Now I was standing in front of that same goblin.

"Oh my god," I said, almost giddy. "This is such great news."

"I know. I really turned my life around, thanks to you. I got a job. Got a new girl. I don't even gamble anymore, and it's all thanks to you. You really are a hero."

"Then you can be my hero and get me out of this."

Glorbal's nose scrunched up. "Oh, no. This is awkward. You're making it about business. I just wanted to catch up."

"I'm about to spend an awful long time here in Hell, Glorbal, getting my face melted off. This is about more than business for me."

"Trust me, I know. I know. It's not a great way to go. The best one is lust, I think. No flames at all. I mean, they screw you with rusty swords and the like, but Hell, at least you're getting some action, right?"

"Listen, Glorbal. I need you to get me out of this. It's not a coincidence that you are here right now, is it? It can't be."

Glorbal made a few notes in his book. "Listen, here's what I'll do for you. Usually, you gotta go right back in when your flesh regenerates, but I'm gonna give you a whole hour break from the torture every single day. That's a pretty sweet deal if you ask me."

"That is not a sweet deal, Glorbal. I saved your life. You owe me."

"Sorry, Julia," Glorbal said, snapping his fingers. "It's the best I can do."

"No! No! No!" I screamed as the two demons lifted me and carried me to the pits. I kicked and screamed, trying to get away, but they were too strong.

"It's a damn shame," Glorbal said. "Still, it's good to see you."

The demons grabbed me by either arm. They cocked me back like I was in a slingshot and flung me into the flames. In seconds, my skin bubbled over and popped in my ears, and my eyes melted in their sockets. I screamed, but there was no sound—the flames had burned out my esophagus. I wanted to blackout, but my consciousness could not escape this torture. I had to experience every single second of it. Forever.

CHAPTER 7

Oh god.

It burns.

It burns!

Let it go. It will be over in a—oh god! Oh god! *Why?*

I can't think—Ahhhh! All I feel is pain, all I am is pain.

Calm down!

It—*owwww*. It hurts so bad!

Breathe. Just breathe—

AHHHHHHH!

***

Months.

Days.

Years.

Minutes.

I have no idea how long I've been in this pit. They burn us. They rip off our skin. Then, they pull us out to let it all regrow again.

Every day, an hour. One single hour when I'm not in excruciating pain.

The worst hour.

I touch my fingers. I touch my toes. I remember the world. I feel almost human. I am almost human. Just when I learn to breathe again and open my mouth to relax, it starts again.

It never stops. The demons inside the pit skewer me with a trident, raise me into the air . . . roast me like a marshmallow over a fire.

I kick. I scream. I beg for death—

Death never comes—

No. It comes. It comes over and over again. It comes for me every day—every time I blink—every time I think it may be the last time, I am mistaken.

Fifty-eight minutes. It's been fifty-eight minutes. I keep track in my head. Two minutes to escape the blazing inferno.

When the bitter air brushes against my raw nerves, I wince in pain—nothing but the pain when you come out of the flames.

Then tendons form. Organs reshape. The air touches them, and I want to die—except I am already dead. Muscles cover the organs, and the slight touch is no longer agony, just a dull ache—then the skin, the skin covers the muscles—and I am whole.

It always starts as a scream. Then, it moves to a whimper. It is torture to remember. In the pain, I forget everything. I forget being human. I forget the universe exists. All that remains is pain.

And I fear going through it again—until they come for me—and it is time.

All around me. Everywhere. Charred bodies whimper out in pain. I envy them. They never have relief. Never remember existing without pain, never remember their old life.

The demon readies its pitchfork and looks at me. He sees me. It's time again. Oh god. It's time. I want to run. I want to escape.

There is no escape.

The pitchfork skewers my stomach and raises me high into the air. I take one last look at the bowels of Hell, surrounded by charred flesh that is no more human than a burnt marshmallow, and I descend into flames.

***

"Yield!" a monster shouts to its prey. My eyes have not come back yet. They are the last to form—I wish they would never come.

I do not need to see the pits. There is no hope in them.

Without my eyes—I am somewhere else. I am anywhere else.

The fire—it feels like it takes forever—but when I watch people burn—with my eyes—it is only a moment—then, the torture begins.

Torture is not in the burning—torture is in the healing.

The burning—you lose yourself. In the healing, you regain yourself—inch by inch—moment by moment—bone by bone.

The agony dulls, then—the moment there is hope—it begins again.

What kind of god—

What kind of demon would torture us like this?

—it is not fair—it is not fair—it is not fair—

Oh god. It's time to start.

The demon comes for me.

Please let it stop.

***

An hour. It had been a whole hour.

But no one has come for me. They didn't look at me.

What is happening? Why aren't they coming for me? It has been an hour. I know. I counted. The moment my eyes grew back—it was always the last thing. An hour. Exactly sixty minutes. Yet. They do not come. Why won't they come?

Come for me already! Come! Are you too pussy to come for me? Are you too scared? Do you know that I don't care anymore—that I welcome the pain—that I long for it now?

No.

Please.

Don't come. Don't come. I don't want you to come.

Shut up.

Shut up. Shut up. Do not come.

I am not ready.

I pull my hands onto my knees and rock slowly. Why won't they come?

Stop. Stop. Stop. Maybe this is life now. Maybe they will never come for me. Maybe I will be okay. Maybe—

—oh, god.

He turned to me. He looked at me.

No. No.

NO!

His trident is in the air. Oh god. It is going to skewer me. Oh, god, it just did!

Stop. Take me out of the air.

I'm not ready.

NOT READY!

Stop. Stop. STOP!

***

I forgot how to cry. I forgot how to moan. I forgot how to exist.

There is only fire. There is only flame. It is everything.

Flame. Rebirth. Flame. Rebirth. Flame. Rebirth.

I am reborn in fire over and over again. I can feel it cleanse my body. I must be clean. I need to be clean. CLEAN ME!

No. Stop. Don't look at me. Stop walking here. There is still time. It hasn't been an hour yet. My eyes. I still cannot see. There is still an hour. I must have that hour. Give me that hour!

You are weak. You are vile. How can you be so pathetic? I must be cleansed of you. Cleanse me!

"Oh, god," I spoke the words out loud, the sound a pile of ash leaving my mouth. It was the first words I'd spoken in . . . was it years? I didn't even know I could speak anymore. I didn't know I could do anything but burn and heal, burn and heal, burn and heal.

—they are all looking at me.

Oh, god. They see me.

Good—cleanse me!

***

"Come with me," a demon said in perfect English. I hadn't been asked to do anything in so long I didn't know what to do for a moment. Then, I placed my hands under me and pushed up.

"W-where . . .?"

"Do not speak," the demon said, his voice brimming with anger.

I didn't say another word. The demon climbed the stone stairs carved into the edge of the pit, and I trailed behind him. Another demon followed two steps behind us. Above me, I felt the cool breeze of Hell.

***

"I'm afraid I made a mistake," Glorbal said when I stood in front of him.

"M-m-m-mistake?" I replied, nearly forgetting how to speak.

He nodded. "I'm afraid so. See, you're not progressing as fast as the other prisoners."

"Pro-gress-ing?"

Again, he nodded, this time with an impish frown on his mouth. "See, you're supposed to burn fast, forget yourself, and then be sent to Soul Mountain for the rest of eternity to writhe away your existence after you have forgotten everything."

"Pro-gress-ing?"

"See," Glorbal sighed, "you've made some progress, but just not enough, and that's my fault. You see, I gave you that hour reprieve. We think that's what's doing it. They used to give all sorts of reprieves and even moved you souls around back in the day, but there's just not enough time for that now. We have to move souls quickly.

There's too many new souls to waste time fiddling around with the old ones."

"Please," I sputtered. "Don't—"

"Listen, I'm doing a favor for you. I'm not gonna cut down your time, but if you say another word down there, I'll have to—"

"Promise. Nothing."

"Seriously, this is the worst part. Once you succumb to the flames, it will be easier, I promise you. Or at least that's what they tell me."

"No. Please."

Glorbal furrowed his brow. "You look horrible. I guess that's a good sign."

***

I struggled every step back to the bottom of the pits. I wanted to scream, cry out. I wanted to do all those things, but I knew that I couldn't. They wanted me to lose my sanity and my humanity.

"Move!" the demon said behind me, pushing me down the rest of the stairs. He didn't have to worry about hurting me. After all, I was already dead. The moment I bounced up, another demon skewered me with a trident and turned me toward the flames.

I was no longer afraid of the flames. And now I knew what I had to do.

I had to protect my humanity, no matter the cost.

***

Oh, god. It was so much worse than I remembered. The burning—the screaming—I thought—but I wasn't ready—I thought I was ready—I wasn't—

Quit being a baby.

Liberate yourself.

The fear. The pain. It's all gone. We are reborn and reborn again. We are nothing, and we are everything, all at once.

Succumb to it. Embrace it. Love it.

I can't. I can't. I can't. Stop thinking like that. Humans fear fire. They fear pain. They fear flames. Every time, every hour, it feels like I am into the flames again. I've stopped counting my sixty minutes. They no longer give it to me.

—They place me in the flame over—over—never ending—it never stops—I can feel myself slipping—I can feel myself wavering.

Wavering is good. Give in to it. It will be over once we are reborn. Give in.

—That sounds nice—

***

A cold hand grabbed me in the dark. I wasn't ready. I wasn't reborn. I wasn't healed. Stop. Please. Stop.

Wherever you are taking me, stop!

There was a clang of steel.

My ears weren't fully formed, and my eyes were still just nerves in a socket, but I heard the clangs.

Moving again. Up the stairs, bumping each one as I went. Then, a nickering sound, the soft hair of a mane brushed me as I was heaved onto a horse.

Something bumped me—snapped the reigns. Screams behind me, then the sound of a gallop. The wind on my charred skin was like being burned all over again. All the old pain in a new way.

But I felt the hooves gallop under me, and the hot furnace of the pits fell into the distance. I didn't know where I was going, but I was moving free from the flames. Nothing I ever felt again could be as bad as that.

"Rest," a voice whispered on the breeze. "Sleep."

CHAPTER 8

I don't know how I slept on the back of that horse, but I did, and I had no idea how long I slept, but I finally woke up atop a crusted pile of my blood on a hard, thin bed made from an even harder mattress.

"Mmmmm," I moaned. When I moved, I realized I was connected to an IV dripping bright pink liquid into my veins. "What is—"

A short, gray-haired man with thick glasses and a bushy beard waddled over to me. "Don't move. Do you hear me? Do not move!"

I laid back down at his command. If there was one thing the pits of Hell taught me, it was to follow orders. I was very good at that now.

"What's happening to me?" I said, my speech slurred so badly I could barely understand myself.

The old man examined the bag and IV line. "You are being given an IV drip. These chemicals will allow you to regenerate. Now that you have left the pits, you can no longer regrow your skin. Luckily, I have a cure for that."

I looked down at my body. Crusted black burns encased my legs. My arms were red and raw, muscles exposed to the air.

"Is that why I can see? In the pits, my eyes always grew back last."

"Yes," he said. "The process works differently here than down in the pits, but the results are the same. Truth be told, your soul is what needs to regenerate. All of this nonsense with how you look is just a construction of the mind."

I stopped looking at my charred limbs and peered at the man. "Who are you?" I asked.

"It's best if you don't know." A woman wearing a purple sundress entered the room. "If you knew that, you'd be more wanted than you are now."

"Wanted?"

"Well, sure," the old man said. "You can't just escape the pits of Hell and expect to get away with it. What kind of reputation would that give the demons, huh?"

"And why are you wanted?"

The woman rubbed the old man's head. "Cuz he's the one that helps 'em all, doesn't he?"

"All of them? I'm not the only one that escaped the pits of Hell?"

"Not many do, I'm afraid, but enough I'd wager that Old Scratch doesn't want to take any chances."

I laughed lightly. It hurt my tender stomach to move even a bit. "He likes that nickname."

"Who?" the woman said. "The Prince of Lies?"

"He doesn't like that one as much," I replied groggily.

"Just rest," the old man said, smiling at me. "It will all be better soon."

I wanted to keep my eyes open, but the lids felt heavy. Before long, I was off to sleep, wondering what the hell was happening but far from complaining about it.

***

"Wake up," the woman said to me. "It's time for food."

"Don't disturb her, woman!" the old man said. "She doesn't even need to eat."

The woman sat down at the side of my bed with a tray. On it sat a bowl of hot soup and gravy-covered mutton of some unknown type. "I know that, but eating is good for the soul. Come on, love."

I looked down at my body. My leg was almost completely healed up, even if my arm was still a ragged assortment of muscles. It hurt to move, but I took a spoonful of the soup. Even though I couldn't taste anything, the feeling of warmth in my stomach made me smile in a way I never thought I would again.

"Doesn't that feel good?" the woman said.

I slurped. "I've had worse feelings."

"I know you have, love," she said, turning to the old man. "See, I told you she could use some food."

"It doesn't matter if she eats or not, you daft woman. It's the chemicals that are going to do their thing."

The woman started to stand, but I stayed her with my hand. "Thank you. What's your name?"

"Oh, my dear. I told you—"
"I know you are trying to protect me, but please. I must know."

"Very well. I'm Gloria, and that over there is Horace."

Horace waved at me. "Hello. I try not to tell everyone, you know. Who knows what kind of people escape the pits."

"Thank you for telling me." I took another big swallow of soup. "This really is great soup, Gloria."

"It makes ya feel human, don't it?"

I nodded. "It does."

"Well, anything we can do to that end, dear. It's just lovely to have some company. I have to deal with this crankypants all day."

"Crankypants!" Horace shouted. "I'm sorry that I'm in Hell, love, and that does bring out the worst in me, but I'm making the best of a bad situation, I think, yeah?"

Gloria rolled her eyes. "Sure ya are, dear."

I finished the soup and lay back down. "I'm sorry. It's delicious. I just have to—"

"Sleep," Horace said. "That's what I've been saying. It's the best medicine."

The bickering continued, creating a pleasant din that lulled me back to sleep.

***

The next time I woke, I felt better than I had in years. I looked down at my arm, and it was completely healed. My legs were completely intact as well. I felt like I could run a million miles and never stop.

"You're up!" Gloria shouted. "Horace! She's up!"

"I see her. I see her." Horace waddled over to me. "How do you feel?"

"I honestly . . . feel great."

Horace nodded, checking the IV. "Good, good. Well, then the chemicals did their job. You look right as rain."

He pulled the IV out of my arm, and I pushed myself up on the bed and stood up. Behind me, my wings fluttered fast to steady me on my feet.

"I don't know if you should be standing yet, love," Gloria said, worried.

Horace flicked his wrists at her. "Don't be daft, woman. She's fine. Look at her. Healthy as a horse."

"Is that true, love? Horace's work sometimes has some unintended consequences."

"Yeah, like healing her," Horace scoffed.

I wiggled my fingers and my toes. I turned my head to one side then the other. "I feel great, actually. Better than I have in . . . as long as I can remember."

"See, woman," Horace said. "I told you I fixed it."

I sat down at the table. Gloria was at the stove boiling a kettle. "Tea, dear?"

"That would be lovely."

"She makes a good pot," Horace said, sitting next to me. "I'll give her that. Probably why I keep her around. It's the only thing I can still taste in this blasted place."

"Oh, hush," Gloria said, blushing slightly.

"How did you—" I started. Then I stopped, thinking better of myself.

"How'd we end up out here in the middle of nowhere?" Gloria asked. "Is that what you want to know?"

I nodded. "It's been on my mind, yes. Most magical folk are in Dis. Does that mean you aren't—"

"Monsters?" Horace said. "You can say it. We don't mind. I'm actually a dwarf. You can tell by my little stubby legs and all. Gloria here is a Gorgon. Ain'tcha, love?"

I noticed then that Gloria wore a bonnet on her head. "That's right. Usually, my head is quite a fright, so I wanted to make sure I hid it away while you got better. People have a problem with my lovelies, but my snakes are what saved your life."

"Really?" I asked.

"Certainly," Horace said. "Milking them is the base for that concoction I made for you. It's amazing what magic still works in Hell. Totally unpredictable."

"Yes," I nodded. "Last time I was here, I realized that unicorn horns still had magic in them."

"Do they now?" Gloria asked, bringing the pot to a boil. "That's a might bit fascinating. Unicorns have a better reputation than Gorgons, I'm afraid."

"People think the worst of Gorgons," Horace said. "Even magic folk. But it's not true, you know. None of it. They can't just turn you to stone by lookin' at 'em. That's just a horrible rumor."

Gloria nodded, pouring out a cup of tea. "Got plenty of us killed, though, even before humans started hunting us for sport."

"That's sad," I said. I started to ask her more questions about her background, but the door slammed open, and a very frazzled Akta burst inside, red-faced and panting.

"We have to go," Akta said. "Now."

Akta was my kin, my great ancestor, and she saved me multiple times the last time I was in Hell. It appeared as though she was doing so again.

"Why the hurry, love?" Gloria said. "Sit down and have some tea."

Akta shook her head. "Another time. They are coming. I may have twenty minutes on them, maybe. You have to go. I brought back two extra unicorns for you. Pack what you can and get out of here."

Horace glanced at Gloria. They exchanged a knowing look that told me this wasn't the first time they'd had to run. They had made a home for themselves here, but from the look of love on their faces, they were all the home they needed.

Gloria smiled at Akta. "We'll be gone. Don't you worry about that."

"I'll send word when we're settled again," Horace added.

Akta nodded. "I'll try to get them to follow me to give you some more time. I'm sorry for this, all of it."

"Don't worry about it, love," Gloria said with another smile.

Akta pulled me to the door before I had a chance to say goodbye. I took one last look at the old couple sitting at their table and hoped that helping me didn't doom them.

CHAPTER 9

"Keep up!" Akta shouted.

"I'm trying!" I could barely stay upright on the unicorn Akta brought for me as we galloped away from Horace and Gloria's house. I had felt wonderful there, nearly recovered, but the constant up and down of the unicorn's gallop made my head spin like I drank too much wine.

I looked back toward the little house and watched a gang of demons descend upon it. "Are they going to be okay?'

"There's nothing you can do for them now!" Akta shouted, turning down an old dirt road. The wall of bodies, ever-present in Hell, moaned at us.

"Where are we going?" I asked.

"Away!" she replied. "Quit worrying. Save your strength, and just keep up!"

***

We rode for hours until Akta stopped in front of a large cave carved into a rock wall. From its lip, I saw walls of moaning humans stretch far into the horizon, and sheer cliffs ascended above it to Hell's ceiling.

The last time I was in Hell, Dis, the biggest city in Hell, filled the horizon and the plains of Hell stretched for leagues upon leagues. Now, I couldn't even see a mile in any direction without being confronted by a wall of limbs and other assorted body parts.

"Come," Akta said, lighting a torch and walking into the cave.

I followed her, my wings fluttering behind me. Akta lit the torches along the walls until, eventually, the whole cave was lit with flickering lights. A mountain of treasure filled the room, piled into great, misshapen heaps. There were heavy weapons and armor from assorted centuries and dynasties and even stores of those ancient leather-bound books I always loved to page through when I was in Aziolith's cave.

I paused, mid-step. "Where are we?"

"Somewhere they won't think to look. Aziolith was a great friend to you but an enemy to me. They will never think that I brought you to his den. They will never even know I kept tabs on him."

"This is where Aziolith lived?"

Akta nodded, placing the torch in a pile of ornate chairs in the middle of the room she used for kindling and sitting down next to them. "He was feared, even in Hell. Every demon knew his name and quaked at the sound of his footsteps."

"Are you sure it's safe if he was so well known?"

"Nowhere is safe, Julia. Nowhere in Hell will ever be safe for you, but we can't move on until you rest. I took you from Horace too soon, and there is a difficult road ahead. If your body is not ready for it, then the demons will surely find you."

"I don't understand," I said, sitting next to Akta. "I felt so good before, and Charlie told me if I were dead, I would never be tired again."

"He never went through the pits of Hell. It's true, your body doesn't feel tired. Your mind, on the other hand, and your spirit are both depleted. Horace did what he could, but you went through a great ordeal, and the only way to fix it is rest."

I had more questions, but Akta had no interest in answering them. I laid back on a pile of silk tapestries and closed my eyes.

***

I woke to the sound of Akta searching through Aziolith's collection of weapons and armor. She had already pulled out a pile of obsidian weapons and armor and was fluttering up and down the horde of treasure, tossing items as she went.

"There it is!" Akta shouted from the top of a heap.

She landed on the ground gracefully and sat down at the fire she'd made of broken Tudor dynasty furniture. "I knew I would find you," she said, admiring the long dagger with a hooked shape and engraved handle.

"What is that?" I asked.

Akta looked startled for a moment as if she'd forgotten I was there but quickly regained her composure. "It is a dagger; one Lucifer has been looking for, for a long time. Do you remember him mentioning it the last time you were here?"

"Vaguely," I replied, yawning.

"Lucifer said that only five weapons in all the solar system can kill him, right?"

I nodded, stretching my limbs out with another yawn.

"One is in Heaven, locked in God's vestibule. Two others are safe in the dungeons of Hell. Then there is the Dagger of Obsolescence. If you stab Lucifer in the heart with it, he will die. He once had it but lost it long ago. He's searched for centuries but never found it again. I have always thought it was here, in Aziolith's cavern, as it was Lucifer who cheated Aziolith to acquire it in the first place but had no reason to search for it until today."

"So . . . what?" I asked. "We're going to kill Satan?"

"No. We are going to offer it as a gift in return for your freedom."

She handed me the knife. It was lighter in my hand than I expected. The blade was curved, with black runes inlaid on either side of it. It was well balanced, and the rough leather grip felt good in my hand. I slashed it left and right across from me.

"That's a pretty good plan," I heard a voice say behind me. "Too bad you'll never get to it."

I turned around and saw Charlie, the monstrous, little imp that tried to sell me twice the last time I was in Hell. He was blocking the opening of the cave with demons lined up on either side of him. He clopped on his hind legs, so proud of himself that it oozed out of him.

"Charlie!" I shouted, scrambling to my feet.

"You did good, getting this far," Charlie said, walking forward. "Further than anyone has in a long time, but unfortunately, this is the end of the line, toots. Nobody ain't never escaped me, and they ain't gonna start now."

"What about Imogen?" I asked. "The banshee who tore out your partner's larynx and got away from you?"

Charlie opened his mouth to speak, but he held back for a moment, thinking. "That don't count, cuz Satan blew her apart." He smiled. "So, I've got a perfect record, far as I'm concerned."

Akta stepped forward, gripping two daggers in her hands. They were familiar. In fact, they looked exactly like the daggers I'd relinquished to the Black Gate during my last tour of Hell.

"I do not want to hurt you, imp," she growled. "But I will."

"I do desperately want to hurt you," I added. "So please, come at me."

Charlie snapped his fingers, and four of his demons rushed forward. I soared into the air and stabbed one of them through the temple. The demon disintegrated immediately, leaving behind nothing but a pile of ashes.

I stared at the blade. "Nice."

Akta stabbed a demon in the chest and kicked it to the ground, then pulled her dagger out of its chest and sent it up the jaw of the next. Green blood sprayed out of the top of its head where the weapon protruded.

Another demon charged at me. I spun in the air and stabbed it in the back as it ran past. It disintegrated like the other one. Charlie snapped his fingers, and the remaining six demons rushed us.

I flew back toward the piles of loot and grabbed another dagger. The lopsided heap of treasure teetered to one side, and I pushed it over onto the demons as they tried to climb toward me. While they righted themselves, I stabbed one in the stomach. It evaporated, and I stuck the dagger in the next demon's throat, then tossed my other dagger into the final demon's eye.

There was a pile of demons at Akta's feet when I looked up, and she sauntered toward Charlie. He tried to snap his fingers and vanish, but Akta flung two small daggers at him. They stuck perfectly, one into each of his hands, preventing his escape.

"Now you are going to help us, little whelp," Akta said, digging her knives deeper into Charlie's hands and pinning him to the wall of the cavern. "How do I find Yilir?"

"You don't wanna do that," Charlie replied, his eyes bulging with fear.

"I'll decide what I want to do," Akta hissed at him. "Now talk, or I will skin you alive. The last time we met, I was not well versed with torturing an imp, but I promise you I have studied up since then."

"She don't wanna be found, all right?" Charlie shouted. "That's why Charon can't see her in the mirror, cuz she doesn't want to be found."

"That is not the question I asked, Charlie."

Yilir was the creator of the Mirror of Yilir, which held the power to see any being in Hell or Earth with just a thought. We had traded it to Charon last time I was here in return for safe passage across the molten lava that surrounded Satan's palace…or was it magma?

"I say we just vaporize him," I said, holding up the Dagger of Obsolescence, which had made such quick work out of so many demons.

"No!" Charlie's voice came out as a squeal. "Don't vaporize me. I can talk. I can talk."

"Then talk, maggot," Akta said, each word soaked in venom.

Charlie dropped his eyes low. "I lied to you before, and I feel bad about it."

"That would be a first," I scoffed.

"Yilir isn't hiding herself from Charon. She's hiding herself from everyone. The truth is that Yilir . . . is the mirror. She bound her soul inside of it. Charon can't find her because he's holding her, every hour of every day."

"How do I free her?" Akta said.

Charlie looked Akta dead in the eyes. "And what if she don't wanna be found, huh? What then?"

"That's not the question I asked, Charlie," Akta said, grabbing the Dagger of Obsolescence from my hand and sticking it into his face. "Quit playing games with me!"

"There's a summoning circle, all right! Jesus, put that thing away."

"I'll put it away when you tell me the truth. Where do I find the incantation?"

Charlie wasn't good at telling the truth, but he was very good at telling people what they wanted to hear. "It's in a book. It's in a book I stole from Aziolith centuries ago. It's how I knew about the mirror to begin with."

"And where is this book?" Akta asked.

"In my flat, in Dis. But you'll never get it. The guards will be on you the second you show up at the city gates."

"Then it's a good thing we're not showing up at the city gates," Akta replied. "You're going to snap us right into your apartment."

"No way. That's against the rules. I can't just be bringing souls places without a reason. I'll get fired."

Akta pressed the Dagger of Obsolescence into Charlie's shoulder. "Either you do it, or you get turned into dust. One or the other. Doesn't matter to me."

Charlie let out a deep sigh. "You drive a hard bargain, sister. I don't think I got any other choice. Looks like you got yourself a deal."

"Don't listen to him. His deals are meaningless."

Akta smiled. "I know they are, but if I recall, you once told me that you had to go with your gut, and I think this is our best option."

"Why do we even need Yilir?"

"Because we'll never get through the Black Gate without Charon's help, and she was Charon's price."

"It looks like we don't have a choice then," I said.

"No," Akta replied. "It doesn't seem as though we do." She pulled the daggers out of Charlie's hands and stuffed them back in her belt.

"You ladies drive a hard, painful bargain," Charlie said, sticking out his bloody hand. "But a fair one."

"Just remember," Akta said, holding the Dagger of Obsolescence tight to Charlie's throat. "You mess up, and I won't hesitate to end you."

I grabbed onto Akta's hand, and she grabbed onto Charlie's claw. With a devious grin, the imp snapped his fingers, and the three of us vanished.

CHAPTER 10

I had been to Dis once before. It was the biggest city in Hell—the only city for all I knew. It was where all of Hell's monsters resided, from the demons who tortured lost souls to the orcs that pulled our carts to the pits of Hell and other fairy folk who were hunted to extinction on Earth thousands of years ago and wound up in Hell.

Dis was an intersection of worlds, where medieval thatched roofs butted up against the modern skyscrapers like the one Charlie lived in with his two children. Demons who worked assignments on Earth preferred the conveniences of the modern world, while those who hadn't left Hell in centuries felt more at home in the thatched homes and cobblestone streets of the past.

The last time I was in Charlie's apartment, he drugged my vodka, hogtied me to his couch, and sold me to a dark lord trying to start an Apocalypse. That was bad enough, but I was angrier that he acted like my friend the whole time he rolled out his devious agenda. I wouldn't be taken in by his charm this time. He was a conniving, devious trickster who would turn on his own mother if it gave him a leg up. I refused to give him the chance. Not again.

Akta, Charlie, and I reappeared in the middle of Charlie's living room. Two young imps with tails too big for their bodies screamed as we materialized in front of their TV.

"It's okay, kids," Charlie said. "These are Daddy's friends."

Charlie led us through the apartment and down a long hallway. He opened a door which led into a small room with a dingy bed and tiny desk on opposite walls and a large bookcase in the middle, filled with ancient leather-bound books.

"Close the door behind you," Charlie said. "My kids are real nosy."

I shut the door behind us, dulling the children's laughter coming from the living room. "Where is it?"

"Take it easy," Charlie replied, pulling out one of the old books. "It's not like these are paperbacks, you know."

"Just hurry up," I said.

"I want to be sure of something," Charlie said, thumbing through the pages of the book. "I want to be sure that no matter what happens, my kids are off-limits."

"If you just do what you promised," I replied, "there will be no reason to involve your kids, Charlie."

The imp shook his head, flipping through another book. "Just promise me that no matter what happens, my kids are off-limits."

I nodded. "You have my word."

"And you?" Charlie pointed at Akta. "You gotta promise, too."

"I don't give my word to demons."

"Imps," he said, disgusted. "I'm an imp, not a demon. And if you want this book, then you will promise me."

Akta held up the Dagger of Obsolescence. "Or I could just cut out your heart and find the book myself."

"Joke's on you there, toots. I don't have a heart."

"That explains a lot," I muttered. "Just promise him already so we can get out of here, Akta."

Akta threw up her hands. "Fine. Your children are off-limits."

Charlie smiled and handed me the book in his hands, and pointed at the illuminated text. "There. Right on that page. That's the good news. You wanna know the bad news?"

I sighed. "Yeah, Charlie. Let's hear it."

"I was stalling this whole time, 'til I could get a team in place to take you out. Sorry about that, but don't forget. You gave me your word."

Charlie vanished with the snap of his fingers, and in the next second, a dozen hoofed feet stomped into the apartment, shaking the ground under us.

"That little jerk!" I shouted.

Akta handed me the book and used the butt of her dagger to smash open a window over the desk. "About what I expected. Let's go!" She pushed me onto the ledge, and I fluttered away from the window to make room for her. Once I was safely in the air, Akta leaped out to join me. I heard a snarling sound and turned back. A big, meaty ogre had latched onto her leg. Behind it, a dozen more beef-faced ogres growled and clawed at her.

"Get off me!" Akta shouted. She slashed at the ogre's arm with her dagger, and it disappeared into ash. Hundreds of fireballs shot at us from the ground as she flew toward me.

"We can't stay in the air for long!" I shouted. "They'll gun us down."

"I have a plan," Akta replied. "Follow me."

Akta zipped past me, and I struggled to keep up. She moved like a graceful bird, flying alongside the fireballs and dodging them. I looked more like a soggy bumblebee as I wiggled and waggled away from the fireballs.

***

"Let me in," Akta said, banging on a door in the middle of a darkened alley.

Footsteps clomped down the stairs at a rapid pace, almost as if they were falling down them. When the door opened, a familiar face stared at me. It was Clovis, the kindly elf who helped me the last time I was in Hell. We had used his house to interrogate Charlie once, before the little imp kidnapped me for the second time in as many days.

"My gods, Akta. You'll wake the dead with that thumping."

"That was the idea, old friend," she said, grabbing Clovis's hand firmly. "We need your help."

"You are always welcome here," Clovis replied. "Come in."

Akta brushed past him and revealed me standing in the alley behind her, smiling at him. "Hi."

"My word," Clovis said, pulling on his tiny, round spectacles. "Is that Julia Freeman? What has brought you to Hell this time?"

I sighed. "Death, I'm afraid."

"She is the reason we are here, old friend," Akta said, starting up the stairs. "And why we need your help."

***

"That is a harrowing story," Clovis said as we sat around the dining room table.

The last time I came to Clovis's house, I didn't understand why somebody would have a kitchen and a dining room if they never had to eat. Now that I was dead, I understood it more. There was a certain comfort in feeling alive, and one of the things that living people did was eat.

"You really escaped the pits of Hell?" Beatrice added in, enraptured by every word of my story. "That's crazy."

Beatrice was Clovis's little daughter. Both had been dead for thousands of years, but Beatrice died first, when she was just a little girl, after being stabbed through the heart in a dark alley.

"I know," I replied. "I still can't believe it."

"That is why we are here, though," Akta said to Clovis. "We must get to Lucifer and request clemency for Julia. He is the only one who can prevent her from being hunted all her days. To do so, we must get out of Dis. Can you help us?"

"Of course, we can. Right, Dad?" Beatrice said. "My dad can do anything."

Clovis sighed. "What you are asking . . . it could endanger everything we hold dear."

"I know it's a lot, my old friend," Akta said, "but you know the horrors contained in the pits. I must do all I can to save Julia from that torment. Can you live with yourself knowing my kin will suffer for all eternity?"

"Can you live with putting me and mine at risk?"

Akta looked down. "I am sorry, my friend. I ask too much. There are others who can help me escape the city, but none I trust as much."

Akta pushed up from the table and turned away, but Clovis grabbed her arm. They stared at each other for a long while, communicating in the way that only old friends can until they both nodded at each other.

"I made a pact to protect you and yours," Akta said. "I plan to honor that pact."

"And mine to you," Clovis said. "There is a smuggler. He brings my shoes to markets across Hell. I will bring you to him."

"You are a good man," I said, unable to look him in the eyes. "Thank you for this. I can't tell you—"

Clovis held up his hand. "Don't mention it. Ever."

***

Clovis dressed me in rags before we left his house. My clothing was too modern and glamorous for Hell, and I stuck out like a sore thumb. If we were to avoid detection, I would have to blend into the surroundings.

"You're a real idiot, idiot," Beatrice told me as she wrapped me in another layer of rags.

"I know," I sighed. "I blame my mother."

"You should," Beatrice replied, smiling. She handed me a satchel to carry the book I stole from Charlie.

After they dressed me, Clovis left Beatrice at home despite her whining. It was dangerous work he did, leading two fugitives through the streets of Dis, and he wanted to make sure Beatrice was safe. I understood that.

Clovis guided us out of the house and through the winding roads of Dis. It was early in the day, and other vendors weren't set up on the streets selling their wares yet. In fact, there were very few monsters in the streets as we weaved our way through.

Finally, we stopped in front of a stable with thick brambles overgrowing the old, wooden fence. Even though most buildings were ancient, the house stood out to its neighbors. It was more run down than most.

"Follow closely, and don't say a word. If Gregor knew the truth, he would sell you in a moment for the reward."

Clovis led us around the back of the house and into a barn that stood apart from the ramshackle stable. Inside, a dozen unicorns fed on hay while a tall, thin elf played the flute between them.

"Gregor!" Clovis said, smiling at the smuggler. "You haven't lost your skill with a tune."

Gregor turned around and stowed his flute. "Another run so soon, old friend? How fast do you work?"

Clovis shook his head. "I'm afraid I have other cargo for you this night."

He pointed at Akta and me. I looked down at the ground, careful not to reveal my face. I had seen more than a dozen wanted posters of us throughout the streets of Dis, and I was not interested in having anyone collect on them.

"My friends need safe passage out of Dis," Clovis said, pulling a money purse from his belt. He dipped his hand inside and pulled out a gold coin. It had a pentagram carved on it that was surrounded by fire. He handed it to Gregor. "No questions asked."

"It will cost you more than this, old friend," Gregor said, examining the coin.

"And I have more for you." Clovis tossed the bag to him.

Gregor caught the purse and gave it a squeeze, massaging it with his rough hands. "What is their bounty?"

"No bounty. Just . . . domestic troubles."

Gregor smiled. "You are a terrible liar."

"But a good client," Clovis replied. "This is half your fee. You get the other half when you return. Akta will tell you where to go, and she will give you a token to prove you have fulfilled your mission. When you return that token, you will receive the rest of the money."

"You don't mince words, Clovis," he said. "I respect that. We leave right away. Let me saddle up the unicorns and collect the rest of my next haul."

"Very well," Clovis said, shaking hands with the man.

Clovis walked over to me and shook Akta's hand. Akta pulled him in for a hug, something I had never seen her do before.

"I owe you, old friend."

"You owe me nothing. One day this debt will be repaid, and I will owe you. That is how friendship works."

Akta let go of her hug, and Clovis turned to me. I squeezed him tightly around the neck, near tears at his generosity. "You have no idea how much this means to me."

He looked into my face. "Just make it count, okay?"

"I swear," I replied, letting him go.

"This lovey-dovey crap is all well and good," Gregor said, "But maybe instead of having a touching moment, you can help me out here, so we can leave sooner."

Clovis waved and disappeared back into the shadows of the street. Akta and I walked toward Gregor and helped him prepare to lead us out of the city.

CHAPTER 11

Gregor really was as good as Clovis made him sound. He smuggled us out of the city without any issue. Akta and I had to lie under a pile of greasy hay while he moved his cart slowly through the town, but soon enough, we were through the city gates and into the countryside.

"It's safe now!" Gregor poked at the pile of hay.

I popped my head up and turned back toward the city, expecting to see it in the distance, but what I saw was nothing but the familiar walls of bodies on either side of me. I instinctively pulled the satchel with Charlie's book close to my body to protect it.

"Which exit did we leave from?" Akta asked, crawling into the front of the cart beside Gregor.

Gregor snapped the reins, and the two unicorns whinnied as they sped to a gallop. "North gate. Centaur there likes money more than he likes his job."

"Good. Then we should just stay on this road for half a day until it bends to the river."

"You mind telling me where we're going?" Gregor asked.

"Yes, I do. I'm sure you would like to know. However, I've long since grown past the ability to trust a smuggler."

"Please," Gregor replied. "Haven't you heard the phrase 'Honor among thieves'?"

"We're not thieves," I said, turning to the front of the cart.

"No, darlin'," Gregor said. "I know you're not a thief. You look like the kind of person who got mixed up in something she doesn't understand."

"You have no idea," I said, mumbling to myself.

"Just sit down and get some rest," Akta said to me. "It's a long road ahead of us."

It was a long road behind us too, but I didn't argue. I pulled Charlie's book from the satchel where I had stashed it and started to read. It was all in an ancient language I didn't understand, but at least the pictures were nice to look at and helped distract me from the souls all around me.

***

"Why do so many people use unicorns here?" I asked after several hours of silence. "Aren't there other creatures that can pull carts?"

"Of course, there are," Gregor said. "But none of them are as fast as a unicorn or as loyal. I still can't believe you hunted them to extinction."

"I did not!" I replied, indignant.

"Oh, I know it wasn't you. It was . . . well, part of you at least. If you're anything like your friend here, then you're part fairy folk, but I can tell by your voice you're more human than anything. Besides, you reek of the fire pits."

"I do not!"

"It's not my place, ma'am. I don't know what you heard about me, but I ain't gonna turn you in. Do you know what kind of criminals I get riding in the back of that cart? If I turned 'em all in, I wouldn't have much of a business."

Akta straightened in her seat. "We are not criminals."

"Probably true," Gregor said, pointing at me. "But if I had to peg it, I would say you're the lady that escaped the pits of hell. That's the only type of person I could see Clovis paying top dollar for, after all."

I pulled off my hood, revealing my face to Gregor. "You are very good at this."

"It's just thousands of years of practice, little lady." He smiled. "Now, put that hood back on. These demons know who to look out for as well."

The demons on either side of the road had been eyeballing us since we left Dis. They busied themselves loading bodies onto the great wall of souls, but I could see them stealing glances.

"Up here," Akta said, pointing to the fork in the road. "Take a right."

Gregor gave a grunt. "Whatever you say."

"Actually," I heard a familiar voice say. "Maybe you should stop." Charlie had materialized in the road in front of the cart.

"Do not stop!" Akta shouted, jumping from her seat.

"Demons of Hell," Charlie said, lifting his hands into the air. "Stop your work. These are traitors to our lord, Lucifer. This one escaped from the pits of Hell, and these others helped her escape! Get them!"

And like that, a hundred demons turned from their work and stomped toward us as a group, circling us closer with each step they took.

"This isn't good!" Gregor said.

I leaped over the front of the cart, helped along by my wings, and landed on the back of one of the unicorns. "I hope this works."

Charlie and his demons pressed in closer. I placed my head onto the unicorn's horn and made a wish . . . I wished that the wall of souls would come tumbling down and crash all over the demons so that we could get out of there.

Instantly, a shockwave rumbled underneath the plains and knocked the demons to the ground. When they looked up, the wall of souls on either side of them teetered and cascaded down upon them.

"No!" Charlie shouted.

I leaped from one unicorn to the other and pressed my head against its horn. I wasn't sure if unicorns could grant infinite wishes or not, but I didn't want to find out I was wrong while a billion souls fell on top of me.

"Where are we going?"

Akta was zipping above us, dodging bodies, but landed on the cart when I called out to her. "I can't tell you!

"Screw keeping it a secret, tell me now!"

Akta stole a glance at Charlie and his demons struggling beneath the weight of charred human bodies, then shook her head and said, "The pass of Kalet."

"I wish to be safe from this cascade of souls, safe at the pass of Kalet," I mumbled at the unicorn.

We vanished into thin air, just as the wall of souls became a river of souls and drowned all the demons in its path, including Charlie.

***

The cart landed with a crunch in an empty pasture with a bridge at its far end, which traversed a river of molten lava...magma...whatever it was called. A dock sat beside the bridge. On the dock, the dark gondolier Charon, with his two, beady, golden eyes peering out at us from beneath his cloak, stood motionless in his boat.

Gregor pulled the reins on his unicorns, and they lurched to a stop. "What the hell just happened?"

"Oh, you didn't know they could do that?" I asked, dismounting the beast and hopping to the ground.

Behind us, a small portion of the wall of souls had fallen. I could see the stalactites of Hell once more peeping out behind them.

"Well done." Akta patted me on the back as we walked toward the boat. Charon groaned as we got closer to him. "You're late. The dark lord expects me."

"He'll wait," Akta replied. "Do you have what I asked for?"

Charon reached into his cloak and pulled out the silver-handled Mirror of Yilir and two white flowers. "The mirror and two winter lilies. An odd request."

Akta took them from Charon and gave me the lilies. "Give these to Gregor. Tell him that his job is done. He should present them to Clovis for the remainder of his payment. Meanwhile, I will set up the incantation from the book."

I pulled the book out of my satchel and handed it to Akta. She flipped it open and studied a drawing, then started to carve the image into the dirt with her dagger. While she worked, I walked over to Gregor and held the flowers out to him.

"These are for you. Take them to Clovis and get the rest of your payment."

"Are you crazy?" Gregor looked at me with wide eyes. "I can't go back that way. They'll kill me."

"Then go another way," I said.

"You know," he said, snatching the lilies from my hand. "I knew I should never have helped you ladies, but I just can't say no to a pretty face, you know? Ah well, I was sick of Dis anyway."

"Where will you go now?" I asked.

"I have plenty of loot and some other things to smuggle. I'll be okay until I get back to the city, and don't worry about Clovis and Beatrice. They'll never get tied back to this. I swear it."

"Thank you, Gregor. You're a better man than Hell should allow." I turned back to Akta as Gregor galloped away. She had finished carving into the ground and had placed the mirror in the center of the circle. Taking a step back, she turned to Charon.

"This is the moment of truth. I hope it works," she said, wiping dirt off her dagger. She reached for the book she'd set aside.

"For your sakes," Charon said. "I agree."

Akta gave me a quick smile and then dug her nose into the book. "Evestra Italhir Megastin. Evestra Italhir Megastin. Evestra Italhir Megastin. Dark witch of the sacred forest. Come. Come. Evestra Italhir Megastin. Evestra Italhir Megastin. Evestra Italhir Megastin."

The ground quaked, and a bright blue light flashed from the mirror, flickering over and over again, faster and faster with each recitation of the incantation.

"Julia!" she shouted. "Join me."

"Evestra Italhir Megastin," we both shouted. "Evestra Italhir Megastin. Evestra Italhir Megastin. Evestra Italhir Megastin."

The ground let out a great quake that shook the valley. A blue beam shot up into the sky. From its light, an object fell to the ground with a thud. When the light dissipated, all that remained was a woman with long, elven ears dressed all in white. Her skin was lighter than alabaster, and her eyes were as blue as a clear sky.

"Yilir?" Charon said, his voice shaking.

The woman looked up at him, and their eyes met. A faint smile grew on her face. "My love?"

CHAPTER 12

"Why would you wake me up, my love?" Yilir said, grasped in Charon's embrace. "Don't you know they will be after us again?"

Charon pulled back slightly to look her in the face. "You do not know, do you?"

"Know what?" Yilir replied, staring deeply into Charon's eyes, unfazed by the fact he was little more than cloth and yellow, burning eyes.

"The gods have abandoned Earth. Only Bacchus remains, and he is in Heaven, far removed from the dealings of Hell."

Yilir inhaled deeply. "You mean . . . could it be true? Could the curse of our love be lifted after all this time?"

"Alas, I am still bound to my duties as the ferryman. Nothing can stop that except for a reprieve from Hades himself."

"And yet," Yilir said, stepping into the boat, "my curse is lifted."

"Not quite," Akta said, picking up the mirror from the ground. "Your soul is still bound to this mirror. If it is destroyed, so will you be."

Akta handed the mirror to Yilir, who nodded graciously for it. "Thank you. I will keep it safe."

"Our love, however," Charon said, caressing Yilir's face with his bony hands, "may continue now."

"That is the most wonderful news," Yilir said, hugging Charon tightly.

"And now, Akta of the forest," Charon grumbled, "you would like me to honor your half of our deal."

"I would," the pixie said. "Take my kin to Lucifer's palace and assure no harm comes to her."

"It will be done," Charon said. "Come, Julia. We have a meeting to attend."

I turned to Akta. "You're coming with me, aren't you?"

Akta shook her head. "I have taken you as far as I can. There will be others tracking you down, and I will keep them busy. You must go and go now. Charlie and his demons will not rest easy until they have you. I cannot protect you, but Charon can. While you are on his boat, nothing can harm you."

"You have saved me more times than I can count," I said, grabbing Akta's hands. "I can never repay you."

"Then don't," Akta replied, shaking free of my grasp. "If you want to repay me, then do not fail. Understood?"

"I won't."

Akta handed me the Dagger of Obsolescence and the book we stole from Charlie. "Give the dagger to Lucifer. It is payment for your soul."

I nodded. "I will."

Akta wasn't one for long goodbyes, and she turned from me without another word. I stepped onto Charon's boat as he pushed off the docks into the molten lava.

As we pulled away, I heard the screams of demons in the distance. They sounded pissed off, and the rumbling of their feet got louder as they neared. Akta pulled out her daggers and prepared for battle.

From the path, a hundred demons, led by Charlie, rushed into the field, snarling and pissed. They barreled toward the river en masse like a swarm of locusts. Akta fluttered into the air as the horde descended upon her.

"Akta!" I shouted, turning to the ferryman. "Go back! We have to help her."

"I was given strict instructions to assure you weren't harmed. I cannot let you leave this boat, and if you do, I will continue without you. Make your choice. Save yourself or your kin."

The boat wobbled beneath my feet when I stood up to defend Akta, but Yilir caught me by the arm. "She fights to defend you. If you return to that shore, you will negate everything she did for you."

I knew she was right, but I couldn't stop the guilt welling up in my throat at the thought of Akta risking her life to save me yet again.

"Sit, little one," Charon said. "Akta is a great warrior. You will see."

I did what he said, sitting down again and turning to watch Akta as she dropped a smoke bomb on the snarling demons. With one last look at me, she smiled and zipped away across the bridge. Charlie stood up when the dust cleared and stared after me. There was nothing he could do to me while I was on Charon's boat, and he knew it. All he could do was glare at me while I disappeared into the mist of the molten lava.

***

We moved through the lava for a long while. None of us had anything to say. I stared out at the festering lake while Yilir lost herself in Charon's eyes. Charon, for his part, took turns staring out at the lava before us and back again into Yilir's loving gaze. It was hard to see any emotion in the yellow, burning eyes of his face, but if I watched closely, I could see them soften when he looked on Yilir.

"We will pass The Gate of Ulthar in a couple of minutes," Charon said. "This is the most treacherous part of our path. While none can be harmed while they are in my boat, the gate cannot allow any to pass with weapons that might harm the Devil."

I looked down at the dagger in my hand. "I definitely have one of those."

"I have only shepherded one past the gate before, and we were lucky to leave with our lives. It was made with the old, strong magic of the first gods, Zeus, and his ilk, but so was I. I do not know which is more powerful or who will break in battle."

"It will be okay, my love," Yilir said, stroking Charon's bony skeleton hand. "Nothing can harm us now."

I watched the two of them, then looked back at the gate. My heart thudded against my rib cage, and a sense of dread came over me. I needed a distraction. "So how did you two . . . get together?" I asked.

Yilir's face clouded for a moment as she looked for the memories. There was a smile on her face. "It was sixty thousand years ago."

"Give or take a few centuries," Charon added, cocking his head beneath the cowl of his cloak.

"The world was still young, and gods still roamed the land."

"So many gods everywhere."

"Can I tell it, honey?" Yilir asked.

"Sorry."

I laughed. It was nice to know that even death and thousands of years didn't change couples.

"Charon was the king of the kingdom of Urthan on a planet far from here. I was his chief architect. Together we built a paradise so grand that the gods gifted us immortality to work for them. In their service, we built the most beautiful palaces the gods had ever seen across every corner of the universe. By the time we reached this planet, we were madly in love with each other, but neither had the nerve to tell the other. Then, Charon was offered a bride in the siren Thelxiepeia, but he refused and instead ran away with me."

"Anubis found out," Charon said. "He discovered that we planned to wed against his wishes and cursed us both. I was sent to the afterlife to live as a ferryman. First on the river Styx, and then as the personal chauffeur for Velaska and Lucifer."

"I was cursed to be Anubis's personal concubine for all time. Luckily, I was an excellent sorcerer." Yilir picked up the mirror. "I was able to cheat death, in my way."

"Quiet," Charon said. "We pass by the gate. If the red eye finds that you have the dagger, it will surely destroy us all."

The Gate of Ulthar rose before us a thousand feet in the air. I had passed through it with Akta only a few years prior. It didn't look like much more than a black gate, but it could expand and contract at will to keep out those that wished to harm the Devil. Once, it blocked fifty legions of angels from passing through it. The last time I was here, I had to lay all my weapons at the feet of Cerberus to pass. Now, I was trying to sneak past with Charon and a dagger that could kill the Lord of Hell himself.

We would have all held our collective breaths if we had any to hold, but instead, we just watched intently at the gate as the bejeweled eye gazed back and forth with its red beam. Even from a thousand feet above, I saw it twist and turn when we passed.

"Crap. It found us."

It wasn't more than a second before we were wrapped in its red gaze, which narrowed on our boat. I felt the skin sheer off my body, and even Charon fell onto his knees.

"What's happening?" I shouted.

"We. Are. Unworthy." Charon choked out the words. "Now—it will blow us into oblivion."

The gate bellowed as the beam charged up to fire on us. Then, a bolt of red lightning descended upon us.

"No!" Yilir screamed. She jumped in front of us and held up her mirror, which emitted a blue wall of energy that expanded around the boat like a shield. As the gate's beam pushed toward our boat, the blue forcefield collapsed and cracked, but it held. The beam, fighting against the mirror, pushed the boat forward until it was past the black gate. Once we were past the gate, the beam stopped. Yilir slumped over.

"Yilir!" Charon wailed. "My love. What have you done?"

I looked down to see the mirror cracked in half. It fell from Yilir's hand onto the hull of the boat. Her once crimson lips were light pink, and her ice-blue eyes faded to a dull gray. Charon leaped to her as she fell, cradling her in his arms.

"My love. My life . . ." Yilir said. "I will always love you. Always."

With those simple words, Yilir broke apart into flecks of blue light, swirling and twinkling against the sky before the mirror recaptured her beauty and drew her back into it forever.

I looked over at Charon, not knowing what to say. Would he cry? Would he curse? Was he going to kick me out of the boat? He did nothing. Letting out a sigh, he turned back to the front of the boat and kept pushing forward. Lucifer's castle, looming in the distance, grew closer with every stroke he took.

"Are you...okay?" I asked him after too long a pause.

Charon let out a rattling sigh. "I had my love for one hour longer than I ever thought I would see her again. My heart is broken, but it is happy as well. Happy I found her, if even for a short while."

I dug into my pocket and pulled out the book which brought Yilir back. "This is what we used to pull Yilir back from the brink. It's yours now. If anything can bring her back, it is in these pages."

The ferryman just stared ahead. "Thank you, little one, but now I would like to concentrate on fulfilling my end of the bargain. We do not need two lost souls today." Charon looked up toward the castle, then pushed with all the frenzied force and speed of a man who had just lost everything.

I put the book aside and gulped a few times. I knew that soon I would meet Old Scratch himself.

CHAPTER 13

The river emptied into a massive molten lake swirling with eddies. Charon guided us through the bubbling lava to the Devil's castle, which sat upon an island in the middle of the lake, its obsidian frame jutting into the sky.

Akta once told me the Devil's castle was the perfect defensive position. There was nothing behind it but sheer rock face, so it kept all of Hell in front of it. With The Gate of Ulthar blocking the way and its unnavigable molten lava lake, the castle could withstand an attack from the gods themselves.

I had to admit, though, I was less than impressed by the construction. While the onyx façade was impressive, it was cracked and warped from centuries of neglect. The black bones that interlocked to form the door were splintered and cracked.

As we neared the dock, I couldn't shake the feeling that the castle was looking at me. The wide and tall door of bones looked like a mouth ready to unhinge its jaw and swallow me up. Above it, two towers stared at me like soulless eyes, tracking us as we pulled up to the dock.

"Thank you," I said to Charon, stepping out of the boat. "I know you risked much to get here, and I appreciate it."

"I risked nothing more than you."

"Maybe, but it is my life to save, not yours."

Charon pushed off from the dock. He picked up the cracked mirror and held it close to his bosom. "Think nothing of it."

With one more push from his oar, Charon disappeared into the mist. I turned to the castle. A hundred massive steps separated me from my destiny. When I came here the last time, the stairs took a brutal toll on me. Between the heat of Hell and my inability to fly—the magic wouldn't work because I wasn't dead—I had nearly passed out and stumbled into the molten lake.

This time, I unfurled my wings and fluttered into the air with ease. I hopped onto each step lightly and propelled myself back into the air until I could take several steps at a time. The heat prevented me from getting much lift, though, which explained why Akta hadn't been able to fly us both when I was struggling to climb the stairs. It also explained why angels couldn't make it over the lake, either.

I made quick work of the stairs and ascended to the doorstep of Lucifer's palace, where the splintered bones inlaid in the massive door rose ominously above me. I pressed against them with all my strength. The bones crackled and popped as they gave way, and I stepped inside.

The black bone motif continued into the foyer of the castle. Short candles flickered on the walls, barely illuminating the darkness. On either side of a black rug in front of me, suits of black armor stood guard, the last line of defense against an intruder. Two of the suits didn't have weapons, a reminder of our last visit. Akta had stolen a broad sword off one of the suits while I'd taken a lance. This time, I didn't need a weapon. I already had one, a pretty important one. But I wasn't here to fight. I was here to beg.

I hovered into the air and made my way down the dark corridor until it opened into a massive throne room. Along every wall, the fire from big, bright torches blinded me for a moment as my eyes adjusted from the darkness into the light.

The golden portrait frames hanging on every wall were empty, except behind me, where there were gigantic paintings of Lucifer in battle. As I walked down the black carpet toward the throne, I noticed that the frames weren't empty by mistake; someone—or something—had ripped out the paintings. The canvas remnants left behind flapped in the slight breeze.

The throne itself was made of bones piled high into the air. And it was vacant. Lucifer was nowhere to be found. I walked toward the back corner of the room, where I once found Kimberly huddled in a corner, and made my way through an open doorway next to the throne.

The next room was decorated with red wallpaper adorned with golden tridents. In the middle of the room, a roaring fireplace burned in front of an empty leather chair with a bottle of scotch sitting next to it.

"This is excellent," a voice boomed from across the castle. "My compliments to the chef."

I recognized the voice even though I had only heard it once before. The voice of the Devil isn't one you forget easily. I walked through the room and into a small corridor lit with candles that shone on the tapestries lining each wall. These were not of Lucifer but of a great bearded man, barrel-chested, clad in golden armor.

"I couldn't eat another bite," Lucifer's voice boomed down the hallway. "Oh, is there dessert?"

I made my way slowly down the hall toward the bright light at the end of it. Guarding the end of the hallway was another painting of the bearded man, standing with a regal smile. One hand sat confidently at his hip while another was pressed against a table behind him.

The hallway emptied into a room awash with light from an opulent chandelier and two hundred candles. A long dining table, holding every meat and sweet imaginable, ran the length of the room. It was a feast for a hundred people, yet only one sat at the table. Lucifer stuffed his fat face with a custard pie. He didn't bother with silverware, content to grab hunks with his hands and stuff them into his mouth.

"You've really outdone yourself tonight!" Lucifer shouted at no one in particular with a mound of cake in his mouth. "This is delicious."

I stepped onto the ground, folding my wings. I hoped that the creaking of the floorboards would alert him to my presence, but he was too enraptured by his sweet treats. Finally, I cleared my throat.

Lucifer looked up from his cakes, confused but not alarmed. He shook off his burgundy mane of crumbs as he stared at me with his yellow, glowing eyes. "Who are you?"

I stepped forward. "I'm sorry to intrude on your dinner, but—"

"This isn't my dinner," Lucifer said. "This is more a mid-morning treat . . . Hang on, I recognize you."

I took another step forward. "Yes, sir. We met once before—"

He smiled, food plastered between his pointed teeth. "The pixie, right?"

"That's right. I came with Akta to deliver Kimberly back to Earth."

Lucifer sniffed the air. "Funny. You smell different— oh, did you die?"

"Unfortunately, sir. Yes. A cult leader slit my throat."

"*Tsk tsk*. It wasn't one of mine, was it?" Lucifer asked, gently touching his chest.

"No, sir. I'm not sure who they were, actually, but they weren't trying to summon you."

The Devil let out a relieved sigh, waving his hand. "Oh, good. I hate it when they do that. So much work, and then they're disappointed that I won't help them."

"It sounds horrible."

Lucifer beckoned me forward. "Please, come and sit. Come and sit. I so rarely have visitors, especially returning ones."

I really didn't want to sit. I wasn't hungry in the least, but I also didn't want to seem rude, especially when I was dealing with the Devil. Especially when I was about to ask a big favor.

"Thank you," I said, taking a seat next to him.

The chairs sat higher than I could reach without jumping, and they were heavy to move. Heavier than any chair I've ever sat on in my life.

"Here," Lucifer said, pushing over a tart to me. "Eat. Eat. My cooks always make too much."

I picked up the tart and took a bite. It tasted . . . like sand. No, sand has a taste. It tasted like nothing, just like everything else I've eaten since I died.

"It's—" I didn't know what to say. I wanted to say it was delicious to appease him, but I also didn't want to lie.

"Ah, yes," Lucifer said, noticing my dilemma. "I forgot. You cannot taste anything, can you?"

I shook my head. "I'm afraid not, sir."

"A pity. A pity. An eternity in Hell, and you can't taste any of it. I've always thought that was the biggest pity."

"Not the constant torture?" I said before I could stop myself.

"Hmm," Lucifer said hesitantly. "You know, that would also be a strong negative."

"I certainly didn't enjoy it."

"Well, I would think not," Lucifer said, standing. "Otherwise, it would not be torture."

"I suppose that's true."

Lucifer sighed a deep sigh. "I suppose we should get on with it, then."

"Get on with what, sir?"

"What you need from me. I know you need something. You'll apologize if I indulged myself for a moment and thought you might be a guest who simply wanted my company, but I haven't had one of those in eons."

"I'm sorry."

"Oh, it's not your fault," Lucifer said, shrugging. "It is the burden of ruling. Everyone needs something from you."

"It sounds horrible."

Lucifer wiped his mouth with a napkin. "It IS horrible. But it is my curse. Now, what do you need? You've come a long way, and you must need something big."

I reached into my belt and pulled out the Dagger of Obsolescence. "I come to present you a gift worthy of an audience with you."

"This should be good. What is it, a painting? I have plenty of those."

I laid the Dagger of Obsolescence on the table and slid it to him. "No, it is the dagger you have searched for. One of only four objects that can kill you in the whole solar system."

Lucifer's eyes went wide as he picked up the dagger. "Could it be? This . . . I have searched for so long . . . where did you find it?"

"It doesn't matter." I waved my hand. I wanted to keep Aziolith's secret. "What matters is that it is yours."

I could see the tears welling up in Lucifer's eyes. "Thank you, little one. Wow, you must have one big ask if you bring me this. Let's hear it."

"I want to stop being tortured."

Lucifer laughed. "Now that is rich! Oh, I thought it would be something easy. I can't just end your torture, my dear. It is for an eternity."

I pushed the wings out of my body. "Yes, but I feel as though I have been miscategorized. See, I am a pixie, and thus, a monster. As you know, monsters are not tortured in Hell; they just live and work here."

"Hmmm, you make an interesting point," Lucifer said. He snapped his fingers, and an enormous ledger slammed onto the table, sending plates and food flying into the air and crashing onto the floor. "What was your name?"

"Julia Freeman."

Lucifer ran his clawed fingers across the pages. "And you said you died from a cult using your blood to open a portal to Hell?"

"Summon a beast from Hell, but yes."

He flipped a few more pages. "Ah yes, here is it. Oh my, only three-millionths pixie blood. That's not very much, is it?"

"No, but it is more than a drop. Enough for me to have these wings. Do you see these things? Humans don't have them."

Lucifer looked up. "Yes, yes. That is a nice parlor trick. Oh, this is interesting. Very interesting."

Lucifer ran over to a rotary telephone in the corner of the room. He picked it up and dialed three numbers. "Yes, retrievals? Have you caught the mhrucki yet? No. Well, that's a shame. What's taking—? Yes, I know you're short-staffed. Just cancel it for the time being, okay? Thank you."

"What's happening?" I asked when he hung up the phone.

"It turns out that the monster that cult summoned has been extraordinarily hard to catch in both Hell and on Earth. Angels can't find it. We can't find it. All we know is that bodies have been turning up without souls all over Stubbins, Colorado, and the surrounding area. Nasty business."

"Bodies without souls?"

"Yes, you see. Every soul has a body unless they are here—or in an interdimensional rift, but one of those hasn't opened in ages. I have a proposition for you. If you find this mhrucki for me, I will let you live out the rest of your days in Dis. Deal?"

Lucifer held out his hand, but I was hesitant to take it. "How powerful is that dagger?"

"Well, I don't really do power rankings, but I would say it's one of the most powerful weapons in the universe. Maybe top thousand."

"That doesn't sound so high."

The Devil gave me an impatient look. "In the whole universe, dear. All of it. Do you know how many weapons there are in the universe? A lot."

"And how important is finding this mhrucki to you?"

"Well, much less important, but it is a hassle. Get enough bodies without souls, and people start talking, you know? Angels come down to Earth and hassle my demons. They yell. It's a whole thing."

I crossed my arms. "And letting me go free costs you...nothing, right?"

"Well, right. Who cares if one less soul is condemned to eternal torture? Not me."

I grinned. "Then I want something else."

"Excuse me? I'm giving you everything you asked for. What else is there?"

"I want my mother to be saved as well. She didn't do anything wrong. She's just as much pixie as I am."

Lucifer grumbled under his breath. "Very well. I will find your mother, as well, and end her suffering. Should you succeed, she will be allowed to live in Hell with you."

"And Kimberly."

"No." Lucifer flipped through his book. "She is not down here."

"What?"

"Yes, she is one of the souls that vanished. Her body is up there, being kept alive unnaturally, but her soul is nowhere to be found. Not in Hell, not in Heaven, not even in the Dream Realm. In fact, that's how I'm sending you back."

"You're sending me back into her body?"

"Well, I can't send you back into yours. It's dead and rotting in a ditch somewhere. It would cause a fright. She is alive, and aside from some muscle atrophy, just fine."

I thought for a moment. "Okay, then I want her to be immune when she gets here in the future, hopefully after a long life."

Lucifer sighed. "Very well, your mother, you, and Kimberly will all be spared eternal torture. Is there anything else?"

"Amnesty for Akta and everyone else who helped me get here."

"All for a little dagger," Lucifer said with a deep sigh. "Very well. It is done, but that's it."

I held my hand out, and Lucifer grabbed it. "Then you have yourself a deal."

"Happy hunting! And do remember, your deal is contingent on the mhrucki coming back. If you die before it returns, all bets are off."

Lucifer snapped his fingers, and everything went black.

CHAPTER 14

My eyes fluttered open. Somewhere nearby, a heart monitor beeped rhythmically. My eyes focused for a moment, and I saw Kimberly's mother, Adelaide, sitting in a chair near me. Apparently, I was in a hospital bed.

Adelaide jumped out of her seat when she made eye contact with me. "Nurse!" she shouted out the door before rushing back to the bed. "Kimberly. Kim. Kim. Can you hear me? Can you hear me?"

Kim? Why was she calling me Kim? Why was she even here? Then I remembered what Lucifer said. He couldn't send me back into my body because it was dead, decaying in a ditch somewhere. I was in Kimberly's body. Because her soul was gone, I could inhabit it.

A portly nurse rushed into the room.

"Kimberly!" she said. "Can you hear me? Nod your head if you can hear me."

I nodded slowly. The nurse held my eyes open as she shone a light into them. "Pupil dilation is normal."

She looked at the heart monitor. "Heart rate is normal. Pulse normal. Looks like we have a miracle. Welcome back, Kim."

***

They kept a trach tube down my throat for the rest of the day. It was hard to do anything but breathe, and it was boring. All I could do was fret about my mission. I had to find the mhrucki and get her back to Hell before I died again. Yet, all the hospital would let me do is sit and wait. What the hell was a mhrucki, anyways?

"Kim," Adelaide said. "Oh, baby girl…I am so happy to see you again." She could barely choke the words out through her tears. She blew her nose loudly into a tissue that looked like she'd been using it for a month. "I thought we'd lost you." She let out a high-pitched squeal then fell into silent sobs.

The truth was, though, she had lost Kim. The person lying on the bed wasn't who she thought it was. It was me, and I had to hide that fact from her. When she stopped talking, I leaned back in my bed and closed my eyes. I smelled the sterile hospital air and was so happy that I didn't smell any sulfur. Not even a little bit.

***

The skin burned off my body, and I watched it crackle with my own eyes as they fell into my skin, and all I saw was black. In the blackness, my terror continued. My muscles smelt of burnt flesh as they disintegrated.

I kicked and screamed, and then I was awake. Adelaide rushed over to try and help. She caressed my head and placed a cold compress on me. It was nice and motherly, like what my own mother would have done given the chance, but as far as I knew, my own mother was in Hell being tortured for her sins. The longer I waited, the longer my mother's torture would continue.

The doctor said I had been in a coma for three months. Assuming Kimberly went into a coma the same night they slit my throat open, that meant I had only been in Hell for a few months. It felt like forty lifetimes. More.

Meanwhile, Mama had been dead for eight years. If she had been in Hell that whole time—oh, my poor Mama. I had to save her.

***

The next morning, they took the tubes out of my throat, and I could talk for the first time. My mouth was itchy and dry, and they gave me ice chips to rehydrate. Adelaide doted over me like only a mother could, but I didn't have the heart to tell her the truth. The truth would kill her, and I needed to avoid killing anybody else until I found the mhrucki.

I started to think about what would happen if I didn't find the monster. What if I just lived out the rest of my life in Kimberly's body? She was a good student and athlete. She would likely get a scholarship to college, and I could have a second chance at life, away from the constraints of these places like Chandler and Stubbins.

But I couldn't do it. I couldn't live with the possibility my mother was suffering in Hell. I couldn't let Kimberly end up in limbo. This wasn't my body after all, and I had no right to claim it, no matter how tempting it was.

Besides, one day Kimberly's body would die, and then I would end up back in Hell, and I had no interest in incurring the wrath of Lucifer when I got there.

***

Two days later, I was standing up and walking around the room. My legs were shaky, but I didn't know if that was from atrophied muscles in Kimberly's legs or because I forgot how to walk with human legs during my time in Hell. Everything felt heavier now. Each step I took, I felt like I was carrying bowling balls. The effects of gravity weighed me down more than they ever had when I was in my own body.

I spent hours in front of the mirror, marveling at my own reflection. Kimberly was so smooth. Her face didn't have any wrinkles. Her nose was smaller than mine and pointier as well. Her lips were fuller, but her cheeks were thinner. While my face had been wide and short, hers was thin and long. The only thing we had in common was the way our ears stuck out of our heads. I had always hated my ears, though I never noticed Kimberly's. Now I was sure she hated hers as well.

"You know, vanity is the mother of all sin," Adelaide said. She'd walked in on me glaring at the mirror.

"Sorry, Ade—mom," I replied. "I'm just trying to get used to all of this, you know, and looking at myself helps me remember."

"You don't remember anything that happened before the accident?"

I shook my head. I figured it was easier to claim amnesia than to piece together what happened in Kimberly's life. I knew some of her past, but I didn't know enough to pass for Adelaide's daughter.

"I know you're my mom," I said. "That's about it, though."

I wondered, as I lied through my teeth if that was really all amnesia was, souls lying about what they remembered so that they could inhabit other bodies. I looked over at Adelaide. Watching her daughter struggle pained her, I could tell, but I could also see great relief in her face. Her baby would soon be home with her.

***

"Where's Dad?" I asked as we finally drove home after a torturous week of rehab at the hospital. One week at the hospital. That must have been about a day in Hell. If it took me another week to find the mhrucki, it meant that Mama only had to suffer for one more day, and then she would be free.

"Dad hasn't taken your . . . he hasn't dealt so well with what happened to you," Adelaide said.

"Does he take anything well?"

I had practiced calling Adelaide "Mom" and Tommy "Dad" every night when I was alone in my hospital room. It became easier to see Adelaide as my mother as she nursed me back to health, but Tommy wasn't much of a dad. He never visited me once while I was in the hospital.

"No, he doesn't." Adelaide had a sad smile on her face. "But I'm sure he'll be happy to see you."

"I doubt it."

"He loves you," Adelaide said. "You know that deep down, even if you don't remember it."

***

It was late when Adelaide pulled up to her house—our house. The television blared against its too-thin walls, glinting against the windows. She got out of the car first, and I followed close behind.

"Your dad—he doesn't understand any of this stuff, so he's not gonna take kindly if you don't remember him. Just smile and wrap him in a big hug, okay? Even if you don't mean it. Got it?"

She was trying to keep the peace, just like always. I wanted to argue with her, but this wasn't the time. I was more tired than I could ever remember being and all I wanted to do was lie down in bed and dream.

But I couldn't sleep. I hadn't slept since waking up in Kimberly's body. Every time I closed my eyes, I saw the pits of Hell. I would never go back to them, even if it meant stabbing myself with Lucifer's dagger first.

"Hello, Tommy! Look who's here!" Adelaide said with a big smile as we entered the house.

Tommy was in the same cheese-stained, white tank top I'd seen him in every time I came to the house. Rain or shine. Cold or hot, he was always in the same wife-beater. I wondered if he showered with it. Then again, I wondered if he showered at all.

I put on my fakest smile and held out my arms wide. "Hi, Dad!"

Tommy's eyes went wide at the sight of me as if he was looking at a ghost. He stood up and wrapped his arms around me.

He stood there for a long time, and I was pretty sure he was sniffing me, which I thought was a little weird for a grown man to do. I figured that was probably just the way he cried. Sometimes people cry funny. At least he showed some emotion, and I could give him credit for that.

***

After a wordless meal of frozen pizza and Coke, I took the longest shower of my life. The hot water cleansed my aching bones and washed away the dreaded memories of Hell. With every step I took on Earth, the lingering thoughts of Hell moved further into my memory, though I couldn't shake them completely.

When the hot water trickled into my eyes, I instinctively squeezed them shut. That's when I saw the demons, laughing as they skewered me with their tridents and roasted me over the flames. I snapped my eyes open and refused to close them again, even if the soap and water stung my eyes.

For whatever it was worth, when I was in Hell, I didn't dream of the pits. I didn't dream of my torture. I didn't dream at all. Even while recovering at Horace's house, when I slept for days at a time, there was no dreaming. Now that I was back in Kimberly's body, all I did was dream.

And who knew how long I would dream of my torture? A week? A month? A year? I couldn't deal with reliving my torture. I would prefer a quiet life in Hell to this any day. Right there, I vowed that I would stay up as long as it took to find the mhrucki and never close my eyes again, not even to blink until it was captured.

After my shower, I went into Kimberly's room and looked around. I hadn't been in it for a very long time, and not much had changed. The walls were still painted bright pink, like when I first saw it when Adelaide was looking so desperately for her daughter. The posters had changed— Duran Duran and Huey Lewis had replaced the Beatles and David Cassidy—but the same stuffed animals were still on her bed. I don't know how she lived in such a ridiculously girly room, but it wasn't my place to judge. I was only here to find the mhrucki.

I was changing into a nightgown when the shadow of Kimberly's father fell over me. Tommy stood in the doorway, grinning like an idiot. If he tried anything with me, I would happily knock him into next week.

"Can I do something for you, T—Dad?"

He didn't answer. He just took a deep whiff of the room and turned up his nose, never taking his eyes off me. Then, he went right back to grinning.

"Can you leave then, so I can finish getting ready for bed?" I stood in front of the mirror, frowning, and ran a brush through my wet hair.

He didn't move, though. He stood in the doorway watching me, cocking his head with every movement I made.

I couldn't take anymore. This was too weird. "Get out, Tommy!" I shouted.

That's when he lunged for me. He grabbed my hands and twisted them until I had no choice but to drop to my knees in pain.

"Stop!" I pleaded. "Let go."

I knew Kimberly had it rough and that Tommy knocked Adelaide around. I had no idea he'd ever raised a hand to Kimberly—and the night she came home from the hospital? What kind of person does such a thing?

I glared into his face, thinking of ways to get away from him, and then watched in horror as he unhinged his jaw. A long, black tongue slithered out of his mouth. Saliva oozed between its sharp teeth as it snarled at me.

Maybe he wasn't a person, after all. My soul was beginning to separate from my body. It felt as if I was being unglued from Kimberly, like pulling two pieces of flypaper apart. My soul struggled to stick to my body as Tommy's mouth vacuumed my soul away.

I was about to die again. I couldn't even last one week back on Earth. Kimberly had been a champion. Her body deserved better than this. Clearly, I was just a girl who had no business being alive and every reason to be charred mercilessly for the rest of eternity.

No. I wouldn't let it go down like that. I planted my feet under me and kicked up into Tommy's crotch. He dropped my arms, and I ran backward toward the window, but I couldn't pull it open before he charged at me again.

I pushed the wings out of my back and flipped backward in the air, kicking Tommy right in the jaw as I did. He flew back against the dresser and smashed the back of his head into the corner.

Blood oozed out everywhere. Except . . . it wasn't red. It was green. And it burned the dresser; the drops corroded whatever they landed on. The mhrucki's eyes turned bright red, and his jaw unhinged again. He hissed at me as I took a few cautious steps closer, and when he swung at me, his claw caught me in the arm. I felt the skin rip open, and when I looked down at the gaping wound, Tommy tackled me into the dresser and then ran out the door. I chased after it, but it flung open the front door and disappeared into the night.

CHAPTER 15

"I have something to tell you . . ." That's how I started talking to Adelaide. Once Tommy—or the mhrucki—took off, I pulled her out of the house and dragged her to a nearby hotel. She refused at first, naturally, but when she looked into my eyes and saw how terrified I was, she relented.

The poor woman had no idea what was going on. She thought her daughter had just gone crazy and she couldn't find her husband. Once we got into the room, I couldn't hide it anymore. I told her everything. And when I was done, she slapped me across the face.

"How. Dare. You!" she shouted. "You got my daughter thrown into a coma, and then you come back to what? To steal her body?"

"Not exactly, Adelaide." I took a deep breath. "I know you're pissed. I would be pissed, too."

"You have no idea what I am! *Where* is my daughter?"

I put my face in my hands. "She is in . . . that thing."

She smacked me upside my head repeatedly, with both hands. "What do you mean 'that thing'? You aren't making any sense!"

I grabbed her hands and pulled her thumbs toward me, forcing her to the floor. "That's enough. Do not hit me again. Do you understand?"

Adelaide nodded through the pain. "Yes—ow, yes!"

"You're going to get the cops called on us." I let go of her.

"Good."

"No! Not good. If you want your daughter back, the cops are very bad for us. Do you want your daughter back?"

She sobbed into her hands. "Yes. Yes, of course, I do."

"Good. I want her back, too."

"Why?" she asked. "If it's so bad down there, then why do you want to go back?"

I groaned. She wasn't understanding this. "I don't want to go back, Adelaide. But I have to go back. Eventually, even Kimberly will die, and then I'll be right back to where I started. At least right now, I have a way out if I can find that monster."

"A way out . . . for you and Kimberly? And your mom?"

I sighed. "For the three of us. Yes, Adelaide."

She looked down at the ground, letting all of this new information sink in. It took a long time. Finally, she asked, "Will you take care of her?"

"For the rest of eternity."

Adelaide wiped her eyes and gave a final sniff. "Then what do we need to do?"

"First things first. I need to get Kimberly's pixie dust back, so I can talk to Aziolith. Can I borrow your keys?"

She crossed her arms. "You don't have a license."

"Fine," I replied. "But before we go, I need to eat something. Can we stop to get food?"

***

I had never eaten so much in all my life. I ordered three cheeseburgers and two milkshakes, along with a mountain of fries. Who knew anything could ever be so good? After being in Hell and not being able to taste a single thing, every flavor exploded in my mouth. The salt from the fries mixed with the savory juice from the burger and blended perfectly with the sweet from the shake. It was Heaven.

"You're going to get my daughter fat," Adelaide said, watching me eat.

"I'm sorry, but you don't know how horrible the food in Hell is."

"What is it like?" she asked. "Hell?" She knew I had been to Hell before but never asked me about my previous dalliance when I rescued Kimberly as a little girl. I think it was too close to home. It would have killed her to know what kinds of things her little daughter went through and what she saw.

"The pits of Hell were endless torture. All day. Every day. Well, except one hour—just long enough to regenerate, feel human, and then lose everything all over again. I don't know how other pits were, but that . . . wasn't very fun at all."

Adelaide sighed. "No. I don't imagine it will be."

"Hey," I said. "When I get back, I'm going to ask about you, too. All right?"

"Yeah," she said, trailing off. "But what about all the other people? The millions upon millions of others stuck being tortured down there?"

I placed my hand on hers. "We can't think about that, okay? We're just two people. We can't change Hell. No one person can. But we can do what's right for your daughter and my mother, okay?"

"Okay."

***

Adelaide pulled up to the mansion where I had lost my life. My gut went tight when I looked at the building, and I had trouble breathing. I clenched the dashboard and tried not to throw up as my whole body convulsed.

"Are you okay?" Adelaide pushed back the hair from my face.

I nodded through grimaced breaths. "It's just . . . have you ever felt complete terror before?"

"Too often," she said with a knowing sigh. I knew she was talking about Tommy, and I wondered for a moment if she was happy that he was gone or sad about it.

I caught my breath and steadied myself. "Wait here for me," I said, getting out of the car.

"Be careful," she replied. "That's my daughter's body you have there."

I slammed the car door closed without responding. I couldn't promise I would be safe. Last time I was here, I died. That's about the least safe thing that you can do. I was done making promises.

My feet dragged as I walked closer to the mansion. Even my wings didn't want to lift me into the air. It was as if I quadrupled in weight since I exited Adelaide's car; the heaviness of my death weighed me down.

Something was different about the house. When I was here before, trained snipers and guards patrolled the grounds, but there was none of that this time. I pulled myself up to look over the fence and didn't see a single human. Granted, the last time I was here, there was a cult meeting which likely meant greater security, but to have not one guard?

I flapped my wings and landed on the branch of a big oak tree next to the brick wall. I hopped up into the canopy to get a good look at the house and confirm my suspicions. When I poked my head out above the tree, I could see across the roof of the house and into the backyard. Thank god Kimberly's eyesight was as least as good as mine. I scanned the whole yard and saw not one single person around the exterior of the house.

Confident that I was alone, I fluttered down to the yard and walked directly to the front door. An eerie silence pervaded the property. I could hear my feet crunch against the ground and then echo under the hollow boards of the porch as I made my way up to the front door.

Do I knock? What do you say to the person that killed you and gave your protégé's soul to a monster? I tried the knob, and much to my surprise, the door swung open. I took a hesitant step inside, fearing that I was walking into a trap. This was too easy. But who would lay a trap? Nobody knew I was even alive.

The floor was covered in blood. Not just mine, either. I counted at least four different crusted blood spots. In the midst of all the bloodstains sat the marble slab they laid Kimberly on as a sacrifice. It must have worked because here I am, chasing down the monster they summoned.

"Hello?" a weak voice called out from the top of the stairs. "Hello?"

I very nearly jumped out of Kimberly's skin at the sound. Once I had composed myself, I floated into the air and made my way above the bloody summoning circle, onto the landing of the second floor. I expected to see a maid, butler, or some form of servant inside, but the house remained hollow and silent.

"Is somebody there?" the voice continued from the end of the hall.

I slowly made my way down to the end of the hall, past the paintings of stuffy old men hanging on the walls. The mansion did not feel warm and inviting, not even in the light of day, and as I neared the room, its darkness stifled me. Still, I could do nothing but press on, hoping to find answers.

The door opened into a spacious bedroom. All the black drapes were drawn shut. Only a small lamp illuminated the large canopy bed in the middle of the room. On it, a feeble man quivered under the covers.

"Please," he said, beckoning. "Come closer, child." Lying there enveloped in the perfect center of the bed, he looked like a tiny, innocent baby. But this man was not innocent. This was Edgar, the old man that killed me.

"Hello, Edgar," I said, my voice filled with vile contempt.

"Do I—" he began. Then the bedside lamp revealed my face, and he tried to scramble away from me. "Oh no. Please, don't kill me."

"Why not?" I replied. "You sacrificed me, Edgar."

"I did," he replied, pulling his sheets to his chin like a frightened child. "But you can be more merciful than me."

"Tell me why you did it, Edgar, and I will consider it."

Edgar looked down at his frail skin. "You do not know the pain of growing old, child. It is a burden I wish on no one."

"We all age, Edgar," I said, crossing my arms. "And we all die."

Edgar struggled to breathe. Every word carried more pain than the last. "Yes, so they say. But why? It is so unnatural, death. I spent my life building this fount of knowledge, all these riches, and here I am wasting away in this empty house, with everything I know locked inside my brain. All alone. It's a pity, don't you think?"

"So, what?" I snarled at him. "You decided to go against the natural order."

"I chose to improve the natural order, child," Edgar said, rolling toward me weakly. "Those I chose for the summoning were all great men, who had done great things. They deserved to continue their missions."

"Even if it meant sacrificing my friend and me? And others?"

"Yes," Edgar said, nodding his head meekly. "You— you have done so little, child. You did not deserve life more than those I gave it to. Or, well, tried to give it to."

"It didn't work, did it?"

Edgar's eyes misted. "It started fine. Pixie blood opened the gate and summoned the mhrucki. She took your soul and then was supposed to use her power to give me life. With every soul she took, she was supposed to give us life."

"But it didn't work out like that, huh?"

"She turned on us immediately. I tried to bind her to me, but she refused. She . . . slaughtered everyone . . . leaving only me, and then she vanished."

"Why did she leave?"

Edgar dropped his head and wept. His shaking shoulders loosened a talisman hanging on a cord around his neck. He reached for it, and I recognized the design through his bony fingers.

It was a coin engraved with a pentagram that was surrounded by fire. I had seen it before, in Hell. It was a coin of Dis; the quan if I remembered correctly. I grabbed hold of it and yanked, snapping the cord that held it around his neck.

"What are you—"

"This is payment for my life," I replied. "Pray I don't take more."

"You deserve to kill me, and I deserve to die."

I grinned at him. "I know what awaits you on the other side, old man, and every time I think of my death, I will think of you, burning in Hell forever, with no hope of escape. That is your punishment."

"Forever?"

I nodded. "Until the end of time. Now, how do I stop this mhrucki?"

"Forever?" the old man repeated, squeezing his sheets as the tears fell down his face.

"Hey!" I snapped my fingers in his face. "How do you send this mhrucki back to Hell?"

The old man looked up at the ceiling. "Forever!"

It was useless. I'd broken him, and I wasn't sure I would have liked what he had to say anyway. After all, he could summon the monster, but he couldn't contain it. I would have to find another person for that—or another being—but that was going to be hard to do without pixie dust. I already tried vanishing without it, but Kimberly's mind wasn't ready for such an advanced skill…yet.

An old leather bag caught my eye on the nightstand. No kidding . . . it looked just like Kimberly's pixie dust bag. I pulled it open, and, sure enough, inside was Kimberly's pixie dust.

"I'm taking this, too." I turned to leave, then stopped. "Oh, one more thing, where did you bury Julia's body?"

CHAPTER 16

Adelaide followed the directions Edgar gave me, which took us to a farmhouse.

"Do you want me to come with you?" she asked.

"No," I said, shaking my head. "I need to do this alone. Go back to the hotel. Don't open the door for anybody. I hope this is the last time I ever see you."

"I hate to say it," Adelaide replied, lingering on her daughter's face for a long moment, "but I feel the same way."

"I will make sure Aziolith knows that Kimberly is my heir and ask that he welcome her as he welcomed me."

Adelaide nodded. "Alright, well…good luck, then."

Edgar said they buried my body in a shallow grave on the other side of the creek behind the farmhouse. The place had been abandoned for some time, and once Adelaide pulled away, there was nothing but the sound of rushing water to take my mind off visiting my own grave.

I hopped over the creek at its narrowest spot and continued to the back corner of the meadow. When I neared the forest forming the border of the property, the grass parted, and I saw ten unmarked graves laid in front of me. Edgar didn't know which mine was, and it didn't matter. The tears were real all the same.

My body would never be mourned. It would never have a funeral. It was, for all time, lying in a dirt patch in an abandoned plot of land. If a developer came one day to dig up the place and found my withered bones, they would barely think twice before discarding it in an unmarked grave somewhere else, and that was the best-case scenario.

Most likely, I would be forgotten, if not in this generation, then once Kimberly died for sure. I would decay into oblivion.

With these thoughts keeping me company, I collapsed onto the grave and cried for I don't know how long. By the time I rose, it was dusk. My body was numb, and I was parched. I had no more tears for myself, and when I stood again, I felt better. I had mourned my life, and now I could move on with my death.

There was still work to do. I clasped the bag of pixie dust in my hand and pulled out a handful. Closing my eyes, I imagined Aziolith's cavern. Every inch, every rock, and every piece of treasure. When I could picture it all clearly in my head, I threw the pixie dust and vanished.

I reappeared in the middle of Aziolith's cave. Huge mounds of gold lined the walls, interspersed with jewels, armor, books, and all manner of treasure. I once estimated that his wealth rivaled the queen of England, but I think I might have been selling him short.

In front of me, Aziolith slept, cocooned around a roaring fire. His fiery, red scales heaved up and down with each breath. Kimberly had been here with me before, but only a couple of times, and I wasn't sure that Aziolith would remember her.

"Hello, Julia of Chandler," Aziolith said without looking up. "What news have you of the outside?"

I sighed loudly enough that he turned to me. "Julia is dead," I said.

"Oh," Aziolith said. "I'm sorry. You smell just like her."

"Yes, there is a reason. She has overtaken this body to help capture a mhrucki who escaped Hell. Once the mhrucki is captured, she—well, I—will go back to Hell. Forever."

Aziolith stood and ambled toward me. "That doesn't make me happy, Julia. Did I not tell you to be careful?"

"You did, and I tried, but everybody has their day, Aziolith. You have lived long enough to see many people die."

"Perhaps. But she—you were always special to me."

I laid my hand on Aziolith's talon. "And you were special to me, too."

"Of course, I was," the dragon said, his lips curling upwards. "Just look at me. I am magnificent."

I laughed and felt grateful for my friend. "I have a favor to ask of you."

"Of course, you do," Aziolith said, smiling. "It wouldn't be you if you didn't have a favor."

"The girl, the one who inhabits this body. She is also special to me, and she—"

Aziolith held up a clawed hand to stop me, midsentence. "She is welcome any time."

I nodded, trying not to cry. "Thank you."

The dragon wrapped his giant, scaled claw around me and pulled me close. "There there, my dear. There there."

"I can't believe this is the end. I can't believe I'm going to die and be forced to live in Hell forever."

"Maybe it won't be forever," Aziolith said. "Maybe they'll stir up an Apocalypse, and then you'll be back here."

"Maybe." I wiped the tears away. "Oh, my god. Hell is the worst!"

"That's what I've been telling you."

"I mean, it was pretty bad when I was there last time, but at least I had some hope I would leave. Coming back and knowing I have to spend an eternity there? Goddamn, that's a tough pill to swallow."

"Come," Aziolith said, leading me to a roaring fire at the center of his cavern. "If you are to die, then let us talk one last time until we run out of things to say."

My eyes brimmed with tears again. "I'd like that."

***

I don't know how long we talked, but eventually, I fell asleep tucked in the dragon's arms. It was the first time I slept, really slept, since I'd returned to Earth, and the first time I didn't dream of Hell. When Aziolith had slept for all that time after being summoned to Chandler, I remember that he woke up often, screaming about his time in Hell. I would try to calm him down when I was able. The warm touch of a friend was often enough to send him back to sleep, and now he returned the favor.

When I woke, I felt fully rested and refreshed. I pulled myself out of Aziolith's arms and searched through the mountains of treasure for a weapon that could kill a mhrucki.

"You're going to want to look in a different stack," Aziolith said, yawning. "There are no good weapons in there."

"Do you know how to kill a mhrucki?"

The dragon shrugged. "The same way you kill anything. Stab it in the heart with the right weapon. But you have to find it first, and that's trickier. Mhrucki can shapeshift into any human they see, making them almost impossible to spot."

"How do you spot them?"

"I don't know. There's probably a book around here somewhere that can tell you if I didn't burn it for kindling, but who knows how long it will take you to find it."

I threw up my hands, exasperated. "Do you have any idea what I should do now?"

"I do, but you aren't going to like it," he sighed. "You need to find Charlie."

He was right. I didn't like his plan, but he was also right that it was the best course of action. The only demons who knew how to catch a mhrucki worked in Retrievals, and the only person I knew who worked in Retrievals was Charlie, the snake who sold me out, tried to send me back to the pits, chased Akta, and did nothing but lie to me.

I didn't have many options. And I knew where Charlie hung out while he was on Earth, which was pretty often. Charlie loved Earth. He'd hole up drinking at a bar set up inside a little house in Scotland, a place that was like a waystation for demons. Angels, too, actually.

A hundred and fifty-ish years ago, the current owner's grandfather's father summoned a demon by accident when he was making a sandwich, and they struck up a friendship. With that friendship, they brought about more demons, and those demons brought the attention of angels. Soon, angels and demons stationed on Earth frequented Frank's house when they needed to get away from the minutiae of their job.

I had been there a couple of times before and always found Charlie wallowing in a pint. With one final hug, Aziolith gave me an obsidian dagger to take care of the Mhrucki. Then I set off to meet with Charlie and figure out how to track the thing down.

***

I appeared outside of an unassuming street in an unassuming part of Scotland. It could have been any street anywhere, and I wouldn't have known the difference; that's how plain it looked. The only way the house looked different was that if you tilted your head to one side, you could see a purple forcefield encasing it, with red and blue hexes floating around inside the barrier.

Aziolith once told me if I walked through the forcefield full steam ahead, nothing would happen to me. Even though it had worked, I was scared to do it again. After all, if I didn't make it, I would be vaporized in an instant.

On the other hand, I didn't have a choice. I took a big step forward and rushed toward the barrier. For a moment, it held me back, like a rubber band, but then it gave way and sent me tumbling forward toward the front door. I brushed myself off and walked inside.

The place was as much of a ruckus as I'd ever seen it. Demons and angels sang drinking songs along the wooden tables in the front of the house, while Frank served them pints of ale in the back.

"I was wondering when you'd show up here." Charlie was looking at me with a wide smile, drinking a pint of beer.

"I would avoid talking to you if I could."

"Sit down," Charlie said, motioning to the empty stool across from him.

"I—"

"I know what you want. Let me see the weapon."

I pulled the obsidian dagger out of my belt and placed it on the table in front of him. Charlie picked it up and examined it closely. He ran his finger across the blade, and it drew blood.

"Good," Charlie said, pushing the dagger back to me. "It will work nicely, but you gotta know that a mhrucki's heart is in her stomach. Don't go for the chest. That's a rookie mistake."

I tucked the weapon back in my belt. "Thank you, but how do I—"

"How do you find her?" he asked. "They have an insatiable hunger, and they like their victims young. When they take a victim, they leave them comatose. Follow the string of comas, and it will lead you right to her."

"What will happen—when I kill her?" I asked.

"All the souls she ate will exit her body. Those who are dead will be sent to Hell for judgment. The others will wake up as if they just had a bad dream."

"And me?"

"You'll be kicked out and, without a body, return to Hell."

"I can handle that," I said.

"Yeeaaah, you might think differently in the moment. You hesitate, and the mhrucki will eat your soul, and you'll be stuck in its stomach forever. If you think Hell is bad, you haven't felt pain until you get digested by a mhrucki for a million years."

I nodded. "Then I won't hesitate."

"Yeah, we'll see. You've got spirit, toots. I'll give you that."

"There is one more thing, though."

"How do you see the mhrucki?" Charlie asked my question for me. "There's a simple rune that can give you the sight. It will burn whenever a mhrucki is close."

He held up his hand, revealing a distinct brand on his palm. It was a triangle with a pentagram in the center and a different shape at each corner: a heart in the upper left, a goat in the upper right, and a trident at the bottom. When Charlie closed his hand and opened it again, the mark was gone. "It's how we find escaped monsters and lost souls. That mark will let you see if someone's living on Earth who oughta be in Hell. Touch her once and reveal her true form, then stab her in the gut quickly before she can fully transform. Once she's transformed, toots, you won't be able to kill her before she slaughters you."

"How do I get a mark like that?"

"I can give it to you." Charlie leaned back and took a sip of beer. "For a price."

"Of course, there's a price. What is it this time?"

"Forgiveness," Charlie said, looking me in the eyes. "Hell is long and lonely, Julia. You will need a friend down there."

I sighed. "You were only doing your job, I suppose."

"And doing what I gotta do to survive. You'll be one of us soon if you can pull this off, and there is one thing we don't do in Hell. We don't turn against our own."

"You realize you are literally helping me turn against your own right now, right?"

"We're also hypocrites, Julia. Stay with me."

"I . . . forgive you."

"Once more, with feeling."

"Fine," I shouted. "I forgive you, all right? I forgive you."

Charlie grabbed my hand and opened my palm. "That's all I wanted to hear. Now, this is going to hurt—a lot. Try not to scream. The neighbors hate that."

A beam of fire shot out of Charlie's hand and seared into my skin. I wanted to scream and rip my hand away, but I kept my composure. I thought of Hell and the excruciating pain I felt there. Compared to that, getting branded was a cakewalk.

CHAPTER 17

It didn't take long to figure out that there was a concentration of teenagers falling into a coma at Kimberly's high school. Thirteen students in the past three months had been hospitalized with no rhyme or reason as to why. Some blamed it on an E-coli outbreak, while others said it must be a bad flu, but nobody knew the truth.

Of course, they didn't, and I didn't blame them. Who would believe that a giant mhrucki was sucking the souls out of their children? That's not something science would tell them. It's the sort of thing you take on faith, and those sorts of things end up in crackpot journals and newspapers that you find in the checkout line at the grocery store.

Then again, I found those types of magazines had the most truth in them. They were the ones that reported the demon dog attack, and they wrote about the portal opening in Chandler. They were the ones that broke every important story in my life since I first discovered my powers.

Walking into the school that day was a bit like déjà vu since I hadn't been inside a school since I left Chandler. Even though I'd been a teacher, walking under the archways of Stubbins High brought me back to my days as a student, when school was the only hope to get me out of Colorado.

"Good morning, Miss Kimberly." A big, fat man smiled at me as I walked through the doors. "So good to have you back."

That smile had to be unnatural, and yet my hand didn't sting as I walked toward him. Adelaide and I spent the previous night reconstructing Kimberly's schedule from memory. My job was to get through the day posing as

Kimberly and hope that by the end of it, something would make my hand ache.

I didn't have to wait long. When I pushed through the halls, looking for my classroom, my hand started to burn. I turned around, searching frantically for the source, but there were hundreds of students in the halls and teachers guiding them to class. I couldn't pick out the mhrucki without causing a scene, and for a girl who just came back to school after being in a coma, screaming about a mhrucki was probably not the best idea. I would just have to bide my time.

***

Any desire to return to my youth or take over Kimberly's body forever vanished as I went through her day. I had been a teacher for a while and a student before that, but it had been almost a decade since I stepped foot inside a classroom, and…did teachers forget how to teach?

Seriously. Everything they said was so boring…even the stuff that I *knew* was interesting because I taught it, like medieval history, sounded so dull coming from Kimberly's teacher. The woman just droned on and on. I could barely keep my eyes open. It was the worst. I hoped that I was not like that in my classroom.

None of the students were mhrucki, though, as my hand didn't burn at all until lunchtime.

Not until I reached the cafeteria.

The moment I stepped into the big room, my hand started to tingle. I had decided during third period to use the pain like a beacon. With all the students sitting down in one place, and teachers standing around watching them, I could simply bide my time walking around and finding my target.

My first thought was that one of the teachers was the culprit, but a quick walk around the outer edge of the cafeteria didn't ring any alarm bells. I made sure to brush past every one of them, too, hoping that my touch would reveal their true identity.

"Are you lost, hon?" a female teacher with big glasses and bad teeth said to me. "There are seats all over."

"Sorry. Just trying to catch my bearings."

She smiled wide with sympathy for the coma kid. Her baked bean teeth showed across her alabaster face, but she was no mhrucki. After ruling out the teachers, only the students remained. It made sense. Students don't have to talk, and teachers do. What better way to hide in plain sight than as an unassuming, shy kid?

I paced up and down the rows from the front to back and left to right. When I approached the furthest back corner of the room, I saw a table, empty save for one small girl with pigtails. My hand started to burn something fierce. It burned so badly that I thought I was going to lose the tray clutched in my hand.

I moved toward the small girl, knowing what she was and knowing I only had one shot to stop her. If I hesitated for even a moment, she would pounce on me. Placing my tray next to her, I rifled through my bag until I clutched the dagger tightly. It would be hard for Kimberly to explain killing a student, but when a dozen souls came out of its mouth, I figured she would be okay. I didn't have time to work out all the details.

"Excuse me," I said.

The girl had been watching me from the corner of her black eyes, and now she looked directly at me. Immediately, she knew what was happening, but it was too late. I laid my hand on her head, and the pigtailed little girl stretched into a ten-foot-tall, hissing monster with seven black, gelatinous arms which flapped around.

The students and teachers fled as I took my dagger and jammed it into the mhrucki's stomach. Its body pulsated and shrank before a blinding light burst forward, shining over the cafeteria and knocking me backward. Outlines of bodies flew through the walls of the cafeteria. For a moment, I saw Kimberly smile at me through a white halo around her body, and then she smacked into me, and I was gone, into the darkness.

***

"Julia," I heard Lucifer's low voice say. "Wake up."

I was back in Hell, in the dining room in the Devil's castle. There was an old woman smiling at me. I did a doubletake before I realized it was my mother.

"Mama!" I shouted, rushing into her outstretched arms. "Oh, Mama, it's good to see you again."

I didn't mind the smell of sulfur in the air or how it permeated Mama's clothes. She squeezed me tightly and pressed her cheek against mine. "It's good to see you too, baby."

Tears welled in my eyes as I stared at her face, so much older than it had been on Earth. So much pain in her eyes. So much death in her face.

"She will take more time to recover," Lucifer said. "I pulled her out from the wall as soon as possible, but I'm afraid Hell will leave a strain on her that will stay with her forever."

I turned to him. "Thank you."

"There is no need to thank me. This was our bargain."

"About that? I have another favor to ask of you."

"Of course, you do." Lucifer lifted his eyes to the ceiling.

"Did you know that Kimberly's mother is also a pixie? And she helped me an awful lot during this trip."

Lucifer grumbled. "Even though you caused quite a scene today—one my cleanup crew will be dealing with for days—you honored your commitment. I will grant Kimberly's mother the same clemency as I granted yours if she ends up here. Mostly because I don't think there's anything I could do to stop you from rescuing her."

"Then," I said, "I guess we are done here."

Lucifer let out a weary sigh. "Of course, you are. I mean, who would want to spend time with me if they didn't need something from me?"

"Oh, Julia," Mama said. "Let's stay with the nice man. Maybe he can tell us a story."

"Mama, that's Satan. He's not really nice."

"He brought us back together, didn't he?" Mama squeezed my hand.

I took a seat at the table and grabbed a tart. "All right, Lucifer. We don't have a lot of plans for the rest of eternity. How about you tell us a story?"

Old Scratch grinned. "I don't mind if I do."

***

If you enjoyed that, jump ahead a few decades and find out what happens in the years after the Apocalypse in *Conquest,* which combines Kimberly, Akta, Julia, and Katrina into one epic adventure.

***

Here's a preview of *Conquest.*

CONQUEST

Book 9 of The Godsverse Chronicles

By:
Russell Nohelty

Edited by:
Leah Lederman

Proofread by:
Katrina Roets & Toni Cox

Cover by:
Psycat Covers

Planet chart and timeline design by:
Andrea Rosales

CHAPTER 1

Kimberly

Location: Earth

I dropped a pinch of pixie dust in the tunnels under Trafalgar Square in London and vanished. One of the great benefits of being a pixie was the ability to travel around the world in an instant. We were hunted to the point of extinction and had to keep our heads on a swivel, but as long as you had a pouch of pixie dust, you could stay one step ahead of the monsters and demons who hunted you.

And on a good night, you could hunt them.

That was my job. Specifically, I hunted the ones that preyed on my kind. I was very good at it—some said I was the best, and those people had both good taste and a keen eye. Truly, I was exceptional.

In my two hundred years of life, I had captured and banished over a thousand demons and, by extension, saved hundreds of pixies from being sacrificed for any number of dark plans. Pixie blood was good for that sort of thing. Of course, for every fairy I saved, another one fell. I tried to focus on the ones I saved, not the ones I'd failed to protect. If I let that burden weigh on me, I would never get out of bed in the morning.

When I reappeared, I was in Seattle, the home of the most amazing coffee in the world and the current location of the demon Thriaska. He'd built a lair somewhere in the city, and it was my responsibility to find it. He was the latest in a long line of demons hunting my people, and I was looking forward to sending him back to Hell. You couldn't kill a demon, but you could banish them. Inevitably, some human would use the wrong summoning spell so that, once again, that demon was free to terrorize Earth.

"Where are you, Thriaska?" I muttered under my breath. "Enjoy your freedom because tonight you're going back to Hell."

It wasn't wise to use pixie dust in the open, so I chose to use my legs and hoof it to the coffee shop where I was meeting my informant. I enjoyed walking. It allowed me to think, and the chill reminded me that I was alive. I smelled the crisp cold in the fall air that whipped past my face. There had been a storm recently, and the ground was still wet with rain.

Two miles down the cold, damp street, I turned into a little coffee shop. One thing that survived was coffee, even during the Apocalypse, and afterward, it became one of the most precious goods on Earth, transforming Seattle into one of the most important cities on the planet.

Honestly, I preferred Seattle at the end of the twentieth century when it was known for grunge music and gloomy days more than for coffee and tech billionaires. I'd gone to college in Seattle, back when things like education mattered to me. That was another life, over two centuries ago. Before the Apocalypse.

It was just like it sounds: all the pious men and women were raptured to Heaven while everybody and everything else was stuck on Earth to deal with the consequences. And there were extreme consequences. The dead rose from their graves. Demons invaded our planet. Nations collapsed. There was nothing we could do except learn to survive in the new normal.

I was there, and I remembered everything. I had only been immortal for a decade at that point and was sure I would not survive the horrors, but I got strong quickly. I had forgotten much about my ancient life, but the Apocalypse was still raw in me.

"Good evening!" a squat girl with a nose ring said from behind the counter. "What can I get you?"

"Hi," I replied. "Large coffee, extra shot."

She nodded and went about pouring the coffee. When she was done, I brought it to a table in the corner and waited. My contact was late. She was always late. She had been around since the beginning, so little things like time didn't matter much to her.

I had an infinity to fill, so I didn't usually begrudge anyone a few minutes. Heck, hours or weeks. But tonight, time mattered a lot to me; in fact, it was everything. Thriaska had kidnapped a pixie girl earlier that morning, and it was only a matter of time before he killed her like he'd killed the others.

Pixie blood was quite possibly the most valuable resource on earth, save for unicorn horns or dragon scales. Both of those monster species became extinct long ago, while pixies molded into society quite well. We were really, really good at blending in. We looked like humans—save for our pointy ears—we smelled like humans, walked and talked like humans.

Some of us even took human mates, like my mother did. Others just kept their heads down and used their magic carefully. In any case, it was my job to keep pixies safe, even if it meant hunting demons and monsters to the ends of the Earth, one at a time, until they learned that we were off-limits. Monsters had thick skulls, and it often took caving them in before they got the message.

The bell over the shop door rang, and a cloaked woman walked into the shop. I eyed her as she walked across the room and muttered something to the waitress. After a moment, the barista poured a drink, and the woman brought it to her mouth.

"This is divine," she said with a sweet smile, belying that she was anything but what she appeared. "Is there anything better than good coffee?"

"Good, right?" I asked as she came toward me.

Lilith had been around since the beginning of everything. She was Adam's first wife but refused to lay with him unless they were equals and was thus banished from the Garden of Eden, which forced her to make a deal with a demon.

She pulled off her hood and let down her long, dark hair. Her thin lips creaked up, accentuating the wrinkles under her soft, brown eyes. "Best in Seattle. So much better than that Starbucks monstrosity they used to make here. Remember that? What was that thing called, a Frappuccino?"

"I think so."

"Yuck. Sugar water, if you ask me. This though, just the perfect amount of bitterness, like you, my dear."

"I'll take that as a compliment, Lilith," I said. "After all, I run on spite and bitterness."

"And coffee, darling," she replied. "Of course, perhaps I shouldn't complain about them too much. Back in my day, I would have killed for sugar water. All we had were figs and apples."

I nodded. Starbucks was the reason Seattle was a bastion for coffee, but they couldn't survive the Apocalypse. Almost nobody did. Some days, in my shame,

I wished for it to come again, if only so humanity would remember what it was like to cower in true fear and the feeling of relief that came over us when the demons vanished.

Life was different after the Apocalypse, for a while at least. People were nicer. Food tasted sweeter. The world looked brighter. I thought maybe humanity's better nature would take hold of them.

But it didn't last.

Eventually, the stories turned into legends. Those who had seen the horror with their own eyes died off, leaving the next generation, who birthed the next generation…the truth vanished to memory, just a footnote in a textbook. The world rebuilt itself in hope and prosperity and then fell to war, only to be rebuilt again. The cycle continued until little remained of the world I remembered.

I took a long sip of coffee. "This is better than Starbucks ever was."

She nodded. "Much better, darling. Much, much better."

Enough coffee talk. "Did you find him?" I asked.

Lilith sighed. "You are probably the rudest girl I have ever met. Did you know that?" She relished being a demon. She didn't see them as evil, just misguided and misunderstood, the same way humans and fairies were. Some of them were downright polite. She didn't think that a few bad apples should spoil the bunch.

"Yes, but I don't care. He's going to kill again, and soon. If he kills one of my people while I'm sipping coffee with you, I'll never forgive myself."

Lilith took a long sip of her coffee. "Why not? It's not like they'll go to Hell. Not really, at least."

She wasn't wrong, technically speaking. While dead pixies were sent to Hell, they weren't punished like humans. Being monsters, they got off on a technicality and were able to work the land, in the auspices of Hell, at the Devil's behest.

"They're still slaves."

"Potato, potahto," Lilith said. "I'm just saying, if another pixie died, it wouldn't be so bad. They'd get out of here, at least." She swirled her hand in a circle, looking at the shop around her.

I chuckled and took my own sip of coffee. "If you hate it so much, why don't you go back? Or to Mars, or Venus? Or Europa?"

I didn't understand much about the inner workings of Hell, but I knew enough demons to know that in the last two hundred years, the Devil had made deals to annex land for Hell on multiple planets in the solar system, easing the tension that led to the Apocalypse in the first place.

"I know you're joking," Lilith said. "But please don't be so cavalier. First off, those satellite Hells are much too cold and remote for me, and second…Hell doesn't have coffee. I desperately need coffee in my life."

"I understand that." I took another sip of coffee. "So… Thriaska? Where is he?"

Lilith's eyes flashed. "Fine. I'll take you to him so that you can have your revenge, okay? You know you used to come to me for advice and counsel, instead of just information. I miss the days when we would just…talk."

My eyes dropped to my hands in my lap. "I'm sorry. It's just—" But I didn't feel like finishing my sentence. I had a job to do, and I hated apologizing for it. "Can we go?"

"Yes," Lilith said. "After I finish my coffee."

I grumbled. "Fine, but if she dies before we get to her, or Thriaska escapes, I'm sending you back to Hell tonight."

Lilith smiled. "You can surely try."

***

If you liked this preview, make sure to pick up *Conquest* today.

ALSO BY RUSSELL NOHELTY

NOVELS
My Father Didn't Kill Himself
Sorry for Existing
Gumshoes: The Case of Madison's Father
Invasion
The Vessel
The Void Calls Us Home
Worst Thing in the Universe
The Marked Ones
The Dragon Scourge
The Dragon Champion
The Dragon Goddess
The Sleeping Beauty
The Wicked Witch
The Fairy Queen
The Red Rider

COMICS and OTHER ILLUSTRATED WORK
The Little Bird and the Little Worm
Ichabod Jones: Monster Hunter
Gherkin Boy
How NOT to Invade Earth

www.russellnohelty.com

1000 BC – BETRAYED [HELL PT 1]
/PIXIE DUST
500 BC – FALLEN [HELL PT 2]
200 BC – HELLFIRE [HELL PT 3]
1974 AD – MYSTERY SPOT [RUIN PT 1]
1976 AD – INTO HELL [RUIN PT 2]
1984 AD – LAST STAND [RUIN PT 3]
1985 AD – CHANGE
1985 AD – MAGIC/BLACK MARKET HEROINE
1985 AD – EVIL
1989 AD – DEATH'S KISS
[DARKNESS PT 1]
2000 AD – TIME
2015 AD – HEAVEN
2018 AD – DEATH'S RETURN [DARKNESS PT 2]
2020 AD – KATRINA HATES THE DEAD
[DEATH PT 1]
2176 AD – CONQUEST
2177 AD – DEATH'S KISS
[DARKNESS PT 3]
12,018 AD – KATRINA HATES THE GODS
[DEATH PT 2]
12,028 AD – KATRINA HATES THE UNIVERSE
[DEATH PT 3]
12,046 AD – EVERY PLANET HAS A GODSCHURCH
[DOOM PT 1]
12,047 AD – THERE'S EVERY REASON TO FEAR
[DOOM PT 2]
12,049 AD – THE END TASTES LIKE PANCAKES
[DOOM PT 3]
12,176 AD – CHAOS